The organs of **J.S.Bach**

CHRISTOPH WOLFF & MARKUS ZEPF

The organs of J.S.Bach

A HANDBOOK

Translation by
LYNN EDWARDS BUTLER

Introduction by
CHRISTOPH WOLFF

PUBLISHED IN COOPERATION WITH
THE AMERICAN BACH SOCIETY

UNIVERSITY OF ILLINOIS PRESS
urbana, chicago, and springfield

Originally published as *Die Orgeln*
J. S. Bachs: Ein Handbuch
Edition Bach-Archiv Leipzig
© Evangelische Verlagsanstalt,
Leipzig/Bach-Archive Leipzig, 2006.
Second edition, 2008.

This publication is sponsored by the American
Bach Society and produced under the guidance
of its Editorial Board. For information about the
American Bach Society, please see its web site at
www.americanbachsociety.org.

Frontispiece: Naumburg, St. Wenceslas's Church:
Hildebrandt organ (photograph, 2006)

Library of Congress Cataloging-in-Publication Data
Wolff, Christoph.
[Orgeln J. S. Bachs. English]
The organs of J. S. Bach : a handbook /
Christoph Wolff and Markus Zepf;
translation by Lynn Edwards Butler;
introduction by Christoph Wolff. — Rev. ed.
p. cm.
Published in cooperation with the
American Bach Society.
Includes index.
ISBN 978-0-252-03684-2 (hard cover : alk. paper)
ISBN 978-0-252-07845-3 (pbk. : alk. paper)
1. Organ (Musical instrument)—Germany—History—
18th century. 2. Bach, Johann Sebastian, 1685–1750.
I. Zepf, Markus, 1972– II. Title.
ML576.3.w6613   2012
786.5'1943—dc23   2011039540

contents

It is with pride and delight that the American Bach Society, in conjunction with the University of Illinois Press, issues this English translation of *Die Orgeln J. S. Bachs: Ein Handbuch* by Christoph Wolff and Markus Zepf. For some time now the society has wanted to expand its printing ventures beyond its well-established hardcover series *Bach Perspectives*. The present volume, which addresses one of the most important aspects of Bach's musical life in a comprehensive yet accessible manner, offers a perfect opportunity to place a German publication of great interest before a new, English-speaking audience.

In compiling their new handbook, Wolff and Zepf have been able to set the record straight on many aspects of the organs under consideration, with regard to both their historical evolution and their present state. The opening of Thuringia and Saxony through the fall of the Socialist government, the reunification of Germany in 1990, and the recent enlightened restorations of many surviving instruments have resulted in a wealth of new information on the churches, organs, and organ makers of Bach's world. In a number of instances, the degree of preservation—and loss—of buildings and instruments can be addressed in a forthright way for the first time since World War II. Wolff and Zepf have been able to document what's old and what's new. They have also drawn on the flood of new research that has taken place as many once-inaccessible archives have opened their doors to outside scholars.

One cannot imagine a better constellation of scholar-performers for the present project. Christoph Wolff, preeminent Bach expert and author of the monumental biography *Johann Sebastian Bach: The Learned Musician*, and Markus Zepf, organ specialist and diligent researcher, form a formidable team of authors. Lynn Edwards Butler, organ scholar and former longtime director of the Westfield Center, is a skilled translator with a broad knowledge of historical organ practices and terminology. All three are experienced organists, familiar with early instruments through performance and examination.

Indeed, they have played most of the extant organs described here and are familiar with their features firsthand.

Favorable for this undertaking, too, is the long-standing connection between the American Bach Society and the University of Illinois Press, publisher of *Bach Perspectives*. The opportunity to work with the seasoned and supportive UIP team of Willis Regier, director, and Laurie Matheson, senior acquisitions editor, allowed the project to move forward in a smooth and fruitful way.

It is the hope of the American Bach Society that *The Organs of J. S. Bach* will serve as a useful reference book for organists, Bach scholars and devotees, and general music enthusiasts. Containing a great deal of information in a portable form, it is envisioned not only as a *vade mecum* for the personal library, but as a travel companion for the suitcase, as well—a guidebook whose stop lists and color photographs, especially, whet one's appetite to observe, hear, and play the extant instruments described therein.

Bach was first and foremost an organist. He won youthful fame through his virtuoso performances and extensive knowledge of organ building. The earliest extant examples of his handwriting are tablature copies of organ music by Buxtehude and Reinken, and his final years show him publishing and revising organ chorales. From the beginning to the end of his life, he was engaged with organ music and the examination, inauguration, and design of new instruments. May the present survey, set forth in English for the first time, serve as a friendly and informative guide to the instrument whose playing, as Quantz put it, "was brought to its greatest perfection" by Johann Sebastian Bach.

George B. Stauffer
General Editor, American Bach Society

preface to the English Edition

It is almost sixty years since the appearance of Werner David's excellent book *Johann Sebastian Bach's Orgeln* (Berlin, 1951). Out of print since the 1960s and not available in many music libraries, David's study was the first to offer a conveniently referenced overview of the instruments that were important to the organist and organ expert Johann Sebastian Bach. In the decades since then, however, the state of our knowledge has changed considerably. Not only have additional instruments been identified with which Bach had direct or indirect contact, but also very detailed information regarding the organs themselves is now available. For these reasons, a reworking of the material presented in such exemplary fashion by David has long been overdue, especially since no study has replaced it. Finally, and not least, the numerous tours now being undertaken to historical Bach organs in what used to be a region largely cut off by the Iron Curtain of the Cold War period make the need for such an updated, expanded, and reliable guide all the more obvious.

Like David's book in its time, the present handbook attempts to present the current state of knowledge. To this end, additional new materials have been gathered, assessed, and organized into a comprehensive handbook. The format has been expanded to include not only the instruments played by Bach, presented alphabetically by location with appropriate biographical and organological material, but also the so-called reference organs. The latter, whose selection is limited to instruments from Bach's narrowest circle, have a significance that should not be underestimated, both with respect to rounding out the theme of the book and to generally broadening our understanding of Bach's organ world. Like David, we have included Bach's examination reports and testimonials, since only these afford a concrete look at what was, for Bach, an essential activity as organ expert and examiner. In addition, emphasis has been placed on the contributions and significance of individual organ builders, especially those with whom Bach had close contact—an aspect not treated by David.

I first made plans to write this book in the 1960s in connection with my organ study at the Hochschule für Musik in Berlin. I was first encouraged by discussions with Michael Schneider, my organ teacher and fatherly friend. Since then my understanding of historical organs has been significantly enlarged by, above all, Luigi Ferdinando Tagliavini, Gustav Leonhardt, Ton Koopman, the late Ewald Kooiman, Harald Vogel, the late Charles Fisk, and John Brombaugh—although this list represents only a small number of my organist and organologist friends. As it turns out, the old plan for a handbook of Bach's organs could be realized only after various crucial requirements were met.

Especially important have been the recent proper restoration of the most important instruments, access to the central German organs that has been possible only since the demise of the communist-run German Democratic Republic in 1989–90, and, finally, the realization that a handbook of historical Bach organs should be a task for the Bach-Archive Leipzig, whose directorship I assumed in 2001. The crucial turning point came, though, when I was able to win over my former doctoral student Markus Zepf, a colleague just as interested in, and knowledgeable and enthusiastic about, the project as I. Without him this project would again have come to nothing. His preparation of the basic material—especially of the organological information in Part I and the information regarding the organ builders in Part III—is an essential and central contribution.

In a spirit of friendly cooperation, three colleagues and friends carefully read major portions of the German original manuscript for this book: Winfried Schrammek, former director of the Museum of Musical Instruments, University of Leipzig, unmatched in his knowledge of the historical central German organ landscape; Jean-Claude Zehnder, who taught for decades at the Schola Cantorum in Basel and who, as organist, was entrusted with all of the still-existing organs that are described here; and Kristian Wegscheider, master organ builder and restorer in Dresden, whose substantial experience in the field of original instruments is difficult to surpass. All three provided valuable, constructive criticism, and their knowledge and suggestions were included in the final version. It must be expressly stated, however, that any errors that may remain are entirely the responsibility of the authors.

A special thank-you is due as well to my colleagues at the Bach-Archive Leipzig. Michael Maul undertook considerable archival research and completed the list of organists from Bach's time. Marion Söhnel's editorial assistance was of benefit to this book, and Miriam Wolf diplomatically coordinated the people involved and the necessary planning of the work. Not to be overlooked is the Evangelische Verlagsanstalt Leipzig, represented by Annegret Grimm, who—especially with the extensive undertaking of acquiring all the photographic materials—demonstrated active support for the "Edition Bach-Archiv Leipzig."

Considerable interest in an American edition arose soon after the book was published in 2006, but it took several years for the plan to come to fruition. From the very beginning, however, I had envisioned as translator Lynn Edwards Butler. Our collaboration had begun in the mid-1970s when she was one of the two founding directors of the Westfield

Center. It culminated in a most memorable American organ tour through Thuringia and Saxony, organized by Lynn's Westfield Center and covering much of the ground surveyed in this book. The tour took place in the early fall of 1989, the very time at which a political change seemed imminent, even though its direction was still unknown. A few months later, the German Democratic Republic was gone and the unparalleled riches of the central German organ landscape became freely accessible. I am most grateful to Lynn not only for her expert translation, but also for the many improvements to the updated original text of the second German edition of 2008—emendations based on her own organological knowledge and experience.

The American edition includes additional pictorial material and provides new color photographs for most of the historical instruments still in existence. It also presents a slightly revised "Introductory Sketch" with a brief new section on Bach and the liturgical use of the organ.

I wish to express my gratitude to George B. Stauffer, distinguished Bach scholar and general editor for the American Bach Society. Lynn's involvement and George's editorial oversight clearly made this a better book. Deep-felt thanks are also due to the American Bach Society and Mary Jewett Greer, its current president, for providing support without which this publication would not have been possible. Finally, I have to say that I am pleased and proud to be surrounded in this project by Markus Zepf, Lynn Butler, George Stauffer, and Mary Greer—a truly remarkable and congenial team of enthusiastic scholars and friends.

Christoph Wolff

Bach—organist, composer, organ expert
An Introductory Sketch

It was hardly by chance that the obituary drafted only a few months after Johann Sebastian Bach's death and later published in volume 4 of *Musikalische Bibliothek* (Leipzig, 1754) referred in its title to the "World-Famous Organist . . . Court Composer, and Music Director" (NBR, no. 306; BDOK III, no. 666). The author and publisher of the obituary no doubt took into account the fact that the extent of Bach's fame and special renown as organ virtuoso was much greater during his lifetime than his limited recognition generally. And it was no exaggeration to use the term "world-famous." After all, in March 1750—before Bach's death—Padre Giovanni Battista Martini of Bologna had written in a letter: "I consider it to be superfluous to describe the singular merit of Sig. Bach, for he is thoroughly known and admired not only in Germany but throughout our Italy" (NBR, no. 385; BDOK II, no. 600). This sounds like an exaggeration, and probably is. However, it cannot be forgotten that Padre Martini owned a number of Bach manuscripts and prints, including a copy of *Clavier-Übung* III (Leipzig, 1739), one of Bach's most important organ works.

Bach's historical position as organist was recognized soon after his death. The Prussian court musician Johann Joachim Quantz, discussing the development of the art of organ playing in his *Versuch einer Anweisung die Flöte traversière zu spielen* (Berlin, 1752), referred to such figures as Froberger, Reinken, Buxtehude, Pachelbel, and Bruhns, noting at the conclusion: "Finally the admirable Johann Sebastian Bach brought it to its greatest perfection in recent times" (NBR, no. 350; BDOK III, no. 651). In Quantz's view, the "art of organ playing" included both performance and composition. As a flute virtuoso and composer for his instrument, Quantz understood only too well that one's technical skill on an instrument affected one's compositional concepts, and vice versa. This was also true for Bach. From childhood onward, his instrumental orientation and vocal background complemented each other, just as his keyboard skills were supplemented by his string experience and augmented by a compositional focus that eventually included the widest possible spectrum of musical instruments and human voices. All of this was supported by a deep knowledge and keen awareness of technological and physiological details and balanced by intellectual discipline and temperamental sensitivity.

The foundation for Bach's systematic approach to his musical undertakings was firmly established before he started his career. Nevertheless, the years in Arnstadt and Mühlhausen and the early years in Weimar, when easily managed duties coexisted with considerable personal freedom and economic security, offered this gifted, highly motivated, industrious, and ambitious musician ideal opportunities for extensive practicing, reflection, and composition. Above all, by a stroke of luck he had access in Arnstadt (where he held his first position) to a brand-new and perfectly functioning instrument constructed by one of the best and most advanced organ builders of his time. The instrument boasted a modern well-tempered tuning that offered no limits to his harmonic experiments and that did not require—as church organs then did of most organists—that he constantly repair it. For four critical years of his artistic life, from 1703 to 1707, he had an ideal—one might even say a more than perfect—performance laboratory at his disposal in which he could strengthen and expand his virtuosity and, as a composer, build and develop his harmonic fantasy and tonal ideas. In addition, Bach enjoyed early on the encouragement, recognition, and support of respected and influential older colleagues, among them in particular the organists Georg Böhm, Johann Adam Reinken, and Johann Effler, and the organ builder Johann Friedrich Wender.

Already as a young organist, and to no less an extent as a mature player, Bach was interested in the entire gamut of musical genres, whether chorale-based or not, contrapuntal or free, written in a few voices or many. By approximately 1714–15, he had investigated practically all of the various ways in which organ and keyboard music could be composed: from the various types of organ chorales (such as large-scale fantasias, chorale partitas or variations, and chorale fugues) to the wide spectrum of genres common to both the organ and harpsichord (such as canzona, passacaglia, toccata, prelude, fantasia, fugue, sonata, and concerto). Added to this was his never-ending interest in the compositional technique of others, from the earliest to the very latest repertoire. Bach's library eventually contained collections as old as Elias Nicolaus Ammerbach's *Orgel oder Instrument Tabulatur* (Leipzig, 1571), of which he owned no less than three copies, and Frescobaldi's *Fiori musicali* (Rome, 1635), of which he prepared a handwritten copy in 1714, as well as works of German, French, and Italian masters of the late seventeenth and early eighteenth centuries. He also assembled compositions not only of his contemporaries, but also of the generation of his students—all of which allowed him to grapple with the most diverse technical and stylistic challenges.

By no later than 1710, when he was twenty-five years old, Bach had mastered all the technical demands of organ and harpsichord playing. What remained was to set standards for the future. As a thoroughly conventional work written before 1710 reveals, moreover,

Bach already operated at the very pinnacle of compositional technique. This is seen in even a glance at the artistic demands of a piece such as the Passacaglia in C Minor, BWV 582, and quite apart from the technical demands that performing such a uniquely large-scaled work requires. The same can be said of the basically new aesthetic premise of his small-format compositions, as demonstrated in the motivically compact structure and formal symmetry of the chorale "Herr Christ, der ein'ge Gottessohn," BWV 601, also written before 1710 and later included in the *Orgel-Büchlein*. In both works, the inclusion of obbligato pedal parts demonstrates Bach's independent development of the pedal far beyond Buxtehude's basic approach. Bach also took new paths in organ playing and composition in other equally exemplary works, such as the large preludes and fugues of the Leipzig period, the trio sonatas, or the chorale repertoire of *Clavier-Übung* III. Over and over again, he explored new territory, in both performing technique and composition. The organist and organ composer Bach maintained these innovative tendencies in his art right until the end of his life, as can be seen in the *Canonic Variations on "Vom Himmel hoch,"* written in the late 1740s.

The repertory of Bach's organ works genuinely reflects the important role of the church instrument in the Lutheran worship service. The "Order of the Divine Service in Leipzig" that Bach entered in the score of Cantata BWV 61 for the First Sunday in Advent 1723 (NBR, no. 113) indicates three "preluding" functions of the organ within the service: playing preludes (1) at the beginning of the service, (2) for the chorales sung by the congregation, and (3) for the cantata. Chorale-based preludes served the purpose of introducing the melody of the hymn to the congregation, free preludes could be played at the opening of the service (and by implication at its conclusion), and the prelude for the cantata was supposed to provide cover for tuning the instruments and to establish the pitch for the ensemble performance.

Not mentioned in Bach's note is the organ's accompanimental function. While in Thuringian towns like Eisenach, Arnstadt, Mühlhausen, or Weimar the organ traditionally accompanied hymns, congregational singing in Leipzig and throughout Saxony remained unaccompanied until the later eighteenth century. On the other hand, the participation of the large, west-end organ in the continuo group of the cantata orchestra, although self-evident, is worth stressing. Bach's assigning the organ an obbligato function for a series of cantatas in 1726–27 (e.g., BWV 49, 146, 169, 188), and thereby featuring the instrument within the orchestra in an unprecedented and particularly prominent way, undoubtedly grew out of this continuo practice.

It is important to understand that service playing by professional organists, the "Figural-Organisten," was always done *ex tempore*. Only the less accomplished or amateur players, the "Choral-Organisten," who often worked under the supervision of the main town organist, would ordinarily have read from music. Bach himself would have improvised any kind of free or chorale-based prelude. (For a reference to Bach accompanying the congregation, see the Altenburg entry.) Therefore, the majority of Bach's extant organ works were written for his activities as a recitalist, which involved a great variety of preludes, toccatas, fantasias, and fugues, as well as a broad spectrum of organ chorales. The smaller, shorter, more functional, and technically less demanding pieces within the repertory appear to have been written for pedagogical reasons or for the use of "chorale organists" unable to improvise.

Organ and organ music, the critical area of experimentation for the young Bach, remained an absolutely essential point of orientation also for the middle-aged and older Bach. A special attribute in pieces like the Brandenburg concertos or the Weimar and Leipzig vocal works with their instrumental dimensions, is that over and over again, in comparison to similar compositions by his contemporaries, they allow Bach's identity as organist to be recognized. Even in his compositions for orchestra and vocal ensemble, Bach understood how to "register," often with the goal of creating new tonal experiences. This can be seen quite clearly in the scoring of four violins in the cantata "Gleichwie der Regen und Schnee," BWV 18, the use of four different instruments (recorder, oboe, viols d'amore, and viol da gamba) in the cantata "Tritt auf die Glaubensbahn," BWV 152, the scoring of two viols d'amore with lute in "Betrachte, meine Seel" in the St. John Passion, or the use of corno da caccia with two fagottos in "Quoniam" in the B-Minor Mass.

Bach's interest throughout his entire life was not just in the sound, and sound combinations, of individual instruments, but also in the building and development of new musical instruments of all kinds. His name is connected with the improvement and sale of fortepianos built in the Silbermann style, with the lute-harpsichord of his Jena relative Johann Nicolaus Bach, with the oboe da caccia and bassono grosso of the Leipzig instrument maker Johann Heinrich Eichentopf, and with the violoncello piccolo of the Leipzig court lute maker Johann Christian Hoffmann (who named Bach executor of his will). This hands-on, experimental side of the musical fraternity was not merely enjoyable for Bach—he must have found himself entirely in his métier. From his earliest school days, his primary interest had been the organ. The Ohrdruf organ-building workshop of Georg Christoph Stertzing may have provided Bach's first insights into the practical side of organ building, for during the time that he was a student in the Ohrdruf Lyceum, Stertzing was making preparations for building the organ for Eisenach's St. George's Church. At that time it was Thuringia's largest instrument, an organ whose disposition was devised by Bach's relative Johann Christoph Bach. Bach remained in contact with the elder Stertzing; in 1716, only a few months before Stertzing's death, he examined the instrument Stertzing had started in Erfurt's St. Augustine's Church.

Bach's vast practical experience with the organ, his intense and wide-ranging self-education, his innate curiosity, and his active contact with skilled and experienced organ builders made him an organ expert of the first rank. His undisputed competence was recognized at an early point, and he exploited it all his life, both to his own advantage and to the advantage of others. That Bach was involved time and again, even into his later years, with proposals for a wide range of organs, rebuilds, and repairs is an aspect of his professional life that should not be underestimated. His experience is highly unusual in the history of music and has clear implications for understanding important connections in his musical art.

At his first organ examination in 1703 at the New Church in Arnstadt, when Bach found himself at the age of eighteen judging the work of Johann Friedrich Wender, a master organ builder some thirty years his senior, the result was not generational conflict but rather a lasting relationship based on reciprocal respect. This close relationship then extended to Wender's son, whom Bach advised as late as 1735 in Mühlhausen. Well-established acquaintance with a large variety of instruments in Thuringia and north Germany, and also, no doubt, the reading of the writings of Andreas Werckmeister, formed the foundation for Bach's expertise. His technical knowledge was probably augmented through his close relationship with Wender, who enticed Bach from Arnstadt to Mühlhausen and at the same time dissuaded Bach's distant cousin Johann Gottfried Walther from competing for the position (Wolff 2000, 102). A similar ongoing and productive relationship can be seen later in Bach's dealings with the young Heinrich Nicolaus Trebs in Weimar or with Zacharias Hildebrandt in Leipzig.

Bach's written examination reports impressively demonstrate thoroughness, a deep understanding of the material, and comprehensive knowledge of the construction and use of the organ. Not even the smallest detail escaped his attention. The Mühlhausen renovation project, for which Bach's report has survived, demonstrates in particular how highly Bach valued the organization, specific character, and balancing of an organ's stops. He paid special attention to the gravity of the instrument, which ideally would be provided by a new "Untersatz," a 32' register. But he also had the idea of strengthening the gravity further by enlarging the resonators and replacing the shallots of the existing Posaune 16'. He also recommended replacing the existing Gemshorn with a "Viol di Gamba 8', which will blend admirably with the present Salicional 4' in the Rückpositiv." He specified a wide variety of materials for the pipes, demanding "good 14-worthy [87.5%] tin" for the three "Principalia" in the facade of the "new little Brustpositiv." In addition, he requested that a "Stillgedackt 8', which is perfect for accompanying concerted vocal music," be built from "good wood" because then it would sound "better than a metal Gedackt."

In his report on the Hildebrandt organ in the St. Wenceslas's Church in Naumburg, which he and Gottfried Silbermann examined in 1746, Bach wrote that in a proper examination "every part specified and promised by the contract—namely, keyboards, bellows, wind chests, wind lines, pedal and keyboard actions along with their various parts, registers, and stops, both open and stopped, as well as reeds" needs to be inspected to see that everything is "really there." In the same report he remarked that the examiners have inspected whether "each and every part has been made with appropriate care" and whether "the pipes have been properly built from the materials promised." He recommended, however, that the organ builder "go through the entire instrument once more, stop by stop, in order to achieve more evenness in the voicing as well as in the key and stop actions."

The Scheibe organ in the University Church in Leipzig had similar problems, and Bach recommended taking appropriate precautions against the "occasional wind surges" and correcting the "uneven voicing" so that the "lowest pipes in the Posaunenbass 16' and Trompetenbass 8' do not speak so roughly and with such a rattle, but with a pure and firm tone." In addition, higher standards were to be met so that the organ's playing action is "somewhat lighter" and "the keyfall . . . not so deep." The report on the Scheibe organ also shows that Bach was in a position to delve into basic construction problems. He criticized the case of the organ and the fact that "it is difficult to reach each part," but showed sympathy for the organ builder, who "was not granted the additional space he had desired in order to arrange the layout more capaciously." He also recommended that "as far as the window rises up behind it, the organ should be protected from further threats of weather damage by means of a small wall or a strong piece of sheet iron placed inside the window."

"Despite all of this knowledge of the organ," the obituary notes, "he never enjoyed the good fortune, as he used to point out frequently with regret, of having a really large and really beautiful organ at his constant disposal. This fact has robbed us of many beautiful and unknown inventions in organ playing that he would otherwise have written down and displayed in the form in which he had them in his head" (NBR, no. 306; BDOK III, no. 666). The instruments Bach had at his disposal in Arnstadt, Mühlhausen, and Weimar were comparatively medium-sized organs. It is therefore understandable that the organist position available in 1720 at St. Jacobi in Hamburg must have been tempting to Bach, even if there was an even better organ at Hamburg's St. Catherine's Church. In Leipzig, Bach certainly would have had unhindered access to the large Scheibe organ (III/48) in the St. Paul's Church. But it is also true that it was not actually his instrument. If it had been, he most certainly would have written more organ works during the Leipzig years. On the other hand, the number of organ compositions by Bach that has been transmitted is astonishingly high. Beyond this, there remains the fact that Bach's organ compositions were never conceived entirely for a specific instrument. Rather, from the beginning the composer took for granted that his works would be played on various organs. It is thus all the more instructive from the point of view of modern interpreters, listeners, and organ enthusiasts that the spectrum of historical organs in Bach's world be considered in its full breadth, diversity, and beauty.

March 21, 1685	Is born in Eisenach as eighth and youngest child of Johann Ambrosius and Maria Elisabeth Bach
1685–95	Grows up in Eisenach; attends German and Latin schools; associates with city organist Johann Christoph Bach
1696–1700	Attends Lyceum in Ohrdruf and is tutored by his eldest brother, Johann Christoph Bach, who had studied with Johann Pachelbel; makes copies (not surviving) of works of Pachelbel and Froberger, among others; before 1700, prepares tablature copy of Buxtehude's large chorale fantasy "Nun freut euch, lieben Christen g'mein," BuxWV 210 (fragment survives); writes his first organ compositions ("Neumeister Collection") and makes his first contacts with organ builder Georg Christoph Stertzing, who at the time had his workshop in Ohrdruf
March 1700 – ca. Easter 1702	Studies with Georg Böhm in Lüneburg and is choral scholar at St. Michael's School; makes visits to Johann Adam Reinken in Hamburg
1700 (dated)	Prepares autograph tablature copy of Reinken's organ chorale "An Wasserflüssen Babylon"
Fall 1702	Successfully applies for the town organist post in Sangerhausen (successor to Gottfried Christoph Gräffenhayn); because of interference by the duke in Weißenfels, the post is given to another applicant
December 1702– June 1703	Serves as lackey and musician at the private chapel of Duke Johann Ernst of Saxe-Weimar. Position obtained by mediation of the Weimar court organist, Johann Effler, a Bach-family friend; probable that primary activity was serving as Effler's assistant

| July 1703 | Examines and dedicates the Wender organ at the New Church in Arnstadt |

Organist at the New Church in Arnstadt

August 9, 1703	Accepts appointment as organist at the New Church in Arnstadt
November 1705– February 1706	Takes four-month-long study trip to Dieterich Buxtehude in Lübeck; he presumably heard and participated in performances in December 1705 of Buxtehude's oratorios *Castrum doloris*, BuxWV 134, and *Templum honoris*, BuxWV 135
ca. 1705–06	Pens autograph of Prelude and Fugue in G Minor, BWV 535a
November 28, 1706	Examines the Albrecht/Erhardt organ in Langewiesen
1706–08	Tests the Wender organ in Ammern (?)
April 24, 1707 (Easter Sunday)	Auditions for the organist position (successor to Johann Georg Ahle) in the free imperial city of Mühlhausen, probably with a performance of the cantata "Christ lag in Todesbanden," BWV 4

City Organist in Mühlhausen

July 1, 1707	Begins as city organist at St. Blasius's Church in Mühlhausen; ancillary position at the Bridge Church (Brückenkirche)
February 1708	Presents plan for renovating and enlarging the organ at St. Blasius's
June 1708	Is offered position of court organist in Weimar (successor to the retiring Johann Effler)

Court Organist in Weimar

July 1708	Begins as court organist and chamber musician at ducal court in Weimar
ca. 1709–12	Makes his own copy of Nicolas de Grigny's *Premier livre d'orgue* (1701)
October 26, 1711	Examines and dedicates the Trebs organ in Taubach
1712–14	Oversees the rebuilding by Heinrich Nicolaus Trebs of the castle church organ
November– December, 1713	Auditions for the position of organist and music director of the Church of Our Lady in Halle (successor to Friedrich Wilhelm Zachow)
ca. 1713	Autograph of *Orgel-Büchlein*, BWV 599–644 (majority of entries)
1714	Copies Girolamo Frescobaldi's *Fiori musicali* (1635)
February 1714	Rejects the position in Halle
March 2, 1714	Is appointed concertmaster in Weimar, while retaining court organist position

ca. 1714–17 (?)	Prepares autograph of arrangement of Vivaldi's Concerto in D Minor, BWV 596, and the organ chorale "Nun komm, der Heiden Heiland," BWV 660a
April 28 – May 2, 1716	Examines (with Johann Kuhnau and Christian Friedrich Rolle) the Contius organ at Church of Our Lady, Halle (Saale)
July 31, 1716	Examines the Stertzing/Schröter organ at St. Augustine's Church, Erfurt
March 1717	In Gotha, briefly replaces the ailing court kapellmeister and court church organist, Christian Friedrich Witt; performs a passion
August 1, 1717	Accepts appointment as court kapellmeister in Köthen; begins service at the end of December
Fall 1717	Travels to Dresden; wins contest with Louis Marchand by default

Court Kapellmeister in Köthen

after December 2, 1717	Begins service in Köthen
December 16–18, 1717	Examines the Scheibe organ in St. Paul's Church, Leipzig
November 1720	Applies (by invitation) and successfully auditions for the position of organist (successor to Heinrich Friese) at St. Jacobi, Hamburg, with concerts at St. Jacobi and at St. Catherine's (Reinken is a member of the audition committee), probably including a performance of the cantata "Ich hatte viel Bekümmernis," BWV 21; return trip on November 23
before December 19, 1720	Withdraws from the Hamburg candidacy
July – beginning of August 1721	Visits Gera, probably in connection with the building of the Finke organs in the Castle Chapel and St. Salvator's Church
April 19, 1723	Accepts position of cantor at the St. Thomas School and music director in Leipzig (successor to Johann Kuhnau)

Thomascantor and Music Director in Leipzig

May 30, 1723	Begins work in Leipzig
November 2, 1723	Examines and dedicates the Hildebrandt organ in Störmthal with performance of the cantata "Höchsterwünschtes Freudenfest," BWV 194
ca. 1723–24	Autograph of Fantasia in C Major, BWV 573
May 30 – June 6, 1725	Examines and dedicates the Finke organ in St. John's Church, Gera; tests the organ in St. Salvator's Church

September 19–20, 1725	Presents two recitals on the Silbermann organ at St. Sophia's Church, Dresden, partially along with the court chapel musicians
1726–28	Is advisor for the new organ at St. Jacob's Church, Sangerhausen (?)
1727–31	Pens autograph (fair copy) of the Prelude and Fugue in B Minor, BWV 544, and partial autograph of the Prelude and Fugue in E Minor, BWV 548
Between 1729 and 1741	Probably visits the Casparini organ in Görlitz
December 1729	Examines candidates for the position of organist at St. Nicholas's, Leipzig; Bach student Johann Schneider is successful
September 14, 1731	Presents recital on the Silbermann organ at St. Sophia's, Dresden
November 12, 1731	Examines the Schmieder organ in Stöntzsch; a further, final examination takes place on February 4, 1732
September 21–28, 1732	Examines and dedicates the Stertzing/Becker organ at St. Martin's Church, Kassel; recital with Anna Magdalena Bach, performs Toccata in D Minor, BWV 538
ca. 1733	Prepares fair copy of the trio sonatas, BWV 525–530; autograph of the Prelude and Fugue in G Major, BWV 541
June 23, 1733	After an audition the previous day at which he may have performed BWV 541, son Wilhelm Friedemann is chosen as organist of St. Sophia's Church, Dresden
June 1735	Travels to Mühlhausen; advises Wender regarding new organ for St. Mary's Church; successful audition by his son Johann Gottfried Bernhard for the post of organist there
June 22, 1735	On the return trip from Mühlhausen, tests the organ in Weißensee
December 1, 1736	Performs two-hour dedication concert of the new Silbermann organ in Our Lady's Church, Dresden
January 14, 1737	Son Johann Gottfried Bernhard is chosen as city organist in Sangerhausen
December 1737	Examines the Schäfer organ in Weißensee (?)
1739–42, 1746–47	Revises the "Great Eighteen Chorales," BWV 651–68 (partial autograph manuscript)
before September 7, 1739	Plays the new Trost organ in the court church in Altenburg
St. Michael's Fair, 1739	Publishes *Clavier-Übung* III
ca. 1742	Drafts disposition for a new Trebs organ in Berka

before December 13, 1743	Examines (with Zacharias Hildebrandt) Scheibe's organ for St. John's Church, Leipzig
1743–46	Planning and building of the Hildebrandt organ for St. Wenceslas's Church, Naumburg
April 16, 1746	Son Wilhelm Friedemann becomes organist and music director of the Market Church in Halle
August 7, 1746	Examines the Scheibe organ in Zschortau
September 24–28, 1746	Examines (with Gottfried Silbermann) the Hildebrandt organ in St. Wenceslas's Church, Naumburg
May 1747	While on a visit to the Prussian court, plays the Wagner organs in Potsdam churches
November (?) 1747	Examines the renovated organ at St. Thomas's, Leipzig
1747	Publishes the *Canonic Variations on "Vom Himmel hoch,"* BWV 769
1747–48	Publishes *Sechs Choräle von verschiedener Art* ("Schübler chorales"), BWV 645–50; autograph (only a fragment survives) of Fugue in C Minor, BWV 562/2
January 12, 1748	Writes letter of recommendation for organ builder Heinrich Andreas Contius
September 1748	Bach's son-in-law Johann Christoph Altnickol becomes organist at St. Wenceslas's in Naumburg
June 1749	Communicates with Heinrich Andreas Contius concerning plans for a new organ at the Franciscan Church, Frankfurt (Oder)
October 3, 1749	Is recommended by Johann Jacob Donati Jr. as consultant for a new organ in Hartmannsdorf, near Dresden
June–July 1750 (?)	Revises the chorale "Wenn wir in höchsten Nöten sein," BWV 668a, under the title "Vor deinen Thron tret' ich hiermit," BWV 668
July 28, 1750	Dies in Leipzig, at 8:15 in the evening

Lübeck

Hamburg

Elbe

Bremen

Lüneburg

BRANDENBURG

Celle

Berlin

Frankfurt (Oder)

Oder

Hannover

Brunswick

Havel Potsdam

Bückeburg

Magdeburg

Weser

Zerbst

Köthen

Göttingen

Sangerhausen

Halle

Elbe

Kassel

Sondershausen

Leipzig

SAXONY

Mühlhausen

Unstrut

Weißenfels

Eisenach

Gotha Erfurt Weimar

Naumburg

Dresden

Wechmar Dornheim

Jena

Zeitz

Altenburg

Ohrdruf Arnstadt

Gera

Suhl

Rudolstadt THURINGIA

Meiningen

Gehren

Schleiz

White Elster

Karlsbad

BOHEMIA

Werra

Coburg

Saale

Frankfurt (Main)

Lahm

Prague

Schweinfurt

Main

Rhine

Vltava

Nuremberg

0   100 km

■ = places where Bach lived
▲ = places Bach visited
△ = places with Bach-reference organs
● = Bach-family places
○ = reference location

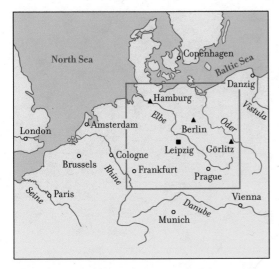

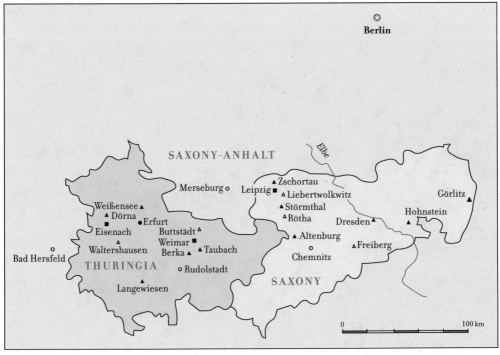

the organs of **J.S.Bach**

PART ONE

The Organs of J. S. Bach

Preliminary Remarks

Churches. Historical information concerning the churches in which the organs are situated is meant to provide a basic orientation, since the size, disposition, care, and use of an organ depends on external conditions such as the architecture of the space and who is in charge of the organ (e.g., the court or the city). Details of the history of the church are provided only when they are of importance to the organ itself (e.g., Hamburg/St. Jacobi, 1714, collapse of the vault over the organ; destruction of the building in 1944 [the organ was in storage]).

Organs. Organ descriptions are specific to their condition at the time the organ was encountered by Johann Sebastian Bach. Dates of construction of earlier and later instruments are mentioned only when they have direct relevance to the state in which the instrument was known to Bach. In cases where the instruments were enlarged and changed over several centuries, such as Hamburg/St. Catherine's or Lüneburg/St. John's, the essential developmental stages are cited.

Dispositions. Dispositions represent their configuration at the time the organs were encountered by Bach; each is provided with the date the disposition was recorded, as well as the size (number of manuals/number of stops) of the organ. The spelling of stop names follows the historical sources, except that the number of ranks in multiranked stops is given in Roman numerals next to the name of the register. Manuals are numbered from bottom to top.

Pitch. Only for recently renovated organs is dependable information available regarding pitch. During Bach's time, it was highly variable compared to the modern standard pitch of $a^1 = 440$ Hz at $15°$ C ($g^{\#1} = 415$ Hz, $g^1 = 391$ Hz, $b^{b1} = 495$ Hz). (Note: For the frequencies given in Part I, Sections A and B, if not specifically otherwise noted, pitches are based on a room temperature of $15°$ C.) Historical data cited from organ-building contracts is limited to indications of the use of Kammerton, a pitch standard imported to Germany from France around 1700 and which during Bach's time was considered an exception to the norm. A Kammerton pitch of a^1 = 415 Hz (also called Dresden Kammerton), about one half tone below modern standard pitch, was the most prevalent, but pitches up to a whole tone lower, a^1 = 408–392 Hz (low or French Kammerton), are also documented. In central and north German church organs of the seventeenth and eighteenth centuries, the prevalent pitch was Chorton (also called Cornetton), preferred because of the greater tonal brilliance it afforded, and predominantly set at a^1 = ca. 465 Hz, around a half tone higher than modern standard pitch. Pitches of up to a whole tone higher (high Chorton) are also documented, however, such as a^1 = 476 Hz (Silbermann, Freiberg/Cathedral) and a^1 = 495 Hz (Schnitger, Hamburg/St. Jacobi).

The existing pitch differences of the time posed problems in performance of concerted music—that is, when vocal and instrumental ensembles performed church music together. The most practical solution, and the one preferred by Bach, was to transpose the figured bass or continuo part assigned to the organ. Organ builders confronted the problem in various ways. In 1738, Christian Friedrich Wender, for example, provided the organ for Mühlhausen's St. Mary's Church with two Kammerton couplers. Gottfried Silbermann noted in numerous proposals that organs in low Kammerton required longer pipes, which resulted in higher costs.

Temperament. Information regarding temperament is given only for restored instruments. Each and every organ builder had (and has) his own system of tempering, and these temperaments are not unequivocally recoverable from surviving pipes. In the seventeenth and early eighteenth centuries, organs in Germany were tuned in meantone (where pure thirds were emphasized); starting around 1700, modifications to this system began to be made in newly built instruments. Irregular (well-tempered) tunings that allowed performance in all keys, set according to Andreas Werckmeister, Johann Georg Neidthardt, and other music theorists, were gradually established. In the circle of the young Johann Sebastian Bach, the organ builders Johann Friedrich Wender and Georg Christoph Stertzing, as well as the organists Johann Christoph Bach, Johann Effler, Dieterich Buxtehude, and Johann Kuhnau, were prominent advocates of well-tempered tunings. During the renovation of Jena's Collegiate Church organ (built 1690) by Zacharias Thayßner, Johann Nicolaus Bach, organist of Jena University, called temperament "the most noble [attribute] of an organ." In his expert's report of 1704, he demanded the retuning of the apparently meantone organ to allow for performance in "diatonic–chromatic–enharmonic" keys—that is, in all keys. The retuning of the organ (II/25) was accomplished in less than ten days (Maul 2004b, 160–61).

Some organs still tuned in meantone—such as the organ built in 1704 by the Donats for Leipzig's New Church—had a "Lieblich Gedackt 8' for concerted music," a stop that was set in a milder temperament than the rest of the organ in order to allow for a greater range of harmonic possibilities. Nothing is known about the temperament of the organs in Leipzig's two principal churches. Because of their Chorton pitch, organ parts for the cantatas were written at a pitch one tone lower than parts for the other instruments. According to Bach's original performance materials, a piece in C minor would have been played by the organist in B♭ minor, for example, or a piece in E♭ major would have been played in D♭ major, a practice the organs had apparently allowed since the time of Kuhnau.

For the use of a pure meantone temperament, as described, for example, by Michael Praetorius in the second part of his *Syntagma musicum* (Wolfenbüttel, 1619), it is necessary for the organ to have subsemitones (split sharps) for the pitches e♭/d♯ and g♯/a♭. Such subsemitones are rarely to be found in Bach's world at the turn of the seventeenth to the eighteenth centuries, however. On the other hand, a short-octave bass (where the lowest C, D, and E are played by the keys E, F♯, and G♯) or the absence of the low C♯ in an otherwise complete lowest octave was common into the middle of the eighteenth century, since compositions mostly did without these pitches.

Missing chromatic keys in the lowest octave are indicated by "CDEFGA–c^3" or "CD–c^3," for example, whereas complete keyboard compasses are indicated as "C–c^3." Any changes to the manual compasses are indicated—for example, 1714 in Lüneburg/St. Michael's or 1733 in Lübeck/St. Mary's.

Wind supply. The wind supply in seventeenth- and eighteenth-century organs was provided exclusively by wedge bellows that were hand or foot pumped. Historical wind pressures are given in only rare cases, such as for Altenburg/Court Church or Naumburg/St. Wenceslas's. Modern wind pressures for restored or renovated organs are given in millimeters on the water gauge (mm WC).

References. The literature and archival sources cited form the basis of this study and do not represent a complete bibliography. In order to provide an easily readable text, the author/date system is used for citations, which under (a) relate to the churches and organs, and under (b) relate to Johann Sebastian Bach. There is no discussion of varying views held by researchers or of contradictory statements in the literature.

Abbreviations:

Bp	=	Brustpositiv
Bw	=	Brustwerk
Hw	=	Hauptwerk
HinW	=	Hinterwerk
Op	=	Oberpositiv
Ow	=	Oberwerk
Ped	=	Pedal
Pos	=	Positiv
T	=	transmission
Uw	=	Unterwerk
W	=	Werk (Hauptwerk)

Organs with a Proven
Connection to Bach

Altenburg

There is evidence that Johann Sebastian Bach visited Altenburg at the beginning of September 1739, probably for an informal examination of the just-completed court organ, as well as to play the organ during a church service. According to the court record of September 7, 1739, "the well-known kapellmeister Bach, of Leipzig, was heard at the organ, and, in passing, judged that the organ's construction was very durable, and that the organ builder had succeeded in giving to each stop its particular nature and proper sweetness" (BDOK II, no. 453). Bach's participation in what was a successful examination and acceptance of the organ on October 26, 1739, in the presence of Gottfried Heinrich Stölzel, kapellmeister in Gotha, while apparently planned, never materialized.

Regarding Bach's organ playing during the church service (probably on September 6, 1739, the Fifteenth Sunday after Trinity), an anonymous "ear-witness" later reported: "Few are in a position to guide a congregation as old Bach could do, who one time on the large organ in Altenburg played the creedal hymn ["Wir glauben all an einen Gott" (We all believe in one God)] in D minor, but raised the congregation to E♭ minor for the second verse, and on the third verse even went to E minor. But only a Bach could do this and only the organ in Altenburg. Not all of us are or have that" (BDOK V, no. C1005a).

Organists of the court church included Gottfried Ernst Pestel (1681–1732) and Christian Lorenz (1732–48). Bach's student Johann Ludwig Krebs took over the position in 1756 and held it until his death in 1780.

Court Church (St. George's)/Schlosskirche St. Georg

Gothic hall church, completed 1473. Baroque furnishing of the interior in 1645–49 according to designs by Christoph Richter; the two fifteenth-century stone balconies were retained.

Organ: Newly built 1733–39 by Tobias Heinrich Gottfried Trost on recommendation of Duke Friedrich II of Saxe-Gotha-Altenburg. With assistance from the court sculptor Johann Jeremias Martini, the instrument was placed on the north balcony of the choir. Numerous alterations in the nineteenth and twentieth centuries. Eule Orgelbau restored the organ in 1976 to its 1739 condition.

Disposition 1739/1976 (II/37)

Hauptwerk (I)	Oberwerk (II)	Pedal
Groß-Quintadena 16' (T)	Geigenprincipal 8'	Principalbaß 16'
Flaute traverse 16' (T)	Lieblich Gedackt 8'	Groß-Quintadena 16' (T)
Principal 8'	Vugara 8'	Flaute traverse 16' (T)
Bordun 8' (T)	Quintadena 8'	Violonbaß 16'
Spitzflöte 8'	Hohlflöte 8'	Subbaß 16'
Viol di Gamba 8'	Gemshorn 4'	Octavenbaß 8'
Rohrflöte 8'	Flauto dolce II 4'	Bordun 8' (T)
Octava 4' (T)	Nasat 3'	Octava 4' (T)
Kleingedackt 4'	Octave 2'	Mixtur VI–IX (T)
Quinte 3'	Waldflöte 2'	Posaune 32'
Superoctava 2'	Superoctava 1'	Posaune 16'
Blockflöte 2'	Cornet V (from g°)	Trompete 8'
Sesquialtera II	Mixtur IV–V	
Mixtur VI–IX (T)	Vox humana 8'	
Trompete 8'		
Glockenspiel c^1–c^3		

Particulars: Hw Trompette 8' reconstructed from four surviving Trost pipes.

Accessories: Hw tremulant; Ow tremulant; bellows signal.

Couplers: Manual shove coupler; wind coupler (Hw/Ped).

Compass: C–c^3 (manuals); C–c^1 (pedal).

Wind pressure (1739): manuals 30°, pedal 29°.

Wind pressure (1998): manuals 70 mm WC, pedal 68 mm WC.

Wind supply (1739/1998): four bellows to the manuals; two larger bellows for the pedal.

Pitch (1998): Chorton (468 Hz at 18.2° C).

Temperament (1998): Neidhardt I.

Literature: (a) Dähnert 1983, 19–25; Friedrich 1989; Friedrich 1998; Dehio 2003, 15–17. (b) BDOK II, nos. 453 and 460; BDOK V, no. C1005a; Schulze 1981, 32–42; Wolff 2000, 143, 145, 532; Wolff 2005a, xix.

1. Altenburg, Court Church:
Trost organ (photograph, 1985)

2. Altenburg, Court Church:
Trost organ (photograph, 1985)

Ammern

During either his Mühlhausen or Weimar period, Johann Sebastian Bach likely tested the Wender organ in Ammern, three miles north of Mühlhausen.

Church of St. Vitus/Kirche St. Vitus

Choir-tower church in the cemetery, presumably built around 1270. Hall church with wooden barrel-vaulted ceiling and two tiers of galleries on three sides; completely renovated at end of eighteenth century.

Organ: 1706–8, new organ (I/13) by Johann Friedrich Wender; disposition altered during construction (Octav Baß 8' replaced Fagottbaß 8'); exact disposition unknown. 1712, rebuild by Wender. 1859, new organ (II/15) by Johann Friedrich Große. Nothing from Bach's time survives.

Archival Source: Stadtarchiv Mühlhausen, *Chronik. Fragment 1533–1802*, Sign. 61/18, fol. 91v.

Literature: (a) Hunstock 1997, 85; Haupt 1998, 104; Dehio 2003, 33. (b) Kröhner 1995, 83–91.

Arnstadt

Johann Sebastian Bach was organist of the New Church from August 1703 until June 1707. Sometime prior to July 13, 1703, Bach, who had just turned eighteen, visited from Weimar at the order of the consistory of the count of Arnstadt in order to inspect and "play the new organ in the new church." Manifestly impressed with his abilities, the consistory straightaway offered Bach the position of organist at the New Church; the appointment was made on August 9, 1703. Bach remained there for only four years, after which he moved to St. Blasius's Church in Mühlhausen. It can be assumed that he was also familiar with the organs in the other Arnstadt churches and that from time to time he played them. His successor at the New Church was his cousin Johann Ernst Bach, who had substituted for him in 1705–6 during his trip to visit Dieterich Buxtehude in Lübeck. After Johann Ernst Bach, Johann Wilhelm Völcker was organist from 1728 to 1737.

Along with Erfurt, Arnstadt was a primary workplace of the Bach family of musicians during the seventeenth and eighteenth centuries. The brothers Heinrich and Christoph Bach worked in Arnstadt as organists and musicians to the court and city from 1641 and 1654, respectively. Heinrich Bach was city and court organist for decades, and his sons Johann Christoph and Johann Michael began their musical careers by assisting their father as organists at the Arnstadt court chapel of Count Schwarzburg in 1663–65 and 1665–73, respectively. Johann Christoph Bach, the older brother of Johann Sebastian, substituted for the ailing Heinrich Bach in Arnstadt in 1688–89. In 1692, Christoph Herthum, Heinrich Bach's son-in-law and Johann Christoph Bach's godfather, took over as city organist, serving both the Upper Church and the court chapel; he held the position until his death in 1710. He was succeeded by his son-in-law, Andreas Börner, who in 1703 (on the same day as Johann Sebastian Bach) was appointed organist of Our Lady's Church; earlier, while the Wender organ was under construction, Börner had played for the church services in the New Church. After the death of his father-in-law, Börner also took over the duties at the Lower Church.

New Church/Neue Kirche (since 1935, Johann Sebastian Bach Church)

Baroque hall church with barrel vault and two to three tiers of galleries, newly built in 1676–83, replacing St. Boniface's Church, which had been destroyed by a major city fire in 1581; remains of the oldest parish church in Arnstadt are integrated into the choir. Centrally located building with the largest seating capacity of the city's three churches.

Organ: 1699–1703, organ newly built in the students' balcony (third gallery) by Johann Friedrich Wender, financed in part by a bequest from the Arnstadt businessman Johann Wilhelm Magen; inspection report does not survive. 1709, painting of the organ case; 1710 and 1713, repairs and improvements by Wender. Rebuilds and enlargements in the late eighteenth and nineteenth centuries. 1913, new organ (III/55) by Steinmeyer Orgelbau using some stops and the case from Wender's organ. 1938, organ moved to the first gallery by Wiegand Helfenbein. 1997–99, restoration by Hoffmann Orgelbau and erection of the Steinmeyer organ in the first gallery; also, reconstruction and placement of the Wender organ in the third gallery. Wender pipework was reused and his playing action and key desk reconstructed. The original key desk, restored many times, has been held since 1864 as part of the Bach memorial located in a museum in the immediate vicinity of the church, the Haus "Zum Palmbaum" (House of the Palm Tree).

Disposition 1703/1999 (II/21)

Oberwerk (II)	Brustwerk/Positiv (I)	Pedal
Principal 8'	Stillgedacktes 8' (o)	Sub Baß 16'
Viola di Gamba 8' (o)	Principal 4'	Principal 8'
Quintadehna 8' (o)	Spitzflöte 4'	Posaunen Bass 16'
Grobgedacktes 8' (o)	Nachthorn 4' (o)	Cornet Bass 2'
Gemshorn 8' (o)	Quinta 3'	
Offene Quinta 6'	Sesquialtera doppelt [II]	
Octava 4' (o)	Mixtur III [1'] (o)	
Mixtur IV 2' (o)		
Cymbel II [1'] (o)		
Trompete 8'		

Particulars: o = register with at least 50 percent historical material. For Hw Principal 8' and Quinta 6', as well as Bw Principal 4', Quinta 3', and Sesquialtera, just one Wender pipe in each register was preserved. Subbaß 16' was reconstructed after the same stop in Horsmar (Wender, 1694); Trompete 8' and Posaunen Bass 16' are modeled on Lahm/ Itzgrund (Herbst, 1728); Cornet Bass 2' is modeled on Abbenrode (Contius, 1708).

Accessories: Ow tremulant; Ow cymbelstern.

Couplers: Bw/Ow, Ow/Ped.

Compass: CD–c^3 (manuals); CD–c^{1}d^1 (pedal).

Wind supply (1999): four wedge bellows (manual pumping mechanism and electric motor).

Wind pressure (1999): 72 mm WC for all divisions.

Pitch (1999): Chorton (465 Hz at 18° C), determined from surviving pipework.

Temperament (1999): unequal (well-tempered), determined from the original Gemshorn 8'.

Archival Source: Thüringisches Staatsarchiv Rudolstadt, Konsistorium Arnstadt, Nr. 1336, fols. 73 and 79–80.

Literature: (a) Wenke 1985, 82–85; Hoffmann 1999, 478–83; Preller 2002, 138–46. (b) NBR, no. 15, BDOK II, nos. 7–8; Wolff 2000, 77–101; Wollny 2005, 83–94.

3. Arnstadt, New Church: Wender organ. The Steinmeyer organ is on the lower gallery behind the grill (photograph, 1999)

4. Arnstadt, New Church: Wender organ (photograph, 1999)

5. Arnstadt, New Church: Original key desk of the Wender organ in its condition (natural wood, detached from the organ) after the last restoration (photograph, 1999)

Upper Church/Oberkirche (also Church of the Barefoot Friars/Barfüßkirche)

Single-nave hall church with barrel vault, built 1250. Formerly a Franciscan cloister church, it became the city's principal church and home of the superintendent after the city fire of 1581. Side galleries and church pews added during the sixteenth century and in 1715–16 are partially preserved.

Organ: 1611, new organ by Ezechiel Greutzscher. On July 16, in the presence of territorial lords, the organ was "examined and found to be competently built (*tüchtig*) by five organists and an organ builder" (Archiv Arnstadt, 394-02-1). 1666, repairs by Ludwig Compenius; 1678, rebuild by Christoph Junge. 1708, organ enlarged by Georg Christoph Stertzing with input from the city organist, Christoph Herthum. Later enlargements and rebuilds. 1847, new organ (III/45) by Ratzmann Bros.; the organ in the St. Michael's Church in Ohrdruf served as model. 1901, rebuild by Wilhelm Sauer (Frankfurt/Oder). Nothing from Bach's time survives.

Disposition 1708 (II/22)

Ober Werck [II]	Rück Positiff [I]	Pedal Clavier
Quintaden 16'	Grobgedackt 8'	Subbaß 16'
Principal 8'	Principal 4'	Quintaden Baß 16'
Grob Gedackt 8'	Hohl Flöte 4'	Fagott Baß 16'
Stillgedackt 8'	Quinta gedackt 3'	Cornet Baß 2'
Octav 4'	Sexta [$1^3/_5$']	Flöten Baß [1']
Quinta 3'	Super Octav [1']	
Mixtur VI	Lieblich gedacktes regal 8'	
Cimbal III		
Brustwerk		
Rausch Pfeiffen		
Krumbhorn 8'		

Accessories: tremulant; cymbelstern.

Couplers: "im Rück Positiff" [Rp/Ow, Rp/Ped].

Compass: CDEFGA–g^2a^2 (manuals); CDEFGA–c^1 (pedal).

Wind supply: four bellows.

Archival Sources: Thüringisches Staatsarchiv Rudolstadt, Konsistorium Arnstadt, *Die Orgel in der Oberkirche zu Arnstadt, 1610–1713*, fol. 31r/v (disposition of 1708 transmitted by Christoph Herthum). Stadt- und Kreisarchiv Arnstadt, Bestand 394-05-2; 394-02-1.

Literature: (a) Adlung 1768, 197–98; Haupt 1998, 76; Dehio 2003, 52–53. (b) *See* New Church.

Our Lady's Church/Liebfrauenkirche (Lower Church/Unterkirche, also Morning Church/Frühkirche)

Three-aisled, late Roman–early Gothic basilica built 1180–1330; burial place of the counts of Schwarzburg. Along with Naumburg Cathedral, the most important medieval church building in Thuringia.

Organ: 1624, new organ by Ezechiel Greutzscher, inspected by Johann Krause (Sondershausen); 1704, repairs by Johann Christian Stertzing. 1979, new organ (II/27) placed on the southern crossing pier by Schuke Orgelbau (Potsdam). Nothing from Bach's time survives.

Archival Source: Stadt- und Kreisarchiv Arnstadt, Bestand Nr. 394-02-1, *Organist u. Orgelb. Georg Raabe.*

Literature: (a) Haupt 1998, 76; Dehio 2003, 49–51. (b) BDOK II, no. 11.

Court Chapel/Schlosskapelle

1700, dedication of the renovated court chapel in Neideck Castle, which served in 1684–1716 as the princely residence and had been modernized in 1694–95; all that remains from the Renaissance castle (built 1553–60 by Gerhardt van der Meer) is the tower. Nothing is known about the organ.

Literature: (a) Dehio 2003, 54–55.

Berka (Bad Berka)

Johann Sebastian Bach's "disposition for the organ [II/28] in Berga" has been transmitted (BDOK II, no. 515). However, the instrument actually built by Heinrich Nicolaus and Christian Wilhelm Trebs was reduced to thirteen stops by Bach's student Johann Caspar Vogler, court organist in Weimar. The larger, twenty-eight to thirty-stop organ was apparently never built. Bach may well have been acquainted with the Berka church; that he participated in the inspection of the organ on completion of the first phase is not as likely. Johann Caspar Ludwig was organist ca. 1750.

St. Mary's Church/Marienkirche

Baroque hall church with two tiers of galleries, built 1739–43 according to plans of architect Johann Adolf Richter, replacing a medieval church that had been torn down.

Organ: 1742–43, new organ (thirteen stops) by Heinrich Nicolaus and Christian Wilhelm Trebs as well as Johann Christian Immanuel Schweinefleisch; probably the disposition was drastically reduced to save costs. Extensive revisions in the nineteenth and twentieth centuries. 1988, removal of organ. 1989, new organ (II/26) by Gerhard Böhm in modified original case.

Proposed disposition 1741–42 (II/28)

"Disposition of the organ in Berga, drawn up by Mr. Sebastian Bach of Leipzig and built by organ maker Trebs" (manuscript, ca. 1742)

Hauptwerk (I)	Brustwerk (II)	Pedal
Quintadena 16'	Quintadena 8'	Suppaß 16'
Principal 8'	Gedackt 8'	Principal 8'
Flöte 8'	Principal 4'	Hohlflöte 4'
Gedackt 8'	Nachthorn 4'	Posaun Baß 16'
Gemshorn 8'	Quinte 2²/₃'	Trompete 8'
Oktave 4'	Oktave 2'	Cornett 4'
Gedackt 4'	Waldflöte 2'	
Quinta 2²/₃'	Tritonus [Terz 1³/₅']	
Naßat 2²/₃'	Cimpel III	
Oktave 2'		
Seßquialter II		
Mixtur V		
Trompete 8'		

Couplers: Bw/Hw, Hw/Ped.
Wind supply: three bellows.

Disposition ca. 1750 (II/14)

"A nice organ with 30 registers, but not all of them have attained perfection . . . the ones that work are the following":

Unter Manual	Ober Manual	Pedal
Quintadena 16'	Gedackt 8'	Sub-Baß 16'
Principal 8'	Principal 4'	Flöten-Baß 8'
Octava 4'	Nachthorn 4'	Posaunen Baß 16'
Octava 2'	Oktava 2'	
Mixtur IV	Sesquialter II	
Cymbel III		

Archival Sources: Bach-Archiv Leipzig, Go. S. 123, fol. 33 (disposition, ca. 1742); Hauptstaatsarchiv Weimar, F 171 (Gottfried Albin de Wette), fol. 159. Information from Stadtarchiv Bad Berka, 2005 (disposition, ca. 1750).

Literature: (a) Lehfeldt 1893, 98–99; Löffler 1931, 140–43; Rubardt 1961, 495–503, esp. 499; Haupt 1998, 95; Häfner 2006, 291–93. (b) BDOK II, no. 515.

Dörna

St. George's Reformed Church/Ev. Kirche St. Georg; *see* Mühlhausen, former "Brücken-hof" Church/Brückenhofkirche

Dresden

There were several visits to Dresden by Thomascantor Bach in connection with concert appearances as organist: 1725 and 1731 in St. Sophia's Church, 1736 in Our Lady's Church.

On two consecutive days, September 19 and 20, 1725, "the *Capell-Director* from Leipzig, Mr. Bach," concertized on the Silbermann organ in St. Sophia's. "Very well received by the local virtuosos at the court and in the city . . . in the presence of the same, he performed for over an hour on the new organ in St. Sophia's Church preludes and various concertos, with intervening soft instrumental music (*doucen Instrumental-Music*) in all keys" (NBR, no. 118, BDOK II, no. 193). According to this report, then, Bach appears to have played, among other things, organ concertos with string accompaniment (probably including the early version of BWV 1053) and demonstrated the capabilities of the organ and its temperament by playing in all keys.

On September 14, 1731, at three o'clock in the afternoon, he gave another concert "in the presence of all the court musicians and virtuosos," an event that was marked by a laudatory poem to Bach published in the Dresden newspapers (NBR, no. 307, BDOK II, no. 294). According to a report of the same event from a Hamburg newspaper, "the famous virtuoso and organist, Bach, obligingly performed" not just once, "but on various occasions" (BDOK II, no. 294a). Bach's 1731 visit to Dresden coincided with the first appearance of Dresden's new court kapellmeister, Johann Adolph Hasse, and the premiere of his opera *Cleofide* on September 13.

In late November/early December 1736, Bach spent time in the residential city in connection with his successful appointment on November 19 as "Electoral Saxon and Royal Polish Court Composer." On December 1, "from 2 until 4 o'clock in the afternoon," he was heard "with particular admiration on the new organ in Our Lady's Church in the presence of the Russian Ambassador, Baron von Kayserlingk, and many persons of rank, as well as a large company of other persons and artists" (NBR, no. 191, BDOK II, no. 389). The Silbermann organ had been completed and examined only a few days before.

After the conversion to Catholicism of the Saxon elector August I, St. Sophia's functioned as the Protestant court church in which Lutheran church services were held. Christian Petzold was court organist and organist of St. Sophia's until 1733. He was succeeded by Wilhelm Friedemann Bach, who remained in the position until 1746. The first organist of Our Lady's Church was Johann Heinrich Gräbner, who held the position until his death in 1739, and was succeeded by his son, the Bach student Christian Heinrich Gräbner, who had already begun substituting for his father in 1733. The Bach student Gottfried August Homilius was organist of Our Lady's from 1742 to 1755.

St. Sophia's Church/Sophienkirche

Two-aisled Gothic hall church from the fourteenth century; after profanation in 1541, the church was newly dedicated as "Sophienkirche" by the countess and widow Sophia in

1602. Church and organ destroyed in World War II; only portions of the interior decoration are preserved.

Organ: 1718–20, new organ (II/30) by Gottfried Silbermann; case design attributed to George Bähr. Changes by Johann Gottfried Hildebrandt in 1733, including laying a "better-sounding temperament." 1816, equal temperament applied by Johann Andreas Uthe. 1874–75, organ renovated and moved by Carl Eduard Jehmlich to the west end; a fifth bellows was added. Destroyed 1945.

Disposition 1720 (II/30)

Hauptwerk (I)	Oberwerk (II)	Pedal
Bordun 16'	Quintadena 16'	Principal-Bass 16'
Principal 8'	Principal 8'	Sub-Bass 16'
Spitz-Flöte 8'	Grobgedackt 8'	Posaune 16'
Rohr-Flöte 8'	Quintadena 8'	Trommete 8'
Octav 4'	Octava 4'	
Spitz-Flöte 4'	Rohr-Flöte 4'	
Quinta 3'	Nasat 3'	
Oktav 2'	Oktav 2'	
Tertia 1⅗'	Quinta 1½'	
Cornet V, from c¹	Sifflet 1'	
Mixtur IV 2'	Mixtur III	
Cymbel III 1'	Vox humana 8'	
Trompete 8', divided	Unda maris 8' (from a⁰)	
Clarinen 4'		

Particulars: Ow Unda maris 8' was added in 1747 by Johann George Silbermann and David Schubert (who worked for the Silbermann shop) at the recommendation of the court organist of the time, Johann Christoph Richter.

Accessories: tremulant (Hw); Schwebung (Ow tremulant).

Couplers: shove coupler, Ow/Hw; wind coupler, Hw/Ped (*Bassventil:* coupler using an extra pallet box).

Compass: CD–d³ (manuals); CD–c¹ (pedal).

Wind supply: four bellows (two to manuals, two to pedal).

Pitch: Dresden Kammerton (a¹ = ca. 415 Hz).

Temperament: apparently modified meantone.

Literature: (a) Adlung 1768, 212; Dähnert 1980, 86–87; Dehio 1996a, 133–34; Greß 2001, 141–43. (b) NBR, nos. 118, 191, 193, and 307, BDOK II, nos. 193, 294, 294a, and 389; Wolff 2000, 318, 365, 369, 371, 497.

Church of Our Lady/Frauenkirche

Baroque square-shaped central-plan church, constructed according to plans drawn up by George Bähr, the city's master architect, to replace a medieval church. 1726, laying of

6. Dresden, St. Sophia's
Church: Silbermann organ
(photograph, 1930)

7. Dresden, St. Sophia's
Church: Design drawing
for the organ case,
attributed to George Bähr
(colored pen-and-ink
drawing, ca. 1718)

the foundation stone; 1734, dedication of partially constructed building; 1738, completion of the sandstone dome; 1743, completion of the entire building. Church and organ destroyed in World War II; 1998–2005, "archeological reconstruction" of the church according to Bähr's corrected plans.

Organ: 1732–36, new organ by Gottfried Silbermann. Examination on November 22, 1736, by concertmaster Johann Georg Pisendel; Theodor Christlieb Reinhold, cantor of Holy Cross Church; and Johann Heinrich and Christian Heinrich Gräbner; dedication on November 25. Rebuild and enlargement by Johannes Jahn (Dresden) in 1912; destroyed 1945. 2003–5, modern organ (IV/67) built by Daniel Kern and placed behind a reconstruction of the original facade. Nothing from Bach's time survives.

Disposition 1736 (III/43)

Hauptwerk (II)	Brustwerk (I)	Obewerk (III)	Pedal
Principal 16'	Getackts 8'	Quinta dena 16'	Groß Untersatz 32'
Octav Principal 8'	Principal 4'	Principal 8'	Principal Pass 16'
Violdigamba 8'	Rohr Flöte 4'	Getackts 8'	Octaven Pass 8'
Rohr Flöte 8'	Nasat 3'	Quinta dena 8'	Octaven Pass 4'
Octava 4'	Octava 2'	Octava 4'	Mixtur VI
Spitz Flöte 4'	Gemshorn 2'	Rohrflöte 4'	Posaune 16'
Quinta 3'	Quinta 1 1/3'	Nasat 3'	Trompeten Pass 8'
Octava 2'	Sufflett 1'	Octava 2'	Clarin Pass 4'
Tertia 1 3/5'	Mixtur III	Sesquialtera 4/5',	
		1 3/5' from c¹	
Mixtur IV 2'	Chalmeaux 8',	Mixtur IV	
	from g°		
Cymbel III 1'		Vox humana 8'	
Cornett V, from c¹			
Fagott 16'			
Trompette 8'			

Accessories: tremulant (Hw); Schwebung (tremulant to Ow); tremulant (Bw).

Couplers: shove couplers, Ow/Hw and Bw/Hw; wind coupler, Hw/Ped (*Bassventil*: coupler using an extra pallet box).

Compass: CD–d³ (manuals); CD–c¹ (pedal).

Wind supply: six bellows.

Pitch: Dresden Kammerton (a¹ = ca. 415 Hz).

Temperament: well-tempered.

Literature: (a) Adlung 1768, 212; Löffler 1925, 96; Dähnert 1980, 68–71; Müller 1982, 158–73; Greß 1994; Greß 2001, 153–56. (b) NBR, nos. 190–91, BDOK II, nos. 388–89; *see* St. Sophia's Church.

8. Dresden, Our Lady's
Church: Silbermann organ
(photograph, ca. 1930)

Eisenach

Johann Sebastian Bach was baptized in St. George's Church in Eisenach on March 23,
1685. His father, the town music director and court musician Johann Ambrosius Bach,
was, according to his employment contract of 1671, required to be in attendance in the
Eisenach churches on "all Sundays and feast days, before and after the sermon at the early
and afternoon church services, as directed by the cantor." Ambrosius's cousin, Johann
Christoph Bach, was city and court organist in Eisenach from 1665 to 1703.

Johann Sebastian Bach knew the Eisenach organs from his childhood there; in later
visits to his birthplace (among others, in 1732 in connection with a trip to Kassel), he got
to know the Stertzing organ (completed 1707), which at the time was Thuringia's largest
instrument (it serves as the model for the modern "Bach-organ" in Leipzig's St. Thomas's
Church). Johann Christoph Bach's successor as organist of St. George's was his nephew
Johann Bernard, who held the position until his death in 1749. He was succeeded by his
son Johann Ernst, who had studied with his uncle Johann Sebastian in Leipzig.

St. George's Church/Georgenkirche

Three-aisled medieval hall church, badly damaged in 1525 during the Peasants' War. New nave with two tiers of surrounding galleries built 1560–61; third gallery added 1672. Eisenach's city church; also the court's church during residencies of the dukes of Saxe-Eisenach.

Organ: 1696–1707, new organ (IV/58) by Georg Christoph Stertzing according to the disposition developed over time by Johann Christoph Bach. (The earlier instrument was built 1576 by Georg Schauenberg using an organ from the former Franciscan church.) 1719, completion of the richly carved facade. 1725, repairs and enlargement (addition of pedal Posaune 32' on its own wind chest, among other things) by Johann Friedrich Wender. 1840, new organ by Holland (Schmiedefeld); 1982, new organ (III/60) by Schuke Orgelbau (Potsdam) using the original case; otherwise nothing from Bach's time survives.

Disposition 1707 (IV/58)

Oberwerk (III)	Brustwerk (IV)	Oberseitenwerk (II)	Unterseitenwerk (I)	Pedal
Bordun 16'	Grob Gedackt 8'	Quintathön 16'	Barem 16'	Großer Untersatz 32'
Principal 8'	Klein Gedackt 4'	Großoktav 8'	Still Gedackt 8'	Principal 16'
Violdigamba 8'	Principal 2'	Gemshorn 8'	Quintathön 8'	Subbaß 16'
Rohrflöte 8'	Super Gems- hörnlein 2' + Quinta 1½'	Gedackt 8'	Principal 4'	Violon 16'
Quinta 6'	Quint-Sexta II	Principal 4'	Nachthorn 4' II	Octav 8'
Oktav 4'	Sifflöte 1'	Flute douce II 4'	Spitzflöt 4'	Gedackt 8'
Flöte 4'		Hohlflöth 4'	Spitzquint 3'	Super Octav 4'
Nassat 3'		Hohlquint 3'	Octav 2'	Flöte 4'
Superoctav 2'		Octav 2'	Schweitzerflöth 2'	Bauernflöte 1'
Sesquialtera III		Blockflöte 2'	Rauschquinte 1½'	Mixtur VI 4'
Cymbel III		Sesquialtera III 2'	Super Octävlein 1'	Posaun Baß 16'
Mixtur VI 2'		Scharf IV	Cymbel VI	Trompete 8'
Trompete 8'		Vox humana 8'	Regal 8'	Cornet 2'
				Glockenspiel 2'

Particulars: Ow Sesqualtera III consists of 4', 2⅔', 1⅗'; Brustwerk Quint-Sexta consists of 1⅓', ⅘'.

Accessories: cut-off valves for Ow, Oberseitenwerk, and Unterseitenwerk; tremulants in Oberseitenwerk, Unterseitenwerk and Pedal; two cymbelstern (stars and bells operable separately).

Couplers: Oberseitenwerk/Unterseitenwerk, Ow/Ped.

Compass: C–e^3 (manuals), C–e^1 (pedal).

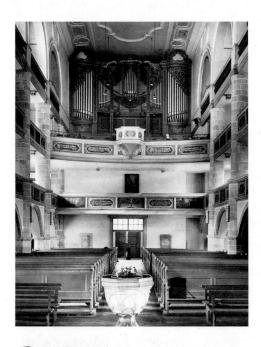

9. Eisenach, St. George's Church:
Holland organ in historical case
(photograph, ca. 1920)

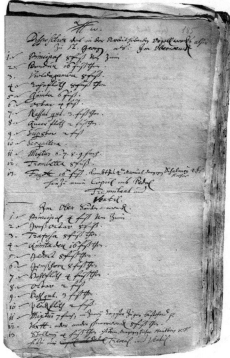

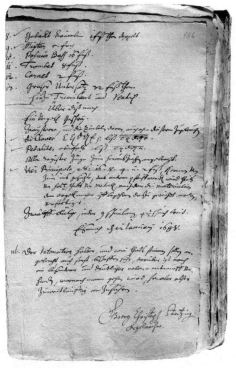

10. Eisenach, St. George's Church: Organ disposition in the hand of Johann Christoph Bach
(left page); signature of Georg Christoph Stertzing (right page), 1698

Wind supply: twelve bellows (Untersatz 32' and Octav 16' on separate chest with wind supplied by two bellows).

Archival Source: Thüringisches Staatsarchiv Weimar, Bestand Eisenacher Archiv: Konsistorialsachen no. 246, *Die nöthige Reparatur und Veränderung der Orgel in der Kirche zu S. Georgen, 1696–1724.*

Literature: (a) Adlung 1768, 214; Lehfeldt 1915, 217–18; Wolfheim 1915, 230; Oefner 1996; Sterzik 1998, 38–47; Butler 2004, 42–60; Böhme 2005, 63–69; Butler 2008, 229–69. (b) BDOK II, no. 1; Nentwig 2004; Wolff 2000, 17–31 and elsewhere.

Erfurt

From his youth onward, Johann Sebastian Bach was well acquainted with the city of Erfurt, hometown of his parents and the place where numerous members of the Bach family worked as musicians. Bach's older sister, Marie Salome Wiegand, lived in Erfurt from 1700 until her death in 1728. Johann Christoph, Bach's older brother, studied there between 1685 and 1688 with Johann Pachelbel, organist at the Prediger Church, and his initial post was that of organist of Erfurt's St. Thomas's Church. Pachelbel's predecessor in Erfurt was Johann Effler, who was later Bach's predecessor as court organist in Weimar and who, during his Erfurt time, regularly played with Johann Ambrosius Bach. The organists of St. Augustine's Church were Paul Effler (son of Johann) from 1666 to 1716 (from 1713 he was assisted by the Erfurt cathedral organist Georg Erasmus Leubing), Sebald Mockwitz from 1716 to 1721, and Johann Christoph Wackernagel from 1722 to 1748.

In 1716, Johann Sebastian Bach, court organist and director of music in Weimar, and the Arnstadt organ builder Johann Anton Weise examined the new organ in St. Augustine's Church. According to their report dated July 31, 1716, Schröter's first instrument had "turned out so well" that "it is not to be doubted in respect to such further work as he shall undertake, that he will likewise complete it industriously and untiringly" (NBR, no. 62, BDOK 1, no. 86). Bach had been acquainted with organ builder Stertzing since his time in Ohrdruf.

St. Augustine's Church/Augustinerkirche

Gothic hall church, built in the fourteenth century as an Augustine Eremite monastery church; became Protestant in 1525, but the monastery (where Martin Luther was a monk) remained in possession of the Augustine order until 1556. Major changes in the seventeenth to nineteenth centuries. 1849, used by the Erfurt Union Parliament; interior destroyed. 1854, dedication of the reconstructed neo-Gothic church.

Organ: 1716, new organ begun by Georg Christoph Stertzing was completed by Johann Georg Schröter. Rebuild in 1753, removal of the organ in 1850. 1939, new organ (opus 2555, III/49) by E. F. Walcker & Cie. Nothing from Bach's time survives.

For Bach's organ report, *see* Part II.A.

Disposition 1716 (III/39)

Hauptwerk (I)	Mittelclavier (II)	Oberpositiv (III)	Pedal
Quintatön 16'	Bordun 16'	Quintatön 8'	Principal 16'
Principal 8'	Principal 8'	Flötentraversière 8'	Subbaß 16'
Gemshorn 8'	Gedackt 8'	Gedackt 8'	Violone 16'
Gedackt 8'	Rohrflöte 8'	Principal 4'	Oktave 8'
Flötentraversière 8'	Hohlflöte 4'	Gedackt 4'	Posaune 16'
Violdigamba 8'	Spitzflöte 4'	Oktave 2'	Trompete 8'
Oktave 4'	Nasat 3'	Flageolet 1'	Cornet 4'
Oktave 2'	Waldflöte 2'	Scharpp IV	
Sesquialtera II	Sifflöte 1'	Sesquialtera II	
Mixtur VI	Quinta 1½'		
Cymbel III	Vox humana 8'		
Trompete 8'			

Accessories: tremulant; cymbelstern with bells at various pitches; glockenspiel g–c³; two cut-off valves.

Coupler: pedal coupler.

Compass: C–e³ (manuals), C–e¹ (pedal).

Literature: (a) Adlung 1768, 218; Haetge 1931, 65–74; Haupt 1998, 100; Sterzik 1998, 38–47. (b) NBR, no. 62, BDOK 1, no. 86; Wolff 2000, 30–31, 143, 483, 527.

Gera

From both Köthen and Leipzig, Johann Sebastian Bach made various trips to Schleiz and Gera, residences of the counts of Reuß. On a return trip in 1721 from a guest appearance in Schleiz, the secondary residence of the Reuß counts, Bach may have inspected the new organ in the court chapel at Osterstein Castle, as well as the organ-in-progress at St. Salvator's Church. Thus he may have influenced the decision also to award the large contract for the organ in St. John's Church to the organ builder Finke.

Bach spent time in Gera from May 30 until June 6, 1725, probably in connection with another guest performance at Osterstein Castle, residence of Heinrich XVIII, count of Reuß-Gera. He was accompanied by two others (probably Anna Magdalena Bach and the barely fifteen-year-old Wilhelm Friedemann) and was paid a handsome honorarium in the amount of 30 talers for approving the organs in the churches of St. John's and St. Salvator's. Bach dedicated the large organ at St. John's on June 3, the First Sunday after Trinity. The lavish expenditures for his lodging and food (including wine, spirits, coffee, tea, sugar, and tobacco) indicate preferential treatment of a prominent guest.

City and court organists were Emanuel Kegel, 1698–1724; Simon Dobenecker (see BWV Anh. II 85 and 101), 1726–28; Sebald Petzold, 1728–39; and August Heinrich Gehra, 1739–89. Organists of St. Salvator's were Simon Dobenecker, 1720–26 and Ludwig Heinrich Kegel, son of the St. John's organist, 1726–78. Christian Ernst Friederici, who had apprenticed with Silbermann, founded an organ and keyboard instrument workshop in Gera in 1737; Friederici assisted Bach with his *Clavier-Übung* III (1739) project.

St. John's Church (City Church)/Johanneskirche (Stadtkirche)

The city church, and Gera's oldest. The medieval building burned completely in 1780; remains were cleared away in the nineteenth century.

    Organ: Built 1721–25 by Johann Georg Finke to replace the instrument built 1646–47 by Ludwig Compenius and examined by Samuel Scheidt. Organ destroyed by the fire of 1780 (as were all relevant materials in the church archives).

Disposition (III/42) according to Adlung (1768)

Hauptmanual	Seitenwerk	Brustwerk	Pedal
Gedackter Untersatz 16' (T)	Gedackt 8'	Eng Gedackt 8' (narrow)	Principalbaß 16'
Großquintatön 16' (T)	Principal 4'	Quintatön 8'	Subbaß 16'
Principal 8' (T)	Nachthorn 4'	Wald- or Dolkanflöte with double mouth 4'	Violdigambenbaß 16'
Violdigamba 8' (T)	Flöte douce II 4'	Nachthorn 4'	Bordun 16' (T)
Bordun (wide) 8'	Gemshorn 4'	Principal 2'	Quintatönbaß 16' (T)
Gemshorn 8'	Gedackte italienische Quinte 3'	Quinte 1½'	Principalbaß 8'
Gemsquinte 6'	Oktave 2'	Oktave 1'	Oktave 8' (T)
Oktave 4'	Sesquialtera 1³/₅'	Mixtur III 1'	Violdigamba 8' (T)
Rohrflöte 4'	Gemsquinte 1½'		Posaunen- Untersatz 32'
Cylinderquinte 3'	Mixtur IV 2'		Posaunenbaß 16'
Sesquialtera 1³/₅'	Krummhorn/ Hautbois 8'		Trompetenbaß 8'
Superoctave 2'			Cornetbaß 2'
Mixtur VI 2'			
Fagott 16'			
Trompete 8'			
Vox humana II 8'			

    Particulars: According to Adlung (1768): Hw Fagott 16' resonators of tin-plated sheet metal. Vox humana II 8' "has 96 pipes. One half, of metal, is a flue; the other half, of sheet metal, is a reed. Both stand on one channel." (*Cf.* Vox humana 8' (Ow) in Trost organ in Waltershausen.) Gedackt 8' (Seitenwerk) and Principal 8' (Ped) made "from pear wood, the languids and mouths sheathed with tin." Flöte douce 4' in the Seitenwerk "doubled throughout, with 96 pipes: 48 stopped, of metal; and 48 open, of pear wood." Pedal Violdigambenbaß 16' "from wood; with each key three pitches are heard [that is, the 16' pitch as well as overtones at the octave and the fifth]." Pedal Trompetenbass 8' resonators "of sheet iron; shallots made of wood from the Wild Service tree, boiled in linseed-oil; shallot openings covered with parchment; tuning wires adjusted with screws."

Accessories: tremulant set to a ⅝ measure; two large cymbelsterns, one on either side; kettledrum; cut-off valve.

Couplers: "to all three manuals"; Hw/Ped.

Compass: CD–c³ (manuals); pedal includes low C♯ but compass unclear

Wind supply: five wedge bellows.

Literature: (a) Adlung 1768, 229–30; David 1951, 57. (b) BDOK II, nos. 183 and 183a; Maul 2004a, 101–19; Wolff 2000, 143, 529; Wolff 2005a, xxi.

St. Salvator's Church/Salvatorkirche

Baroque hall church built 1717–20 according to plans of the Saxon architect David Schatz; rebuilt after the 1780 fire and dedicated in 1783.

Organ: Built 1720–22 by Johann Georg Finke; disposition unknown. Organ and all records destroyed in the city fire of 1780. Since 1905, an Art Nouveau case has held an organ by Ernst Röver. Nothing from Bach's time survives.

Literature: (a) Dehio 2003, 443–44; Haupt 1989, 61. (b) BDOK II, no. 183; Maul 2004a, 101–19.

Castle Chapel/Schlosskapelle

Chapel in the main wing of Osterstein Castle in Gera-Untermhaus, a residential palace from the sixteenth century, completely remodeled in 1717–35; destroyed in World War II.

Organ: Built 1719–21(?) by Johann Georg Finke under commission of Heinrich XVIII, count of Reuß-Gera. Contract dated September 19, 1719, is for a one-manual organ with nine stops; it was enlarged in August 1720 by the addition of a Posaunenbass. New organ built in nineteenth century by Gebr. Poppe; original facade survived until 1945. Nothing from Bach's time survives.

Disposition 1720 (I/10)

Manual		Pedal
Quintathön 8'	Gemßhorn 4'	Sub Bass 16', wood
Grobgedackt 8', wood	Quinta 3'	Posaunenbass [16']
Principal 4'	Octava 2'	
Kleingedackt 4', wood	Mixtur III	

Particulars: The Quintathön 8' was partially reused from the previous organ.

Pitch: Kammerton.

Literature: (a) Maul 2004a, 105, 108–9.

Görlitz

Johann Sebastian Bach must have visited the Casparini organ in Görlitz between 1729 and 1741. The exact travel dates are unknown, but in his travel diaries, Johann Andreas Silbermann, who was shown the Casparini organ by David Nicolai in 1741, noted: "The old, famous Mr. Bach of Leipzig did not judge this instrument unfairly when, in discussing it with my cousin [Gottfried Silbermann], he called it a 'horse organ,' because one has to be strong as a horse to play it" (BDOK II, no. 486). Organists of the city church were Christian Ludwig Boxberg (a former student of the St. Thomas School, Leipzig) from 1702 to 1729 and Bach student David Nicolai from 1730 to 1764.

Church of St. Peter and Paul's/Peter- und Paulskirche

Five-aisled Gothic hall church, completed 1497. Trusses and interior decoration that were damaged by fire on March 19, 1691, were restored by 1712.

Organ: Built 1697–1703 by Eugenio and Adam Horatio Casparini, who returned to Germany from Padua in order to take on the project, bringing with them what they had learned in Italy. Repairs by David Decker Sr. in 1717; rebuild by David Decker Jr. in 1727. Various rebuilds up through 1845. 1894, new organ (III/53) by Schlag & Söhne; 1928, new organ (IV/89) by Orgelbau Sauer; 1995–97, new organ by Mathis Orgelbau using original Casparini case. Some wood pipes of the Onda maris 8' from Casparini were reused; otherwise, nothing from Bach's time survives.

Disposition 1703 (III/57)

Hauptwerk [I]	Oberwerk [II]	Brustpositiv [III]	Pedal:
Principal 16'	Quintatön 16'	Gedackt 8'	**Großer Seitenbass**
Principal 8'	Principal 8'	Principal 4'	Großprincipalbaß [32']
Violdigamba 8'	Onda maris 8'	Oktave 2'	Posaune 16'
Rohrflötquinte 6'	Oktave 4'	Plockflöte 2'	Oktavbaß 16'
Superoktave 4'	Gedackte Fleute douce 4'	Quint Nasat 1½'	Gemshornbaß 8'
Gedackt Pommer 4'	Spitzfleute 3'	Sedecima 1'	Großquintbaß 6'
Salicet 4'	Sedecima 2'	Scharf Mixtur 1'	Jubalflöt 4'
Offen Flöte 3'	Glöckleinton 2'	Hautbois 8'	Scharf II
Quinta 3'	Super Sedecima 1½'		Bauernflöt 2'
Plockflöt 2'	Cymbel II		Mixtur minor V
Rauschpfeife II 2'	Scharf 1'		**Kleiner Seitenbass**
Vigesima nona 1½'	Cornetti 8'		Tromba 8'
Mixtur III 1'			Jungfernregal 4'
Zynk II 3'			Jubal 4'
Bombart 16'			Cymbel II
Vox humana 8'			**Hinteroberbaß**
			Contrabaß 16'
			Jubalflöt open 8'
			Krumhorn 8'

Superoktavbaß 4'
Hinterunterbaß
Bordun 16'
Fagotti 16'
Quintatönbaß 8'
Mixtur major XII

Accessories: Revolving suns with four bells (c–e–g–c); nightingale; Vogelgesang (bird-song); Tamburo (drum) 16'; cuckoo; tremulant; cut-off valves to all divisions; cut-off valves to the two angels over the Brustpositiv; bellows signal.

Compass: CD–c^3 (manuals); CD–d^1 (pedal).

Wind supply: seven bellows.

Pitch (according to J. A. Silbermann, 1741): Cornetton (Chorton).

Literature: (a) Boxberg 1704; Adlung 1768, 232–33; Dähnert 1980, 130–34; Seeliger 1992, 16–18; Dehio 1996a, 371–75; Lade 1997; Scherer-Hall 1998, 43–48. (b) BDOK II, nos. 266–67, no. 486; Schaefer 1994, 168–71.

Gotha

Although there are no concrete dates for a visit before 1717, Johann Sebastian Bach must have been well acquainted from his youth with Gotha, a city located on the road between Eisenach and Erfurt that was the residence of the dukes of Saxe-Gotha. In March of 1717, Bach briefly substituted for the ailing Christian Friedrich Witt, who had been court kapell-meister and organist of the Castle Church in Gotha since 1693. Witt died on April 3, 1717. On Good Friday, March 26, 1717, Bach conducted a musical passion at the Castle Church.

Castle Church/Schlosskirche

One-aisled Baroque hall church, dedicated 1646 and rebuilt 1695–97; stucco work by Johann Samuel and Johann Peter Rust. Singers' gallery added ca. 1800. Court church until 1918, and at times burial place for the dukes of Saxe-Gotha.

Organ: Newly built in 1692 by Severin Hohlbeck and placed on an eastern gallery above the pulpit and altar. Changes in the eighteenth and early nineteenth centuries. New organ by Johann Friedrich Schulze in 1856, using the Hohlbeck case; otherwise, nothing from Bach's time survives.

Disposition (II/35) according to Adlung (1768)

Hauptwerk (I)	Brustwerk (II)	Pedal
Quintatön 16'	Quintatön 8'	Subbaß 16'
Bordun 16'	Lieblichgedackt 8'	Oktave 8'
Principal 8'	Principal 4'	Schweizerbaß 1'
Grobgedackt 8'	Kleingedackt 4'	Posaunbaß 16'

11. Görlitz, Church of St. Peter and Paul's: Mathis organ in
historical case of the so-called sun organ (photograph, 1997)

12. Gotha, Castle Church:
Case of the Hohlbeck organ
(photograph, 1926)

Hauptwerk (I)	Brustwerk (II)	Pedal
Violdigamba 8'	Sesquialtera [II]	Trompetbaß 8'
Oktave 4'	Oktave 2'	Cornetbaß 2'
Spielflöte 4'	Traverse 2'	
Quinte 3'	Sedetz 1²/₃' [!]	
Oktave 2'	Nasatflöt 1¹/₂'	
Sexta	Mixtur	
Blockflöte 1'	Dulcianregal 4'	
Mixtur	Geigenregal 4'	
Trompete 8'	Dulcianregal 16'	
	Knopfregal 8'	
	Singendregal 4'	

Particulars: In the Bw, Dulcianregal 16', Knopfregal 8', Singendregal 4' on a separate chest with its own cut-off valve.

Accessories: tremulant; cut-off valves for Bw and Pedal; Vogelgesang (birdsong); cymbelstern; bellows signal.

Couplers: Permanent pedal coupler ("Coupler to Manual that cannot be uncoupled").

Literature: (a) Adlung 1768, 234; Lehfeldt 1891, 66–67; Ernst 1983, 13; Dehio 2003, 488. (b) Wolff 2000, 178, 527, and elsewhere.

Halle (Saale)

After the death in August 1712 of Friedrich Wilhelm Zachow, organist and music director of the Market Church, Johann Sebastian Bach was offered the position. He auditioned successfully in December 1713 but, after a lengthy delay, declined the position in March 1714, whereupon he was promptly appointed concertmaster in Weimar. On July 30, 1714, the church board named Gottfried Kirchhoff organist of the Market Church; his successor was Wilhelm Friedemann Bach, who served from 1746 to 1764.

Construction of the Contius organ had begun in 1712, and Bach was able to witness the instrument's progress in 1713. It is likely, though, that he was already involved with the project, since Zachow was unable to see the project through. The completed instrument was thoroughly examined by Bach, Johann Kuhnau, and Christian Friedrich Rolle on April 29 and 30, 1716. The detailed report, written by all three examiners and dated May 1, the day of the festive dedication, is preserved (NBR, no. 59, BDOK 1, no. 85). During the same visit, Bach would have taken the opportunity to acquaint himself with the small 1664 Reichel organ that stands prominently displayed above the altar. Tradition has it that Zachow taught organ playing to the young Georg Friedrich Händel on this instrument.

Market Church of Our Lady/Marktkirche Unser lieben Frauen

Late-Gothic hall church, built 1529–39 using the old church towers of the Churches of St. Gertrude's and St. Mary's from 1121 and 1141, respectively. Interior decoration from after 1550.

Large Organ: 1712–16, new organ by Christoph Contius. 1843, rebuild by Johann Friedrich Schulze; 1897, new organ by Wilhelm Rühlmann. 1984, new organ (III/56) by Schuke Orgelbau (Potsdam) reusing the original case; otherwise, nothing from Bach's time survives.

For Bach's organ report, *see* Part II.A.

Disposition 1716 (III/65)

Hauptwerk (I)	Oberwerk (II)	Brustwerk (III)	Pedal
Principal 16'	Bordun 16'	Quintatön 8'	Untersatz 32'
Quintatön 16'	Principal 8'	Gedackt 8'	Principal 16'
Oktave 8'	Gedackt 8'	Principal 4'	Subbaß 16'
Rohrflöte 8'	Violdigamba 8'	Flöte douce 4'	Oktave 8'
Gemshorn 8'	Oktave 4'	Nachthorn 4'	Gedackt 8'
Quinte 6'	Blockflöte 4'	Quinte 3'	Quinte 6'
Oktave 4'	Querflöte 4'	Nasat 3'	Oktave 4'
Spitzflöte 4'	Quinte 3'	Oktave 2'	Nachthorn 4'
Quinte 3'	Oktave 2'	Waldflöte 2'	Quinte 3'
Superoktave 2'	Spitzflöte 2'	Spitzflöte 1'	Superoktave 2'
Sifflöt 2'	Waldflöte 1'	Terz 1³/₅'	Waldflöte 1'
Terz 1³/₅'	Terz 1³/₅'	Mixtur IV	Mixtur VII

Mixtur VI	Mixtur V	Cymbel II	Cymbel IV
Cymbel III	Cymbel III	Ranket 8'	Posaune 32'
Trompete 16'	Fagott 16'	Oboe 4'	Posaune 16'
Trompete 8'	Vox humana 8'	Cymbelstern	Trompete 8'
			Schallmey 4'
			Cornet 2'

Accessories: two cymbelsterns; revolving sun in the Ow; Vogelgesang (birdsong; built by Contius for the last time in Halle); Bw tremulant.

Compass: CD–c^3 (manuals); CD–c^1 (pedal).

Wind supply: ten bellows.

Wind pressure: 32–33°.

Literature: (a) Adlung 1768, 239; Serauky 1939, 479–83; Stüven 1964, 118. (b) NBR, no. 59, BDOK I, no. 85; BDOK II, no. 76; Wolff 2000, 136, 143, 151, 155, 187, 207–8, 484, 527, and elsewhere.

Small organ: Built 1663–64 by Georg Reichel; positioned over the altar. Dedicated February 15, 1664, with sermon by Johann Gottfried Olearius, later Bach's superintendent in Arnstadt. Various repairs and rebuilds; organ's pitch was lowered by two whole tones during repairs in 1875. 1972, restoration by Schuke Orgelbau (Potsdam); 1982, organ tuned in quarter-comma meantone.

13. Halle, Market Church: Schuke organ in historical case (photograph, 2007)

14. Halle, Market Church: Reichel organ (photograph, 2007)

Disposition 1664/1972 (I/6)

Manual
Grob Gedackt 8'
Principal 4'
Spillflöte 4'
Octava 2'
Sesquialtera II [$1^3/_5$' + $1^1/_3$', with no repetitions]
Superoctav 1'

Compass: CD–c^3
Wind supply: three bellows.
Pitch (1972): Chorton (three half tones above A = 440).
Temperament (1982): meantone.
Literature: (a) Mundt 1907/8, 392; Serauky 1939, 297; Lützkendorf 1991, 166–78; Brandt 1996, 14–18.

Hamburg

According to Carl Philipp Emanuel Bach, his father "journeyed now and again to Hamburg, to hear the then famous Organist of St. Catherine's, Johann Adam Reinken" during the time Bach was a choral student at St. Michael's in Lüneburg in 1700 to 1702 (NBR, no. 306, BDOK III, no. 666). The bonds to Hamburg apparently remained strong. After the death of his wife Maria Barbara, Bach became interested in the vacant organist position at the St. Jacobi Church, and in November 1720 he made a trip to Hamburg, where he played the organs both at St. Jacobi and at St. Catherine's. According to the obituary, Bach was heard

> for more than two hours on the fine organ of St. Catherine's before the Magistrate and many other distinguished persons of the town, to their general astonishment. The aged Organist of this Church, Johann Adam Reinken, who at that time was nearly a hundred years old, listened to him with particular pleasure. Bach, at the request of those present, performed extempore the chorale "An Wasserflüssen Babylon" at great length (for almost half an hour) and in different ways, just as the better organists of Hamburg in the past had been used to do at the Saturday vespers. Particularly on this, Reinken made Bach the following compliment: "I thought this art was dead, but I see that in you it still lives" (NBR, no. 306, BDOK III, no. 666).

The chorales on "An Wasserflüssen Babylon," BWV 635a and 635b, should be viewed in this context. Apparently Bach also played the Fugue in G Minor, BWV 542/2, in 1720, for Mattheson cited the theme and countersubject in his *Grosse General-Baß-Schule* of 1731. Original source evidence suggests that a performance of the cantata "Ich hatte viel Bekümmernis," BWV 21, likewise probably took place in Hamburg.

Bach was chosen as organist but did not accept the position, remaining for the time as kapellmeister in Köthen; Johann Joachim Heitmann was called instead. In 1768, Carl Philipp Emanuel Bach became cantor at the Hamburg Johanneum and music director of Hamburg's five principal churches, a position he held until his death in 1788. His predecessor was his godfather, Georg Philipp Telemann, who had held the position from 1721 to 1767. As cantor and music director, Emanuel was responsible for festive concerted music at St. Catherine's and St. Jacobi.

Johann Sebastian Bach apparently never forgot Reinken's instrument. As his student Johann Friedrich Agricola reported in his annotations to Adlung's *Musica mechanica organoedi* (1768):

> In the organ of St. Catherine's in Hamburg there are 16 reeds. The late Capellmeister, Mr. J. S. Bach in Leipzig, who once made himself heard for two hours on this instrument, which he called excellent in all its parts, could not praise the beauty and variety of tone of these reeds highly enough. It is known, too, that the famous former Organist of this church, Mr. Johann Adam Reinken, always kept them in the best tune . . .
>
> The late Capellmeister Bach in Leipzig gave assurance that the 32-foot Principal and the pedal Posaune in the organ of St. Catherine's in Hamburg spoke well and quite audibly right down to the lowest C. But he also used to say that this Principal was the only one of that size with these good qualities that he had ever heard (NBR, no. 358, BDOK III, no. 739).

Principal Church of St. Catherine's/Hauptkirche St. Katharinen

Three-aisled Gothic hall church, completed 1426. Church and the parts of the organ that had not yet been put in storage were destroyed in World War II; 1950–56, modernizing rebuild by architects Hopp and Jäger.

Organ: 1520, rebuild of an existing organ by Marten de Mare; 1534, repairs by Jacob Iversand. 1543, substantial work by Gregorius Vogel (a III/43 disposition is transmitted). 1551–52, Rückpositiv added by Hendrik Niehoff and Jasper Johannsen. Between 1559 and 1629, the organ was cared for by the Scherer family of organ builders, who in 1605–6 built a new case and a partially new organ. 1630–31, Gottfried Fritzsche added a seven-stop Brustwerk presumably played by the Oberwerk (III) keyboard. Further rebuilds by Friedrich Stellwagen in 1644–47 and Joachim Richborn. 1671–74, Johann Friedrich Besser apparently provided a fourth keyboard, eight new bellows, and Principal 32' and Posaune 32' in the Pedal. At the recommendation of organist Anton Heinrich Uthmöller, the disposition was enlarged in 1738–40; further rebuilds continued into the twentieth century. Case and wind chests destroyed in 1943. 1962, new organ (IV/75) by Emanuel Kemper, who reused some of the original pipes that had been placed in storage. 2008–12, reconstruction by Flentrop Orgelbouw of the organ and organ gallery as Reinken knew them, using original pipework that has been partially preserved.

15. Hamburg, St.
Catherine's Church:
Niehoff/Johannsen/
Stellwagen organ
(photograph, ca. 1900)

Disposition 1721 (IV/57)

Werck [II]	Rückpositiv [I]	Oberwerk [III]	Brustwerk [IV]	Pedal
Principal 16'	Principal 8'	Principal 8'	Principal 8'	Principal 32'
Quintadena 16'	Gedackt 8'	Hohlflöte 8'	Octava 4'	Principal 16'
Bordun 16'	Quintadena 8'	Flöte 4'	Quintadena 4'	Sub-Baß 16'
Octava 8'	Octava 4'	Nasat 3'	Waldpfeiffe 2'	Octava 8'
Spitzflöte 8'	Blockflöte 4'	Gemshorn 2'	Scharff VII	Gedackt 8'
Querflöte 8'	Hohlflöte 4'	Waldflöte 2'	Dulcian 16'	Octava 4'
Octava 4'	Quintflöte 1⅓'	Scharff VI	Regal 8'	Nachthorn 4'
Octava 2'	Sifflet 1'	Trommete 8'		Rauschpfeiffe II
Rausch-Pfeiffe II	Sesquialtera II	Zincke 8'		Cimbel III
Mixtura X	Scharff VIII	Trommete 4'		Mixtura V
Trommete 16'	Regal 8'			Groß-Posaun 32'
	Baarpfeiffe 8'			Posaune 16'
	Schallmey 4'			Trommete 8'
				Krummhorn 8'
				Schallmey 4'
				Cornet-Baß 2'

Accessories: tremulants in W and Rp; two cymbelsterns, drum, Vogelgesang (bird-song); cut-off valves to all divisions.

Couplers: Rp/W, Ow/W, W/Ped.

Compass: CDEFGA–c^3 (manuals), CDE–d^1 (pedal).

Wind supply: sixteen bellows.

Literature: (a) Klée Gobert 1968a, 101–54; Niedt 1721, 176–77; Vogel 1997, 95–108; Seggermann 2001, 142–50; Grapenthin 2007, 169–98. (b) NBR, nos. 306 and 358, BDOK III, nos. 666 and 739; Adlung 1768, 187 and 288; Wolff 2000, 60–65, 211–16, and elsewhere; Wolff 2005, xviii, xxiii; Maul/Wollny 2007, xxi–xxxv.

Principal Church of St. Jacobi/Hauptkirche St. Jacobi

Three-aisled Gothic hall church, completed 1360. Collapse of the vault over the organ in 1714; building destroyed on June 18, 1944 (organ was in storage). 1951–59, modern reconstruction according to plans of architects Hopp and Jäger.

Organ: 1512–16, new organ by Jacob Iversand and Harmen Stüven; 1546, repairs by Jacob Scherer; 1588–92, rebuild by Hans Scherer I; 1605, rebuild by Hans Scherer I and II; 1635, renovation by Gottfried Fritzsche; 1655, rebuild by Hans Christoph Fritzsche. 1689–93, new organ by Arp Schnitger using twenty-five registers from the previous organ. 1721, repairs and rebuild by Otto Diedrich Richborn; 1760, repairs and rebuild by Johann Jacob Lehnert; further rebuilds in eighteenth and nineteenth centuries. The Schnitger facade pipes were sacrificed toward the end of World War I (1917); the instrument was brought into playing condition again by Hans Henny Jahnn and Karl Kemper in 1926–30. 1942, pipework and wind chests were placed in storage; 1948–50, provisional rebuild by Kemper (organ placed on the ground floor); 1961, the Kemper-altered organ was placed in a new case on a newly built middle-aisle gallery. A modern Kemper organ was installed in the south aisle beside the Schnitger organ. 1989–93, reconstruction of the Schnitger organ of 1693 (key desk copied from Lübeck cathedral), with extensive restoration by Jürgen Ahrend of what had remained from the original organ.

Disposition 1721 (IV/60)

Werck (II)	Rück Positiv (I)	Ober Positiv (III)	Brust Positiv (IV)	Pedal
Principal 16'	Principal 8'	Principal 8'	Principal (wood) 8'	Principal 32'
Quintadehn 16'	Gedackt 8'	Rohrflöht 8'	Octav 4'	Octava 16'
Octava 8'	Quintadehna 8'	Hohlflöht 8'	Hohlflöht 4'	Subbaß 16'
Spitzflöht 8'	Octava 4'	Spitzflöth 4'	Waldtflöht 2'	Octava 8'
Gedackt 8'	Blockflöte 4'	Octava 4'	Sexqualtera II	Octava 4'
Octava 4'	Naßat 3'	Naßat 3'	Scharff IV-VI	Nachthorn 2'
Rohrflöht 4'	Octava 2'	Gems Horn 2'	Dulcian 8'	Mixtur VI-VIII
Flachflöht 2'	Siffloit 1½'	Octava 2'	Trechter Regal 8'	Rausch Pfeiff III
Super Octav 2'	Sexqualtera II	Scharff IV-VI		Posaune 32'
Rausch Pfeiff III	Scharff VI-VIII	Cymbel III		Posaune 16'

16. Hamburg, St. Jacobi
Church: Schnitger organ in its
original position on the west
wall (photograph, ca. 1860;
organist Heinrich Schmahl
stands in the aisle)

Mixtur VII-IX	Dulcian 16'	Trommet 8'		Dulciane 16'
Trommet 16'	Bahr Pfeiffe 8'	Vox Humana 8'		Trommet 8'
	Schallmey 4'	Trommet 4'		Trommet 4'
				Cornet 2'

Accessories: Main cut-off valve; cut-off valves for all divisions; two tremulants; two cymbelsterns; one Totentrommel ("death" drum).

Couplers: Bp/W, Op/W.

Compass: CDE–c³ (Rp); CDEFGA–c³ (W, Op, Bp); CD–d¹ (Ped)

Wind supply (1721): twelve bellows.

Wind supply (1993): six bellows, all with wind pressure of 80 mm WC.

Pitch (1993): Chorton, a¹ = 495 Hz.

Temperament (1993): modified meantone (⅕ Pythagorean comma).

Literature: (a) Praetorius 1619, 168–69; Niedt 1721, 175–76; facsimile of the 1720 disposition in Reinitzer 1995, 147; Hepworth 1905/6, 258–64; Klée Gobert 1968b, 155–234; Busch 1993, 156–61. (b) NBR, no. 81, BDOK II, no. 102; NBR, no. 306, BDOK III, no. 666; *see* also St. Catherine's Church.

17. Hamburg, St. Jacobi Church: Schnitger organ after restoration
and reconstruction (photograph, 1993)

Hohnstein (Saxon Switzerland)

See Stöntzsch.

Kassel

Johann Sebastian and Anna Magdalena Bach traveled to Kassel at the end of September 1732 to examine the new organ in the St. Martin's Church, whose builder was well known to the Thomascantor. The trip occurred scarcely three weeks after their youngest daughter, Christiana Dorothea, one and a half years old, was buried on August 31, 1732. The couple arrived on September 21 and put up at the Gasthaus Stadt Stockholm. According to the report in a Kassel newspaper from September 22:

> The great and costly organ in the Collegiate Church of St. Martin, or the so-called Great Church, on which work has been going on for almost three years, has finally been adapted to the mode of today and brought to perfection by the organ builder, Mr. *Nicolaus Becker*, of Mühlhausen. When this organ, in accordance with the orders of High Authority, has been examined by the famous Organist and Music Director Mr. Bach of Leipzig, with the help of the Court and Town Organist here, Mr. Carl Möller, in the hope that it will pass the desired test, it is to be played fully next Sunday, God willing, in public assembly, and inaugurated with musical harmony. (NBR, no. 157, BDOK II, no. 316)

Bach's organ recital took place in the presence of the prince of Hesse-Kassel, who especially admired and complimented the artist on his pedal playing, removing a ring from his finger and presenting it to Bach (BDOK II, no. 522). A notation of the Kittel student Michael Gotthard Fischer on his copy of the Toccata and Fugue in D Minor (Dorian), BWV 538, claims that the piece was "played at the examination of the large organ in Cassel." There are no further details regarding Bach's program, which may have included a solo cantata performed by Anna Magdalena Bach. In Kassel, Bach not only was remunerated very well, he also was entertained by the prince and provided with a servant who waited on him and his wife during their eight-day stay.

St. Martin's Church/Martinskirche

Built in the fourteenth–fifteenth centuries as collegiate church for the Hesse residence; secularized in 1526; from 1529, a Lutheran parish church; from 1567, burial site of the landgraves of Hesse. Church and organ destroyed in October 1943. 1954–58, modern rebuilding of the church.

 Organ: New organ (III/33) built 1610–12 by Hans II and Friedrich Scherer; renovations 1662–64 by Ludwig Compenius. 1717, repairs by Andreas Jacobus: new Posaune 16' (to replace Scherer register that had been destroyed by "lead sugar" (*Bleizucker*) and reworking of Trompetbaß and Cornetbaß; the Rückpositiv, "which had been unusable for many years," was brought "again into good condition for playing" (Carspecken 1968). 1730–31, enlargement of organ by Johann Friedrich Stertzing; new stops included Vox humana and probably Posaune 32'. After Stertzing's death in 1731, Wender's son-in-law Johann Nikolaus Becker completed the instrument in 1732; the 1732 disposition is unknown. Presumably on the advice of Bach, whose report is not preserved, the bellows were set lower in 1733. 1797–1801, major renovation. 1837, a disposition of III/42 is recorded. 1896, completely new organ (III/38) by Friedrich Ladegast. Nothing survives from the earlier organ.

Disposition (III/33) from before 1730 (Dresden Ms.)

Rück-Positiv (I)	Ober-Werck (II)	Ober-Positiv (III)	Pedal
Principal 8'	Principal 16'	Hohl Pfeiffe 8'	Principal 32'
Gedackt 8'	Quintadena 16'	Principal 4'	Octav Principal 16'
Quintadena 8'	Octava 8'	Gemßhorn 4'	Untersatz 16'
Octava 4'	Hohl Pfeiffe 8'	Nasat 3'	Gedackt 8'
Quer-Pfeiffe 4'	Flöthen 4'	Wald-Flöthe 2'	Rausch-Pfeiffe III
Mixtur VI	Rausch Pfeiffe III	Zinck III [4'?]	Posaune 16'
Scharff IV	Mixtur VIII	Cymbel II	Trompeta 8'
Krumbhorn 8'	Scharff	Trompeta 8'	Cornet 2'
Meßingen Regal 8'			

Accessories: strongly beating tremulant; softly beating tremulant; cymbelstern; tamburo (drum); cut-off valve for each division.

Couplers: manual coupler; coupler Hw/Ped.

Literature: (a) David 1951, 60; Smets 1931, no. 104; Bernsdorff-Engelbrecht 1967, 113–26; Carspecken 1968, 47–63; Fock 1939/1997, 49–54. (b) NBR, no. 157, BDOK II, no. 316; BWV, entry for BWV 538; Wolff 2000, 24 and 208.

Köthen

In August 1717, Bach was called as court kapellmeister to the prince of Anhalt-Köthen. In this position, which he held until April 1723, he was responsible for the music in the city churches only on rare occasions. Nevertheless, in that he had organ students (among others, his nephews Johann Bernhard Bach and Bernhard Christian Kayser), it seems likely that he would have used Köthen's various instruments at least for teaching. The fragmentary autograph entry of the Fantasia in C Major, BWV 573, in the first keyboard album for Anna Magdalena Bach (1722), no doubt belongs in this pedagogical context.

Bach and his family belonged to the Lutheran congregation of St. Agnus's Church, where, from 1721 on, Bach rented a seat in the women's section for his wife Anna Magdalena. For the Calvinistic-reformed princedom, St. Jacob's Church functioned as cathedral

18. Kassel, St. Martin's Church: Scherer-Becker organ with historic facade pipes and no Rückpositiv (photograph, ca. 1880)

church and princely interment site. It was there, then, that in March 1729 Bach's funeral music was performed for his former employer, Prince Leopold of Anhalt-Köthen. In addition, performances of sacred vocal works of Bach (among others, BWV 21 and 199) have been verified as having taken place in Köthen in 1717–23, even though in what context they took place remains unclear.

Organists at St. Jacob's were Johann Jacob Müller (also composer and fifth-class teacher in the reformed school) from 1713 to 1721 and Friedrich August Martini from 1732 to 1781. Christian Ernest Rolle worked as organist at St. Agnus's (his dates are confirmed for the years between 1718 and 1727); he also was a member of the court kapelle. Thereafter, until 1758, although apparently irregularly and possibly in rotation with Kayser (see below), the organist was Johann Christoph Rosenkranz.

Bach's Köthen student Bernhard Christian Kayser went with his teacher to Leipzig in 1723, continued his instruction with Bach, undertook the study of law at the university in 1724, and for a number of years was apparently one of Bach's closest associates, perhaps even serving for a time as Bach's private secretary. Returning to Köthen, he functioned there from 1733 at the latest as "lawyer to the court and government" as well as "chamber musician" and court organist, for a time probably also as organist of St. Agnus's Church, of which he was a member. Important copies of Bach works stem from Kayser, including, for example, the Prelude and Fugue in E Minor, BWV 548, which attests to Kayser's musical capabilities.

St. Jacob's Church/Jacobskirche

Three-aisled Gothic hall church built 1400–1518 (already in use by 1488). Lutheran services began ca. 1527, reformed services in 1589; as a result, the high altar and sculptures were removed by no later than 1596. From the end of the sixteenth century, reformed city and cathedral church. 1866–69, rebuild of the church interior.

    Organ: 1674–76, new organ (II/25, spring chests) by Zacharias and Andreas Thayßner. 1697, Andreas Thayßner added a manual coupler, and in 1703–4 he made additional improvements. 1713–14, repairs by Johann Georg Müller; 1717–18, repairs by David Zuberbier; 1735, repairs by Johann Georg Zippelius. 1746, repairs by Johann Scheibe, who also proposed a renovation. A number of renovation proposals were made by Johann Christoph Zuberbier, who recorded the disposition in 1756 and in 1766–68 carried out a rebuild. 1877, new organ (III/47) by Friedrich Ladegast. In Köthen's Heimatmuseum, all that is preserved from the Thayßner organ is the central tower and a rounded outer tower with its carvings.

Disposition 1756 (II/25)

Hauptwerk [II]	Rückpositiv [I]	Pedal
Quintathön 16'	Quintathön 8'	Principalbaß 16'
Principal 8'	Gedact 8'	Subbaß 16'
Gemshorn 8'	Principal 4'	Posaunenbaß 16'
Gedact 8'	Gedact 4'	Trompete 4'
Octava 4'	Gemshorn 4'	Cornettin 2'
Quinta 3'	Quinta 3'	
Sesquialter	Octava 2'	
Super-Octava 2'	Flöta 1'	
Mixtur IV	Mixtur III	
Trompete 8'	Fagott [16'?] or	
	Schallmey [4'?]	

    Coupler: manual coupler.
    Compass: CD–c³ (manuals), CD–c¹ or CD–d¹ (pedal).
    Wind supply: three bellows.
    Literature: (a) Haetge 1943, 142–67; Henkel 1985, 5–28; Grohs 2000, 307–9. (b) König 1963/64, 53–60; Wolff 2000, 187–235 and elsewhere; Wolff 2005, xxi–xxii, xxvii.

19. Köthen, St. Jacob's Church: Thayßner organ (photograph, ca. 1860)

St. Agnus's Church/Agnuskirche

Baroque hall church, built as the Lutheran city church in 1694–99 at the wish of the Lutheran princess Gisela Agnus of Anhalt-Köthen. 1748, addition of a surrounding gallery by the court carpenter, Höhne; 1849, rebuild of the church's interior.

Organ: 1707–8, new organ (II/27?) by Johann Heinrich Müller, dedicated Easter Monday 1708; funded by a gift of 1,000 talers made in 1699 by Princess Gisela Agnus of Anhalt-Köthen. Various repairs carried out 1734 and 1742 by Johann Christoph Zuberbier. The Rückpositiv disposition is recorded as part of a Zuberbier cost estimate; he added a Vox humana. Later rebuilds. Wilhelm Rust visited the organ in 1865. 1881, new organ (III/33) by Wilhelm Rühlmann. Nothing from Bach's time survives.

Fragmentary disposition ca. 1740 (II/27) according to Hartmann and Zuberbier

Hauptwerk [II]	Rückpositiv [I]		Pedal
(Ten Stops)	(Ten Stops)	Quinta 3'	(Eight Stops)
Principal 8'	Quintaton 8'	Octava 2'	Posaunbaß 16'
Trompete 8'	Gedackt 8'	Spitzflöte 2'	
	Principal 4'	Tertia 1³⁄₅'	
	Floute douce 4'	Mixtur III	

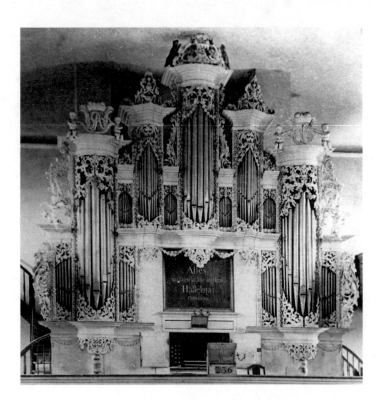

20. Köthen, St. Agnus's
Church: Müller organ
(photograph, ca. 1880)

Accessories: Hw tremulant.

Coupler: manual coupler.

Compass: C–? (manuals); C–d¹e¹f¹ (pedal, according to Rust).

Wind supply: four bellows.

Literature: (a) Hartmann 1799, 19–20; Rust 1878, vii–ix; Haetge 1943, 167–72; Klotz 1950, 189–201; Henkel 1985, 5–28; Dähnert 1986, 3–24. (b) BDOK II, nos. 86, 92, 103; König 1963/64, 53–60; *see* St. Jacob's Church.

Palace Church/Schlosskirche

1597–1608, construction of castle with chapel; 1731, rebuild of chapel according to plans by Johann Michael Hoppenhaupt Sr. After 1869, no church services took place there, and the room was rebuilt. 1963, reconstruction of the chapel; 1988–91, restoration as Baroque gallery church (galleries taken from the reformed church in Oberbeuna, built in 1725 by Hoppenhaupt).

Organ: 1731–33, new two-manual organ by David Zuberbier; the disposition of the previous instrument is unknown. By 1865, when Wilhelm Rust visited, only remnants remained. 1991, installation by Orgelbau Wieland Rühle of an organ by Johann Christoph

Zuberbier that had been built in 1754 for the church in Thurau/Anhalt (but from 1715 had been housed in the Köthen Historical Museum).

Disposition 1733 (II/13)

Hauptwerk [I]	Brustwerk [II]	Pedal
Quintaten 8'	Gedackt 8'	Sub Baß 16'
Viol di Gamba 8'	Quintaden 4'	Octaven Baß 8'
Prinzipal 4'	Prinzipal 2'	
Quinta 3'	Quinta 1½'	
Octava 2'		
Tertia 1³/₅'		
Mixtur III 1'		

> **Coupler:** manual coupler.
> **Compass:** C–e³ (manuals); C–e¹ (pedal).
> **Wind supply:** two bellows.
> **Pitch:** Kammerton.
> **Literature:** (a) Rust 1878, ix; Dauer 1992; Rühle 1992.

Langewiesen

At the end of November 1706, Bach traveled from Arnstadt to the small town of Lange-wiesen (near Gehren) to examine an organ. (Langewiesen is the birthplace of his first wife, Maria Barbara, and the place where at one time his father-in-law, Johann Michael Bach, worked.) The organ examination, which took place on the First Sunday of Advent (November 28), was carried out by Bach, Johann Kister (city organist from neighboring Gehren), and city councilman Fidler, also from Gehren. Neither the examination report nor the disposition of 1706 has survived. Johann Christian Thalacker was cantor and apparently also organist of Our Lady's from 1693 to 1746.

Church of Our Lady/Liebfrauenkirche

Baroque hall church with surrounding galleries, erected 1675–80 from what remained of the old city church after a fire.

Organ: 1706, new organ by Johann Albrecht and Johann Sebastian Erhardt. 1794–95, rebuild by the Wagner Bros., who recorded the original disposition. 1845, new organ (II/18) by Johann Friedrich Schulze. Nothing from Bach's time survives.

Disposition (II/20) before rebuild in 1794

Hauptwerk (I)	Positiv (II)	Pedal
Quintadena 16'	Quintadena 8'	Subbaß 16'
Principal 8'	Gedackt 8'	Violonbaß 16'

Hauptwerk (I)	Positiv (II)	Pedal
Gemshorn 8'	Spiel Flöte 4'	Principal Baß 8'
Violdigamba 8'	Quinta 1½'	Hohlfloeten Baß 4'
Octave 4'	Mixtur IV 1'	Posaunen Baß 16'
Tertia 1½' [!]	(English) Tremulant	
Quinta 3'		
Octave 2'		
Mixtur IV 2'		

Particulars: According to Seidel, an English tremulant gives delicate stops, such as the Vox humana, "a soft waver (*ein leichter Tremulant*)."

Coupler: manual coupler.

Compass: C–c^3 (manuals); C–c^1 (pedal).

Wind supply: four bellows.

Archival Sources: Stadtarchiv Langewiesen, Bestand 3478; Thüringisches Hauptsta-atsarchiv Rudolstadt, Bestand Unterkonsistorium Gehren, Nr. 351: *Die Erbauung eines neuen Orgelwerckes in der Kirche zu Langewiesen betr., 1784–1801*, fol. 35r (disposition in January 1794).

Literature: (a) Seidel 1844, 97–98; Dehio 2003, 749. (b) BDOK II, no. 18.

Leipzig

Six years before the beginning of his tenure in Leipzig as cantor and director of music from 1723 to 1750, Bach visited Leipzig at the invitation of the rector of the university in order to test the new organ in the university church of St. Paul's. After the successful examina-tion, Daniel Vetter, the sixty-year-old organist at St. Nicholas's who was responsible for overseeing the organ-building project, wrote:

> At the request of the honorable University the instrument was examined on December 16, 1717, by the kapellmeister from Köthen, Mr. N. [*recte:* J. S.] Bach, with no major defect, and judged in such a way that he could not praise and laud it enough, especially its rare stops, recently invented, and not to be found in very many places (BDOK I, no.87).

Beginning in 1723, Bach held overall responsibility for the music in Leipzig. Even though he held no position as organist, he played the organs in the city every now and again, used them for teaching, oversaw their upkeep, and concerned himself with filling the city's organist positions. During Bach's tenure, the following were organists: At St. Thomas's, Christian Gräbner until 1729, Johann Gottlieb Görner after 1729; at St. Nicholas's, Johann Gottlieb Görner until 1729, the Bach student Johann Schneider from 1730; at the New Church, Georg Balthasar Schott until 1729, the Bach student Carl Gotthelf Gerlach after 1729; at St. Paul's, Johann Christoph Thiele. Bach had close contact with the Leipzig organ builders Johann Scheibe and Zacharias Hildebrandt.

The organs in the two principal churches of St. Nicholas and St. Thomas were used primarily during worship services and were also used to accompany Bach's cantatas, passions, and other sacred works. They played a special role in those cantatas in which Bach treated the organ as a concertizing instrument, himself playing the solo parts and giving over ensemble direction to the choir prefects. This can be seen especially in the cantatas "Wir müssen durch viel Trübsal in das Reich Gottes eingehen," BWV 146 (Jubilate Sunday, May 12, 1726); "Geist und Seele wird verwirret," BWV 35 (Twelfth Sunday after Trinity, September 8, 1726); "Gott soll allein mein Herze haben," BWV 169 (Eighteenth Sunday after Trinity, October 20, 1726); "Ich geh und suche mit Verlangen," BWV 49 (Twentieth Sunday after Trinity, November 3, 1726); "Ich habe meine Zuversicht," BWV 188 (Twenty-first Sunday after Trinity, October 17, 1728); and "Wir danken dir, Gott, wir danken dir," BWV 29 (municipal election, August 27, 1731).

The only new organ built in Leipzig during Bach's tenure was for the Church of St. John, located just outside the city gates. The disposition for this new organ by Scheibe must certainly have been developed with Bach's assistance. Bach and Zacharias Hildebrandt tested the new organ in the fall of 1743. The Bach student Johann Friedrich Agricola later reported that this organ "was recognized as flawless by Mr. C[apell]. M[eister]. Joh. Seb. Bach and Mr. Zacharias Hildebrandt after perhaps one of the strictest investigations ever suffered by an organ" (BDOK III, no. 740). Organists at St. John's were Johann Michael Steinert, 1694–1731; Johann Gottlieb Reinicke, 1731–47; and Johann Georg Hille, 1747–66.

St. Paul's or University Church/Paulinerkirche or Universitätskirche

1485, completion of the rebuild of the medieval monastery church to a late Gothic hall church; 1539, secularization of the monastery; 1543, surrender of the monastery holdings to the university; August 12, 1545, dedication of the church by Martin Luther. 1710–12, Baroque refurbishing of the interior; nineteenth century, neo-Gothic remodeling. Only lightly damaged during World War II, the church was demolished by the East German communist regime on May 30, 1968; construction of an "Aula with Vestry," a contemporary interpretation of the former University Church, began in 2007.

Organ: 1528, new organ (II/15) by an unknown builder placed in the middle of the south wall; rebuilds 1626–27 by Josias Ibach and 1627–28 by Heinrich and Esaias Compenius. 1710, university initiated negotiations with Gottfried Silbermann for a new organ, which nevertheless was never built. Instead, the university continued with its plan to have Johann Scheibe carry out a major rebuild and expansion of the existing instrument, which Scheibe already had moved to the west side of the church in 1710. 1716, completion of what at the time was the largest organ in electoral Saxony; 1717, examination by Bach. Rebuilds in later eighteenth and nineteenth centuries; 1841–44, new organ (III/56) by Johann Gottlob Mende.

For Bach's organ report, *see* Part II.A.

21. Leipzig, St. Paul's Church: Scheibe organ (copper engraving, ca. 1720, with notes in the hand of Johann Andreas Silbermann: "The case is painted white, here and there a little goldleaf.")

Disposition 1717 (III/48 plus six transmissions) according to Sicul

Hauptwerk (II)	Hinterwerk (Echo) I	Brustwerk (III)	Pedal
Groß-Principal 16' from pure tin in facade (T)	Lieblich getackt 8' (wood)	Principal 8' from pure tin in façade	**Transmissions:** Groß-Principal-Bass 16' (T)
Groß-Quinta-Tön 16' (T)	Quinta-Tön 8'	Viol di Gamb naturell 8'	Groß-Quinta-Tön 16' (T)
Klein Principal 8' (T)	Fleute deuce 4'	Grob getact wide-scaled 8'	Octav-Bass 8' (T)
Fleute Allemande 8'	Quinta decima 4'	Octav 4'	Octav-Bass 4' (T)
Gems-Horn 8'	Decima nona 3'	Rohr-Flöte 4'	Quint-Bass 3' (T)
Octav 4' (T)	Holl-Flöte 2'	Octav 2'	Mixtur-Bass V–VI (T)
Quinta 3' (T)	Viola 2'	Nassat 3'	**On the small Brust-Pedal chests:**
Quint-Nassat 3'	Vigesima nona 1½'	Sedecima 1'	Groß hell-Quinten-Bass 6' of pure tin in facade
Octavina 2'	Weit-Pfeiffe 1'	Schweitzer-Pfeiffe 1'	Jubal-Bass 8'
Wald-Flöte 2'	Mixtur III	Largo [Larigot] [1⅓']	Nacht-Horn-Bass 4'
Große Mixtur V–VI (T)	Helle Cymbal II	Mixtur III	Octav-Bass 2'
Cornetti III	Sertin [Sordin] 8'	Helle Cymbal II	**On large wind chests to either side:**
Zinck II			Groß Principal-Bass 16' of pure tin in facade
Schalmo [Chalumeau] of wood 8'			Sub-Bass 16'
			Posaunen-Bass 16'
			Trompeten-Bass 8'
			Holl-Flöten-Bass 1'
			Mixtur-Bass IV

Particulars: A visitor to the organ in 1736 described some of the stops as follows (Dresden Ms., 43):

Chalumeau: stopped reed, voiced softly and sweetly, imitating the instrument.

Fleute Allemande: narrow-scaled open wood, somewhat sharply voiced, imitating the traverso.

Weite Pfeiffe: open metal, very widely scaled, sharply voiced, also called Glöcklein-Thon.

Sertin: stopped reed; nevertheless because of its sharp intonation it resembles the muted trumpet called Sertin or the stop most organ builders call Sordun.

Largo: wide-scaled, open 1½' similar to Glöcklein-Thon.

Schweitzer Pfeiffe: very narrow, open, sharply voiced.

Jubal: principal-scaled, open but dull-voiced.

Große Hell-Quinten Bass: wide-scaled, with a somewhat high cut-up, very loud although reverberant and melodious.

The same source indicates that the keyboards and stop names were color-coordinated: blue for the Hinterwerk, red for the Brust.

Accessories: tremulant; cut-off valves to each division; cymbelstern; bellows signal.

Compass: CD–? (manuals); CD–c^1 (pedal).

Wind supply: six bellows.

Literature: (a) Praetorius 1619, 116; Sicul 1718, 195–97; Dähnert 1980, 182–84; Schaefer 1994, 156–58; Hütter 1995, 483–677; Butler/Butler 2006, 285–306; Butler 2011, 89–91. (b) BDOK I, no. 87; NBR, no. 72, BDOK II, nos. 87–89; Wolff 2000, 143–44, 184, 187, 221, 316, 318.

St. Nicholas's Church/Nikolaikirche

Three-aisled hall church, erected 1513–25 to succeed the oldest parish church of the city. 1628–30, addition of west-end student gallery; 1735, addition of two tiers of galleries. 1784–97, classical refurbishing of the interior.

Organ: 1479, first mention of an organ in the west gallery of the southern side-aisle. 1597–98, new organ (II/27) by Johann Lange; 1608, repairs by Joachim Zschugk; 1625–26, renovation of the case; 1638–39, repairs by Andreas Werner to damage incurred during the Thirty Years' War. 1693–94, enlargement by Zacharias Thayßner to III/36. 1724–25, renovations by Johann Scheibe; 1739–40, repairs by Zacharias Hildebrandt. 1741, organ is visited by Johann Andreas Silbermann. 1750–51, organ is put into perfect condition again by Zacharias and Johann Gottfried Hildebrandt. 1785–87, dismantling of the old organ (usable parts incorporated into the town church organ in Taucha) and new organ (III/49) by Gebr. Trampeli. 1862, entirely new organ (IV/85) by Friedrich Ladegast; 2003–4, restoration and enlargement (V/103) by Eule Orgelbau.

Disposition (III/36) according to J. J. Vogel (ca. 1700)

Oberwerk (II)	Rückwerk (I)	Brustpositiv (III)	Pedal
Quintatön 16'	Grobgedact 8'	Quintathon 8'	Untersatz 16'
Principal 8'	Principal 4'	Principal 4'	Octavbaß 4'
Grobgedact 8'	Gemshorn 4'	Sesqualtera II	Posaunenbass 16'
Gemshorn 8'	Quintathon 4'	Quinte 3'	Trompetenbaß 8'
Octava 4'	Viola di Gamba 4'	Octava 2'	Schallmeyenbaß 4'
Nazard 3'	Nazard 3'	Mixtur III	Cornetbaß 2'
Quinte 3'	Octava 2	Schalmey 4'	
Superoctava 2'	Mixtur IV		
Waldflöte 2'	Sesquialtera		
Mixtur VI	Bompart 8'		
Fagot 16'			
Trompete 8'			

22. Leipzig,
St. Nicholas's
Church: Lange organ
(watercolor by Carl
Benjamin Schwarz of
the "Former Organ in
the St. Nicholas Church
in Leipzig" 1785)

Particulars: Johann Andreas Silbermann (Schaefer 1994) lists Quinte 1½' instead of Viola di Gamba 4' (Rp) and Quinte 1½' instead of Quinte 3' (Bw), as well as Octava 8' instead of Octavbaß 4' (Ped). Tin-plated iron resonators in the Schalmey 4' (facade, Bw) and in the pedal reeds. Cornetbaß 2' with wooden blocks and boots. The stops were "iron drawknobs in slots."

Accessories: tremulant; Vogelgesang (birdsong); cymbelstern.

Couplers: "no pull-down pedal" (Silbermann).

Compass: CD–c³ (manuals), CD–d¹ (pedal).

Wind supply: four large single-fold bellows.

Pitch: Chorton.

Literature: (a) Vogel n.d., 97; Dähnert 1980, 180–82; Schaefer 1994, 171–73; Magirius 1995a, 337–473. (b) BDOK II, no. 180.

St. Thomas's Church/Thomaskirche

Three-aisled hall church, built 1482–96 for the Augustinian monastery that had existed since 1212. 1498, completion of a stone choir gallery; 1570–71, addition of galleries on the north and south sides; 1632, construction of two musicians' galleries for town pipers and art fiddlers on the north and south sides of the choir gallery. End of the nineteenth century, removal of Baroque additions and renovation of the interior in neo-Gothic style. 1949, Johann Sebastian Bach's alleged remains were moved from the Bach-Gellert vault in St. John's Church to a new tomb located at the entrance to the choir.

Large Organ: First evidence of an organ dates from 1384. 1511, new organ (likely II/21) by Blasius Lehmann; rebuilds during the sixteenth century; 1598–99, enlargement by Johann Lange to II/25. 1670–71, enlargement of Brustwerk from two to nine stops by Christoph Donat and sons. 1721–22, major rebuild by Johann Scheibe; 1730, during Bach's tenure, organ was cleaned and through-tuned (the temperament was "no longer accurate"), and the Pedal Posaune 16' was strengthened, again by Scheibe; 1739–40, Scheibe provided new twenty-four-note pedal keyboard (probably CD–c^1); 1747, major repairs by Scheibe. 1755, rebuild (III/39) by Christian Immanuel Schweinefleisch; he built new chests for the Rückpositiv and Pedal and eleven new stops (three for the Rückpositiv and eight for the Pedal). 1772–73, Schweinefleisch's student Johann Gottlieb Mauer moved the Rückpositiv into the main case as an Oberwerk division; 1794–95, rebuild by Gebr. Trampeli; further rebuilds between 1808 and 1847 by Johann Gottlob Mende. 1889, completely new organ (III/63) by Wilhelm Sauer, who also enlarged the organ to III/83 at the wish of Karl Straube in 1908. In addition to the Sauer organ, in 1998–2000 a new "Bach organ" (IV/61) by Gerald Woehl was installed in the north balcony; its disposition is modeled on the Stertzing organ in Eisenach's St. George's Church, while the case is modeled after the Scheibe organ for Leipzig's St. Paul's Church.

Disposition (III/35) according to J. J. Vogel (ca. 1700)

Oberwerk (II)	Rückpositiv (I)	Brustwerk (III)	Pedal
Principal 16'	Principal 8'	Grobgedackt 8'	Sub Baß 16'
Quintatön 16'	Quintadena 8'	Principal 4'	Posaunen Baß 16'
Principal 8'	Lieblich Gedacktes 8'	Nachthorn 4'	Trommeten Baß 8'
Spielpfeife 8'	Traversa 4'	Nasat 3'	Schallmeyen Baß 4'
Octava 4'	Spitzflöte 4'	Gemshorn 2'	Cornet 2'
Quinta 3'	Klein Gedackt 4'	Sesquialtera	
Superoctava 2'	Violin 2'	Zimbel II	
Sesquialtera II	Schallflöt 1'	Regal 8'	
Mixtur VI–IX	Rausch Quinta II	Geigenregal 4'	
	Mixtur IV		
	Krumbhorn 16'		
	Trommet 8'		

23. Leipzig, St. Thomas's Church: Mauer organ (drawing, 1772–73)

Accessories: tremulant; Vogelgesang (birdsong); cymbelstern.

Compass: CD–c³? (manuals); CD–c¹ (pedal).

Pitch: Chorton.

Literature: (a) Vogel n.d., 111; Dähnert 1980, 184–86; Schrammek 1983b, 46–55; Magirius 1995b, 153–335; Wolff 1998, 20–22; Sprondel 2000, 390–93; Wolff 2005b, 9–20. (b) BDOK II, no. 561; *see* St. Paul's Church.

Small Organ: 1489, new construction as swallow's-nest organ on the south wall; rebuilds during the sixteenth century; 1630, enlargement by Heinrich Compenius. 1639–40, organ was moved by Andreas Werner and Erhardt Müller to a new gallery over the triumphal arch. Inscription on the organ doors: "SANCTUS, SANCTUS, SANCTUS / DOMINUS DEUS ZEBAOTH" (Holy, holy, holy art thou, Lord God of hosts), along with the year it was built on the left, "F[ecit]. 1489," and the year it was rebuilt or repaired on the right, "R[eparavit]. 1639." 1665, six stops added by Christoph Donat; 1720–21, repairs by Johann Scheibe. 1727–28, Zacharias Hildebrandt brought eight stops into playing condition. 1740–41, dismantling of the disintegrating organ by Johann Scheibe. Bach used the swallow's-nest organ for performances of multichoir works, as, for example, in the Magnificat with the Christmas interpolations, BWV 243a, or in the St. Matthew Passion (1736) for the third choir in the first part's introductory and concluding choruses.

Disposition (II?/21) according to J. J. Vogel (ca. 1700)

Rückpositiv [I]	Oberwerk [II]	Brustwerk [II?]	Pedal
Lieblich Gedackt 8'	Principal 8'	Trichterregal 8'	Subbaß 16'
Principal 4'	Gedackt 8'	Sifflöt 1'	Fagott 16'
Hohlflöte 4'	Quintatön 8'	Spitzflöte 2'	Trompete 8'
Nasat 3'	Octave 4'		
Octave 2'	Rauschquinte II 3'		
Sesquialtera II	Mixtur IV–X		
Dulcian 8'	Cymbel II		
Trompete 8'			

Wind supply: six bellows.

Pitch: Chorton.

Literature: (a) Vogel n.d., 111; Dähnert 1980, 186. (b) *see* St. Paul's Church.

St. John's Church/Johanniskirche

1582–84, new building after the church had been destroyed in 1547; 1894–97, new building using the tower from 1749. 1894, discovery of the alleged remains of Johann Sebastian Bach and Christian Fürchtegott Gellert, which were then interred in two new sarcophagi in a tomb directly in front of the altar. Considerable damage to the building during World War II (1943); the ruins were exploded in May 1963. (The Bach bones had already been moved to St. Thomas's in 1949.)

Organ: 1553, purchase of a positive; 1656, installation by Christoph Donat of a small organ that had been in the St. Nicholas Church. 1694–95, new organ (I/10) built by Johann Tobias Gottfried Trost (Manual: Gedackt 8', Quintatön 8', Prinzipal 4', Gedackt 4', Quinte 3', Oktave 2', Sesquialter II, Mixtur III; Pedal: Subbaß 16', Prinzipalbaß 8'). 1742, the old organ was sold to the church in Laußig (Eilenburg County) and Johann Scheibe built a new organ using pipes from the small organ of the St. Thomas Church; Bach's organ report unverifiable. Further rebuilds during the eighteenth and nineteenth centuries; 1893–94, removal of the organ during a church renovation. 1899, organ's key desk and organ bench purchased by Paul de Wit (of Leipzig); after 1926 they were housed in the Music Instrument Museum of Leipzig University (Inv.-Nr. 262). After restoration in 2009 by Marcus Stahl, Dresden, they are now on display in the Bach Museum of the Bach-Archive Leipzig.

24. Leipzig, St. John's Church: Scheibe organ (photograph, ca. 1894)

25. Leipzig, St. John's Church: Scheibe key desk; rebuilt by Paul de Wit, ca. 1900; restored 2009. Museum for Musical Instruments of the University of Leipzig. Since March 2010 on permanent loan to the Bach Museum Leipzig.

Disposition 1742 (II/22)

Hauptwerk (I)	Oberwerk (II)	Pedal
Quintathön 16'	Quintathön 8'	Subbaß 16'
Principal 8'	Lieblich Gedackt 8'	Violon 8'
Gedackt 8'	Principal 4'	Posaun 16'
Octav 4'	Spielpfeiff 4'	Trompet 8'
Spielpfeiff 4'	Hohlflöt 3'	
Quinta 3'	Octav 2'	
Octav 2'	Weitpfeiff 1'	
Octav 1'	Tertia II	
Mixtur IV		
Cornetto II		

Particulars: "Of special interest . . . is to be noted that by engaging a stop it is possible to play piano and forte on one manual quite extraordinarily well" (SeN, 56; cited in Dähnert 1980, 177).

Accessories: cut-off valves for the manuals; tremulant; bellows signal.

Coupler: Hw/Ped.

Compass: CD–c^3 (manuals); CD–c^1 (pedal).

Wind supply: three bellows.

Literature: (a) SeN, 56; Adlung 1768, 251; de Wit 1899/1900, 989; Dähnert 1962, 85–86, 103; Dähnert 1980, 177–78; Henkel 1986, 44–50; Mai 1995, 809–69. (b) BDOK II, no. 519; *see* St. Paul's Church.

New Church/Neue Kirche

Baroque hall church with surrounding galleries completed 1699, replacing the Franciscan (Barefoot) monastery church build 1488. Replaced in the nineteenth century by the St. Matthew's Church, which was built on the same site; this building was fully destroyed in World War II (1943).

Organ: 1703–4, new organ by Christoph Donat Sr. and Jr., placed on the south gallery above the pulpit; Georg Philipp Telemann was its first organist. 1722, rebuild by Johann Scheibe (the disposition transmitted by Niedt/Mattheson [p. 189] was not built). Further rebuilds beginning in the late eighteenth century; 1847, new organ by Johann Gottlob Mende.

Disposition 1704 (II/21)

Vorderwerk (I)	Hinterwerk (II)	Pedal
Quintatön 16'	Lieblich gedackt 8' zur Music [for concerted music]	Subbaß 16'
Principal 8'	Viol' di Gamba 8'	Posaunenbaß 16'
Grobgedackt 8'	Klein gedackt 4'	Trompetenbaß 8'
Spielflöten 8'	Octava 2'	Schalmeyenbaß 4'

Octava 4'	Nasat 3'
Gedackte Flöte 4'	Spitzflöt 1'
Quinta 3'	
Superoctava 2'	
Gemshorn 2'	
Russflöte 1'	
Mixtur IV	

Particulars: resonators of tin-plated iron in the Trompetenbaß 8' and Schalmeyen-baß 4'.

Accessories: tremulant; bellows signal.

Coupler: manual coupler.

Compass: CD–c^3 (manuals); CD–c^1 (pedal).

Wind supply: four bellows.

Temperament: meantone; however, Lieblich gedackt 8' zur Music: well-tempered.

Literature: (a) Niedt 1721, 189; Schering 1926, 116–17; Dähnert 1980, 179–80; Mai/Küas 1995, 679–96.

26. Leipzig, New Church: Donat organ (detail; copper engraving, ca. 1730)

Lübeck

In the late fall of 1705, Johann Sebastian Bach set out on a journey to Lübeck "in order to listen to the famous organist of St. Mary's Church there, Diedrich Buxtehude" (NBR, no. 306; BDOK III, no. 666); he returned to Arnstadt at the beginning of February 1706. Bach had been granted four weeks' leave, and he had arranged for his cousin Johann Ernst Bach to substitute for him. Nevertheless, because he "stayed about four times longer" than he had requested, he was required to justify himself on February 21, 1706, before the church consistory (NBR, no. 20; BDOK II, no. 16).

None of the details of Bach's stay in Lübeck are known. It appears, however, that the trip was planned to coincide with the performances on December 2 and 3, 1705, of Buxtehude's oratorios *Castrum doloris* and *Templum honoris* (BuxWV 133–34), for which none of the music has survived.

St. Mary's Church/Marienkirche

Three-aisled Gothic brick basilica; nave built 1315–30. Bombed in World War II (1942); the organs and the seventeenth-century music galleries were completely destroyed. 1954, rebuilding of the church using what remained of the interior.

Main Organ: 1377, earliest record of an organ. 1516–18, new organ or substantial rebuild by an otherwise unknown organ builder; the large two-manual instrument included Werk, Unterwerk, and Pedal divisions (the organ never possessed a Rückpositiv). 1560–61, addition of a Brustwerk by Jacob Scherer; 1596–98, substantial rebuild begun by Gottschalk Johannsen (also known as Borchert) and concluded by Jacob Rabe. 1637–41, substantial rebuild and enlargement by Friedrich Stellwagen; organ examination by Heinrich Scheidemann. 1683, Michel Briegel "completely tuned the two organs throughout, not including the reeds," in thirty-one and a half days (Lübeck, Archiv der Hansestadt, St. Marien, I 1a, *Wochenbuch 1678–1685*, fol. 279r). Apparently Buxtehude, who later composed a laudatory poem for Werckmeister's *Harmonologia* of 1702, wanted all three organs (main organ, small organ, rood screen organ) in the same temperament, not least so that they could all be played together (*Castrum doloris*, 1705: dirge accompanied "by all organs"). 1704, three new stops added by Otto Diedrich Richborn. 1721, disposition (III/54) is published by Niedt/Mattheson. 1733–35, rebuild by Konrad Bünting that included rearranging the keyboards as well as filling in the missing notes in the keyboard's compass. 1782, probable tuning in equal temperament. 1851–54, completely new organ (IV/80) by Johann Friedrich Schulze using the original case (nonspeaking pipes were placed in the facade); destroyed 1942. 1968, new organ (V/101) by Emanuel Kemper.

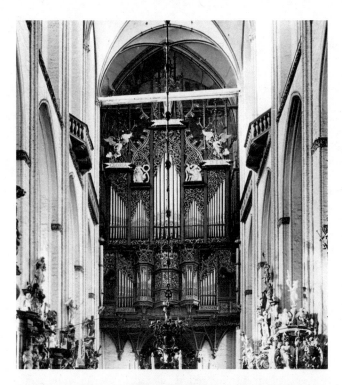

27. Lübeck, St. Mary's
Church: Schulze
organ in historical case
(photograph, ca. 1930)

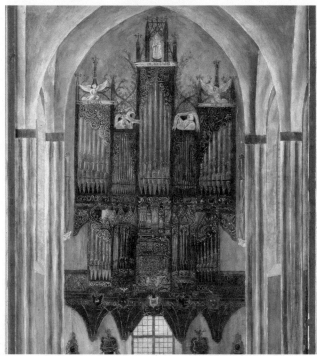

28. Lübeck, St. Mary's
Church: Johannsen/
Stellwagen organ with
original Brustwerk
(painting by Carl Julius
Milde, 1851)

Disposition (III/54) according to Niedt (1721)

Werck (III)	Unterwerk (I)	Brustwerk (II)	Pedal
Principal 16'	Bordun 16'	Principal 8'	Principal 32'
Quintadena 16'	Principal 8'	Gedact 8'	Principal 16'
Octava 8'	Blockflöte 8'	Octava 4'	Sub-Baß 16'
Spitz-Flöte 8'	Hohlflöte 8'	Hohl-Flöte 4'	Octava 8'
Octava 4'	Quintadena 8'	Sesquialtera II	Gedact 8'
Hohl-Flöte 4'	Octava 4'	Feld-Pfeiffe 2'	Octava 4'
Nasat 3'	Spiel-Flöte 2'	Gemshorn 2'	Bauernflöte 2'
Rauschpfeiffe IV	Sesquialtera II	Sifflet 1½'	Nachthorn 2'
Scharff IV	Mixtura V	Mixtura VIII	Mixtura VI
Mixtura XV	Scharff IV–V	Cimbel III	Groß-Posaun 24'
Trommete 16'	Dulcian 16'	Krumhorn 8'	Posaune 16'
Trommete 8'	Baarpfeiffe 8'	Regal 8'	Dulcian 16'
Zincke 8'	Trichter-Regal 8'		Trommete 8'
	Vox humana 8'		Krumhorn 8'
			Cornet 2'

Accessories: cymbelstern; two drums; tremulants in Bw and Ow.

Compass: W and Uw: CDEFGA–c³; as of 1733, CD–c³. Bw: DEFGA–g²a²; as of 1733, CD–c³. Ped: CDEFGA–d¹; as of 1733, CD–d¹.

Wind supply (1707): ten bellows.

Pitch: Chorton.

Temperament (1683): modified meantone (well-tempered?); after 1782, probably equal.

Literature: (a) Niedt 1721, 189; Stahl 1939, 6; Snyder 1985, 427–29, 431–34; Snyder 1986, 175–90; Dehio 1994, 451–65; Belotti 1997, 254; Ortgies 2004, 70–74; Ortgies 2006, 316–36; Snyder 2007, 79–87, 467. (b) NBR, no. 20, BDOK II, no. 16; NBR, no. 306, BDOK III, no. 666; Wolff 2000, 65, 95–98, 208, 526; Maul/Wollny 2007.

Small Organ ("Dance of Death" Organ/"Totentanz" Orgel): 1475–77, new organ (I/P) by Johannes Stephani placed in the northern side chapel, a confessional chapel that since the fifteenth century had housed Bernt Notke's painting *The Dance of Death*. 1557–58, addition of a Rückpositiv division by Jacob Scherer; 1621–22, addition of a Brustwerk and enlargement of the Pedal by Henning Kröger. 1653–55, reworking of the wind chests, among other things, by Friedrich Stellwagen. 1701, overhaul by Hans Hantelmann—according to Buxtehude, the first renovation since Stellwagen's work. 1760, enlargement of the Brustwerk disposition by organ builder Bünting; he also filled in the missing pitches D♯, F♯, and G♯; provided couplers to all manuals; replaced the tinfoil on the facade pipes; and made changes to the case. 1805, organ tuned in equal temperament by Joachim Christoph Kaltschmidt. Ca. 1845, Theodor Vogt writes down what is now the oldest surviving record of the disposition (III/39). 1845–46, rebuild reducing the disposition to thirty-four stops. 1937, modified partial restoration by Karl Kemper;

29. Lübeck, St. Mary's:
"Totentanz" organ after
restoration (photograph,
1937)

reconstructed disposition recorded by Gustav Fock. Organ destroyed World War II (March
1942). 1986, new organ (IV/56) by Alfred Führer using data from exact measurements
taken in 1937.

Disposition 1705 (III/40) as reconstructed in 1937

Hauptwerk [II]	Rückpositiv [I]	Brustwerk [III]	Pedal
Quintade 16'	Prinzipal 8', facade	Gedackt 8'	Prinzipal 16', facade
Prinzipal 8', facade	Rohrflöte 8'	Quintadena 4'	Subbaß 16'
Spitzflöte 8'	Quintatön 8'	Hohlflöte 2'	Oktave 8'
Oktave 4'	Oktave 4'	Quintflöte 1½'	Gedackt 8'
Nasat 2⅔'	Rohrflöte 4'	Scharff IV	Oktave 4'

Hauptwerk [II]	Rückpositiv [I]	Brustwerk [III]	Pedal
Rauschpfeiffe II	Sesquialter II	Krummhorn 8'	Quintadena 4'
Mixtur VI–X	Sifflöte 1½'	Schalmei 4'	Oktave 2'
Trompete 8'	Scharf VI–VIII		Nachthorn 1'
	Dulzian 16'		Zimbel II
	Trechterregal 8'		Mixtur IV
			Posaune 16'
			Dulzian 16'
			Trompete 8'
			Schalmei 4'
			Cornet 2'

Coupler: Couplers date from 1760.

Manual compass: CDEFGA–c^3; from 1760, CD–c^3.

Pedal compass: CDEFGA–d^1; from 1760, CD–c^1.

Pitch: Chorton.

Temperament (1683): modified meantone (well-tempered?); after 1805, equal.

Literature: (a) Ley 1906/07, 280–82; Stahl 1939, 9–11; Fock 1974, 186; Dehio 1994, 451–65; Snyder 2002, 40; Snyder 2007, 81–82, 467.

Rood Screen Organ (Lettnerorgel): Documented use since 1492 for masses in the choir and Marian services in the chapel behind the high altar. 1664, new positive organ by Michel Briegel; 1684, repair and tuning of the organ, which according to Buxtehude "had been very imperfect and impure"; it took Michel Briegel six days. The instrument was used until 1800. In addition, since 1678 there was a *"Doppelt 16 füßiges Regal"*—regal with a 16' register—for performances on feast days and at Abendmusiken (Snyder 2007, 466). 1854, new organ (I/7) by Theodor Vogt, using registers from the dismantled main organ. The case was modeled after the Brustwerk case that had been removed from the main organ. In 1900, Karl Kemper built a new organ (II/15) using the same case. Destroyed 1942.

Pitch: Chorton.

Temperament (1683): modified meantone (well-tempered?).

Literature: (a) Stahl 1939, 11–12; Snyder 2007, 101, 463, and 468.

Lüneburg

From March 1700 until the spring of 1702, Johann Sebastian Bach, supported by a scholarship, studied as chorister at the Latin School of St. Michael's, Lüneburg, at that time the secondary residence of the dukes of Brunswick-Lüneburg-Celle. The Lüneburg connection apparently came through Georg Böhm, who became Bach's organ and keyboard teacher. A very early Bach autograph in organ tablature notation—a manuscript dated 1700 of Johann Adam Reinken's chorale fantasia "An Wasserflüssen Babylon" (By the Flowing Waters of Babylon) copied under Böhm's supervision—proves that already at the beginning

30. Lübeck, St. Mary's:
Center aisle with rood screen
organ (painting by Wilhelm
Stoeltzner, 1856)

of his time in Lüneburg the fifteen-year-old was an unusually advanced performer (Maul/
Wollny 2007). The Lüneburg time also offered the young Bach the opportunity of getting to
know the large north German organs and acquiring further knowledge of organ building.
Bach made various trips from Lüneburg to Hamburg in order to seek out Reinken and
play on his organ at St. Catherine's. (At the time Böhm worked as harpsichordist at the
opera, and Bach's cousin Johann Ernst Bach also was in Hamburg for educational reasons.)

Georg Böhm's organ at St. John's Church in Lüneburg was the best in the city in ca.
1700, although still without a fully developed pedal division. Bach no doubt was strongly
influenced by Böhm and may still have maintained contact while he was in Leipzig. At the
very least, Böhm took part as distributor in Bach's *Clavier-Übung* project.

St. John's Church/Johanniskirche

Five-aisled Gothic hall church, completed before 1370, enlarged 1460–70.

Organ: 1551–53, new organ (III/27) by Hendrik Niehoff and Jasper Johansen. 1576, addition of Untersatz 16' (preserved) to the Pedal (Hinterlade) by Dirk Hoyer. 1586, refurbishing of pedal chests by Matthias Mahn; 1587, repairs by Hans Scherer I; 1633–35, rebuild by Franz Theodor Kretzschmar; 1651–52, enlargement by Friedrich Stellwagen to III/40. At the request of Georg Böhm, Mathias Dropa built a new pedal division in 1712–15 and enlarged the organ to III/47. Numerous changes after 1739. 1952–53, restoration by Rudolf von Beckerath, including replacing the no-longer-preserved mechanical action. 1992, repairs and changes to disposition.

31. Lüneburg, St. John's Church: Niehoff/Johannsen/Dropa organ (photograph, 2000)

Disposition 1710 (III/28)–1714 (III/46; new stops in italic)

Rückpositiv (I)—1710	Rückpositiv (I)—1714	Oberwerk (III)—1710	Oberwerk (III)—1714
Principal 8' (L)	Principal 8'	Principal 8'	Principal 8'
Quintaden 8' (U)	Quintadena 8'	Hohlflöte 8'	Rohr Flöthe 8'
Octave 4' (L)	Octava 4'	Octave 4'	Octava 4'
Hohlflöte 4' (U)	*Wald-Flöthe 2'*		Rohr Flöthe 4' (from Rp)
Sieflöte 1' (U)	Sifflet 1'	Nassat 3'	Nasat 3'
Mixtur (L)		Gemßhorn	Gemßhorn 2'
Scharff (L)	Scharff V-VII	Superoctave 2'	
Sesquialtera (U)	Sesquialtera II	Cymbel	Mixtur V–VI (from Rp)
Regal 8' (U)	*Dulcian 16'*		*Sesquialtera II*
Baarpfeiffe 8' (U)	Baar Pfeiffe 8'	Trommette	Trompeta 8'
Schalmey 4' (U)	Regal 4'		*Krumbhorn 8'*
			Vox humana 8'

Werck (II)—1710	Werck (II)—1714	Pedal—1710	Pedal—1714
			Untersatz 32'
Principal 16'	Principal 16'		*Principal 16'*
	Quintadena 16'		
Octave 8'	Octava 8'	Untersatz 16'	Untersatz 16'
	Gedackt 8'		*Gedackt 8'*
Octave 4'	Octava 4'		*Octava 4'*
	Spitzflöte 4'		*Octava 2'*
Nachthorn 2' [Ped]	Super Octava 2'		Nachthorn 2' (from Werck)
Mixtur	Mixtur VI–VII		*Mixtur VII–VIII*
Scharff	Scharff		*Rauschpfeiffe III*
	Trommette 16'		*Groß Posaune 32'*
			Posaun 16'
Trommette 8' [Ped]	*Dulcian 8'*		Trompeta 8' (from Werck)
	Schalmey 4' (from Rp)		Trompeta 4'
Cornette 2' [Ped]			Cornet 2' (from Werck)

Particulars: Using a Netherlandish model, the principal plenum stops in the Rückpositiv were placed on a lower chest (L = lower chest, *Unterlade*) while the flutes and reeds were placed on an upper chest (U = upper chest, *Oberlade*). According to Praetorius (1619): "3 keyboards; the middle one, for the instrument's largest division, has an entire octave more in the bass than keyboards generally have—that is, another octave below low C, which is coupled to the Pedal and is used with it. Otherwise the 3 Praestants or Principals in the three keyboards are all the same, and not lower than 4-foot [*recte:* 8-foot] tone." Matthias Dropa noted in 1710: "Untersatz 16' only goes to F, and from there the Pedal is coupled to the Manual [*Werck*]. In sum, 27 stops, of which scarcely 18 are fully usable." The Regal 8' in the Rückpositiv, he says: "is worth little or nothing at the top."

Accessories (until 1714): tremulant; cut-off valves.

Accessories (after 1714): cut-off valves to all divisions; main cut-off valve; tremulant; cymbelstern.

Couplers (1714): Rp/W, Ow/W.

Compass: CDEFGA–g^2a^2 (manuals); CDEFGA–c^1 (pedal).

Compass (after 1714): CD–c^3 (manuals), CD–c^1 (pedal).

Literature: (a) Praetorius 1619, 170–71; Krüger 1906, 67–72, 78–80; Smets 1931, 27; Fock 1950, 113, 122–23; Vente 1958, 89; Selle 1970, 59–116, especially 70–77; Vogel/Lade/Borger-KIeweloh 1997, 102–7 and 347–48. (b) BDOK II, no. 5; NBR, no. 306, BDOK III, no. 666; Wolff 2000, 41, 42, 53–66, 70, and elsewhere; Maul/Wollny 2007.

St. Michael's Church/Michaeliskirche

Three-aisled Gothic hall church (fourteenth century) that served as the site of the family vault of the dukes of Brunswick-Lüneburg.

Organ: 1538–52, rebuild of an older instrument on the north wall by Jacob and Hans Scherer; 1551, addition of a new Rückpositiv; 1580, additional work by the Scherers and by Jacob Scherer's son-in-law, Dirk Hoyer. 1683, report from Arp Schnitger on the organ's condition; he found "almost nothing . . . that is still somewhat usable" (Fock 1974, 102). The bold disposition he proposed was never built; instead, in 1705–7 Matthias Dropa built a new instrument (III/43) on the west wall at the base of the tower. Tobias Götterling provided the artful case carvings. Later rebuilds. 1931, new organ (III/49) by Furtwängler & Hammer built into the original case.

Main organ, disposition 1705 (III/32) according to Dropa

"Specification of the old St. Michael's organ. The stops contained therein that are still present are the following:"

Oberwerk [II]	Rückpositiv [I]	Brustwerk [III]	Pedal
Principal 16' usable in the Pedal	Principal 8'	Principal 2'	Principal 16' (T)
Hollflete 16' [Ped]	Quintadena 8'	Waldflete 2'	Nachthorn 2' (T)
Octav 8' [Ped]	Rohrflete 8'	Sexquialtera II	Mixtur IV (T)
Octav 4	Gedact 8	Scharff III–IV	Tromet 8' (T)
Gemshorn 2'	Octave 4'	Regal 8'	Cornet 2' (T)
Nachthorn 2' (T)	Nasat 3'		
Rauschpfeiff II	Gemßhorn 2'		
Mixtur IV (T)	Siflet 1½'		
Tromet 8' (T)	Mixtur IV–V		
Cornet 2' (T)	Schalmei 4'		

Compass: F–g^2a^2 (manuals); D–$b^\flat$ (pedal).

32. Lüneburg, St. Michael's Church: Center aisle with Scherer/Hoyer organ (painting by Joachim Burmester, ca. 1700)

Choir Positive

1662, positive (I/4) is bequeathed from Hamburg; 1701, enlargement by Johann Balthasar Held, reusing the bellows, keyboard, and a Krummhorn 8'. It is likely that, as a matins choir member, Bach regularly played this organ. The existence of the instrument cannot be verified after ca. 1800. 2000, new instrument by Martin ter Haseborg, built according to Held's proposal from the spring of 1701.

Disposition 1701/2000 (I/5)

Manual
Gedackt 8' (*wood*)
Principal 4' (*lowest six pipes are stopped*)
Octav 2'
Sexquialtera II
Klein Krumhorn 8'

Particulars: In the organ built in 2000, two transpositions are possible, for a^1 = 440 Hz and a^1 = 465 Hz, and stops are divided between c^1 and $c\sharp^1$ (at normal pitch).

Accessory: tremulant.

Compass: C–d^3.

Pitch (2000): a^1 = 415 Hz.

Temperament (2000): meantone.

Literature: (a) Fock 1950, 81 and 113; Fock 1974, 102–4, 120–23; Vogel/Lade/Borger-Keweloh 1997, 194–95; van de Linde 2002, 199–218; pers. comm. from Tobias Gravenhorst, August 12, 2005. (b) *See* St. John's Church.

Mühlhausen

On June 15, 1707, Johann Sebastian Bach was appointed successor to Johann Georg Ahle at St. Blasius's Church in Mühlhausen, but by July of 1708 he had already left this post, accepting the position of court organist and chamber musician to Duke Wilhelm Ernst of Saxe-Weimar. In the free imperial city of Mühlhausen, Bach had access to a large, albeit old, organ. He apparently had been given consent from the beginning to have it renovated and enlarged.

As city organist he also was responsible for collaborating with the other churches, and he regularly played church services at the "Brückenhof" Church. In addition to Mühlhausen's two principal churches—St. Mary's (the Ratskirche, which served as the principal house of worship for the city council) in the upper city and St. Blasius's (the superintendent's church) in the lower city—there were more than ten active houses of worship in the town. Bach's responsibilities included the festive music for the annual inauguration of the city council at St. Mary's; his polychoral cantata "Gott ist mein König," BWV 71, is associated with this occasion in 1708, as are two other cantatas from the years 1709–10, neither of which has survived.

Bach departed on friendly terms, and he returned to Mühlhausen on a number of occasions. His relationship to the organ builder Johann Friedrich Wender, who had built the organ in Arnstadt and who probably had recommended Bach to Mühlhausen, likewise remained active for decades. Bach's last documented visit to the free imperial city, in 1735, was in connection with his consultation with Christian Friedrich Wender concerning the new organ for St. Mary's. In addition, his third-born son, Johann Gottfried Bernhard, was a candidate to succeed Johann Gottfried Hetzehenn, organist at St. Mary's, who had died in April of that year. The young Bach was elected as organist of St. Mary's on June 9, while both father and son were in Mühlhausen. An unofficial examination of the new Wender organ by Johann Sebastian Bach is recorded under the date June 16 in the account book of St. Mary's, and it is noted that he and his son "were given a small dinner by the administrator on account of the favorable state of affairs" (BDOK II, no. 365).

St. Mary's Church/Marienkirche

Five-aisled Gothic hall church (fourteenth century); principal church of the upper city. Now used as a museum (Thomas Müntzer Memorial).

Organ: 1564, new organ; 1614, overhaul by unknown builder. 1676, enlargement by unknown builder with assistance from Johann Friedrich Wender. After damage from lightning on October 6, 1720, restoration by Wender (incorporating parts still usable). 1734–38, new organ by Christian Friedrich Wender, probably with advice from J. S. Bach. Later changes; 1821–22, rebuild by Johann Friedrich Schulze. 1891, new organ (III/61) by Wilhelm Sauer incorporating some old stops into a neo-Gothic case (originally intended for Leipzig's St. Thomas Church). Rebuild in 1976. 1993, restoration by Christian Scheffler to the condition of the organ in 1891. Nothing remains of the Wender organ, but an archival photograph of the original organ gallery during the dismantling of the instrument survives.

Disposition 1720 (III/60) according to Dresden Ms.

HauptWerk [II]	Rück-Positiv [I]	OberWerck [III]	Pedal
Bordun 16'	Principal 8'	Salicional 16'	Sub-Baß 32'
Principal 8'	Gedackt 8'	Viola di Gamba 8'	Sub-Baß 16'
Spill-Flöthe 8'	Quintadena 8'	Hohlflöte 8'	Principal 16'
Salicional 8'	Quintadena 4'	Principal 4'	Octava 8'
Octava 4'	Queerflöthe 4'	Fleute douce 4'	Wald-Flöthe 8'
Offene Flöthe 4'	Hohlflöthe 4'	Spitz-Flöthe 4'	Octava 4'
Qvinta 3'	Gemßhorn 4'	Quinta 3'	Qvintadena 4'
Superoctava 2'	Quinta 3'	Wald-Flöthe 2'	Nachthorn 4'
Sexta 4' [3¹/₅']	Superoctava 2'	Tertian 1³/₅'	Superoctava 2'
Waldhorn 2'	Tertia 1³/₅'	Cimbel IV	SubSuperoctava 1'
Sifflet 1½'	Sifflet 1'	Harffen Regal 16'	Mixtura X
Cymbel Mixtur VI	Mixtura VI	Hautbois 8'	Groß-Posaune 32'
Mixtura VIII	Dulcian 16'	Trompeta 4'	Posaune 16'
Sordunen 16'	Krumbhorn 8'		Dulcian 16'
Zinck 8'			Trompeta 8'
			Krumbhorn 8'
			Schallmey 4'
			Cornet 2'

Accessories: tremulant to Hw and Ow; tremulant to Rp; tremulant to Ped; cymbelstern; drum; Vogelgesang (birdsong); bellows signal; cut-off valve for each division; main cut-off valve.

Coupler: manual coupler.

Wind supply: fourteen bellows.

33. Mühlhausen, St. Mary's: Bird's-eye view of the organ gallery from the time
of the dismantling of the Wender organ (photograph, ca. 1890)

Disposition 1738 (III/43) according to Adlung (1768)

Hauptwerk (II)	Rückpositiv (I)	Oberwerk (III)	Pedal
"Is wide-scaled and has quite a magestic sound" (*recht majestätischen Klang*)	"Is somewhat wider-scaled and sounds pungent and delicate" (*schneidend und delikat*)	"Has narrow scaling and a biting voicing" (*eine spitzige Intonation*)	"Has very wide scaling, penetrating strength" (*durchdringende Stärke*), "and beautiful reeds"
Quintatön 16'	*Quintatön 8'	Rohrflöte 8'	Principal 16', tin, facade
Rohrflöte 16'	*Bordun 8'	Principal 4', tin, facade	Untersatz 16', wood
*Principal 8', English tin, facade	*Principal 4', tin, facade	Salicet 4'	Oktave 8'
Violdigamba 8'	*Spitzflöte 2'	Spitzflöte 4'	Gemsquinta 5^1/$_3$'
Gedackt 8'	*Sesquialtera II	Flöte douce 4', wood	Oktave 4'
Gemshorn 8'	*Mixtur III	Ged. ital. Quinte 3'	Spitzflöte 2'
Oktave 4'		Oktave 2'	Rohrflöe 1'
Kleingedackt 4'		Terz 1^3/$_5$'	Mixtur VI 2^2/$_3$'
Quinte 2^2/$_3$'		Cymbel III	Posaune 32', wood
Oktave 2'		Sordino 8'	Posaune 16', wood
Waldflöte 2'			Trompete 8'
Mixtur VI 2'			Cornettin 2'

Scharfe Cymbel III
Basson 16'
Trompete 8'

Particulars: * = register from the previous organ.

Accessories: cut-off valves to all divisions; two tremulants (one slower, one faster); cymbelstern with four bells: c^2, e^2, g^2, c^3.

Couplers: Hw/Ped; Hw/Rp; shove coupler for Ow/Hw; low Kammerton [*Großkammerton*] coupler; normal Kammerton [*Kleinkammerton*] coupler.

Compass: CD–c^3 (manuals); CD–d^1 (pedal); manual keyboards made with ivory and ebony.

Wind supply: three very large bellows for the manuals, three very large bellows for the pedal.

Pitch: Chorton.

Archives: Stadtarchiv Mühlhausen, *Chronik. Fragment 1533–1802*, Sign. 61/18.

Literature: (a) Niedt 1721, 192–93; Adlung 1768, 259–60 [1738 disposition]; Sommer 1882, 66–72; Smets 1931, 28–29 [1720 disposition]. (b) Brinkmann 1950, entry: *Johann Gottfried Bernhard Bach*, n.p.; NBR, no. 176, BDOK I, no. 31; BDOK II, nos. 365 and 372; Wolff 2000, 89–90, 99–100, 102–15, 143, 399–400, 526, and elsewhere.

St. Blasius's Church/Kirche Divi Blasii

Three-aisled Gothic hall church (thirteenth–fourteenth centuries); principal church of the lower city.

Organ: 1560–63, new organ by Jost Pape; 1676, rebuild by Jost Schäfer. 1687–91, partial rebuild and enlargement (II/29) by Johann Friedrich Wender, who settled in Mühlhausen at the time. At Bach's recommendation, organ enlarged by Wender in 1708 to III/37. After various rebuilds, in 1821–23, new organ by Johann Friedrich Schulze using the original case. 1959, new organ by Schuke Orgelbau (Potsdam) according to Bach's disposition of 1708 but enlarged by five stops to III/42.

For Bach's organ report, *see* Part II.A.

Dispositions 1707 (II/29) and 1708 (III/37)

In 1707	As rebuilt in 1708 Ober- and	In 1707	As rebuilt in 1708
Hauptwerk (II)	**Hauptwerk (II)**	—	**Brustwerk (III)**
Quintatön 16'	Quintatön 16'	—	*Stillgedackt 8'*
Principal 8'	Principal 8'	—	*Flöte 4'*
Gemßhorn 8'	*Violdigamba 8'*	—	*Quinte 3'*
Oktave 4'	Oktave 4'	—	*Principal 2'*
Gedackt 4'	Gedackt 4'	—	*Terz 1³/₅'*
Quinte 3'	Quinte 3'	—	*Mixtur III*
Sesquialtera II	Sesquialtera II	—	*Schallmey 8'*

In 1707	As rebuilt in 1708 Ober- and	In 1707	As rebuilt in 1708
Hauptwerk (II)	**Hauptwerk (II)**	—	**Brustwerk (III)**
Oktave 2'	Oktave 2'		
Mixtur IV	Mixtur IV		
Cymbel II	Cymbel II		
Trompette 16'	*Fagotto 16'*, C–c^1		
Rückpositiv (I)	**Rückpositiv (I)**	**Pedal**	**Pedal**
Gedackt 8'	Gedackt 8'	—	*Untersatz 32'*
Quintatön 8'	Quintatön 8'	Principal 16'	Principal 16'
Principal 4'	Principal 4'	Subbaß 16'	Subbaß 16'
Salicional 4'	Salicioanl 4'	Oktave 8'	Oktave 8'
Quintflöte 4'	Quintflöte 4'	Oktave 4'	Oktave 4'
Sesquialtera II	Sesquialtera II	Rohrflötenbaß 1'	Rohrflötenbaß 1'
Oktave 2'	Oktave 2'	Mixtur IV	Mixtur IV
Spitzflöte 2'	Spitzflöte 2'	Posaunbaß 16'	*Posaunbaß 16'*
Cymbel III	Cymbel III	Trompete 8'	Trompete 8'
		Cornetbaß 2'	Cornetbaß 2'

Particulars: Italic = Bach's modifications. Also at his suggestion, new shallots and tongues for the Pedal Posaune 16'.

Accessories: tremulants to all three keyboards; cymbelstern with twelve bells (c, e, g, c); drum; bellows signal.

Couplers: *Bw/Hw;* Rp/Hw; Hw/Ped.

Compass: CD–d^3 (manuals); CD–d^1 (pedal).

Wind supply: four bellows to the manuals, two bellows to the pedal [*three additional bellows*].

Pitch: Chorton.

Temperament: well-tempered (according to Ratte and Rathey).

Literature: (a) Adlung 1768, 260–61; Thiele 1927/28, 142–52; Schrammek 1983a, 18–21; Ratte 2000, 510; Rathey 2001, 163–71. (b) NBR, no. 31, BDOK I, no. 83; Dok II, no. 21; *see* St. Mary's Church.

"Brückenhof" Church/Brückenhofkirche (former St. Mary Magdalene's Church of the Augustinian Convent)

One-aisled monastery church of the order of the Penitence of Holy Mary Magdalene, thirteenth century; after introduction of the Reformation, used as parish church and known as the "Brückenhof" Church. 1680, renovation of the church building, which was damaged by fires in 1689 and 1707. 1843, church closed; 1884, church torn down.

Organ: 1702, new organ (I/7) by Johann Friedrich Wender; 1727, repairs by Wender. 1760–61, repairs by Johann Christoph Wilhelmi; further repairs into the nineteenth century. 1843, organ moved to All Saints; pitch was changed to Chorton from "between

34. Mühlhausen,
St. Blasius's Church:
Schulze organ in historical
case without Rückpositiv
(photograph, ca. 1870)

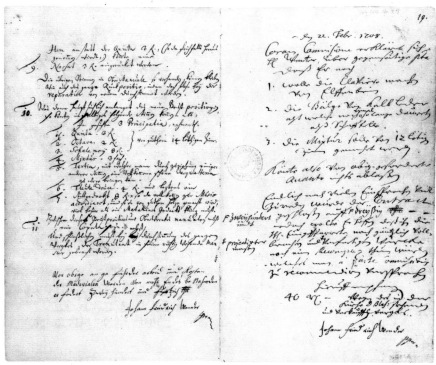

35. Mühlhausen, St. Blasius's Church: Disposition for new organ, 1708. On the left, J. S. Bach's handwriting; in the concluding paragraph, J. F. Wender's quotation in the amount of 250 talers. On the right, comments of the city council after Wender's hearing on February 22, 1708.

Chor- and Kammerton" (Ernst 1987) by organ builder Johann Friedrich Große. 1917, sacrifice of the facade pipes. After secularization of All Saints (now an exhibition hall) in 1920, the organ—only case, action, wind chests, and rollerboard were preserved—eventually came to the St. George's Church (essentially a Romanesque hall church, altered frequently and enlarged in 1713) in Dörna, where Johann Friedrich Wender had been baptized. 1994–2001, restoration by Kristian Wegscheider of what parts survived; he built new pipework using the old scalings.

Disposition 1848–2000 (I/7)

1848	2000
Manual	**Manual**
Gedackt 8'	Gedackt 8'
Principal 4'	Principal 4'
Flöte 4' (conical, wood)	Spitzflöte 4' (metal)
Hohlflöte 8'	Quinta $2^2/3$'
Octave 2'	Octave 2'
Mixtur III 1'	Mixtur III 1'
Pedal	**Pedal**
Subbaß 16'	Subbaß 16'

Particulars: In the 1848 disposition, Flöte 4' was added ca. 1781 and the Hohlflöte 8' replaced Quinte 3'. In the 2000 disposition, scalings were reconstructed from Wender's scale indications on the underside of the toeboards.

Coupler: pedal coupler.

Compass: CD–c^3 (manual); CD–c^1 (pedal).

Literature: (a) Sommer 1882; Ernst 1987; communications from Kristian Wegscheider, 2005. (b) *See* St. Mary's Church.

Naumburg

At the request of the city council, the new Hildebrandt organ was to be inspected in September 1746 "by two well-known capable masters of their craft and experts in the field." Accordingly, "the kapellmeister from Leipzig, Mr. Bach, a highly qualified organist, and Mr. Silbermann of Dresden, an organ builder well known in his field, were selected" (BDOK II, no. 546). They submitted their report to the city council on September 27, affirming that they had "examined and carefully gone through the entire organ part by part" (BDOK II, no. 547). Bach's student and future son-in-law, Johann Christoph Altnickol, took over the post of Naumburg city organist in September 1748; he held the position until his early death in 1759.

36. Mühlhausen, "Brückenhof" Church: Wender organ
now in St. George's Church, Dörna (photograph, 2006)

City Church of St. Wenceslas/Stadtkirche St. Wenzel

Late-Gothic hall church, erected 1426–46 to replace an older parish church (Stadtkirche). 1534–35, addition of student balconies; 1724, decoration of interior in Baroque style and addition of a *Spiegeldecke* (a ceiling with a flat middle section). 1945, war damage on the north and west sides.

    Organ: 1613, new organ (II/38) by Joachim Zschugk placed on north side of the choir. Ca. 1650, organ tuned by Ludwig Compenius to a pitch that was "choir-appropriate" (*chormäßig*); in 1662 he provided a third manual keyboard. 1695–1705, organ moved to the west end, placed in a new case with ornate carvings by Johann Goericke, and enlarged to III/45 by Zacharias Thayßner. 1743–46, new organ by Zacharias Hildebrandt; old case retained. Various changes in nineteenth and twentieth centuries. 1993–2000, thorough restoration by Eule Orgelbau, returning the organ to its 1746 condition.

For Bach's organ report, *see* Part II.A.

Disposition 1746/2000 (III/53)

Hauptwerk (II)	Rückpositiv (I)	Oberwerk (III)	Pedal
Principal 16' (o)	Principal 8' (o)	Bordun 16' (r)	Principal 16' (o)
Quintathen 16' (o)	Quintadehn 8' (o)	Principal 8' (o)	Violon 16' (o)
Octava 8' (o)	Rohr Floete 8' (o)	Hollflött 8' (o)	Subbaß 16' (o)
Spitzflöte 8' (o)	Viol di Gamba 8' (o)	Unda maris 8' (r)	Octav 8' (o)
Gedackt 8' (o)	Praestanta 4' (o)	Prestant 4' (o)	Violon 8' (o)
Octav 4' (o)	Vagara 4' (o)	Gemshorn 4' (+)	Octav 4' (o)
Spitzflöte 4' (r)	Rohrflött 4' (o)	Quinta 3' (o)	Octava 2' (r)
Sesquialtera II (r)	Nassat 3' (r)	Octav 2' (o)	Mixtur VII (r)
Quinta 3' (o)	Octava 2' (r)	Tertia 1³/₅' (r)	Posaune 32' (r)
Weit Pfeiffe 2' (o)	Rausch Pfeiffe II (r)	Waldflöt 2' (r)	Posaune 16' (r)
Octav 2' (o)	Mixtur V (r)	Quinta 1½' (r)	Trompet-Bass 8' (r)
Cornett IV (r)	Fagott 16' (r)	Sif-Floete 1' (r)	Clarin-Bass 4' (r)
Mixtur VIII (r)		Scharff V (r)	
Bombart 16' (r)		Vox humana 8' (r)	
Trompet 8' (r)			

Particulars: (o) = register with more than 50 percent material from Hildebrandt; (r) = register reconstructed completely by Eule; (+) old pipework, but not from Hildebrandt. Although there is a stopknob for Pedal Untersatz 32', it nevertheless was not built by Hildebrandt, because there was not enough room in the Thayßner case, which he retained.

Accessories: tremulant; cymbelstern; bellows signal; Ow tremulant [for Vox humana]; cut-off valve for each division.

Couplers: shove coupler, Rp/Hw; shove coupler, Ow/Hw; wind coupler, Hw/Ped.

Compass: CD–c³ (manuals); CD–d¹ (pedal).

Wind supply 1746/2000: seven bellows.

Wind pressure (1746): 36° (manuals), 40° (pedal).

Wind pressure (2000): 74 mm WC (manuals), 78 mm WC (pedal).

Pitch (2000): Chorton (464 Hz).

Temperament (2000): Neidhardt I (1724).

Literature: (a) Adlung 1768, 263–64; Dähnert 1962, 189–200; Reichling 2000; Werner 2000, 396–402; Schrammek 2001, 27–30. (b) NBR, no. 235; BDOK I, no. 90; BDOK II, nos. 546–51; (b) Wolff 2000, 143–44, 208, 421, 533.

37. Naumburg, St. Wenceslas's Church: Hildebrandt organ (photograph, 2006)

Ohrdruf

After the death of his father in 1695 (his mother had died the previous year), Johann Sebastian Bach moved at the age of ten to live with his older brother and guardian Johann Christoph Bach, transferring from the Latin School in Eisenach to the Lyceum in Ohrdruf. Johann Christoph had worked at St. Michael's Church in Ohrdruf since 1690, serving as city and court organist and also, from 1700, as preceptor of the fifth (and second-lowest) class of the Lyceum (even though he did not finish Latin school). According to the obituary, young Johann Sebastian "laid the foundations for playing the clavier" (NBR, no. 306; BDOK III, no. 666) under Johann Christoph's guidance and at the same time came to know the various organs in Ohrdruf. At that time Georg Christoph Stertzing, who began building the large new organ for the St. George's Church in Eisenach in 1696, still had his workshop in Ohrdruf. Bach's connections to Stertzing and his son are documented into the 1730s.

Upon Johann Christoph's death in 1721, the position of city organist and cantor in Ohrdruf fell to Christoph's son Johann Bernhard, who had studied with his uncle Johann Sebastian. In that position, which he held until his death in 1743, Johann Bernhard was responsible for both St. Michael's and Trinity Church. After 1742 his brother Johann Andreas played for him at Trinity. From 1744 to 1779, Johann Andreas was at St. Michael's, as well; Heinrich Zacharias Frischmuth succeeded Johann Andreas at Trinity, serving there from 1744 to 1774. Johann Andreas Bach was the owner of two handwritten anthologies of organ music by various masters compiled by Johann Christoph Bach around 1700, anthologies that also contain early autographs of Johann Sebastian Bach: the so-called *Andreas Bach Book* (Leipzig, Musikbibliothek, Becker collection III.8.4) and the so-called *Möller Manuscript* (Berlin, Staatsbibliothek, Mus. ms. 40644).

St. Michael's Church/Michaeliskirche

Late-Gothic hall church, completed 1412; it succeeded a St. Michael's chapel that had been erected ca. 724–25 by St. Boniface when he established the Benedictine order in Thuringia. 1753, church destroyed by fire; 1760, new building; 1808, building (again) fell victim to fire. New building completed 1823, but destroyed (except for the tower) during World War II (1945).

Organ: 1683, Heinrich Brunner repaired a positive to which he later added a pedal division; the positive was moved to the newly built Trinity Church in 1714. The new organ (II/19) begun in 1679 by Kaspar Lehmann remained unfinished after the builder died. 1688–90, renovation and enlargement by Heinrich Brunner, likewise never completed. In 1693, at J. C. Bach's request, his teacher Johann Pachelbel evaluated the organ's deficiencies (see Schulze 1984, plates 1/2, for a facsimile of his report), which were never completely remedied during Bach's tenure. The organ was destroyed during the fire of 1753. 1758–60, new three-manual organ by Johann Stephan Schmaltz according to plans of Johann Andreas Bach. Johann Peter Kellner, of Gräfenroda, served as consultant and praised the instrument, noting especially: "Oboe d'amore 8' is an entirely new and especially beautiful stop, one I have found in no other organ, and its inventor, Bach, and its maker, Schmaltz, are to be praised on account of it."

Disposition 1693 (II/21)

Hauptwerk [II]	Rückpositiv [I]	Pedal
Quintadena 16'	Stillgedackt 8'	Principal 16'
Principal 8'	Principal 4'	Subbaß 16'
Grob Gedackt 8'	Flöte 2'	Oktav 8'
Oktave 4'	Nassat 3'	Mixtur III 4'
Quinta 3'	Sesquialtera II	Fagotto 16'
Klein Oktave 2'	Oktave 1'	Cornetto 2'
Mixtur IV 2'		
Cymbel II 1'		
Trompeta 8'		

Compass: CD–c^3 (manuals); CD–c^1 (pedal).

Archival Source: Thüringisches Staatsarchiv Gotha, Gemeinschaftliches Hohenlohisches Archiv, no. 2702.

Literature: (a) Lux 1926, 145–55; Oertel 1950, 7–10; Schulze 1984, 189–90; Dehio 2003, 938; Harder 2005, 154–61. (b) BDOK II, no. 4; NBR, no. 306, BDOK III, no. 666; Wolff 2000, 35–51 and elsewhere.

Trinity Church/Trinitatiskirche

Baroque hall church, erected 1709–14, with two tiers of galleries on three sides; also used as burial site and referred to as "Burial Church."

Organ: 1714, positive (I/5) from Ohrdruf's St. Michael's Church was set up (it had been repaired by Heinrich Brunner in 1679 and had later acquired a pedal division). Johann Christoph Bach played the dedication on June 17, 1714. 1745–47, new organ by Johann Stephan Schmaltz according to plans of Johann Andreas Bach; dedicated on June 27, 1747, with a cantata composed by J. A. Bach. 1814, new organ (II/34) by Georg Franz Ratzmann; rebuilt 1886. 1992, organ returned to its 1814 condition by Förster & Nicolaus. Nothing from Bach's time survives.

Disposition 1714 (I/5)

Manual	Pedal
Principal 8'	Grob Gedackt 16'
Klein Gedackt 4'	
Flöte 2'	
Cymbel	

Compass: CDEFGAB–c^3 (manual)

Archival Source: Thüringisches Staatsarchiv Gotha, Gemeinschaftliches Hohenlohisches Archiv, no. 2689.

Literature: (a) Haupt 1998, 88; Dehio 2003, 938. (b) *See* St. Michael's Church.

Castle Chapel/Schlosskapelle

A chapel in the four-winged Renaissance Ehrenstein Castle, in use from 1665 to 1775 by the counts of Hohenlohe-Oehringen as their secondary residence. 1775, dissolution of the Castle Chapel. Dramatically changed, the building is used partially as a museum.

Organ: No information is preserved.

Literature: (a) Lehfeldt 1898, 85; Dehio 2003, 939–40.

Potsdam

According to Johann Nicolaus Forkel, during his trip to Potsdam and Berlin in 1747 Johann Sebastian Bach was shown all of the organs in Potsdam—instruments built by the Silbermann student Joachim Wagner, whom Bach apparently knew. Wilhelm Friedemann Bach accompanied his father on the trip and Forkel's report is based on Friedemann's recollection of the event. The Berlin newspapers of May 11, 1747, noted of Bach's visit simply that "On Monday, the famous man let himself be heard on the organ in the Church of the Holy Spirit at Potsdam and earned general acclaim from the listeners attending in great number" (NBR, no. 239; BDOK II, no. 554). It is not known whether Frederick the Great, whose chamber-music gathering Bach had attended the previous evening, was among the listeners. It is unlikely.

Garrison Church/Garnisonkirche

Built 1720–22, the church had to be torn down in 1730 because the foundation was sinking. (The organ [II/25] built in 1723 by Joachim Wagner was given by King Friedrich Wilhelm I to the Jerusalem Church in Berlin, where it remained until 1878.) 1731–32, new Garrison Church designed by Philipp Gerlach. The most important sacred building in Prussian Baroque architecture, and used as a "preaching church" by both Lutheran and Reformed congregations, it was a galleried, rectangular room with the pulpit located in the middle of the long side. Bombed April 1945; ruins dynamited in 1968.

Organ: 1732, new organ by Joachim Wagner; changes in the eighteenth and nineteenth centuries. 1898, new organ (III/46) by Wilhelm Sauer using twenty-one stops from the Wagner organ and the original facade. Destroyed April 1945.

Disposition 1732 (III/42)

Hauptwerk (II)	Unterwerk (I)	Oberwerk (III)	Pedal
Bordun 16'	Gedackt 8'	Quintadehna 16'	Principal 16'
Principal 8'	Quintadena 8'	Principal 8'	Violon 16'
Rohrflöte 8'	Rohrflöte 4'	Salicional 8'	Octave 8'
Octave 4'	Nassat 3'	Gedackt 8'	Quinte 6'
Flauto traverso 4'	Octave 2'	Octave 4'	Octave 4'
Quinte 3'	Terz 1³/₅'	Fugara 4'	Mixtur VI
Octave 2'	Sifflöte 1'	Quinte 3'	Posaune 16'
Cornet V	Cimbel III	Octav 2'	Trompete 8'
Scharff V	Vox humana 8'	Waldflöte 2'	Clairon 4'
Cimbel III		Quinta 1½'	Carillon
Fagott 16'		Mixtur IV	
Trompet 8'		Hautbois 8'	

Accessories: tremulant; cut-off valve for each division; tremulant for the Vox humana 8' (Uw); drawknob for fanfaring angels; drawknob for drumming angels; cymbelstern (*Sonnenzug*); bellows signal.

Coupler: manual coupler.

Compass: CDE–c³ (manuals); CD–d¹ (pedal).

Wind supply: six large bellows.

Literature: (a) SeN, 78; Mundt 1925/26, 275–76; Thom 1990, 8–9; Kitschke 1993, 212–18; Schaefer 1994, 162; Dehio 2000b, 782–83. (b) NBR, no. 239, BDOK II, no. 554; Wolff 2000, 208, 425–28, 446, 533.

Holy Ghost Church/Heiliggeistkirche

Built 1725–26 to serve both Lutheran and Reformed congregations; destroyed in April 1945.

Organ: 1730, new organ by Joachim Wagner. 1859, new organ (II/22) by Carl Ludwig Gesell and Carl Schulz. Destroyed April 1945.

Disposition 1730 (II/18 plus four transmissions)

Hauptwerk (I)	Oberwerk (II)	Pedal
Bordun 16'	Quintadöne 8'	Subbaß 16'
Principal 8'	Gedackt 8' (T)	Posaune 16'
Gedackt 8' (T)	Octave 4' (T)	Trompete 8'
Octave 4' (T)	Flöte 4'	
Quinte 3'	Nassat 3'	
Octave 2' (T)	Octave 2' (T)	
Cornett III	Quinte 1½'	
Scharff V	Cimbel III (T)	
Cimbel III (T)	Vox humana 8'	
Trompete 8'		

38. Potsdam, Garrison Church:
Wagner organ above the pulpit altar
(photograph, between ca. 1928 and
1944.)

Particulars: Apparently keyboard was at the side, with the facade over the balustrade of the second balcony. Inscription in the pedal chest (discovered in 1859 by Carl Ludwig Gesell and Carl Schultz): "His Royal Majesty in Prussia, Friedrich Wilhelm, had the organ in this church built by the organ builder Wagner in 1730; also the church was built 3 years previously." (Cited in Kitschke 1993, 210.)

Inscription in the manual chest: "This church, which was previously a government building, was built several years ago, after which His Royal Majesty also gave this organ, which was built in 1730 by the organ builder Joachim Wagner of Berlin, and is the 5th instrument made by him after his new invention." (Cited in Kitschke 1993, 210.)

Compass: CD–c^3 (manuals); CD–c^1 (pedal).

Literature: (a) Wagener 1863/64, 2; Albrecht 1938; Kitschke 1993, 210. (b) NBR, no. 239, BDOK II, no. 554; *see* Garrison Church.

For St. Nicholas's Church/Nikolaikirche, *see* Reference Organs.

Sangerhausen

In the fall of 1702, after finishing his Latin school education in Lüneburg, Johann Sebastian Bach applied for the position of city organist at St. Jacobi Church, a post that had
become vacant upon the death in that year of Gottfried Christoph Gräffenhayn. Bach
was chosen by the city council after a successful audition, but he was not hired due to
the intervention of Johann Georg, Duke of Weißenfels. The position went instead to
Johann Augustin Kobelius, who also served as music director (from 1703 onward) until
his resignation in 1725; his successor, Johann Friedrich Rahm, served until 1736.

Bach retained his connections with Sangerhausen. He was apparently consulted in
1726–28 during the project to build a new organ, and in 1737 he corresponded with the
mayor of the city regarding the vacant organist position. Bach's third son, Johann Gottfried Bernhard, competed successfully for the position and was appointed by city council
on January 14, 1737. He resigned from the position in 1738, scarcely two years later. (In
Mühlhausen, too, Gottfried Bernhard had resigned from the position at St. Mary's Church
after just two years of service.) He left Sangerhausen for parts unknown without notice
to his superiors and leaving debts behind—to the great sorrow of his father. Gottfried
Bernhard died in 1739 in Jena, where he had begun to study law at the university.

St. Jacobi Church/Jacobikirche

Three-aisled late-Gothic hall church completed in 1502. Interior newly decorated ca.
1665 in Baroque style, using in part items from the Augustine Eremite monastery; surrounding wooden galleries are from the early seventeenth century.

Organ: Built 1603 by Ezechiel Greutzscher in an existing case; 1697, brought into
good order by Heinrich Brunner at request of continuo organist Gottfried Christoph
Gräffenhayn. 1726–28, new organ by Zacharias Hildebrandt; case carvings by Valentin
Schwarzenberger. It is likely that Bach was involved in planning the disposition. Organ
was examined at the end of May 1728 and dedicated on June 1. Changes and rebuilds in
the nineteenth and twentieth centuries. 1976–78, thorough restoration by Eule Orgelbau,
recovering the disposition of 1728 and adding three additional pedal stops.

Disposition 1603 (II/24)

Rückpositiv [I]	Oberwerk [II]	Brustwerk [II]	Pedal
Principal 4'	Grob Quintadena 16' [T?]	Regal	Grob Quintadena 16' [T?]
Quintadehn Baß 4'	Grob gedackter Unterbaß 16' [T?]	Octava	Subbaß 16' [T?]
Hoelflöten 2'	Grob Principal 8'	Rauschpfeiffen gedoppelt [II]	Grob Posaunen Baß [16']
Kleine octava 1'	Grobe Octava 4'		Flöten Baß gedeckt [8'?]

39. Sangerhausen, St. Jacobi Church: Hildebrandt organ (photograph, 2007)

Rückpositiv [I]	Oberwerk [II]	Brustwerk [II]	Pedal
Kleine Quinta 1¹/₃'	Grob Gedacktes 4'		Quinten Baß
Zimbeln doppelt [II]	Grobe Quinta 3'		Corneten Baß
Stimme Dulcian	Super Octava 2'		
Arth [Dulcian-like			
stop] [8'?]			
	Mixtur VIII		
	Zimbeln III		
	Zincken 8'		

Particulars: The Subbaß (Unterbaß) was made of metal. Regarding the Grob Quinta-dehna 16': "Like the Subbaß, playable both in the manual and the pedal, with two separate registers [stopknobs]."

Accessories: tremulant to each division.

Coupler: Rp/Ped.

Compass: CDE–c³ (manuals), CDE–f¹ or d¹ (pedal).

Disposition 1728 (II/27)

Hauptwerk (I)	Brustwerk (II)	Pedalwerk
Bordun 16'	Still Gedackt 8'	Prinzipalbaß 16'
Prinzipal 8'	Rohrflöte 8'	Subbaß 16'
Gedact 8'	Violdigamba 8'	Oktavenbaß 8'
Quintadena 8'	Prinzipal 4'	Posaunenbaß 16'
Oktave 4'	Rohrflöte 4'	
Spitzflöte 4'	Nassat 3'	
Quinta 3'	Octava 2'	
Octava 2'	Quinta 1¹/₂'	
Mixtur V	Siflet 1'	
Cimbeln III	Cimbeln III	
Cornet IV		
Trompete 8'		
Vox humana 8'		

Particulars: Subbaß 16' was taken over from the previous organ. Gedacktbaß 8', Choralbaß 4', and Rauschbaß IV were added to the Pedal in 1978.

Accessories: Bw tremulant; tremulant for use with the Vox humana 8'.

Coupler: Bw/Hw.

Compass (1728): CD–c³ (manuals), CD–c¹ (pedal).

Compass (1978): CD–d³ (manuals), CD–d¹ (pedal).

Wind supply: four wedge bellows.

Wind pressure (1978): 76 mm WC.

Pitch (1728): Chorton.

Pitch (1978): a¹ = 440 Hz at 18° C.

Temperament: Equal temperament (1978).

Literature: (a) Schmidt 1882, 61–67; Dähnert 1962, 169–81; Schrammek 1983a, 60–63; Dehio 1999a, 471–72. (b) NBR, no. 203, BDOK I, no. 42; BDOK II, nos. 395–96; Wolff 2000, 67–68, 399, 532, and elsewhere; Wolff 2005, xix.

Stöntzsch (Pegau)/Hohnstein (Saxon Switzerland)

On November 2, 1731, while the organ was being enlarged, Johann Sebastian Bach came to Stöntzsch to evaluate the work. A contemporary report in the church archive notes that at the time "only 6 registers or stops [were] finished as well as 2 bellows." On February 4, 1732, the completed organ was "once again looked at and tested by Mr. Kapellmeister *Bach* and afterward fully paid" (BDOK II, no. 298).

Church

Built 1722, replacing an older church from ca. 1000. To benefit brown-coal strip mining, the church was torn down in 1965; village of Stöntzsch razed.

Organ: 1677–78, new organ (I/5) by Georg Oehme (disposition: Grobgedackt 8', Offene Flöte 4', Principal 2', Mixtur 1½', Dulcian Regal 8', "revolving Cymbel" [= cymbelstern]). 1728–32, enlargement by Johann Christoph Schmieder with counsel from Johann Sebastian Bach; organ moved to the west balcony. 1935, restorative overhaul by Eule Orgelbau. As a result of the town being razed, the organ was dismantled in 1964 by Eule Orgelbau and moved to Hohnstein.

Disposition ca. 1730 (I/9)

Manual	Pedal
Quintadena 8'	Sup Bass 16' (wood)
Grob gedackt 8'	Principalbass 8' (wood)
Principal 4'	
Klein gedackt 4'	
Quinta 3'	
Octave 2'	
Mixtur III	

Particulars: "The Principal is to be placed in the facade in three towers. Keyboard at the front of the organ. Two strong bellows, of good wood and leather, and otherwise well protected, the wind chests, actions and case (*Structuren*), and other work built in a proper and durable manner according to accepted organ building standards, with some carvings and paintings in front in the facade. On account of the lack of room, the pipework to be placed as close together and the case narrowed as much as I can allow it without any damage to the organ (Schmieder manuscript, ca. 1730)."

40. Stöntzsch, church:
Oehme/Schmieder organ now
in the church in Hohnstein
(photograph, 1968)

Hohnstein Church/Kirche Hohnstein

Built 1725–26, hall church with tower (using stones from the enclosure wall of an earlier structure that burned in 1724), designed by George Bähr, architect in Dresden. Surrounding galleries, organ placed above the altar in the choir.

Organ: 1967, Schmieder organ from Stöntzsch (with altered disposition) installed by Eule Orgelbau.

Disposition 1967 (I/14)

Manual		Pedal	
Spitzprinzipal 8'	[1967]	Subbaß 16'	[1732?]
Rohrflöte 8'	[1935]	Principal 8'	[1860]

Manual		Pedal	
Praestant 4'	[1935]	Singend Cornet 4'	[1967]
Gedeckt 4'	[1860]	Rauschpfeife V 4'	[1967]
Nasard 2²/₃'	[1935]	Liebliche Posaune 16'	[1935]
Octava 2'	[1732]		
Tertia 1³/₅'	[1935]		
Mixtur IV 1¹/₃'	[partially 1967]		
Trompete 8'	[1967]		

Coupler: pedal coupler.

Compass: CD–c³ (manual), CD–c¹ (pedal); C♯ added to manual and pedal in 1935.

Wind supply: two bellows (reconstructed 1935).

Wind pressure: 68 mm WC (1935).

Archival Source: Archiv der Superintendentur Borna, no. 5.722, fol. 5 (disposition, ca. 1730).

Literature: (a) David 1951, 101; Dähnert 1980, 156–58; Schrammek 1983a, 42–45. (b) BDOK II, no. 298.

Störmthal

Bach undertook the examination of the new Hildebrandt organ in Störmthal on November 2, 1723, during his first year in Leipzig, at the invitation of Störmthal's patron, Statz Hilmor von Fullen. According to the report, Bach acknowledged and commended the instrument's "soundness and reliability" (BDOK II, no. 163). The organ was dedicated with the performance of the cantata "Höchsterwünschtes Freudenfest," BWV 194, which was heard in two parts, before and after the sermon.

Church

Late-Gothic hall church, completely renovated and rebuilt in 1722, with surrounding galleries; chancel altar in choir. Original condition is almost fully preserved.

Organ: Newly built (I/8) in 1702 as a gift of the patron, von Fullen, who also paid for construction of the gallery for the organ and choir. 1722–23, new organ by Zacharias Hildebrandt, likewise a gift of von Fullen. 1723, painting of the interior and the organ case; 1748, repairs by Hildebrandt. Minor changes in nineteenth and twentieth centuries. 1917, organ brought into playing condition by Eule Orgelbau; facade pipes that had been sacrificed for the war effort were replaced and pitch was lowered to A = 440 by shifting the trackers. 1974, repairs by Eule-Orgelbau. 2000, case painted in its original colors. 2008, restoration by Eule-Orgelbau.

41. Störmthal, church: Hildebrandt organ (photograph, 2000)

42. Störmthal: Title page of the cantata text for the organ dedication (BWV 194)

Disposition 1723/2008 (I/14)

Manual		Pedal
Principal 8'	Octava 2'	Subbaß 16'
Quintadena 8'	Tertia 1³/₅'	Posaune 16'
Grobgedackt 8'	Quinta 1½'	
Praestant 4'	Sufflöt 1'	
Rohrflöte 4'	Mixtur III 1¹/₃'	
Nasat 3'	Cornet III	

Particulars: The Cornett III (from c^1) was added at the request of chamberlain von Fullen. The 2008 restoration included removing a Principalbaß 8' that had been added to the organ by Urban Kreutzbach in 1840, building a new Posaune 16' according to historical models, and restoring the organ's pitch and temperament.

Accessories: tremulant (reconstructed 2008).

Coupler: pedal coupler.

Compass: CD–c^3 (manual), CD–c^1 (pedal).

Wind supply: two bellows.

Wind pressure (2008): 72 mm WC.

Pitch (2008): Low Chorton, a^1 = ca. 462 Hz.

Temperament: Silbermann ⅙ comma.

Literature: (a) Dähnert 1962, 158–64; Barth 1974, 22; Dähnert 1980, 258–59; Dehio 1996b, 364; www.euleorgelbau.de, accessed January 1, 2010. (b) BDOK II, nos. 163 and 164.

Taubach (Weimar-Taubach)

On October 26, 1710, the Nineteenth Sunday after Trinity, Johann Sebastian Bach went to Taubach (now a part of Weimar) to evaluate and dedicate the organ.

St. Ursula's Church/Kirche St. Ursula

Built 1704–5, retaining the choir tower from the fifteenth century; 1849–50, demolition of the church; new church designed by Clemens Wenzeslaus Coudray.

Organ: 1709–10, new organ by Heinrich Nicolaus Trebs; demolished in 1848.

For Bach's examination report, *see* Part II.A.

Disposition 1710 (I/11)

Werk	Pedal
Gedackt 8', metal	Sup Baß 16', wood
Quintathön 8', ½ metal, ½ wood	Principal Baß 8', wood
Principal 4', of good tin	Wald Flöth 2', metal
Quinta 3', metal	

Octava 2', metal
Tritonus $1^3/_5$', metal
Superoctav 1', metal
Mixtur III, metal

    Accessories: cymbelstern, tremulant.
    Coupler: pedal coupler.
    Wind supply: two bellows (9' x 4½').
    Literature: (a) Dehio 2003, 1212; Lehfeldt 1893. (b) NBR, no. 42, BDOK I, no. 84; BDOK II, nos. 50, 50a.

Weimar

In July 1708, Johann Sebastian Bach assumed the position of court organist and chamber musician at the court of Wilhelm Ernst of Saxe-Weimar; in the spring of 1714 he assumed the post of concertmaster, as well. The majority of Bach's organ works stem from the Weimar years. Bach's predecessor was Johann Effler, who held the position from 1678 to 1708 and, until the positions were divided in 1684, served at the same time as city organist. Bach's successors were his two earliest students, Johann Martin Schubart (1717–21) and Johann Caspar Vogler (1721–63).

    Johann Gottfried Walther, a distant relative, was organist from 1708 to 1748 of the City Church of St. Peter and Paul's, where Bach's children born in Weimar were baptized. (Walther's predecessor was Samuel Heintze [1692–1707], his successor Johann Samuel Maul [1748–1802].) On November 27, 1713, Walther stood as godparent at the baptism of the organ builder Heinrich Nicolaus Trebs's son. The court's church services were held from time to time in the City Church, especially at high feasts. At such times, Bach would have had opportunity to play the organ. The organist at the St. Jacob's Church from 1713 to 1765 was Philipp Samuel Alt, who also was a bass in the court kapelle.

Palace Church/Schlosskirche

Built 1651–54 as part of Wilhelmsburg Palace; interior decoration completed by 1658 was designed by Johann Moritz Richter Sr., who also designed the palace church in Weißenfels. The church—named Weg zur Himmelsburg (The Path to Heaven's Castle)—fell prey to flames when the palace burned in 1774.

    Organ: In 1657, Duke Wilhelm IV of Saxe-Weimar inherited the old organ from Erfurt's Church of the Barefoot Friars (Barfüßerkirche) and contracted with Ludwig Compenius to erect the organ in its own space above the altar in the new palace church. The one-manual instrument was heard for the first time at the dedication of the renovated church on May 28, 1658 (its Oberwerk remained essentially unchanged until 1774). Several months later Compenius was contracted to build a second division, a Seitenwerk, which was completed December 18, 1658 (II/20; organ inspection by Adam Drese, court organist and kapell-

43. Weimar, Palace Church: Interior with Compenius organ (gouache by Christian Richter, ca. 1660)

meister). 1707–8, Johann Conrad Weißhaupt built new bellows, new wind chests, and new Pedal stops, and integrated the Seitenpositiv into the organ as Unterwerk. 1712–14, at Bach's request, Heinrich Nicolaus Trebs enlarged the bellows, improved the wind chests, and added new stops. 1719–20 and 1734–38, repairs and/or renovations by Heinrich Nicolaus Trebs. 1756, demolition of the organ because of structural problems with the balcony. The replacement instrument (II/24) was destroyed in the palace fire of 1774.

Disposition 1658 (II/20) according to Schrammek (1988)

Seitenpositiv	Oberwerk	Pedal
Grobgedackt, narrow-scaled [*stiller Mensur*] 8'	Quintadena 16'	Gedackter SubBass 16'
Quintadehna 8'	Principal 8'	Posaunen Bass 16'
Spielpfeife 4'	Gedackt 8'	Fagott-Bass 16'

Sesquialtera	Gemßhorn 8'	
Spitzflöthe 2'	Octava 4'	
Krumbhorn 8'	Klein gedackt 4'	
Trommet 8'	Mixtur	
Schallmeyen 4'	Cymbel	
Glockenspiel		

Disposition 1737 (II/24) according to Wette

Im Unter-Clavier [I]	Im Ober-Clavier [II]	Im Pedal
Principal 8'	Quintathön 16'	Groß-Untersatz 32'
Gedackt 8'	Principal 8'	Sub-Bass 16'
Violdigamba 8'	Gemshorn 8'	Violon-Bass 16'
Kleingedackt 4'	Gedackt 8'	Principal Bass 8'
Octava 4'	Octava 4'	Posaun-Bass 16'
Waldflöt 2'	Quintathön 4'	Trompetten-Bass 8'
Sesquialtera IV	Mixtur VI	Cornett-Bass 4'
Trompette 8'	Cymbel III	
	Glockenspiel	

Particulars: According to the Dresden Ms., Principals 8', tin; Untersatz 32', Sub-Bass 16', and Violon-Bass 16', wood; Posaun-Bass 16', wooden resonators; rest of the stops, metal. Sesquialtera IV "in octaves $2\frac{2}{3}$' and $1\frac{3}{5}$'."

According to Schrammek (1985, 1988), the Untersatz 32' may already have been added during the 1707–8 rebuild.

Accessories: Ow and Uw tremulants; cymbelstern.

Coupler: manual coupler; pedal coupler (Ow/Ped).

Compass (after 1708): CD–c^3 (manuals), C–e^1 (pedal).

Wind supply (1708): eight large bellows.

Pitch: Chorton.

Positive

In 1658, the duke contracted Samuel Bidermann to build a positive for the palace church. It apparently stood behind the altar in the first balcony and was later maintained by Ludwig Compenius and then, from 1712, by court organ builder Heinrich Nicolaus Trebs. The instrument was destroyed, at the latest, by the palace fire of 1774.

Disposition 1658 (I/5)

Manual
Koppel 8', wood
Prinzipal 4', tin
Superoktave 2', tin
Quint [$1\frac{1}{2}$'], tin
Cimbel III, tin

Accessory: tremulant.

Compass: CDEFGA–c^3.

Wind supply: two bellows.

Pitch (1673): Chorton.

Archival Sources: Thüringisches Staatsarchiv Weimar, B 4367a and B 4351.

Literature: (a) Wette 1737, 174–76; Adlung 1768, 282; Lehfeldt 1893, 373–74; Löffler 1926, 156–58; Smets 1931, 70; Jauernig 1950, 49–105; Schrammek 1988, 99–111. (b) Wolff 2000, 66–69, 117–86, 483, 526–27, and elsewhere.

City Church of St. Peter and Paul's (Herder Church)/ Stadtkirche St. Peter und Paul (Herderkirche)

1498–1500, late-Gothic hall church with recessed choir; interior decorated by Johann Adolf Richter in Baroque style in 1726–35, including, among other things, addition of two-tiered galleries above the side aisles.

Organ: 1683, new organ by Johann Bernhardt Rücker. According to the Dresden Ms., however, at the examination Rücker's work "was found to be bad, and because he was not capable of remedying the shortcomings, he therefore fled by night" (Smets 1931, 70). 1685, new organ (II/25) by Christoph Junge using parts from the older organ. 1810–12, new organ (III/44) by Johann Gottlob Trampeli, completed by his nephew Friedrich Wilhelm Trampeli. 2000, new organ (III/53) in partially reconstructed Trampeli case by W. Sauer Orgelbau Müllrose. Nothing from Bach's time survives.

Disposition 1685 (II/25)

Rück Positiv (I)	Oberwerk (II)	Pedal
Grobgedackt 8'	Quintadehna 16'	Sub-Baß 16'
Quintadena 8'	Principal 8'	Posaunen 16'
Principal 4'	Grobgedackt 8'	Trompet-Baß 8'
Klein Gedackt 4'	Gemßhorn 8'	Cornet-Baß 2'
Spill-Flöten 4'	Viol di Gamba 8'	
Viol di Gamba 4'	Octava 4'	
Sesquialtera II	Quinta 3'	
Octava 2'	Octava 2'	
Sifflöth 1'	Mixtur IV	
Cymbel Mixtur III	Cymbel III	
	Trompeta 8'	

Particulars: reed resonators (with the exception of the Pedal Posaune) of tin-plated sheet metal.

Accessories: cymbelstern in Rp; Ow tremulant; Rp tremulant.

Couplers: Rp/Ow; Ow/Ped; Rp/Ped.

Wind supply: six bellows.

Archival Sources: (A) Thüringisches Staatsarchiv Weimar, B 4342 and B 4351.

Literature: (a) Lehfeldt 1893, 333–36; Smets 1931, 70; Dehio 2003, 1315–16. (b) BDOK II, nos. 54, 56; *see* Weimar Palace Church.

St. Jacob's Church/Jacobskirche

1712–13, new Baroque hall church built using parts of the older structure from the twelfth century; interior with three tiers of galleries on three sides. As court musician, Bach took part in the dedication on November 6, 1713. 1728, elevated to garrison church by Duke Wilhelm Ernst; after the city fire of 1774, for a short while it served as the court's church. 1806, Goethe and Christiane Vulpius were married here. After the Napoleonic war of 1816–17, interior was restored. Johann Gottfried Walter's gravestone lies next to the church wall.

Organ: 1721–23, new organ (II/18) by Heinrich Nicolaus Trebs, a gift of Duke Wilhelm Ernst of Saxe-Weimar. After restoration of the church in 1823, new organ placed in the upper balcony by Johann Friedrich Schulze; facade with dummy pipes retained. 1977, new organ (II/17) on the south side of the choir by Gerhard Böhm.

Disposition 1723 (II/18)

Haupt Werck [I]	Brust Werk [II]	Pedal
Gedackt 8'	Quintadena 8'	Sub Baß 16'
Principal 4'	Nachthorn 4'	Principal Baß 8'
Klein Gedackt 4'	Wald-Flöthe 4'	Posaune 16'
Quinta 3'	Flaute douce 4'	
Octava 2'	Sesquialtera II	
Tertia 1³⁄₅'	Principal 2'	
Mixtur III	Cymbel Mixtur III	
Trompeta 8'		

Particulars: Hw Trompeta 8' resonators of tin-plated sheet metal.

Accessories: Hw tremulant; Bw cymbelstern.

Couplers: Bw/Hw, Hw/Ped.

Wind supply: two large bellows.

Literature: (a) Löffler 1926, 156–58; Smets 1931, 71, 135; Haupt 1998, 103; Dehio 2003, 1317–18.

Weißenfels

Bach's connections to Weißenfels date back to 1713. On February 23 of that year, in connection with a hunting party on the occasion of Duke Christian's birthday, and at the request of the neighboring Saxe-Weißenfels court, Bach, court organist in Weimar, conducted the cantata "Was mir behagt, ist nur die muntre Jagd," BWV 208. Bach's second wife, Anna

Magdalena, grew up in Weißenfels, where her father, a trumpeter, was a member of the court kapelle. Bach's links to Weißenfels were strengthened during the Leipzig years; in 1728, Duke Christian named him titular kapellmeister of Saxe-Weißenfels. There is no evidence that Bach played the organ in the Palace Church, although it is likely that he knew the instrument. Palace organists were Christian Edelmann (until 1701), David Heinrich Garthoff (1702–41), and Georg Caspar Mangold (1741–46).

Along with the Herold organ in Buttstädt near Weimar, the organ in the Palace Church of Weißenfels is one of the few instruments of the Bach period with a pedal compass that reached to f¹.

Palace Church/Schlosskirche

Baroque palace church in Augustusburg, a castle with three wings completed 1682 to a design by Johann Moritz Richter, who also built the Wilhelmsburg in Weimar. Royal ownership ended in 1746.

Organ: 1668–73, new organ (II/30; spring chests) by Christian Förner placed in the second (upper) balcony. Georg Friedrich Händel played the organ as a young man in 1693. 1839, new organ (II/17) placed in the Förner case by Johann Friedrich Schulze. 1945, war damage; 1983–85, new organ by Mitteldeutscher Orgelbau Voigt using the Förner disposition and retaining the original case.

Disposition 1673 (II/30)

Brustwerk (I)	Oberwerk (II)	Pedal
Quintadehn 8'	Quintadehn 16'	Sub-Baß 16' of wood
Gedackt 8'	Principal 8'	Principal 8'
Principal 4'	Grob-Gedackt 8'	Octav 4'
Gedackt 4'	Spitz-Flöt 8'	Quinta 3'
Quinta 3'	Octav 4'	Octav 2'
Sesquialtera [1³/₅']	Quinta 3'	Mixtur IV 2'
Octav 2'	Sesquialtera [1³/₅']	Posaunbaß 16'
Mixtur III 1'	Octav 2'	Trompet 8'
Krummhorn 8'	Mixtur IV 2'	Cornet 2'
Schalmey 4'	Fagott 16'	
	Trompet 8'	

Accessories: tremulant to the entire organ.
Coupler: manual coupler.
Compass: CD–c³ (manuals), CD–f¹ (pedal).
Wind supply (1673): three bellows.
Pitch (1673): Chorton.
Pitch (1985): 440 Hz at 15°.
Temperament (2000): slightly unequal.

44. Weißenfels, Palace Church: Interior (photograph, 2006)

45. Weißenfels, Palace Church: Reconstructed Förner organ (photograph, 2006

Literature: (a) Trost 1677; Sommer 1882, 82; Friedrich 2001c, 21–35; Koschel 2002, 9–14; Voigt 2004, 81–87. (b) NBR, no. 44, BDOK II, no. 55; NBR, no. 212, BDOK II, nos. 254 and 462; BWV 208 entry; Wolff 2000, 134–35, 208, and elsewhere.

Weißensee

Bach tested the repaired organ in Weißensee on June 22, 1735, on his return from Mühlhausen, and he was in Weißensee again for the examination of the organ on December 16, 1737. No other visits have been discovered.

City Church of Saint Peter and Paul's/Stadtkirche St. Peter und Paul

One-aisled hall church, built ca. 1180, Protestant since 1539. Interior decoration from 1655, barrel-vaulted ceiling from 1689 to 1691.

Organ: 1735–37, enlargement of the 1624 instrument by four stops to III/32 by Conrad Wilhelm Schäfer; disposition unknown. 1903, new organ (II/21) by Otto Petersilie in the original case with larger-than-life representation of Moses and Aaron.

Literature: (a) Haupt 1998, 95; Braun 1999, 19–33; Dehio 2003, 1362–64; Börner/Schubert 2005.

Zschortau

At the request of the patron Heinrich August Sahrer von Sahr, Johann Sebastian Bach travelled to Zschortau, a short distance from Leipzig, on August 7, 1746, the Ninth Sunday after Trinity. He played and tested the organ and found that "everything has been built capably, carefully, and well" (NBR, no. 235, BDOK I, no. 89). In addition to Bach and Scheibe, Johann Paul Streng, superintendent from Delitzsch, and administrator Andreas Christian Brandes were also present at the organ examination. Bach's report clearly indicates that Scheibe, who probably was born in Zschortau, provided a number of items over and above what was contracted: the wooden stops Quinta Thön 16', Viola di Gamba 8', and Fleute-Travers 4', as well as Super-Octave 1' and "a coupler (*Angehänge*) between Manual and Pedal."

St. Nicholas's Church/Kirche St. Nicolai

Hall church with a Romanesque lateral west tower. Choir, nave, and adjacent sacristy built ca. 1517. Galleries on three sides were added in 1870.

Organ: 1744–46, at request of patron Heinrich August Sahrer von Sahr, new organ (I/13) by Johann Scheibe in west balcony. 1870, instrument moved to a newly built second balcony and a second manual added by Eduard Offenhauer. 1954, instrument moved back to the previous position by Eule Orgelbau. 1984, removal of the second manual by Eule

46. Zschortau, church: Scheibe organ (photograph, 2009)

Orgelbau. 2000, restoration and restitution of the original disposition by Eule Orgelbau. Only organ by Scheibe that has been preserved.

For Bach's organ report, *see* Part II.A.

Disposition 1746/2000 (I/13)

Manual		Pedal
Quinta Thön 16'	Fleute doux 4'	Subbaß 16'
Principal 8'	Hohl Fleute 3', bass	Posaun-Baß 16'
Grobgedackt 8'	Hohl Fleute 3', soprano	Violon 8'
Viol de Gamba 8', bass	Super Octava 2'	
Viol de Gamba 8', soprano	Super Octava 1'	
Octav 4'	Mixtur III–IV 1$^1/_3$'	

Particulars: Viola di Gamba 8' and Hohl Fleute 3' are divided between c^1 and $c^{\#1}$. The Gedackt 4' is called "Fleute Doux" in Scheibe's proposal and "Fleute-Traverse" in Bach's report. In 1744, Scheibe described the Viola di Gamba 8' as "a costly and rare register that cannot be built for less than several hundred talers." Its lowest octaves are made of wood; from $c^{\#1}$ the pipes are metal and slightly tapered. Hohl Fleute 3', stopped metal pipes. Quinta Thön 16', stopped and of wood. Posaunen Baß 16', wide-scaled, with leathered wooden shallots.

Inscription in the Pedal chest: "Johann Scheibe currently organ builder to the honorable Leipzig University 1744" (*Johann Scheibe beÿ/Einer löbl. universitat leipzig/der Zeit Orgelmacher 1744*).

Inscription in the manual chest: "Johann Hinrih Jentz of Leipzig 1745."

Accessories: tremulant (reconstructed 2000); bellows signal.

Coupler: pedal coupler (does not couple the Quinta Thön 16' and Viola di Gamba 8').

Compass: $CD-c^3$ (manual), $CD-c^1$ (pedal).

Wind supply: three bellows (2005, two bellows added that can be pumped either by hand or with an electric motor).

Pitch (2005): Chorton, a^1 = 464.4 Hz at 18° C.

Temperament: unequal.

Literature: (a) Rubardt 1936/37, 272–74; Dähnert 1980, 285–86; Blanchard 1985, 176–79; Theobald 1986, 81–89; Dehio 1996b, 1073; Petzoldt 2000, 280–85, 322–23; information from Eule Orgelbau, 2005; Kaufmann 2006, 404–9. (b) NBR, no. 235, BDOK I, no. 89; BDOK II, no. 545.

Reference Organs
from Bach's World

There is no evidence that Johann Sebastian Bach knew and played the organs cited in the following section. For the majority of these instruments, however, it is highly likely that he did. Beyond that, many of the instruments are particularly important to the history of organ building and provide an essential guide toward an understanding of Bach's instruments.

Berlin

After his visit to Potsdam in 1747, Johann Sebastian Bach proceeded to Berlin. He had previously been in Berlin in 1742, when he had visited his son Carl Philipp Emanuel, who at the time was in the service of Frederick the Great, king of Prussia. Bach's first documented visit to Berlin was from Köthen in 1719, the year in which organ builder Joachim Wagner settled in Berlin. It cannot be proven that Bach got to know the St. Mary's organ in 1747 or on an earlier occasion.

St. Mary's Church/Marienkirche

Three-aisled Gothic hall church, completed in early fourteenth century. Renovated after a fire in 1380. Nineteenth century, addition of rib vaulting as well as walls separating the nave and the tower vestibule. 1893–95, new organ gallery.

Organ: 1720–23, new organ by Joachim Wagner (opus 1); case by Johann Georg Blume, 1723, finished in 1742 by Paul de Ritter. At the request of Friedrich Ludwig Seydel, organist at St. Mary's, the organ was rebuilt in 1800 according to specifications provided by Abbé Georg Joseph Vogler, at which time 1,400 "unnecessary" pipes were removed. The Wagner disposition was partially rebuilt in 1830 by Carl August Buchholz and enlarged by Schlag & Söhne to III/53 with cone chests. 1948, renovation by Alexander Schuke. 2000–2002, partial reconstruction (III/46) by Daniel Kern.

Disposition 1723 (III/41)

Hauptwerk (II)	Oberwerk (III)	Hinterwerk (I)	Pedal
Bordun 16'	Quintadena 16'	Gedackt 8'	Principal-Bass 16'
Principal 8'	Principal 8'	Quintadena 8'	Violon 16'
Viole di Gambe 8'	Gedackt 8'	Octav 4'	Gembßhorn 8'
Rohrflöt 8'	Octav 4'	Rohrflöt 4'	Quinta 6'
Octav 4'	Fugara 4'	Octav 2'	Octav 4'
Spitzflöt 4'	Nassat 3'	Waldflöt 2'	Mixtur VI 2'
Quinta 3'	Octav 2'	Quinta 1^1/$_3$'	Posaune 16'
Octav 2'	Tertie 1^3/$_5$'	Cimbel III 1'	Trompet 8'
Scharff V 1½'	Sifflöt 1'	Echo to Cornet V	
Cimbel III 1'	Mixtur IV 1½'		
Cornet V 8' (from c^1)	Vox humana 8'		
Trompete 8'			

Accessories: Ow tremulant; HinW tremulant; cymbelstern; cut-off valves for each division.

Couplers: Ow/Hw, HinW/Hw.

Compass: CD–c^3 (manuals), CD–d^1 (pedal).

Pitch (1723): Chorton.

Pitch (2002): a^1 = 440 Hz.

Literature: (a) Dehio 2000a, 35–37; Pape 2000, 175–76; Pape 2002, 150–59; Gailit 2002, 140–49. (b) Wolff 2000, 208, 317, 425–31, 446, and elsewhere.

Buttstädt

It is likely that Bach took over responsibility for the Herold organ in St. Michael's Church (an instrument he may have known as early as 1702) from his Weimar predecessor Johann Effler, and in this manner he probably got to know Johann Anton Mylius (librettist, BWV 1127), the superintendent there. Organists in Buttstädt, a city that belonged to the duchy of Weimar, were Johann Paul Friese (from before 1700 until his death in 1721) and Johann Tobias Krebs (from 1721 to 1762), a student of Johann Gottfried Walther and of Johann Sebastian Bach and father of the later Bach student Johann Ludwig Krebs. The important manuscripts that contain organ music transmitted by the Krebs circle (Staatsbibliothek Berlin, Mus. ms. Bach, P 801–803) originated in part in Buttstädt and therefore would have been played on the organ there.

St. Michael's Church/Michaeliskirche

One-aisled hall church with a very deep and high choir, completed 1551. Severely damaged during fire of 1684, the renovated church with three tiers of surrounding galleries was dedicated in 1689; in 1720 it was sumptuously decorated by Franz Domenicus Minetti, a

47. Berlin, St. Mary's Church: Wagner organ after restoration and reconstruction
(photograph, 2002)

48. Buttstädt, St. Michael's Church: Herold organ (photograph, 1976)

Florentine sculptor and painter. The pulpit and altar by court sculptor Friedrich Philipp Puppert (1727) are considered the most important in Thuringia.

Organ: Contract for a new organ signed on July 29, 1696, with Peter Herold, who died in 1700; Finke (Johann Georg? Christian?) completed the instrument in 1701. 1724, at request of Johann Tobias Krebs, and after an evaluation by Johann Gottfried Walter (text cited in Schmidt-Mannheim 2004), repairs by Heinrich Nicolaus Trebs. 1764–66, enlargement by Johann Michael Hartung; numerous changes in the nineteenth and twentieth centuries.

Contract disposition 1696 (II/23)

Ober Werck (I)	Unter Werck (II)	Pedal
Quinta Thön 16'	Gedackt 8'	Sub Baß 16'
Principal 8'	Quinta Thön 8'	Flötgen Bässgen 1'
Gems Horn or so-called Flach Flöte 8'	Principal 4'	Posaunen Baß 16'
Viola di Gamba 8'	Quinta 3'	Cornet Bässgen 2'

Gedackt 8'	Sesquialtera III
Octava 4'	Octava 2'
Quinta 3'	ZimbelStimme III
Super Octava 2'	Trompetten Regal 8'
Sexta	
Mixtur VI	
ZimbelStimme III	

Accessories: tremulant, cymbelstern.

Couplers: Ow/Uw, Ow/Ped.

Compass: CD–c³ (manuals), CD–f¹ (pedal).

Instruction in the contract: "for proper *application* of the fingers and feet, the d in the *pedal* directly under the d¹ in the *manual*, that is, that it is arranged and set according to d¹/d."

Wind supply: three bellows.

Wind pressure: 33–35°.

Literature: (a) Adlung 1768, 206; Zietz 1969; Dehio 2003, 179–80; Schmidt-Mannheim 2004, 155–88. (b) Maul 2005, 7–34.

Erfurt

Along with Arnstadt, Erfurt was the most important city for the musical Bach family during the seventeenth and eighteenth centuries. Johann Bach worked as organist from 1636 to 1673 at the Prediger Church, church of the town council and musical center for the Lutheran citizens of Erfurt, a biconfessional city that at the time was part of the electoral archbishopric of Mainz. His successor was Johann Effler, who previously had been organist in Gehren (where he was succeeded by Johann Michael Bach, later Johann Sebastian's father-in-law). In 1678, Effler became city and court organist in Weimar, where he was succeeded by Johann Sebastian Bach in 1708. Effler's successor in Erfurt was Johann Pachelbel, who held the organist post until 1690 and who taught Johann Christoph Bach of Ohrdruf. Pachelbel's successors as town organist were Nicolaus Vetter, 1690–91; Johann Heinrich Buttstedt, 1691–1727; Jacob Adlung (Johann Nicolaus Bach's student), 1728–62; and Johann Christian Kittel (one of the last students of Johann Sebastian Bach), 1762–1809.

Johann Sebastian Bach often visited Erfurt, the birthplace of his parents, and in 1716 examined and evaluated the organ in St. Augustine's Church.

Prediger Church/Predigerkirche

Three-aisled Gothic Dominican basilica from the thirteenth–fourteenth centuries; with its considerable dimensions, it counts as one of the most important architectural creations of the mendicant order in Germany. After the Reformation, it was Erfurt's principal city church.

49. Erfurt, Prediger Church: Schuke organ
in historical case (photograph, 2007)

Organ: 1572–79, new organ by Heinrich Cumpenius; 1648–49, enlarged by Ludwig Compenius, who also repaired it in 1677. 1740, after a fire, damaged organ rebuilt by Franciscus Volckland. 1977, new organ (IV/56) placed in original case by Schuke Orgelbau (Potsdam).

Disposition (II/30) according to Adlung (1768)

Rückpositiv (I)	Hauptwerk (II)	Pedal
Quintatön 8'	Quintatön 16' (T)	Principal 16'
Gedackt 8'	Principal 8'	Subbaß 16'
Principal 4'	Gemshorn 8'	Violone 16'
Nachthorn 4'	Rohrflöte 8'	Quintatön 16' (T)
Liebliche Pfeife 4'	Violdigamba 8'	Oktave 8'
Sesquialter II 3'	Flötetraverse 8'	Quinte 6'
Oktave 2'	Oktave 4'	Hohlflöte 4'
Scharpquintez III	Sesquialter II	Flachflöte 2'
Trompete 8' (T)	Oktave 2'	Posaune 16'
Schallmey 4' (T)	Mixtur IV-VII	Fagott 16'
	Cymbel III	Trompet 8' (T)
		Schallmey 4' (T)

Adlung (1768) reports: "This instrument is old, and originally built in 1649 by Ludwig Compenius, organ builder in Naumburg. Over time one continued to alter one thing or another, and increase the number of stops, until it eventually reached the following condition." The organ facade carries the following chronostichon: "CoMpenIVm strVXIt fraVDe ex VarIa reprehensVS restItVit VolkLanD VarIe Ist[ud] HoC organVM et aUXit."

Accessories: two cut-off valves, three tremulants, glockenspiel (Hw).

Couplers: manual coupler, pedal coupler.

Compass: CDEFGA–e³ (manuals), CDEFGA–d¹ (pedal).

Literature: (a) Adlung 1768, 224–25; Tettau 1890, 145; Ziller 1935, 22–28; Haupt 1998, 101; Belotti 1999, xix; Dehio 2003, 337–42; Friedrich 2005a, 211; Aumüller 2010, 67, 78, 103.

Frankfurt (Oder)

In 1749, Johann Sebastian Bach conferred with the Halle organ builder Heinrich Andreas Contius (son of Christoph Contius) regarding an organ for the Franciscan Church in Frankfurt (Oder). Apparently at the instigation of Royal Prussian concertmaster Johann Gottlieb Graun, Contius approached Bach in Leipzig for this purpose in April. (No correspondence survives. Bach had previously written a recommendation for Contius that is dated January 12, 1748.) Contius did not receive the contract, however. It may be that Bach was familiar with the Franciscan Church in Frankfurt, for Carl Philipp Emanuel Bach directed the collegium musicum in this Prussian university city from 1734 to 1738.

Franciscan Church (Lower Church)/Franziskanerkirche (Unterkirche)

Late-Gothic church, completed ca. 1525. 1735–36, renovation and addition of galleries. World War II damage was repaired, and in 1967 the building became a concert hall; original woodwork was removed.

Organ: 1749, recommendation and report from Bach regarding the planned new organ for the renovated church; documents untraceable. 1754, new organ by Damm (Thamm); instrument does not survive. 1975, concert organ by Frankfurter Orgelbau Sauer placed in the western bay of the middle aisle. Since 1990, a positive by Wilhelm Sauer (opus 107, built 1866 for the church in Jeeben/Altmark) has been in the choir.

Literature: (a) Wolff 2000, 444; Gramlich 2002, 80–86. (b) BDOK I, no. 51; BDOK II, nos. 582, 586, 589, 590; BDOK V, no. A 90a.

Freiberg

Whether Bach knew Gottfried Silbermann's first large organ, built for Freiberg's Cathedral of St. Mary, or the organ in Freiberg's St. Peter's Church, a parallel instrument to the organ in Dresden's Church of Our Lady, is not known. Nevertheless, it is likely that Bach visited the city where Silbermann had his workshop, for we know from the inventory of Bach's estate that he owned a share in a silver mine in Kleinvoigtsberg, near Freiberg. Bach's student Johann Friedrich Doles, who later held Bach's position in Leipzig, was cantor from 1744 to 1755 in Freiberg, where he was responsible for the vocal music in the cathedral.

Cathedral organists were Elias Lindner (student of Johann Kuhnau), 1711–31, and Johann Christoph Erselius, 1731–72. Organists at St. Peter's were Johann Christian Hennig (student of Daniel Vetter and Jacob Weckmann), 1686–1722; Johann Gabriel Spiess, 1722–37; Johann Georg Glöckner, 1737–42; and Johann Christoph Klemm (student of Johann Gottlieb Görner), 1742–61.

Cathedral of St. Mary/Dom St. Marien

Late-Gothic hall church, completed 1499; west portal ("Golden Door") dates from 1225–30. Interior decoration dates from 1500 and after; following the Reformation, the Cathedral became the burial site for the Albertine branch of the house of Wettin from 1541 to 1694. 1726–28, addition of private boxes under the stone galleries.

Organ: 1710–14, new organ by Gottfried Silbermann. Thomascantor Johann Kuhnau and court organist Gottfried Ernest Pestel (Altenburg) examined the instrument on August 13–14, 1714. On October 25, 1719, Elias Lindner, who had been organist since 1711 and had designed the organ's case and balcony, requested new shallots for the Posaune 16' and that the Pedal Trompete 8' be leathered. In 1738, Silbermann altered the way the organ was pumped and replaced the Oberwerk Nassat 3' with Quintadena 8' and the Oberwerk Terz 1⅗' with Flageolett 1'. At the same time, the case ornamentation was gilded

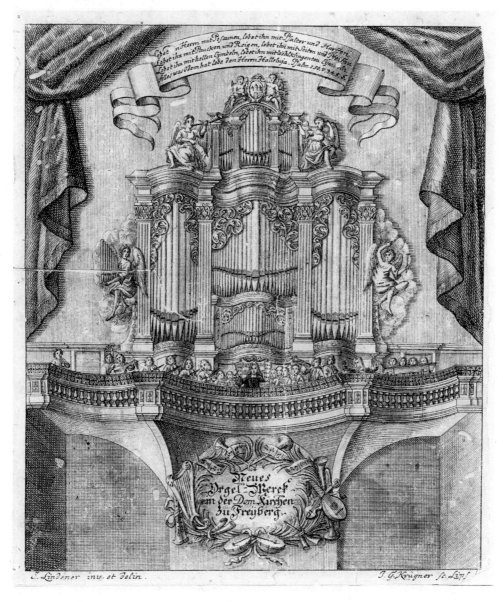

50. Freiberg, Cathedral: Concerted music at the Silbermann organ under direction of
Elias Lindner, cathedral organist and designer of the organ (copper engraving, ca. 1714)

51. Freiberg, Cathedral: Silbermann
organ (photograph, 2006)

by Christian Polycarp Buzäus. Repairs in the nineteenth and twentieth centuries. 1981–83, complete restoration by Jehmlich with assistance from Kristian Wegscheider.

Disposition 1714 (III/44)

Hauptwerk (II)	Brustwerk (I)	Oberwerk (III)	Pedal
"mighty or solemn sound" (gravitätischer Klang)	"delicate and sweet" (delicat und lieblich)	"sharp and pointed" (scharff und spitzig)	"strong and penetrating" (stark und durchdringend)
Bordun 16'	Gedackt 8'	Quintadehn 16'	Untersatz 32'
Principal 8'	Principal 4'	Principal 8'	Principalbaß 16'
Viola di Gamba 8'	Rohrflöt 4'	Gedackt 8'	Sub Baß 16'
Rohrflöt 8'	Nassat 3'	Octava 4'	Octav Baß 8'
Octava 4'	Octava 2'	Spitzflöt 4'	Octav Baß 4'
Quinta 3'	Tertia 1³/₅'	Nassat 3'	Pedalmixtur VI
Super Octav 2'	Quinta 1½'	Super Octava 2'	Posaun Baß 16'
Tertia 1³/₅'	Sufflöt 1'	Tertia 1³/₅'	Trompet Baß 8'
Cornet V, from c¹	Mixtur III	Echo V, from c¹	Clarin Baß 4'

Mixtur IV	Mixtur III
Zimblen III	Zimbeln II
Trompet 8'	Krumbhorn 8'
Clarin 4'	Vox humana 8'

Particulars: Untersatz 32' comprises two stops: Holzgedackt 32' and Holzprincipal 16' on the same toeboard.

Accessories: tremulant to the manuals; Ow tremulant to the Vox humana; Hw and Bw cut-off valves; Ow cut-off valve.

Couplers: shove coupler, Bw/Hw; shove coupler, Ow/Hw; no pedal coupler.

Compass: CD–c^3 (manuals), CD–c^1 (pedal).

Wind supply: six bellows (three bellows for the manuals and three bellows for the pedal); since 1983, electric motor and one magazine bellows for each division.

Wind pressure (1714): 41° = 97 mm WC, manuals; 46° = 109 mm WC, pedal.

Wind pressure (1983): 90 mm WC (manuals), 100 mm WC (pedal).

Pitch (1983): Chorton, a^1 = 476 Hz.

Literature: (a) Dähnert 1980, 104–11; Dehio 1996a, 259–71; Greß 2001, 36–39.

St. Peter's Church/Petrikirche

Late-Gothic church rebuilt 1728–34 after a fire. 1894–96, in place of the two-tiered galleries, a new gallery that projected far into the room. 1974, remodeling; nave and choir separated by a glass wall.

Organ: 1735, new organ by Gottfried Silbermann (built at the same time as the organ for Our Lady's in Dresden). 1855, organ tuned in equal temperament by Johann Gotthold Jehmlich; 1895, organ pitch normalized and the low C♯ added in all divisions; also, addition of Subbaß 16' as well as a Hinterwerk division with pneumatic membrane chest and five registers. 1993, partial restoration by Jehmlich. 2006–7, collaborative restoration by Jehmlich Orgelbau Dresden and Orgelwerkstatt Wegscheider Dresden, returning organ to its 1734 condition; previously unknown Silbermann documents were discovered in the Pedal chest.

Disposition 1735 (II/32)

Hauptwerk (I)	Oberwerk (II)	Pedal
Principal 16'	Quinta Dena 16'	Groß Untersatz 32'
Octav Principal 8'	Principal 8'	Principal Baß 16'
Viol di Gamba 8'	Gedackts 8'	Octaven Baß 8'
Rohr-Flöte 8'	Quinta Dena 8'	Posaune 16'
Octava 4'	Octava 4'	Trompete 8'
Spitz-Flöte 4'	Rohr-Flöte 4'	
Quinta 3'	Nassat 3'	
Octava 2'	Octava 2'	
Tertia 1³/₅'	Quinta 1½'	

Hauptwerk (I)	Oberwerk (II)
Cornet IV, from c^1	Sufflöt 1'
Mixtur IV	Sechst Quint Altra
	[$^4/_5$', from c^1 $1^3/_5$']
Cymbel III	Mixtur III
Fachott 16'	Vox Humana 8'
Trompete 8'	

Accessories: Hw tremulant; *Schwebung* [soft tremulant] to Ow; bellows signal.

Couplers: shove coupler, Ow/Hw; wind coupler, Hw/Ped.

Compass: CD–c^3 (manuals), CD–c^1 (pedal).

Wind supply: four bellows (two to the manuals, two to the pedal).

Wind supply (1734/2007): four wedge bellows that can be pumped by hand or motor.

Wind pressure (2007): 94 mm WC.

Pitch (2007): a^1 = 462.5 Hz at 18° C.

Temperament: Until 1855, modified meantone; 1855–2007, equal; 2007, Neidhardt II 1732 ("for a small city").

Literature: (a) Dähnert 1980, 116–20; Dehio 1996, 277–79; Greß 2001, 101–3; Drechsel 2007.

52. Freiberg,
St. Peter's Church:
Silbermann organ
(photograph, before
1894)

Gotha

Given that the city lies within the triangle Eisenach-Arnstadt-Weimar and close to Ohrdruf, it is to be assumed that Johann Sebastian Bach knew the organs in Gotha. City organists at St. Margaret's Church were Johann Pachelbel, 1692–95; Johann Nicolaus Bremser, 1695–1742; and Johann Ludwig Backhaus, 1742–71. Johann Christoph Bach, Johann Sebastian's older brother, was the first to be offered to succeed Pachelbel; he nevertheless declined the position in order to stay in Ohrdruf.

St. Margaret's Church/Margarethenkirche

Gothic hall church with added choir, completed 1543. Rebuilt 1636–40 after a fire. Since 1652, burial site for Duke Ernst I ("the Pious") and his family. 1725–27, interior decoration in Baroque style. After damage in World War II, restyling in 1951–57 according to Baroque concepts.

Organ: 1652, new organ (III/P) by Johann Moritz and Andreas Weise. In 1687, court organist Nicolaus Körner and chamber organist Christian Friedrich Witt found the instrument "to put it simply, thoroughly bad and ruined . . . so that one cannot cite specific weaknesses, because not even one register, let alone more, is usable" (Ernst 1983, 13). 1688, contract with Johann Moritz Weise for repairs; 1696–98, new organ by Severin Hohlbeck. Changes in the eighteenth and nineteenth centuries. Destroyed in the war; new organ (III/36, op. 313) built 1960 by Alexander Schuke using the partial remains of the original case.

Disposition 1698 (II/25)

Hauptwerk [I]	Brustwerk [II]	Pedal
Quintatön 16'	Lieblich Gedackt 8'	Principalbaß 16'
Principal 8'	Principal 4'	Subbaß 16'
Gedackt 8'	Quintatön 4'	Posaunenbaß 16'
Violdigambe 8'	Nasat Quinte 3'	Trompetenbaß 8'
Oktave 4'	Spitzflöte 2'	Schallmey Baß 4'
Spielflöte 4'	Sief floit 1'	Cornetbaß 2'
Quinta 3'	Mixtur IV 1½'	
Superoktava 2'		
Sexta		
Mixtur VIII 2'		
Dulcian 16'		
Trompetta 8'		

Accessories: Hw tremulant, Bw tremulant, two cymbelsterns.
Coupler: Hw/Ped.
Wind supply: six bellows.
Literature: (a) Ernst 1983, 13; Dehio 2003, 483–84; Schuke 2004, 9; Harder 2005, 155–56.

53. Gotha, St. Margaret's
Church: Schuke organ in
historical case (photo-
graph, 2007)

Gräfenroda

There is no evidence for Johann Sebastian Bach's acquaintance with the Gräfenroda
organ, but he may have advised Kellner on its disposition. From 1732 to 1772, Johann Peter
Kellner was cantor and organist in Gräfenroda, a town southeast of Ohrdruf at the edge
of the Thuringian Forest. (He had already begun to substitute in 1727.) His acquaintance
with Johann Sebastian Bach was of great importance and may have come about through
his teacher Hieronymus Florentinus Quehl, from Suhl. It was strengthened during a visit
to Leipzig sometime before 1730. Kellner later became very active as an organ expert.
Kellner's students included Johann Philipp Kirnberger, Johannes Ringk, and Johann
Ernst Rembt. Kellner and his circle played an important role in the transmission of Bach's
organ music.

St. Laurence's Church/Laurentiuskirche
Built 1731–33 as a Baroque hall church; restored 1839–43. Its important interior decoration survives.

Organ: 1733–36, new organ by Johann Anton Weise; Johann Peter Kellner provided the disposition. Enlargements in 1749 and 1755 by Johann Stephan Schmaltz. Repairs and rebuilds in the nineteenth and twentieth centuries. 1908, new organ by Eifert using some individual pipes and the original case. 1966, new organ by Hartmut Schüssler in the original case, again retaining some original pipework, as well as wind chests and pipes from the Strobel organ in Bad Frankenhausen. 2003–5, reconstruction of the Weise organ by Orgelbau Waltershausen.

Disposition 1736/2005 (H/26)

Hauptwerk (I)	Oberwerk (II)	Pedal
Bourdon 16'	Hohlflöte 8' (t)	Principal Baß 16'
Quintatön 16' (t)	Gedackt 8'	Subbaß 16'
Principal 8' (t)	Principal 4' (t)	Violon Baß 16'
Viol di Gamba 8'	Flauto traverse 4' (t)	Principal Baß 8' (t)
Gedackt 8'	Gemshorn 4'	Traversen Baß 8' (t)
Gemshorn 8' (t)	Octava 2'	Posaun Baß 16'
Octava 4' (t)	Waldflöte 2' (t)	
Octave 2'	Spitzflöte 1' (t)	
Mixtur VI 2' (t)	Mixtur IV 1'	
Scharff III 1' (t)	Vox humana 8'	

54. Gräfenroda, St. Laurence's Church: Reconstructed Weise organ (photograph, 2006)

Particulars: (t) = partially old pipework (in the Ow Waldflöte 2', only one preserved pipe). The Flauto traverse 4' (Ow) is overblowing, as is the Traversen Baß 8' (Pedal). Ow Vox humana 8' was added in 1755; the glockenspiel above the Ow was already installed by 1749.

Accessories: two cut-off valves; twenty-eight-note glockenspiel; cymbelstern; Ow tremulant; bellows signal.

Couplers: Ow/Hw, Hw/Ped.

Compass (1736): C–c³ (manuals), C–d¹ (pedal).

Compass (2005): C–d³ (manuals), C–d¹ (pedal).

Wind supply (1736/2005): five bellows.

Wind pressure: 75 mm WC (manuals), 80 mm WC (pedal).

Pitch (2005): a¹ = 466 Hz.

Temperament: mild meantone (using ⅕ Pythagorean comma).

Literature: (a) Dehio 2003, 506; Harder 2005, 157–60; Friedrich 2005b, 214–18; Stade 2005, 161–64; communication from Waltershausen Orgelbau, 2005.

Lahm (Itzgrund)

Johann Lorenz Bach, who had studied with Johann Sebastian Bach in Weimar from 1715 to 1717, worked from 1718 until his death in 1773 as organist and cantor in Lahm. It is possible that he consulted with his uncle while planning the organ.

Palace Church/Schlosskirche

Hall church with altar and pulpit in the middle of the long side wall (*Quersaalkirche*), built 1728–32 in French Baroque style according to plans of Duke Adam Heinrich Gottlob von Lichtenstein by the Ansbach court building director Karl Friedrich von Zocha. Burial site of the dukes of Lichtenstein.

Organ: 1730–32, new organ by Heinrich Gottlieb Herbst; disposition by Johann Lorenz Bach. Changes in the nineteenth and twentieth centuries, especially under Paul Ott. 1978–83, restoration by Hoffmann Orgelbau.

Disposition 1732 (II/29)

Hauptwerk [I]	Oberwerk (Hinterwerk) [II]	Pedal
Quinta Thöne 16'	Quinta Thöne 8'	Sub-Baß 16'
Principal 8'	Gemshorn 8'	Violon-Baß 16'
Viola di Gamba 8'	Praestanda 4'	Quint grosso 12'
Gedact 8'	Flaut-Traversiere 4'	Principal 8'
Quinta 6'	Sesquialtera II	Getact 8'
Octav 4'	Waldflöte 2'	Octave 4'
Flaut-Douce 4'	Cymbel III ½'	Mixtur V 2'

55. Lahm/Itzgrund, palace church: Herbst organ (photograph, 2007)

Nassat 3'	Vox humana 8'	Posaunen Baß 32'
Super-Octav 2'		Posaunen Baß 16'
Mixtur IV 1'		Trompete 8'
Trompete 8'		

Particulars: Hw Nassat 3', C–c^2 with chimneys, c#^{2}–c^3 conical. Ow Flaut-Traversiere 4', conical.

Accessories: two cymbelsterns; faster and slower tremulants.

Coupler: manual coupler.

Compass: CD–c^3 (manuals), CD–d^1 (pedal).

Literature: (a) Mehl 1953, 78–82; Schindler 1985, 112–21; Dehio 1999b, 561.

Liebertwolkwitz

Liebertwolkwitz's patron was Statz Hilmor von Fullen, who previously had endowed the Störmthal organ. The close relationship between Bach and the organ builder Hildebrandt suggests that Bach may also have been involved with this instrument.

Church

Hall church built 1572–75; heavily damaged by fire during the Battle of Leipzig in 1813; rebuilt 1908 by Julius Zeißig. Two tiers of surrounding galleries; patron's loge on the north side.

Organ: 1724–25, new organ by Zacharias Hildebrandt, "organ builder and citizen of Freiberg" (1724 contract), paid for by "Electoral Saxon and Royal Polish Chamberlain" Statz Hilmor von Fullen of Störmthal. 1766, repairs; 1813, dismantling of the organ. Nothing from Bach's time survives.

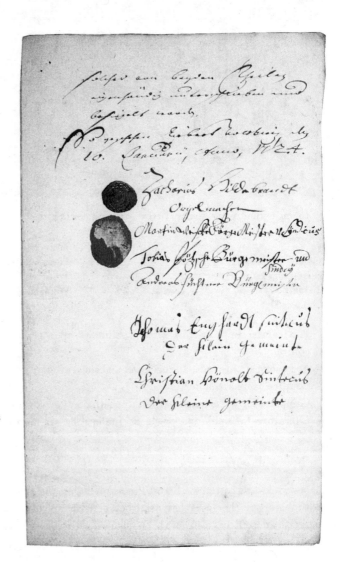

56. Liebertwolkwitz, church: Final page of the organ contract of 1724 with the signature of Zacharias Hildebrandt, as well as Martin Weische, Tobias Götzsche, and Andreas Förstner, majors; also Thomas Enghardt and Christian Hönolt, aldermen

Disposition 1724 (I/13)

Manual		**Pedal**
Principal 8'	Octava 2'	Sub Baß 16'
Grobgedackt 8'	Quinta 1½'	Posaunen Baß 16'
Quintadena 8'	Sufflöt 1'	
Octava 4'	Mixtur III 1½'	
Rohr Flöte 4'	Cornet III	
Quinta 3'		

Accessory: tremulant.
Coupler: pedal coupler.
Compass: CD–c^3 (manual), CD–c^1 (pedal).
Wind supply: two bellows.
Archival Source: Bach-Archiv Leipzig, Rara II, 204.
Literature: (a) Dähnert 1962, 32–33; Dehio 1998, 643–44.

Lübeck

In the winter of 1705–6, Johann Sebastian Bach spent a number of months in Lübeck. The cathedral's organ, which at the time was only six years old and for its time the most modern organ in the city, may have been of particular interest to Bach.

Cathedral/Dom

Gothic hall church, rebuilt 1266–1341 from a Romanesque basilica. Destroyed in World War II; 1966–70, rebuilt in a new form.

Organ: 1696, new organ contracted by Arp Schnitger and built by his longtime associate Hans Hantelmann. "In the year 1699, on the 6th, 7th, and 8th of February, it was examined by Buxtehude, organist at St. Mary's Church, and Johann Jacob Nordtmann, organist here at the Cathedral" (Fock 1974, 160). Case carvings by Johann Jakob Budde. 1892–93, new organ (III/64) by E. F. Walcker & Cie in original case. The key desk from 1696 is preserved in the Saint Annen Museum. 1970, new organ (IV/47) by Marcussen & Son.

Disposition 1699 (III/45)

Rückpositiv (I)	**Werck (II)**	**Brustwerk (III)**	**Pedal**
Prinzipal 8'	Prinzipal 16'	Prinzipal 8' of wood	Prinzipal 16'
Quintadena 8'	Quintadena 16'	Oktave 4'	Subbaß 16'
Gedackt 8'	Oktave 8'	Oktave 2'	Oktave 8'
Oktave 4'	Spitzflöte 8'	Gemshorn 2'	Gedackt 8'
Blockflöte 4'	Oktave 4'	Quinta 1½'	Oktave 4'
Kleinflöte 1'	Rohrflöte 4'	Sesquialtera II	Nachthorn 2'
Sesquialtera II	Nasat 3'	Scharff VI–VIII	Rauschpfeiffe II

Rückpositiv (I)	Werck (II)	Brustwerk (III)	Pedal
Scharff VI–VIII	Rauschpfeiffe II	Dulzian 8'	Mixtur VI–VIII
Dulzian 16'	Mixtur VI–VIII	Schallmey 8', from g	Posaune 32', from F
Trichterregal 8'	Zimbel III		Posaune 16'
	Trompete 16'		Dulzian 16'
	Trompete 8'		Trompete 8'
			Trompete 4'
			Cornet 2'

Accessories: cut-off valve for each division; tremulants in Werck and Pedal; cymbel-stern; drum; bellows signal.

Coupler: Bw/W.

Compass: CDE–c³ (RP), CDEFGA–c³ (W, Bw), CD–d¹ (Ped).

Wind supply: eight bellows.

Literature: Fock 1974, 160–61; Snyder 2002, 38–43; Snyder 2007, 87–88.

57. Lübeck, Cathedral: Walcker organ in historical case (photograph, ca. 1900)

58. Lübeck, Cathedral:
Original key desk of the
Schnitger organ (photograph,
1993)

Merseburg

When Bach was in Halle to examine the Contius organ, the large Wender organ in Merseburg Cathedral was just being completed. Considering his longstanding connections with the Mühlhausen organ builder, Bach may have worked with Wender on the Merseburg disposition. Georg Friedrich Kauffmann was court and cathedral organist in Merseburg from 1710 until his death in 1735.

Cathedral/Dom

Three-aisled hall church, built 1510–17; Roman portions of the building date to the eleventh century.

Organ: 1665, new organ, builder unknown. 1693–1705, enlargement and renovation by Zacharias Thayßner; old case reused. The instrument was assessed negatively by the organ builder Christoph Gloger and by Johann Kuhnau; Kuhnau speaks of a "very large, but pretty much bungled organ" (Engel 1855). 1714–16, rebuild and further enlargement by Johann Friedrich Wender, including addition of a Brustwerk. Johann Nicolaus Becker, Wender's son-in-law, cared for the organ after 1724. 1734–35, repairs by Zacharias Hildebrandt, who added a Vox humana to the Oberwerk. Later rebuilds. 1853–55, new organ (IV/81) by Friedrich Ladegast using twenty-seven registers and six bellows from the previous organ, as well as the case from 1665; the old registers were replaced by Ladegast in 1866. Various rebuilds in the twentieth century. 2002–4, thorough collaborative restoration by Eule Orgelbau, Orgelwerkstatt Scheffler, and Orgelwerkstatt Wegscheider.

Disposition 1717 (IV/66) at the examination by Johann Kuhnau and Gottfried Ernst Pestel (according to Engel 1855)

Brustwerk (I)		Rückpositiv (II)		Großmanual (III)	
Gelinde Gedackt 8'	(maple)	Quinta dena 8'		Rohrflöte 16' (7 lowest pipes wood, rest metal)	
Principal 4'	(t)	Großgedackt 8'	(maple)	Quinta dena 16'	
Salicional 4'	(t)	Quinta dena 8'	(m)	Principal 8'	(t)
Nassat 3'	(t)	Gedackt 8'	(maple)		
		Kammerton		Gemshorn 8'	(m)
Oktava 2'	(t)	Principal 4'	(t)	Großgedackt 8'	(m)
Flachflöte 2'	(maple)	Octava 4'	(t)		
		Kammerton		Quinta 6'	(m)
Superoctava 1'	(t)	Flauto dulce 4'	(maple)	Octava 4'	(m)
Mixtur IV	(t)	Quinta offen 3'	(m)	Kleingedeckt 4'	(m)
		Spielflöte 2'	(m)	Ses qui altera II	(m)
		Octava 2'	(m)	Octava 2'	(m)
		Tertia 2' [1³/₅']	(m)	Mixtur VI	(t)
		Mixtur IV	(t)	Cymbel III	(t)
		Fagott 16'	(wB)	Bombard 16'	(wB)
				Bombard pedaliter	
				Trompet 8'	(wb)

Oberwerk (IV)		Pedal		Hinterwerk to Pedal	
Bordun 16'	(w)	Principalbaß 16'	(t)	Untersatz 32'	(w)
Rohrflöte 8'	(m)	Subbaß 16'	(w)	Violonbaß 16'	(w)
Viola di Gamba 8'	(t)	Oktavenbaß 8'	(m)	Fleute douce 8'	(maple)
Principal 4'	(t)	Quintenbaß 6'	(m)	Nachthornbaß 4'	(m)
Spitzflöte 4'	(m)	Oktavenbaß 4'	(m)	Scharfe Flöte 1' [2'?]	(t)
Gedacktflöte 3'	(m)	Waldflöte 1'	(t)	Rohrflöte 1'	(t)
Octava 2'	(m)	Mixturbaß VI	(t)	Trommetenbaß 8'	(wB)
Rohrflöte 2'	(m)	Posaunenbaß 32'	(wB*)		
		* lowest octave wood		Schallmeyenbaß 4'	(wB)
Tertia 2' [1³/₅']	(m)	Cornettin 2'	(wB)		
Plein seu[!] V–VII	(t)				

59. Merseburg, Cathedral: Ladegast organ in historical case (photograph, 2005)

Oberwerk (IV)

Sordino 8'	(wB)
Schallmey 4'	(wB)
Stahlspiel	

Particulars: (m) = metal, (t) = tin, (w) = wood, (wB) = tin-plated sheet metal.

"In addition there is also a fifth keyboard located on the [church's] lowest balcony, whose stops and other relevant information have been listed above in the Rückpositiv. For these 4 or 5 manuals there are 3 large well-built bellows. *Summa Summarum:* 66 sounding stops, 12 accessories, 10 wind chests, 5 keyboards, 6 bellows" (Engel 1855, 15). Bombard *pedaliter:* "A special stop for the Bombard, to be played in the Pedal, with bells, a cut-off valve, and 2 wind chests" (Engel 1855). Sordino 8': resonators of tin-plated sheet metal with small tin caps, [a stop] that can imitate the *Vocem humanam* (Engel 1855). According to Adlung (1768), Stahlspiel was a four-foot stop and there were two additional Pedal stops, a Posaunenbaß 16' and a metal Oktavenbaß 8' at Kammerton pitch. According to Kuhnau, who examined the organ, "the completed [Merseburg Cathedral] instrument was given over last summer, with everyone delighted by the beautiful variety of its especially quiet (*doucen*) stops and by the light action of the manual keyboards, of which there are four, and by other artful inventions" (Mattheson 1725, 235).

Accessories: cymbelstern (Großmanual); cut-off valve for each division; Oberwerk tremulant.

Manual couplers: Ow/Großmanual, Rp/Großmanual.

Pedal coupler: Ped/Großmanual (according to Adlung, only the front Pedal chests could be coupled).

Wind supply: six large bellows (three to the manuals, three to the pedal).

Pitch: Chorton.

Literature: (a) Mattheson 1725, 235; Adlung 1768, 255–57; Engel 1855, 9–21; Dähnert 1962, 72; Dehio 1999a, 535–46.

Potsdam

According to contemporary accounts, Bach played all the organs in the Prussian capital during his visit in 1747. Thus he may have visited St. Nicholas's Church.

St. Nicholas's Church/Nikolaikirche

Baroque hall church, built 1721–24; portal facade from 1752 to 1755 by Georg Wenzeslaus von Knobelsdorff using Santa Maria Maggiore in Rome as a model. Church burned down in 1795; 1835, new classical central-plan building with cupola.

Organ: 1724, installation and modification (changes are not documented) by Joachim Wagner of the organ that had been built by Johann Michael Röder in 1713 for Potsdam's old Garrison Church. 1795, organ and church burned. 1837, new instrument (II/26) by Gottlieb Heise for the new church.

Disposition 1724 (II/23) according to Kitschke (1993)

Haupt-Werk [I]	Seiten-Werk [II]	Pedal
Quintadoen 16'	Gedackt 8'	Sub-Baß 16'
Principal 8'	Principal 4'	Principal 8'
Octave 4'	Quinta 3'	Octave 4'
Quinta 3'	Octave 2'	Octave 2'
Octav 2'	Tertian 1³/₅'	Mixtur V
Quinta 1½'	Cimbel III	Posaun 16'
Mixtur V	Vox humana 8'	Trompet 8'
Trompete 8'		Trompet 4'

Accessories: Seitenwerk tremulant; cut-off valves for all divisions; main cut-off valve; bellows signal; cymbelstern.

Literature: (a) SeN, 79; Kitschke 1993, 207–10; Dehio 2000b, 779–80.

Rötha

The nearest Silbermann organs to Leipzig were the instruments in Rötha, about ten miles south of the city. We can assume Bach's acquaintance with them, even though they were built before he arrived in Leipzig.

St. George's Church/Georgenkirche

Three-aisled late Gothic hall church, built ca. 1500.

Organ: 1721, new organ by Gottfried Silbermann and Zacharias Hildebrandt for the town's patron, Christian August Freiherr von Friesen. 1796, addition of pedal coupler by Johann Gottlieb Ehregot Stephani. Changes in the nineteenth century. 1917, facade pipes sacrificed. 1979–80, restoration by Eule Orgelbau.

Disposition 1721 (II/23)

Hauptwerk (I)	Oberwerk (II)	Pedal
* Bordun 16'	* Gedackt 8'	Principal Baß 16'
Principal 8'	Quintadena 8'	* Posaune 16'
Rohr-Flöte 8'	Principal 4'	* Trommete 8'
Octava 4'	Rohr-Flöte 4'	
Spitz-Flöte 4'	Nasat 3'	
Quinta 3'	Octava 2'	
Octava 2'	Tertia 1³/₅'	
Cornet III	Quinta 1½'	
Mixtur III	Sifflet 1'	
Cymbeln II	Mixtur III	

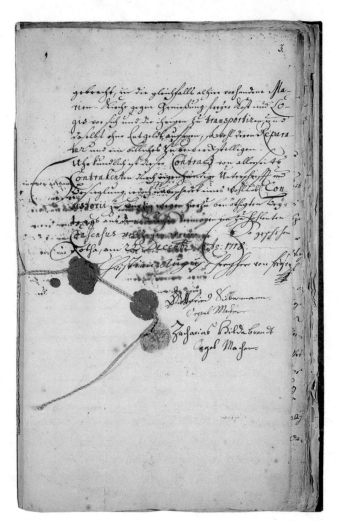

60. Rötha, St. George's
Church: Organ contract
dated December 22,
1718, with signatures
and seals of Gottfried
Silbermann and
Zacharias Hildebrandt

Particulars: * = partially reconstructed wooden pipes, resonators, or boots.

Accessory: tremulant.

Couplers: shove coupler, Ow/Hw; Hw/Ped (permanently coupled until 1793).

Compass: CD–c^3 (manuals), CD–c^1 (pedal).

Wind supply: three bellows (1935: magazine bellows with wind pressure of 76 mm WC).

Pitch (2000): Chorton a^1 = 465 Hz.

Temperament: equal (since 1832).

Literature: Dähnert 1962, 24–25; Dehio 1996b, 865–66; Greß 2001, 52–53.

61. Rötha, St. George's Church: Silbermann/Hildebrandt organ (photograph, 2006)

St. Mary's Church/Marienkirche

Pilgrimage church "of the miraculous pear-tree," erected 1510–20. Interior altered in eighteenth century.

Organ: 1721–22, new organ by Gottfried Silbermann, who added, over and above the contract, a Tertia in the manual and a permanently coupled Pedal Subbaß 16'. Changes in the nineteenth century. 1942, organ stored due to disrepair of the church. 1950, during the Bach celebrations, organ erected first in a hall of the Old City Hall, Leipzig, and then at the Berlin Bach exhibition. 1960, organ returned to St. Mary's in Rötha. 1975–77, restoration by Eule Orgelbau.

Disposition 1722 (I/11)

Manual		Pedal
Principal 8'	Octava 2'	Subbaß 16'
Gedackt 8'	Tertia $1^3/_5$'	
Octava 4'	Quinta $1^1/_2$'	
Rohr Flöte 4'	Sufflet 1'	
Nassat 3'	Cymbeln II	

Accessory: tremulant.
Coupler: pedal coupler (permanently coupled until 1834).
Compass: CD–c^3 (manual), CD–c^1 (pedal).
Wind supply: two bellows (1977: magazine bellows).
Wind pressure (2000): 75 mm WC.
Pitch (2000): Chorton, a^1 = 465 Hz.
Temperament: equal (since 1834).
Literature: Dähnert 1962, 26; Dehio 1996b, 867–68; Greß 2001, 54–55.

Waltershausen

Located between Weimar and Gotha on the trade route from Leipzig to Frankfurt, Waltershausen and the large Trost organ must at some time have been visited by Bach—perhaps on his trips to Kassel in 1732 or Mühlhausen in 1735, for example, by which time the organ would have been completed.

City Church "To God's Help"/Stadtkirche "Zur Gotteshilfe"

Baroque central-plan building, designed by Wolf Christoph Zorn of Plobsheim, built 1719–23 to replace a medieval church; model for Our Lady's Church in Dresden.

Organ: 1722–35, new organ by Tobias Heinrich Gottfried Trost. 1754, apparently enlarged by Ruppert, who is said to have added five previously uninstalled Trost stops. Rebuilds in nineteenth and twentieth centuries. 1996–98, thorough restoration by Orgelbau Waltershausen.

62. Rötha, St. Mary's Church: Silbermann organ (photograph, 2006)

Disposition ca. 1730/1998 (III/47)

Hauptwerk (II)
Portun Untersatz 16' (o)
Groß Quintadena 16' (o)
Principal 8' (o)
Gemshorn 8' (o)
Viol d'Gambe 8' (o)
Portun 8' (o)
Quintadena 8' (o)
Unda maris 8' (o)
Octava 4' (o)
Salicional 4' (o)
Röhr-Flöta 4' (t)
Celinder-Quinta 3' (o)
Super-Octava 2' (p)
Sesquialtera II (o)
Mixtura VI–VIII 2' (r)
Fagott 16' (r)
Trompetta 8' (p)

Pedal
Groß Principal 16' (o)
Sub-Bass 16' (o)
Violon-Bass 16' (o)
Octaven-Bass 8' (o)
Celinder Quinta 6' (r)
Quintadenen-Bass 16' (T)
Viol d'Gambenbass 8' (T)
Portun-Bass 8' (T)
Super-Octava 8' (T)
Röhr-Flötenbass 4' (T)
Mixtur-Bass VI 2' (T)
Posaunen-Bass 32' (r)
Posaunen-Bass 16' (o)
Trompeten-Bass 8' (o)

Brustwerk (I)
Gedackt 8' (o)
Nachthorn 8' (p)
Principal 4' (o)
Flöte douce II 4' (o)
Nachthorn 4' (r)
Gemshorn 4' (t)
Nassad-Quinta 3' (p)
Spitz-Quinta 3' (o)
Octava 2' (p)
Sesquialtera II (p)
Mixtura IV 2' (p)
Hautbois 8' (p)

Oberwerk (III)
Flöte Dupla 8' (r)
Flöte travers 8' (r)
Vagarr 8' (o)
Lieb. Principal 4' (o)
Spitz-Flöte 4' (o)
Gedackt Quinta 3' (r)
Wald-Flöte 2' (o)
Hohl-Flöte 8' (o)
Vox humana 8' (r)
Geigen-Principal 4' (o)

Particulars: (o) = original register, with less than five new pipes; (p) = partially reconstructed register, with more than five new pipes; (r) reconstructed register; (T) = transmission of pitches C–c^1 from Hauptwerk to Pedal. Hauptwerk: Salicional 4', tapered; Unda maris 8', doubled ranks of wooden pipes that share a rear wall and languid chamber. Oberwerk: Geigenprinzipal 4' stands on its own pallet box in the Bw, directly over the keydesk, and can be coupled to the Ow; Hohlflöte 8' and Vox humana 8' originally on the same toeboard, separated in 1998.

Accessories: tremblant doux for all manual divisions; two cymbelsterns (bells from Trost: g–b–d–g and c–e–g–c); bellows signal; cut-off valves allow wind to be provided to the manuals and the pedal separately.

Couplers: Ow/Hw, Bw/Hw, Hw/Ped, Bw/Ped.

63. Waltershausen, City Church "Zur Gotteshilfe": Trost organ (photograph, 1998)

Compass: C–c^3 (manuals), C–d^1 (pedal).

Wind supply: four large bellows. (1998: motors installed that simulate hand pumping; bellows can also be pumped manually. Divided channels separate manual and pedal wind.)

Wind pressure (1998): 73 mm WC.

Pitch (1998): Chorton, a^1 = 466.8 Hz.

Temperament (1998): well-tempered system based on $\frac{1}{5}$ Pythagorean comma.

Archival Source: Trost's description of the organ, Sächsische Landes- und Universitätsbibliothek, Dresden.

Literature: (a) Adlung 1768, 278–79; Heinke 1998, 21–25, 96; Vogel 1999, 1–3, 6; Friedrich 2009, 106.

Overview

An Inventory of the Organs
and Their Parts, Including
Their State of Preservation

The instruments described in Parts A and B are listed here according to their state of preservation and the survival of historical elements from the period. Manual and pedal compasses, when cited, likewise refer to the Bach period. For partially preserved instruments, the third column lists the parts that still exist: C = case; K = key desk, preserved separately; A = action; P = individual pipes; R = register(s); W = wind chest(s). Missing information is noted by —, reference instruments (from Part B) by (B).

Preserved Instruments

Place	Organ	Manual compass	Pedal compass
Altenburg, Court Church	T. H. G. Trost, 1739 (II/37)	$C–c^3$	$C–c^1$
Freiberg, Cathedral (B)	G. Silbermann, 1714 (III/44)	$CD–c^3$	$CD–c^1$
Freiberg, St. Peter's (B)	G. Silbermann, 1735 (II/32)	$CD–c^3$	$CD–c^1$
Halle, Market/Our Lady's	G. Reichel, 1664 (I/6)	$CD–c^3$	—
Lahm/Itzgrund, Palace Church (B)	H. G. Herbst, 1732 (II/29)	$CD–c^3$	$CD–d^1$
Lüneburg, St. John's	H. Niehoff, 1551; (III/28) = condition before Dropa, 1714	$CDEFGA–g^2a^2$	$CDEFGA–c^1$
Naumburg, St. Wenceslas's	Z. Hildebrandt, 1746 (III/53)	$CD–c^3$	$CD–d^1$
Rötha, St. George's (B)	G. Silbermann, 1721 (II/23)	$CD–c^3$	$CD–c^1$
Rötha, St. Mary's (B)	G. Silbermann, 1722 (I/11)	$CD–c^3$	$CD–c^1$
Sangerhausen, St. Jacobi	Z. Hildebrandt, 1728 (II/27)	$CD–c^3$	$CD–c^1$
Stöntzsch (Pegau)	J. C. Schmieder, rebuild ca. 1730 (I/9)	$CD–c^3$	$CD–c^1$
Störmthal	Z. Hildebrandt, 1723 (I/14)	$CD–c^3$	$CD–c^1$
Waltershausen, City Church (B)	T. H. G. Trost, ca. 1730 (III/47)	$C–c^3$	$C–d^1$
Zschortau, St. Nicholas's	J. Scheibe, 1746 (I/13)	$CD–c^3$	$CD–c^1$

Partially Preserved Instruments

Place	Organ	Parts preserved	Manual compass	Pedal compass
Arnstadt, New Church	J. F. Wender, 1703 (II/21)	C, P, K	CD–c³	CD–c¹
Berlin, St. Mary's (B)	J. Wagner, 1723 (III/41)	C, P	CD–c³	CD–d¹
Buttstädt, St. Michael's (B)	Herold/Finke, 1701 (II/23)	C, R	CD–c³	CD–f¹
Eisenach, St. George's	G. C. Stertzing, 1707 (IV/58)	C	C–e³	C–e¹
Görlitz, Church of St. Peter and Paul's	E. and A. H. Casparini, 1703 (III/57)	C, P	CD–c³	CD–d¹
Gotha, Castle Church	S. Hohlbeck, 1692 (II/35)	C	—	—
Gotha, St. Margaret's (B)	S. Hohlbeck, 1698 (II/25)	C (part.)	—	—
Gräfenroda, St. Laurence's (B)	J. A. Weise, 1736/2005 (II/26)	C, P	C–c³	C–c¹
Halle, Market Church	C. Contius, 1716 (III/65)	C	CD–c³	CD–c¹
Hamburg, St. Catherine's	various (1720: IV/57)	R	CDEFGA–c³	CDE–d¹
Hamburg, St. Jacobi	A. Schnitger, 1693 (IV/60)	R, wind chests	CDE–c³; CDEFGA–c³	CD–c¹
Köthen, St. Jacob's	Z. and A. Thayßner, 1676; Disposition 1756 (II/25)	C (part.)	CD–c³	CD–c¹ [d¹?]
Leipzig, St. John's	J. Scheibe, 1742 (II/22)	K, organ bench	CD–c³	CD–c¹
Lübeck, Cathedral (B)	Schnitger/Hantelmann, 1699 (III/45)	K	CDE–c³; CDEFGA–c³	CD–d¹
Lüneburg, St. Michael's	Scherer family, among others (III/32)	C	—	—
Merseburg, Cathedral (B)	enlarged by J. F. Wender, 1717 (IV/66)	C	—	—
Mühlhausen, "Brückenhof" Church	J. F. Wender, 1702; disposition 1848/2000 (I/7)	C, A	CD–c³	CD–d¹
Weißenfels, Palace Church	C. Förner, 1673 (II/30)	C	CD–c³	CD–f¹

Instruments that have not been preserved

Place	Organ	Manual compass	Pedal compass
Ammern, St. Vitus's	J. F. Wender, 1708 (I/13)	—	—
Arnstadt, Upper Church	E. Greutzscher, 1611 (II/22)	CDEFGA–g²,a²	CDEFG–c¹
Arnstadt, Palace Chapel	—	—	—
Arnstadt, Our Lady's	E. Greutzscher, 1624		
Bad Berka, St. Mary's	H. N. and Ch. W. Trebs, ca. 1750 (II/14)	—	—
Dresden, Our Lady's	G. Silbermann, 1736 (III/43)	CD–d³	CD–c¹
Dresden, St. Sophia's	G. Silbermann, 1720 (II/30)	CD–d³	CD–c¹
Erfurt, St. Augustine's	G. C. Stertzing and J. G. Schröter, 1716 (III/39)	C–e³	C–e¹

Erfurt, Prediger Church (B)	Compenius, 1579/1649; rebuild F. Volckland, 1740 (II/32)	CDEFGA–e^3	CDEFGA–d^1
Frankfurt/Oder, Franciscan Church (B)	Damm, 1754	—	—
Gera, St. John's	J. G. Finke, 1725 (III/42)	CD–c^3	C–c^1
Gera, St. Salvator's	J. G. Finke, 1722	—	—
Gera, Castle Chapel	J. G. Finke, 1721 (I/9)	—	—
Kassel, St. Martin's	H. and F. Scherer, 1612; rebuild J. N. Becker, 1730–32 (III/34, Dresden Ms.)	—	—
Köthen, St. Agnus's	J. H. Müller, 1708 (II/27?)	—	—
Köthen, Palace Church	D. Zuberbier, 1733 (II/13)	C–e^3	C–e^1
Langewiesen, Our Lady's	J. Albrecht, J. S. Erhardt, 1706; disposition (II/20) dates to before 1794	C–c^3	C–c^1
Leipzig, New Church	C. Donat, 1704 (II/21)	CD–c^3	CD–c^1
Leipzig, St. Nicholas's	Z. Thayßner, 1694 (enlargement to III/36)	CD–c^3	CD–d^1
Leipzig, St. Paul's	J. Scheibe, 1716 (III/48)	CD–?	CD–c^1
Leipzig, St. Thomas's, large organ	J. Lange, 1599; C. Donat, 1670; Disposition ca. 1700 (III/35)	CD–c^3	CD–c^1
Leipzig, St. Thomas's, small organ	1489; rebuild H. Compenius, 1630; 1665, enlarged by C. Donat; disposition ca. 1700 (II?/21)	—	—
Liebertwolkwitz (B)	Z. Hildebrandt, 1724/25 (I/13)	CD–c^3	CD–c^1
Lübeck, St. Mary's, main organ	Enlarged by F. Stellwagen, 1641; disposition recorded 1721 (III/54)	CDEFGA–c^3; CDEFGA–g^2,a^2	CDEFGA–d^1
Lübeck, St. Mary's, small organ	Enlarged by H. Kröger, 1622; disposition reconstructed 1937 (III/40)	CDEFGA–c^3	CDEFGA–d^1
Lübeck, St. Mary's, rood screen organ	M. Briegel, 1664	—	—
Lüneburg, St. Michael's, positive	J. B. Held, 1701/2000 (I/5)	C–d^3	
Mühlhausen, St. Mary's	J. F. Wender, 1720 (III/60)	—	—
Mühlhausen, St. Mary's	Ch. F. Wender, 1738 (III/43)	CD–c^3	CD–c^1
Mühlhausen, St. Blasius's	J. F. Wender, 1691 (II/29; rebuild 1708, III/37)	CD–c^3	CD–d^1
Ohrdruf, St. Michael's	K. Lehmann, H. Brunner, et al.; disposition in 1693 (II/21)	CD–c^3	CD–c^1
Ohrdruf, Palace Chapel	—	—	—
Ohrdruf, Trinity Church	H. Brunner, 1679 (I/5)	CDEFGAB–c^3	—
Potsdam, Garrison Church	J. Wagner, 1732 (III/42)	CD–c^3	CD–d^1
Potsdam, Holy Ghost Church	J. Wagner, 1730 (II/18)	CD–c^3	CD–c^1

Place	Organ	Manual compass	Pedal compass
Potsdam, St. Nicholas's (B)	Röder/Wagner, 1724 (II/23)	—	—
Taubach, St. Ursula's	H. N. Trebs, 1710 (I/11)	—	—
Weimar, Palace Church	Disposition 1737 (II/24)	$CD–c^3$	$CD–e^1$
Weimar, Palace Church, positive	S. Bidermann, 1658 (I/5)	$CDEFGA–c^3$	
Weimar, City Church	C. Junge, 1685 (II/25)	—	—
Weimar, St. Jacob's	H. N. Trebs, 1723 (II/18)	—	—
Weißensee	C. W. Schäfer, 1737 (II/32)	—	—

PART TWO

Organ Tests and Examinations

Johann Sebastian Bach's Organ Reports

Of the numerous reports written or co-written by Bach in the course of four and a half decades, only seven have been preserved. As the following overview shows, Bach's documented role as adviser and examiner of new and renovated instruments extends to more than twenty instruments. It is certain that he had a hand in many more.

1703	Arnstadt, New Church	J. F. Wender: new organ
1706	Langewiesen, Our Lady's	J. Albrecht and J. S. Erhardt: new organ
1708	Mühlhausen, St. Blasius's	J. F. Wender: renovation
ca. 1708	Ammern, St. Vitus's	J. F. Wender: new organ
1710	Taubach, St. Ursula's	H. N. Trebs: new organ
1712–14	Weimar, Palace Church	H. N. Trebs: renovation
1716	Halle, Market Church	C. Contius: new organ
1716	Erfurt, St. Augustine's	G. C. Stertzing, J. G. Schröter: new organ
1717	Leipzig, St. Paul's	J. Scheibe: new organ
1723	Störmthal	Z. Hildebrandt: new organ
1725	Gera, St. John's and St. Salvator's	J. G. Finke: new organs
1726–28	Sangerhausen, St. Jacobi	Z. Hildebrandt: new organ
1731	Stöntzsch	J. C. Schmieder: renovation
1732	Kassel, St. Martin's	N. Becker: renovation
1735	Mühlhausen, St. Mary's	C. F. Wender: renovation
1739	Altenburg, Palace Church	T. H. G. Trost: new organ
~1742	Berka, St. Mary's	H. N. Trebs: new organ
1743	Leipzig, St. John's	J. Scheibe: new organ
1746	Zschortau, St. Nicholas's	J. Scheibe: new organ
1743–46	Naumburg, St. Wenceslas's	Z. Hildebrandt: new organ

Bach's very first inspection, of the organ in Arnstadt's New Church, took place in 1703 and resulted in Bach being offered an appointment. His last documented examination is dated November 1746. Nevertheless, as late as June 1749, the Thomascantor—a consultant sought after as often by organ builders as by architects—was contacted on the advice of the Prussian court kapellmeister Carl Heinrich Graun concerning the new organ being planned for the Franciscan Church (Lower Church) in Frankfurt (Oder). In October of the same year, the organ builder Johann Jacob Donati Jr. suggested Bach as consultant for a new organ in Hartmannsdorf (BDOK V, no. B586b).

Concerning the inspection of the 1743 Scheibe organ in Leipzig's St. John's Church, for which the report does not survive, the Bach student Johann Friedrich Agricola, in his commentary to Jacob Adlung's *Musica mechanica organoedi* (Berlin 1768), writes that the instrument, "after the strictest examination of an organ that perhaps ever was undertaken, was acknowledged by Mr. Capellmeister Joh. Seb. Bach and Mr. Zacharias Hildebrand, to be above reproach" (BDOK III, no. 740). In his commentary, Agricola also refers to Bach's enthusiasm for the St. Catherine's organ in Hamburg (BDOK III, no. 739), noting especially the quality of its reeds and its 32' stops (Principal and Groß-Posaune), which in his youth had shaped Bach's conception of gravity in an organ. Thus, as early as 1708, Bach specifically requested a 32' pedal stop in the renovation of his Mühlhausen organ. In 1757, Christian Immanuel Schweinefleisch built eight new stops for the pedal division of the St. Thomas organ in Leipzig. His inclusion of an Untersatz 32' seven years after Bach's death during the time that Bach's student Johann Friedrich Doles was cantor represents the granting of what probably had been a demand of the earlier Thomascantor left unfulfilled during his lifetime.

In 1774, Carl Philipp Emanuel Bach gave an account of his father's activities as organ examiner to Johann Nicolaus Forkel, author of the first Bach biography in 1802:

> Never has anyone undertaken organ examinations so strictly and yet so fairly. He understood to the highest degree everything about organ building. If a builder worked honestly, and yet lost money on the project, he would persuade the patron to make a subsequent payment. No one knew how to register an organ as well as he. Often he shocked organists when he wanted to play their instruments, for he drew stops in his own manner, and they believed it was impossible that the way he wanted it would sound well, but they afterward heard an *Effect* that astounded them. These arts died with him. The first thing he did at an organ examination was this: He said, in fun, "Above all I must know whether the organ has good lungs," and in order to test this, he would pull on every speaking stop, and play as full-voiced as possible. At this point organ builders often became pale with fright (NBR, no. 394; BDOK III, no. 801).

A year later, Emanuel once again emphasized to Forkel his father's "special insights into the proper design of an organ, the disposition of stops, and the placing of the same" (NBR, no. 395; BDOK III, no. 803).

In formulating his written reports, Bach—and also Kuhnau, the primary author of the Halle report from 1716—relied on Andreas Werckmeister's *Erweiterte und verbesserte*

Orgel-Probe (Quedlinburg, 1698) for the arrangement of the material and for terminology (Williams 1982). It can be assumed, though, that Bach also knew Werckmeister's previous volume, *Orgelprobe, oder kurze Beschreibung, wie . . . man die Orgelwerke . . . annehmen, probiren, untersuchen . . . solle* (Frankfurt/Leipzig, 1681). In any case, Werckmeister, whose term "well-tempered" he also adopted, decisively influenced Bach's theoretical knowledge.

The following reports are translations of the German texts published in BDOK I. They are drawn for the most part from the *New Bach Reader* but differ from it at times, and the reader is encouraged to compare versions.

1. St. Blasius's Church, Mühlhausen, 1708

(NBR, no. 31; BDOK I, no. 83)

Specification for the new repair of the organ at St. Blasius's:

1. The lack of wind must be remedied by adding three new well-built (*tüchtig*) bellows that will provide sufficient wind for the Oberwerck, the Rückpositiv, and the new Brustwerk divisions.

2. The four old bellows now present must be adapted in order to provide stronger wind pressure to the new 32' Untersatz and the other Pedal stops.

3. The old Pedal wind chests must be removed and re-fitted with such wind lines as allow one to use a single stop alone, or all stops at the same time, without any change in the wind, something that has until now never been possible, and yet is highly necessary.

4. Next, the 32' Sub Bass, or so-called Untersatz, of wood, which gives the best gravity to the whole organ: This stop must now have its own wind chest.

5. The Posaunen Bass must be outfitted with new, larger resonators, and the shallots regulated differently, so that the stop can produce much more gravity.

6. The new glockenspiel desired by the parishioners shall be put in the Pedal. It consists of 26 bells sounding at 4' pitch, which bells the parishioners will acquire at their own expense, and the organ builder will subsequently make them playable.

    As regards the Obermanual, here, instead of the Trompette (which will be removed), there shall be a

7. Fagotto sounding at 16' pitch, which is useful for all kinds of new ideas, and sounds quite delicate in concerted music. In addition, instead of the Gemshorn (which likewise shall be removed), there will be a

8. Viol di Gamba 8', which will blend admirably with the present Salicional 4' in the Rückpositiv. Also, instead of the Quinta 3' (which also will be removed), a

9. Nassat 3' could be fit in.

The remaining stops already in the Obermanual can remain, as can the entire Rückpositiv, although as part of the renovation they must be completely tuned from scratch.

10. As far as the important new little Brustpositiv is concerned, the following stops could be placed in it:

In the facade, three Principalia, namely:

1. Quinta 3'
2. Octava 2'
3. Schalemoy 8'
   all three of the above from good 14-worthy [87.5%] tin.
4. Mixtur III.
5. Tertia, which, by drawing other stops, can make possible a complete and beautiful Sesquialtera.
6. Fleute douce 4'; and finally, a
7. Stillgedackt 8', which is perfect for accompanying concerted vocal music and, being made from good wood, sounds far better than a metal Gedackt.

11. There must be a coupler between this Brustpositiv and the OberWerck manuals. And finally, in addition to a thorough tuning of the entire organ, the tremulant must be adjusted so that it beats at the proper rate.

2. St. Ursula's Church, Taubach, 1711

(NBR, no. 42; BDOK I, no. 84)

Whereas Mr. Heinrich Trebs, the bearer, an organ builder experienced in his art, requests me to give him a testimonial concerning the work he has done in this principality, I have neither been able nor desired to refuse him, since he merits it too well; accordingly I assure the gracious reader of this letter that he has applied his most praiseworthy industry to the work he has done in these parts, and I, as one appointed to inspect the same, have found that both in the fulfillment of the contract and in subsequent work he has proven himself a reasonable and conscientious man, for he agreed to the lowest price and he afterward performed the work agreed upon with the greatest industry.
Weimar, Feb. 16, 1711

Joh. Sebast. Bach,
Court Organist and Chamber Musician

3. Market Church of Our Lady, Halle, 1716

(NBR, no. 59; BDOK I, no. 85)

Since it has pleased the Most Honorable *Collegium Marianum* of the Town of Halle to request in writing that the undersigned appear here the day before yesterday, that is, on the 29th of April last, to examine and investigate in all its parts the large new organ in the Church of Our Lady, constructed by the Grace of God and to His Glory by the organ builder Herr Christoff Cuncius, and to note down whatever we should find that is well done (*tüchtig*) or not so well done therein, and in general make known our judgment; accordingly, in most dutiful response to this most gracious request and the trusting confidence expressed in our experience and skill, we made our appearance here on the appointed day and, after having had the high summons repeated to us orally, undertook in God's Name the examination of the new organ in said Church. To wit, we (1) found the bellows chamber large enough for the bellows and well protected against bad weather, but have also noted that, since the chamber's window faces west, the bellows are exposed to excessive heat from the sun, and therefore a curtain or some other protection against the sun will be needed for the times when the organ is not in use. As for (2) the bellows themselves, which are ten in number (although the builder promised only nine in the contract, perhaps because he thought *quod superflua non noceant* [there would be no harm in abundance], and that an even number was preferable to an odd for the sake of arranging the bellows, which are set opposite each other), they might indeed still demonstrate the specified capacity and the builder's industry, but the wind did not drive the liquid in the wind gauge we applied to the 35 to 40 degrees otherwise required in organs of this size and found in other organs having a good wind supply, but only to 32 or 33 degrees. Accordingly, one observes a shaking in the bellows when the Hauptwerk is played. Nevertheless this would be tolerated if only the Oberwerck, the middle manual, did not shake—for this is counted among the major faults.

But apart from this we found (3) no visible defect in the wind chests, which also withstood the test of having all the keys in both the manual and pedal keyboards pressed down at the same time without our noticing any leakage except a little in the middle manual, which, however, is caused by the toe boards not being screwed in firmly enough, and can easily be corrected. Under the pallets the springs have not been doubled or tripled, such as poor builders often do to prevent ciphers, but all are single. Because of this, the keyboard should be comfortable to play. Yet it will nevertheless be necessary to make it somewhat lighter, at the same time not compromising the quick return of the keys and not causing any ciphering—all of which the master has promised to do. (4) As for the organ's internal layout, clearly it would have been better to have more room, so that everything would not have had to be placed so close together and could be reached more easily. For the rest, (5) all the stops specified in the contract are present and made of the materials there mentioned, except that instead of the specified metal Gemshorn Bass 16' a wooden Untersatz or SubBass 32' has been provided, the size of its pipes making up for not using metal.

Furthermore, the following useful stops have been built over and above the contract:

Spitzflöte	2'
Quinta	3'
Octava	2'
Nachthorn	4'
Quinta, open	6'

These five stops are made of metal.

On the other hand, the following have not been built:

the Fagott Bass, of tin	8'
Gedackt, of metal	4'
Waldflöte, ditto	2'
Rohr Flöte, ditto	12'

Likewise, he has provided two 3-rank Cymbals instead of the two 2-rank ones called for. And however one deals with (6) concerns regarding the alloy of the metal, it is altogether easy to see (and this is fairly commonplace) that in the stops not in the facade there has been more saving of tin than of lead; so that the pipe resonators in the instrument could or should have been somewhat thicker.

It is true that light should play off the pipes standing in the façade, and probably the best part of the good tin has been used for them; that they do not shine must not be blamed on the builder, but on the soot that has fallen upon them.

On the other hand, it is the builder's fault if the sound—because the voicing has left something to be desired, especially of the large pipes—is not audible and clear. This fault is found here in various pipes, among others, in the Subbass 32' and Posaunenbass 32', and also in the other reeds. However, as well as promising to tune the organ here and there, since we found all three manuals still somewhat out of tune, and to set it in the passably good temperament he at one time showed us, Herr Cuncius has also promised to improve the voicing of some of the pipes, something which, indeed, would have been better had it occurred before the examination, and it also would have been better if we could have inspected the parts that are still missing—namely, the

Coupler,
2 Tremulants,
2 Cymbelsterns,
a movable sun operable from a stop in the Oberwerk, and
the Vogelgesang (bird song).

This, then, is what we, the undersigned, in obedience to our duty and in the interest of truth must report concerning this organ. For the rest, we wish it may always perform well, to the honor of the Most High and the especial renown of its Most Noble Patrons, as well as of the whole worthy town, in peace and tranquility, for holy inspiration and devotion, and may it last for many years. Halle, Feast of SS. Philip and James [May 1], 1716

Johann
Kuhnau, mpp [in his hand]
Christian Friedrich Rolle
Joh: Sebast: Bach

4. St. Augustine's Church, Erfurt, 1716

(NBR, no. 62; BDOK I, no. 86)

Testimonial of the Examiners:

Whereas we, the undersigned, have tested the new organ built by Herr Johann Georg Schröter for St. Augustine's, the Lutheran church in Erfurt, having been appointed examiners for this purpose, and have found, after sufficient investigation, that it has been built correctly and diligently according to the contract; moreover, the said Herr Schröter also has requested us not to fail to give testimony to his diligence. Now, therefore, we have sought herewith, as is fair, to gratify his wish, and must add, to his credit, that (as has already been mentioned) he has faithfully fulfilled the terms of the contract drawn up for this work; what is more, it is only proper that he be congratulated on the fact that the first organ he has completed as a master builder has turned out so well, and thus there is no doubt that with respect to any further work he may undertake, that he will likewise complete it diligently and untiringly, applying the knowledge that God has given him. This we neither could nor would refuse him, out of respect for the truth.

Dated Erfurt, July 31, 1716.

(L.S.)   Johann Sebastian Bach,
Concertmaster and Court Organist to the Prince of Saxe-Weimar
(L.S.)   Johann Anton Weise,
Organ builder of Arnstadt

5. St. Paul's Church, Leipzig, 1717

(NBR, no. 72; BDOK I, no. 87)

Since at the desire of Your Most Noble Magnificence Dr. Rechenberg, currently rector of the Most Worshipful University of Leipzig, I have undertaken the examination of the partly newly built and partly renovated organ in St. Paul's Church, I have done this to the best of my ability, noting any faults, and in general as regards the entire organ project, would like to put in writing the following:

1.) As concerns the case, it clearly cannot be denied that it is very tightly confined, and it is thus difficult to reach each part in the event that, with time, something needs repair. Herr Scheibe, builder of said organ, offers as excuse that, first, he did not build [design?*] the case himself and he has had to accommodate the internal layout to it as best he could, and second, he was not granted the additional space he had desired in order to arrange the layout more capaciously.

2.) The usual main parts of an organ—wind chests, bellows, pipes, roller boards and other parts—have been well and carefully built, and there is nothing to call attention to, other than that the wind must be made more steady throughout, so that the occasional wind surges might be avoided. The roller boards should indeed have been secured in frames, in order to avoid ciphering in bad weather, but since Herr Scheibe built roller boards [without frames], as is his custom, and guarantees that this is as good as using frames, this was allowed to pass.

3.) The stops listed in the disposition, as well as everything included in the contract, have been provided, in both quality and quantity, except that two reeds—namely, Schalmey 4' and Cornet 2'—had to be left out at the order of the Worshipful University, and in their place an Octava 2' in the Brustwerk and a Hohlflöte 2' in the Hinterwerck were added.

4.) The various faults revealed in the uneven voicing must and can be improved immediately by the organ builder—that is, that the lowest pipes in the Posaunenbass 16' and the Trompetenbass 8' do not speak so roughly and with such a rattle, but with a pure and firm tone; and then the remaining pipework that is uneven must be diligently corrected and made even, which can be conveniently done when the entire instrument is once again tuned—and indeed, this should happen when the weather is better than it has been recently.

5.) To be sure, the organ's playing action should be somewhat lighter and the keyfall should not be so deep. The very narrowly confined case made it impossible to build the action in any other way, so one must let it go this time, and in any case, it is still possible to play in a manner that one need not fear a key will stick while playing.

6.) The organ builder had to build a new wind chest for the Brust over and above the contract—because the old wind chest that was to have been used instead of building a new one was, firstly, made with a table, and thus twisted and warped, and secondly, was also built in the old manner, with a short-octave bass, missing the remaining notes, which could not be added to it in order for all three keyboards to be the same, and using the old chest would have created inequality (*deformitè* [*sic*]), so it was highly necessary that a new one be built, both to avoid the problems that would soon become troublesome and to keep a fine uniformity (*conformitè* [*sic*]) among the manuals. Even without any reminder

* The verb used here, verfertigen, can mean "to build" and also "to design."

from me, the organ builder is to be reimbursed for the parts newly built over and above the contract, and therefore not lose because of them.

The organ builder also requested that I lodge a complaint with the Most Praiseworthy University regarding various items charged to his account that were not agreed to—namely, among other things, the carvings, gilding, and the fees received by Herr Vetter for his oversight—for which he is not responsible, nor has it ever been customary for the builder to assume these expenses (otherwise he would have calculated his estimate differently). He very respectfully requests likewise not to incur any expense because of them.

Finally, it cannot go unmentioned that (1) at least as far as the window rises up behind it, the organ should be protected from further threats of weather damage by means of a small brick wall or a strong piece of sheet iron placed inside the window; and (2) it is customary and most necessary that the organ builder provide a one-year warranty in order to fully take care of any problems that may occur, which he is willing to do, as long as he is promptly and fully reimbursed for the costs he has incurred over-and-above the contract.

This is what I have found it necessary to make note of as regards the examination of the organ. Placing myself entirely at the disposal of Your Most Noble Magnificence, Dr. Rechenberg, and the entire Worshipful University, I remain,

Your most obedient and humble
Joh: Seb: Bach.
Capellmeister
to the Prince of Anhalt-Cöthen

Leipzig,
December 17, 1717

6. St. Nicholas's Church, Zschortau, 1746

(NBR, no. 235; BDOK I, no. 89)

Since His Highborn Lord, Herr Heinrich August Sahrer von Sahr, Hereditary Liege Lord and Magistrate of Zschortau and Biesen, as Most Respected Patron of the Church of Zschortau has requested me, the undersigned, to go through and examine in said church the organ newly built by Johann Scheibe of Leipzig; and I, in the presence of said Lord of Sahr, painstakingly went through it part by part, tried it out, and carefully compared it with the original contract put before me, drawn up between the inspectors and Herr Scheibe on June 30, 1744; and have found not only that the contract has been fulfilled in each and every way, with everything soundly, diligently, and well built, and with the exception of a few minor problems that Herr Scheibe took care of on the spot, there is nowhere a major fault, rather there are the following stops built over-and-above the contract, namely:

1. Quinta Thön 16', of wood
2. Viola di Gamba 8', of wood

3. Fleute-Travers 4', of wood

4. Super Octava 1', metal

5. A coupler (*Angehänge*) between Manual and Pedal,

all of which were found and adjudged to be well made and good.

Therefore, in the interest of truth, and to the renown of the builder, I have wished to attest to the same over my own signature and with my own seal affixed.

Dated: Zschortau, August 7, 1746.

> Joh: Sebast: Bach.
> Royal Polish and Electoral Saxon
> Court Composer

7. St. Wenceslas's Church, Naumburg, 1746

(NBR, no. 236; BDOK I, no. 90)

Since Your Most Noble and Most Wise Council of the Town of Naumburg has graciously allowed us, the undersigned, the honor of visiting the organ thoroughly repaired and almost completely rebuilt by Herr Hildebrandt and examining it according to the contract made in respect of the same, which was given to us; therefore, we have conscientiously and dutifully done so, and it was revealed that: Each and every part specified and promised in the contract—namely, keyboards, bellows, wind chests, wind lines, pedal and keyboard actions along with their various parts, registers, and stops, both open and stopped, as well as reeds—is really there; also, in general each and every part has been made with appropriate care, and the pipes have been properly built from the materials promised. At the same time it must be mentioned that an extra bellows and a stop named Unda Maris have been provided over the contract. Nevertheless, it will be necessary to encourage Herr Hildebrandt to go through the entire instrument once more, stop by stop, in order to achieve more evenness in the voicing as well as in the key and stop actions. Once again we affirm that this is our conscientious and dutiful testimony, which we have signed with our own hands and corroborated with our customary seals. Naumburg, September 27, 1746.

> *Joh: Sebastian Bach*
> Royal Polish and Electoral Saxon Court Composer
> Gottfried Silbermann
> Royal Polish and Electoral Saxon Court and State Organ Builder

Instructions for Examining Organs

At the beginning of the last century, a manuscript was uncovered during repairs to an organ in a church in Saxony that, according to its title, was based on an oral transmission of the organ builder to the electoral Saxon court, Gottfried Silbermann, who died in 1753. The manuscript, privately owned, comprises sixteen numbered paragraphs and a postscript written on eight pages in small quarto format. Even though the attribution to Silbermann remains doubtful, the instructions nevertheless provide a concise and illuminating enumeration of the main points of an organ test in the middle of the eighteenth century.

This translation is based on the text transmitted in "Eine Erinnerung an den Altmeister des Orgelbaues Gottfried Silbermann," *Zeitschrift für Instrumentenbau* 30 (1909–10), 1133–35.

A Proper and Thorough Guide
as to how an honest organ examiner should
examine a new organ using fundamental principles,
so that he can be justified in the sight of God and the world,
written down as heard from the mouth of the late Mr. Gottfried Silbermann,
formerly Royal Court Organ Builder in Freyberg.

1. First, an organ examiner should and must look at the gallery to determine whether it has a firm foundation and is built so that it can carry an organ with such and such number of registers and that over a long period of time it will not sag, thereby causing irreparable damage to the church (of which enough tragic examples have come to light). A well-informed organ builder will have discernment and be able to assess these matters.

2. The examiner should also pay attention to the design (*Archidectur*), whether the organ case is well proportioned, and especially should notice—as it is customary for a drawing to be available, such a drawing being quite necessary—whether the organ itself agrees with the depiction in the drawing.

3. When ample space is available in a gallery one should take care not to build things too close together; everything—such as the pallets, trackers, and the pipework—should be easy to reach. When an organ is too crowded and something quite minor occurs—as is often the case—and one cannot reach in or only with difficulty and at great pains, then often more harm is done than good. This would be a major fault.

4. The stopknobs must be attached to the shafts precisely and securely so they need not be pulled out even half a foot before the stop has fully actuated the wind-chest slider, for both the stopknob and the slider must begin to move and continue to move exactly together.

5. The toeboards must be screwed to their wind chests neither too tightly nor loosely, for if they are screwed in too tightly, the sliders will pull badly, at times tearing the wood. If, however, they are screwed in too loosely, then the wind leaks from the chest through the toeboards, causing a cipher and robbing the instrument of its power. Care must be taken to find the middle road.

6. The keyboards also must be made in such a way that they are easy to play and do not make a big clattering noise that sometimes is really hateful and irksome, for if the pallet springs are too strong, then they become hard to play, something simply not permitted.

7. There must not be more than one spring for each pallet, for where there are more it is an error attributable to the laziness and inattention of the organ builder and definitely not permitted.

8. There is much one could say about the bellows. They must be built in proportion to the organ; for example, an instrument with 24 to 30 stops would require 3 bellows, 7–8 feet long, 5–6 feet wide. They must be made from really good, flawless wood and leather, and bound by strong horse veins,[1] be made with one fold, and able to be raised rather high, so that the wind lasts that much longer (this is especially advantageous for the pumpers). It is also very good and much better when the intake valves are screwed on beneath the bellows, so if necessary they can be unscrewed and, with the help of a light and half of one's body, one can look around the whole bellows and easily correct a problem. The wood used for the bellows must have a glue solution poured on over and

---

1. Werckmeister refers to covering or binding the bellows with horse veins (*Roß-Adern*): "It is very good when the bellows are well bound and protected with horse veins, and it is best when the horse veins are fastened with wooden brads and glued" (Werckmeister 1698, 3; Krapf 1976, 2). Werckmeister also claims that when horse veins are used it is no longer necessary to use counterweights to ensure the wind pressure remains constant (Werckmeister 1698, 46; Krapft 1976, 37). Adlung describes horse veins as "either straps or horse skin or actual dried horse veins, leg tendons or sinews. They are more durable than common leather which has a tendency to crack" (Adlung 1768, 42; cited in Krapf 1976, 2).

over so that worms will not harm the wood. Also, the bellows must be placed in a location where neither sun nor moon can shine on them, either within masonry walls, or at least in a chamber that can be closed up with boards. The bellows must be placed on a framework that stands at least four feet high that is very securely set up so that one can, if necessary, crawl under it. However, if the bellows rest flat on the floor and not on a framework, this is a major fault because then the bellows pull in dust, feathers, cobwebs, and other dirty things, and blow it along with the wind into the wind-chest channels and from there into the pipework, which causes the pipes not to be able to speak—which is absolutely not permissible. The bellows must work at their peak in an organ, so one must give this appropriate and scrupulous attention.

9. The wind chest is the whole heart—indeed, the primary essence—of an organ, and it should generally be made of very good quality oak that has previously been soaked in a large beer cauldron (so that the vapors settle better on one another),[2] because the degree of accuracy to which the boards must be fashioned cannot be described. One must also use only one kind of wood—oak and nothing but oak—for the wind chest. That is, toeboards, sliders, and the spacers (between the sliders) on the wind chest—everything must be of oak. When this is not the case, the error may not be excused. One also should not assume that a knowledgeable organ builder will necessarily do this, because one still finds organs where the wind chests are made of oak, to be sure, but the toeboards are of linden and the sliders are of pine, which certainly not even a bungler would do, no matter how inexperienced he might be.

10. Now an even more difficult point: At times one finds some pretty large bleed holes bored in the wind chests of organs, or there will be small holes bored in the toeboards next to the pipes, or sometimes even in the metal—and also in the wooden—pipes themselves, below where they stand in the holes of the toeboards. (Mr. Silbermann and Mr. Trost in Altenburg call them "rogue's holes" [*Schelmlöcher*].[3]) Certain unscrupulous organ build-ers make such holes so the "false" wind [i.e., wind leaked through the bad construction] that results from laziness and inattention to their work will escape through these bleed holes, because if this did not happen there would be a terrible cipher—indeed, such an instrument would be unplayable. But an instrument loses its energy and full power in this way. An organ examiner must be on guard here so such careless people do not fool him. Indeed, it is impossible to describe how carefully one must look at and pay attention to every little thing if one does not want to be deceived.

11. The examiner should push off all the stops, have the bellows pumped, and then he should lay both arms on the keyboard so all pallets are opened at the same time. When this

---

2. Adequate moisture content inhibits fungi and insects and also can render wood more permeable.

3. "Rogue's holes" is a rough translation. *Schelmisch* or *schelm*-like means "impish," "mischie-vous," "roguish"; a *Schelm* is a "devil." The term is also used for carrion and can mean a depraved or profligate person.

happens and one hears no run or cipher—that is, no pipes are making a gentle sound—then the wind chest is very good and not to be faulted and the organ builder cannot be praised enough. If one discovers the opposite, however, and there is a run, it is one of the most serious faults, and such an organ builder must know nothing about the bleed holes discussed above, or else he would quickly have seen to it. One can also carry out this test right at the beginning, because when there is nothing heard, then the wind chest is good, but an instrument that has a run, where pipes quietly sound that shouldn't sound, can never ever be brought perfectly into tune. Further,

12. one can pull out all the stops and with doubled chords play continuous sixteenth notes, and if one observes a gulping in the wind, again, it is a fault and the gulping results from a problem in the bellows—in particular, from valves being too small that are inside at the front where the wind goes from the bellows into the channel, a place where one cannot get to, though, without removing the bellows.

13. One also must put neither too little nor too much weight on the bellows; the amount must be established by using the wind gauge. An organ builder or examiner will know how these are made, but to describe all this here would be very complicated.

14. An examiner must have a good understanding of temperament. If it is correct, then all of the stops are checked, one at a time, for accuracy. Normally the temperament is set on the 4-foot Principal, and all the other pipes are tuned to it. In this way one can easily hear what is pure and what is impure, for if a pipe beats, it is not in tune.

15. The Principal must be nicely cleaned and polished like silver. It must also be sharply voiced (*eine scharfe Intonation haben*)—indeed, all the pipework should be. Mr. Silbermann uses the same material for the inner pipes as he does for the Principal in the facade, which of course costs more but also has a better effect than if one uses three parts lead and one part tin—that is, common metal. Finally,

16. the speech of the reeds, such as Regal, Vox humana, and Posaunen-Baß, should not be primitive (*grausam*), but nicely elegant (*fein lieblich*)—especially the Posaunen-Baß, which should speak promptly, not somewhat delayed, which is extremely annoying.

If the shallots of the Posaunen-Baß are made from wood, they must be treated inside with a glue solution so that woodworms do not get in, but if the shallots are metal, this is not necessary, and they are much better, although costlier. The same glue solution must be poured into the Subbaß pipes, also on account of worms, and because the pipes will sound much brighter. If there is a Violdigamben-Baß 16'—which is something incomparably beautiful—then the languids must have a tin lining; the mouth labia, on the other hand, should be made of good pear wood. The same pear wood mouth labia must be used on other pedal stops, such as Violon 16' and Principal 16', in order for them, too, to be properly built.

Certainly the scaling of instruments in large cities must be somewhat wide, especially in the large churches, but of course this will demand more wind. In sum, an organ builder can build a lasting reputation, but he also can discredit himself if he does not consider his conscience. If he has done his best, then it is only right he should be paid well for his work, and also the examiner should be given a nice gratuity.

Note:

As to the bellows, the following is also to be kept in mind: When they are placed below—where this is at all possible—then the wind is always much stronger than when the wind is brought into the organ from above, on the side, or behind the organ.

PART THREE

Organ Builders

Sections A and B give short biographies of organ builders to whom Johann Sebastian Bach had a personal connection or whose organs he came into contact with. Other organ builders and organ-building firms are listed without comprehensive information in Section C. As far as possible, dates of birth and death or of years of business are provided. Under "Organs" in Sections A and B, organs associated with Bach are listed first, followed by additional, complementary instruments. Dates in parentheses relate to the completion of the organ. There has been no attempt to make this directory complete.

Organ Builders with a Personal Connection to Bach

Albrecht, Johann

(d. January 22, 1719, in Coburg)

Presumably journeyman with Christoph Junge, whose organ in Erfurt's Merchants' Church he completed after Junge's death in 1687. Moved his workshop to Coburg. His best-known student was Johann Sebastian Ehrhardt, with whom he built the organ in Langewiesen.

Organs: Part I. A: Langewiesen (new organ, 1706).— Coburg, St. Moritz (rebuild).
Literature: BDOK II, no. 18; Fischer/Wohnhaas 1994, 14.

Becker, Johann Nikolaus

(b. before 1700)

Son-in-law of Johann Friedrich Wender, who presumably trained him to be an organ builder. Becker appears also to have had a close association with Johann Friedrich Stertzing, whose successor he became; in 1724 he took over work in Merseburg Cathedral. In the baptismal book in St. Mary's, Mühlhausen, Becker is called "Royal Hesse Privileged Organ Builder" in 1720.

Organs: Part I. A: Kassel, St. Martin's (rebuild, 1732).— Oberteutschenthal, St. Laurence's (translocation from St. Maxim, Merseburg, 1723; case preserved).
Literature: BDOK II, no. 316; Stüven 1964, 85; Kröhner 1995, 84.

Contius (Cuncius, Cuntzius), family of organ builders

• **Christoph** (b. 1676 in Wernigerode, d. November 8, 1722, in Halle)

According to Gerber, Contius lived in Halberstadt and renovated the Grüningen organ built 1595; he later moved his workshop to Halle.

Organs: Part I. A: Halle, Market Church (new organ, 1716).— Tharschengen (new organ, 1706). Abbenrode (new organ, 1708; restored 1975). Glaucha, St. George's (new organ, 1720).

Literature: Werckmeister 1705; Adlung 1768, 231 (Glaucha disposition); Gerber I, 775; Stüven 1964, 92.

· **Heinrich Andreas** (d. March 27, 1795, in Valmiera, Latvia)

Son of Christoph C., apprenticed with Joachim Wagner, and in 1748 became Christian Joachim's successor as organ examiner in Halle (Saale). He left Halle in 1763, was in Reval (now Tallinn) from 1768 to1771, and was working in Riga in 1783. Johann Sebastian Bach wrote a recommendation for Contius in 1748.

Organs: Part I. B: Frankfurt/Oder (proposal, 1749).— Löbejün, St. Peter's (repairs, 1737). Giebichenstein near Halle, St. Bartholomew's (new organ, 1743). Dieskau, St. Anne's (new organ, 1750). Glaucha near Halle (new organ, 1751). Niemberg, St. Ursula's (various repairs, 1756–61).

Literature: Adlung 1768, 230–31 (Giebichenstein disposition); Stüven 1964, 100, 107, 109, 114, 116, 118; BJ 1977, 137; Grosmane 2003, 43.

Ehrhardt, Johann Sebastian

(baptized October 6, 1676, in Gehren)

As an apprentice, built the organ in Langewiesen with Johann Albrecht, and thereafter was active as an independent builder in Heldburg; he also worked in the area of Coburg.

Organs: Part I. A: Langewiesen (assisted building new organ, 1706).— Gauerstadt (new organ, 1723).

Literature: Fischer/Wohnhaas 1994, 80.

Finke (Fincke, Finck), Johann Georg

(b. ca. 1685, buried May 26, 1749, in Saalfeld)

It is probable that he learned organ building from Peter Herold, Apolda, and that he was working in his workshop before 1700. In Jena after 1707, then in Saalfeld; he became citizen of Neustadt/Orla in 1726. After his death, the Saalfeld workshop apparently was carried on by his son Johann Georg Jr. On the basis of the renovations (enlargements) to the St. Johan's organ in Gera, Kümmerle proposes that Finke took joy in experimentation and was "in multiple ways ahead of his time." Fischer assumes that Johann Christoph Wiegleb was his student.

Organs: Part I. A: Gera, St. John's (new organ, 1725). Gera, St. Salvator's (new organ, 1722). Gera, Castle Chapel (new organ, 1721?). Part I. B: Buttstädt, St. Michael's (new organ, completed 1701?; preserved).— Schwarzburg, parish church (new organ, 1713). Gera, city church, small organ (new organ, 1715).

Literature: Adlung 1768, 271–72; Gerber II, 123; Kümmerle I, 405; Fischer 1969, 39; Fischer/Wohnhaas 1994, 93–94; Friedrich 2001a.

Hildebrandt, family of organ builders

• **Zacharias** (b. 1688 in Münsterberg/Silesia, d. November 10, 1757, in Dresden)
Probably learned joinery from his father; it is not known where he learned organ building. On December 9, 1713, he began working in the workshop of Gottfried Silbermann. They worked together on a number of instruments and both signed the contract in 1718 for the new organ for St. George's Church in Rötha. In 1722 Hildebrandt became a citizen of Freiberg, and he married on September 14 in Langhennersdorf. In the same year there erupted a quarrel with Silbermann, after Hildebrandt, in defiance of their agreement, repaired the St. Peter's organ in Freiberg, and in Störmthal contracted to build a new organ by undercutting Silbermann's quoted price. In 1727 he moved to Sangerhausen, where he stayed for four years; in 1730 he was named "Royal Saxe-Weißenfels Court Organ Builder." In addition to organs, Hildebrandt earned a reputation for his harpsichords and lute-harpsichords built in the years 1738–40. A reconciliation with Silbermann occurred before the examination of Hildebrandt's organ in Naumburg at the latest. In 1750, Silbermann conferred oversight to Hildebrandt of the new organ in Dresden's Court Church. Silbermann's sole heir and nephew, Johann Daniel, took over this position in 1753, and Hildebrandt submitted his disposition for the Church of the Three Kings in Dresden. Hildebrandt became Johann Scheibe's successor as university organ builder in Leipzig in 1749.

Organs: Part I. A: Naumburg, St. Wenceslas's (new organ, 1746; preserved). Sangerhausen, St. Jacobi (new organ, 1728; preserved). Störmthal (new organ, 1723; preserved). Part I. B: Liebertwolkwitz (new organ, 1725). Rötha, St. George's (new organ, 1721; contract co-signed with G. Silbermann; preserved).

Literature: Dähnert 1962; Schrammek 1983a, 60–61; Friedrich 2002.

• **Johann Gottfried** (b. 1724 in Störmthal or Liebertwolkwitz, d. 1775 in Dresden)
Son of Zacharias Hildebrandt, pupil of his father and Joachim Wagner, worked with his father (among other places in Naumburg) and was his father's successor. His workshop was in Dresden.

Organs: Hamburg, St. Michael's (new organ, 1762–71).

Schäfer, Conrad Wilhelm

(b. before 1670, d. after 1737)
Organ builder in Kindelbrück (Thuringia). The earliest reference to his work is from 1685, when he repaired the bellows in the organ in Sömmerda.

Organs: Part I. A: Weißensee, St. Peter and Paul's (enlargement, 1735–37).

Scheibe, Johann

(b. 1680, probably in Zschortau, d. September 3, 1748, in Leipzig)
Married Anna Rosine Hesse in 1705 and from that date was citizen of Leipzig. As university organ builder he was responsible for all the organs in the city; he carried out

major renovations at the New Church, St. Thomas's, and St. Nicholas's, and built a new organ for St. John's. He was contracted to renovate and enlarge the organ in the university's St. Paul's Church in 1710 even though proposals had been received from Christoph Donat Jr. (whose workshop he later took over) and Gottfried Silbermann; Adam Horatio Casparini consulted on the project. From that point he lived in St. Paul's College, the rent for which the university paid in his last years. His organ facades are composed of concave and convex surfaces, crowned with volutes, and give no hint as to the arrangement of the various divisions. According to Johann Friedrich Agricola, Zacharias Hildebrandt and Johann Sebastian Bach gave Scheibe's organ for St. John's in Leipzig one of the most exacting examinations of a new organ ever undertaken (NBR, no. 306; BDOK III, nos. 666 and 740). According to Rubardt, Scheibe was "a particularly characterful individual, a right thinking and articulate man who had justly earned J. S. Bach's high esteem." Johann Adolph, Scheibe's son, launched an attack against Bach and other musicians in 1737 (NBR, no. 343; BDOK II, no. 400; Maul 2010).

Organs: Part I. A: Leipzig, St. Paul's Church (renovation and enlargement, 1710–16; examination, 1717). Leipzig, St. Thomas's (renovation, 1720–22). Leipzig, New Church (renovation, 1721–22). Leipzig, St. Nicholas's (renovation, 1724–25). Leipzig, St. John's (new organ, 1741–43). Zschortau (new organ, 1746; preserved).

Literature: Schering 1926, 257; Rubardt 1963; Klotz 1980a; Dähnert 1980, 308; Henkel 1986, 44–50; Theobald 1986, 81–89; Kaufmann 2000, 404–9; Rubardt 2005; Butler 2011, 87–101.

Schröter, Johann Georg

(b. August 20, 1683, in Berlstedt [Thuringia], d. ca. 1750)

Pupil of J. C. Vockeroth in Berlstedt; from 1712, citizen and organ builder in Erfurt. Became privileged organ builder on October 24, 1716, which gave him the right to repair all "organs in the city and province." Some twenty-two of his organs can be documented in and around Erfurt, of which ten dispositions have been transmitted by Adlung. In 1716 he completed the organ begun by Stertzing Sr. in Erfurt's St. Augustine's Church (which led Löffler to posit a relationship to Stertzing's workshop). Johann Sebastian Bach wrote a recommendation for Schröter in 1716 (NBR, no. 62; BDOK I, no. 86).

Organs: Part I. A: Erfurt, St. Augustine's (new organ, 1716).— Kerspleben near Erfurt (new organ, 1720). Erfurt, All Saints' Church (new organ, 1724). Wandersleben (new organ, 1724). Erfurt, Hospital Church (new organ, 1735). Andisleben (new organ, 1735).

Literature: Adlung 1768; Löffler 1928, 131; Klotz 1980b; Fischer/Wohnhaas 1994, 377.

Schweinefleisch, Johann Christian Immanuel

(b. May 16, 1721, in Mockern, near Altenburg; d. April 15, 1771)

Attended the St. Thomas's School in Leipzig until 1731. Nephew of Tobias Heinrich Gottfried Trost, with whom he apprenticed in 1737–42; he helped build the organ in Altenburg's palace church. In 1742–43, as a journeyman with Heinrich Nicolaus Trebs, he took part in building the organ in Bad Berka. He later worked with Zacharias Hildebrandt. After Scheibe's death in 1748, Schweinefleisch took care of the organs in Leipzig's principal churches. In 1770–71 he installed a new organ in Böhlitz's town church (it had apparently been used as an interim instrument in St. Thomas's, Leipzig, during the rebuild of the main organ by Mauer).

Organs: Part I. A: Altenburg, palace church (assistant on new organ, 1739; preserved). Bad Berka (assistant on new organ, 1743). Leipzig, St. Thomas's (renovation, 1755).

Literature: BDOK II, no. 515. Löffler 1926; Löffler 1931; Friedrich 1989, 69.

Silbermann, Gottfried

(b. January 14, 1683, in Kleinbobritzsch near Frauenstein, d. August 4, 1753, in Dresden)

Son of a court carpenter. His brother Andreas (1678–1743) worked in Alsace from 1699. Werner Müller disproved the story told by Joseph Krömer (under the pseudonym Ludwig Mooser) that Andreas Silbermann had studied with Eugenio Casparini in Görlitz. Gottfried Silbermann received his training from his brother between 1701 and 1705 and ran his brother's Straßburg workshop during his absence in Paris in 1705–7, after which Gottfried himself traveled throughout France. In 1710, in Frauenstein, he signed the contract to build an organ for the cathedral in Freiberg. Friedrich August I (August the Strong), elector of Saxony, named him "Privileged Court and State Organ Builder" in 1723. The only documented meeting with Johann Sebastian Bach is at the examination of the Hildebrandt organ in Naumburg in September of 1746. In 1750, suffering from age and illness, he named his former student Zacharias Hildebrandt as the project manager of the new organ for the catholic Court Church (*Hofkirche*) in Dresden (the organ was completed under Johann Daniel Silbermann in 1755). He adopted Hildebrandt's idea of building space-saving Hinterwerk divisions. In addition to organs, Gottfried Silbermann built harpsichords, fortepianos, and clavichords.

Organs: Part I. A: Dresden, St. Sophia's (new organ, 1720). Dresden, Our Lady's (new organ, 1736). Part I. B: Freiberg, cathedral (new organ, 1714; preserved). Freiberg, St. Peter's (new organ, 1734; preserved). Rötha, St. George's (new organ, 1721; preserved). Rötha, St. Mary's (new organ, 1722; preserved).— Forchheim, parish church (new organ, 1726; preserved). Ponitz, parish church (new organ, 1737; preserved). Dresden, catholic *Hofkirche* (new organ, 1755; partly preserved).

Literature: Adlung 1768; Flade 1926, 1953; Müller 1982; Greß 1989; Schaefer 1994; Schaefer 1995; Müller 1999; Greß 2001; Schaefer/Greß 2001; Silbermann 2006.

Stertzing, family of organ builders

· **Georg Christoph** (b. ca. 1650, buried February 21, 1717, in Eisenach)

Married Anna Dorothea Schnabel, of Gotha, on November 23, 1686, in Ohrdruf, and settled in Ohrdruf in 1690. On April 22, 1691, he was advised by Eisenach's city council of his appointment as overseer of the organs at St. George's, St. Nicholas's, and St. Anne's. From 1696, he was engaged in building a new organ for St. George's. Flade has pointed out that among Stertzing's contemporaries, only Andreas Silbermann in Straßburg, Christian Förner, and Matthias Schuricht also built organs with a low C#.

Organs: Part I. A: Arnstadt, Upper Church (enlargement, 1708). Eisenach, St. George's (new organ, 1707; case survives). Erfurt, St. Augustine's (new organ, 1716; completed by Johann Georg Schröter).— Craula/Wiegleben (new organ, 1687). Berka/Werra (new organ, 1697). Obersuhl (new organ, 1701). Erfurt, St. Peter's (new organ, 1702; since 1811 in Büßleben; partly preserved). Jena, City Church (new organ, 1706). Udestädt (new organ, 1710).

Literature: Adlung 1768, 275–76; Fischer/Wohnhaas 1994, 404; Oefner 1996; Butler 2008, 229–69.

· **Johann Georg** (b. 1690 in Ohrdruf)

Son of Georg Christoph, whose Eisenach workshop he took over.

Organs: Part I. A: Eisenach, St. George's (assisted with new organ, 1696–1707; case survives). Eisenach, St. Nicholas's (new organ, 1718).

Literature: Fischer/Wohnhaas 1994, 404; Oefner 1996, 64.

· **Johann Friedrich** (b. 1681, d. 1731)

Son of Georg Christoph. In his application to the Kassel court in 1714 he referred to work done in Eisenach churches. Married November 26, 1711, in Eisenach, where his son, Johann Friedrich Bernhard, was baptized on November 13, 1712. In 1715 he was living in Kassel, where the previous year he had been named court organ builder. After his death, the organ project in St. Martin's Church in Kassel was completed by Johann Nikolaus Becker.

Organs: Part I. A: Kassel, St. Martin's (enlargement, 1730–31). Hannoversch Münden, St. Blasius's (new organ, 1719–20). Lauterbach (new organ, 1727).

Literature: Fischer/Wohnhaas 1994, 404; Oefner 1996, 63.

Trebs (Tröbs, Trebes), Heinrich Nicolaus

(b. August 10, 1678, in Frankenhausen, buried August 18, 1748, in Weimar)

Son of a cabinetmaker; according to Walther he studied organ building in 1698 with Christian Rothe in Salzungen. After working in Mühlhausen he settled in 1709 in Weimar, where he married the mayor's daughter, Catharine Elisabeth Aulepp, in 1713. Already on February 16, 1711, Bach had provided a recommendation (BDOK I, no. 84) in support of his application to become Weimar "Privileged Court Organ Builder." On November 27, 1713, Bach stood as godfather at the baptism of Johann Gottfried Trebs in Weimar's City Church of St. Peter and Paul's. In Weimar records from 1716, Trebs is described as "court organ builder." According to Walther, he built some twenty organs. Christian Immanuel Schweinefleisch was his journeyman in 1743.

Organs: Part I. A: Bad Berka, St. Mary's (new organ, 1742–43). Taubach, St. Ursula's (new organ, 1709–10). Weimar, palace church (renovations, 1714 and 1738). Weimar, St. Jacob's (new organ, 1723).

Literature: Walther 1732, 614; Gerber IV, 383; Löffler 1926; NBR, no. 42; BDOK I, no. 84; BDOK II, no. 61.

Trost, family of organ builders

• **Tobias Heinrich Gottfried** (b. ca. 1680, perhaps in Halberstadt, buried August 15, 1759, in Altenburg)

Learned handcraft of organ building from his father, Johann Tobias Gottfried; first documented as independent organ builder in 1711. Moved in 1718 to Altenburg, where he was named "Privileged Court Organ Builder" on November 23, 1723. His organs show the change from seventeenth-century dispositions rich in reeds to dispositions rich in the sound produced by flues and multiple 8' stops. In Waltershausen a two-ranked Flöte douce 4' has been preserved that has one rank of conical, open wooden pipes, the other of cylindrical, stopped metal pipes.

Organs: Part I. A: Altenburg, court church (new organ, 1739; preserved). Part I. B: Waltershausen, Church "Zur Gotteshilfe" (new organ, 1735; preserved).—Großengottern, Upper Church (new organ, 1717; preserved). Eisenberg, palace chapel (renovation, 1733; preserved).

Literature: Kümmerle III, 668; Klotz 1980d; Friedrich 1989, 18–20; Friedrich 2009, 102–6.

• **Johann Tobias Gottfried** (b. 1651, apparently in Halberstadt, d. 1721)

Brother of the organist Johann Caspar Trost Jr., who wrote a booklet on the Förner organ in the Augustusburg Castle, Weißenfels. Son of the theologian Johann Caspar Trost Sr., he worked in the workshop of Christian Förner for around ten years, taking part in Förner's new organs in Weißenfels and St. Ulrich's, Halle. Trost may have learned to play the organ from his father.

Organs: Part I. A: Leipzig, St. John's (new organ, 1695). —Belgern (new organ, 1684). Mutzschen (new organ, 1689). Cannewitz (new organ, 1696). Langensalza, Church on the Hill (new organ, 1701). Tonna, parish church (new organ, 1704). Siebleben, parish church (new organ, 1717).

Literature: Adlung 1768, 250; Gerber IV, 395; Friedrich 1989, 13–18.

Wagner, Joachim

(b. April 13, 1690, in Karow near Genthin [Saxony-Anhalt], d. May 23, 1749, in Salzwedel)

His father was a pastor; his brother studied theology (Friedrich Wagner was pastor at St. Michael's, Hamburg, from 1736 to 1760). Wagner learned organ building with Christoph Treutmann, a Schnitger student best known for the organ (III/42) he built in

1734–37 for the monastery church of St. George in Grauhof. Wagner worked two years for Gottfried Silbermann and in 1741 became acquainted with Silbermann's nephew from Straßburg, Johann Andreas Silbermann, when he examined Wagner's organ in St. Mary's Church in Berlin. Wagner settled in Berlin and married Anna Elisabeth Canzer (d. 1739 in Magdeburg). According to Kitschke, Wagner had such a favorable position vis-à-vis contracts that he was able to build primarily new organs, leaving repairs and rebuilds to the numerous members of his profession who were less accomplished. Wagner died while working on the St. Mary's organ in Salzwedel. Among his students were Heinrich Andreas Contius, Halle (Saale), and Johann Gottfried Hildebrandt, Dresden.

Organs: Part I. A: Potsdam, Old Garrison Church (new organ, 1722; since 1730 in Berlin's Jerusalem Church). Part I. B: Berlin, St. Mary's (new organ, 1723; partly preserved). —Brandenburg, Cathedral of St. Peter and Paul's (new organ, 1725). Berlin, Old Garrison Church (new organ, 1726). Brandenburg, St. Catherine's (new organ, 1727). Berlin, St. George's (new organ, 1727). Potsdam, Holy Ghost Church (new organ, 1730). Potsdam, New Garrison Church (new organ, 1732). Treuenbrietzen (new organ, 1741).

Literature: Mundt 1928; Steves 1939; Schulze 1968; Kitschke 1993, 197–202; Kitschke 2011, 200.

Wender, family of organ builders

· **Johann Friedrich** (baptized December 6, 1656, in Dörna near Mühlhausen, d. June 12, 1729, in Mühlhausen)

In 1676, assisted an unknown organ builder in renovating the St. Mary's organ in Mühlhausen, where he settled, probably in 1687 when he was given the contract to renovate the organ at St. Blasius's. His students include his son Christian Friedrich and probably also his son-in-law Johann Nikolaus Becker, and Johann Christoph Dauphin.

Organs: Part I. A: Ammern, St. Vitus's (1708). Arnstadt, New Church (new organ, 1703). Eisenach, St. George's (enlargement, 1725). Mühlhausen, St. Mary's (repair of organ after lightning strike, 1720). Mühlhausen, St. Blasius's (partially new organ, 1691 and 1708). Mühlhausen, Brückenhof Church (new organ, 1702). Part I. B: Merseburg, cathedral (enlargement, 1716). —Bollstedt near Mühlhausen (new organ, 1688–89). Mühlhausen, St. Peter's (new organ, 1710). Mühlhausen, St. Martin's (new organ, 1719). Mühlhausen, St. George's (new organ, 1714).

Sources/Literature: Stadtarchiv Mühlhausen, Chronik, Sign. 68/18–. Adlung 1768; Gerber IV, 543; Großmann 1968; Fischer/Wohnhaas 1994, 464; Kröhner 1995, 85.

· **Christian Friedrich** (baptized March 7, 1694, in Mühlhausen, d. 1740 in Erfurt)

Son of Johann Friedrich, whose workshop in Mühlhausen he took over.

Organs: Part I. A: Mühlhausen, St. Mary's Church (new organ, 1738).

Sources/Literature: Stadtarchiv Mühlhausen, Chronik, Sign. 61/18. —Fischer/Wohnhaas 1994, 464.

Organ Builders from the Sixteenth to Eighteenth Centuries Associated with Bach's Organs

Casparini, family of organ builders

• **Eugenio** (b. February 14, 1623, in Sorau, buried September 17, 1706, in Niederwiesa/Silesia)

Baptized Johann Caspar, he changed his name while working in Italy. He returned to Germany in 1697 to build, with his son, the "sun organ" in Görlitz.

Organs: Part I. B: Görlitz, Church of St. Peter and Paul's (new organ, 1703).

Literature: Boxberg 1704; Flade 1952; Reichling/Janka 2000.

• **Adam Horatio** (b. 1676 in Padua, d. August 11, 1745, in Breslau)

Son of Eugenio. After completion of the Görlitz organ, in 1703 he settled in Breslau. Brought Italian influences into German organ building.

Literature: BDOK I, commentary to no. 87; Flade 1952, 892; Reichling/Janka 2000.

Compenius (Cumpenius), family of organ builders

• **Heinrich Cumpenius** (b. ca. 1530–35, in Fulda, d. May 2, 1611)

Lived in Eisleben, Erfurt, and Nordhausen. Part 1. A: Erfurt, Prediger Church (new organ, 1527–79). —Fritzlar, Cathedral (new organ, 1588–90).

• **Heinrich II** (b. before 1560, d. September 22, 1631, in Halle [Saale])

Son of Heinrich Cumpenius; organist and organ builder in Eisleben; lived in Halle with title of "Organ Builder and Brewer by Authority of the Prince and Archbishop."

Organs: Part I. A: Leipzig, St. Thomas's, small organ (enlargement, 1630).

Literature: Schneider 1937; Klotz 1952; Schlepphorst 2000; Rehm 2002; Aumüller 2010, 67, 78, 103.

• **Ludwig** (b. after 1608 in Halle [Saale], d. February 11, 1671)

Son and student of Heinrich II; became citizen of Naumburg in 1632 and was a citizen of Erfurt from 1652. Also built stringed keyboard instruments.

Organs: Part I. A: Arnstadt, Upper Church (repairs, 1666). Kassel, St. Martin's (renovation, 1664). Naumburg, St. Wenceslas's (renovation, 1662). Weimar, Palace Church (partly new organ using parts of the organ from Erfurt's Church of the Barefoot Friars, 1658). Part I. B: Erfurt, Prediger Church (rebuild, 1649). —Naumburg, Cathedral (renovation, 1632). Gera, St. John's (repairs and enlargement, 1647).

Literature: Klotz 1952; Henkel 1985, 20 (fn. 15); Schlepphorst 2000.

Donat(i), family of organ builders

· **Christoph Sr.** (b. September 30, 1625, in Marienberg, buried August 17, 1706, in Leipzig)

Became citizen of Leipzig in 1662. Trained eight sons as organ builders, including Christoph Jr. and Johann Jacob Sr. (b. June 27, 1663, he later called himself Donati and was active in Zwickau and Altenburg). Approximately twenty organs and some clavichords are documented as being made in his workshop.

Organs: Part I. A: Leipzig, St. Thomas's, main organ (enlargement, 1671). Leipzig, St. Thomas's, small organ (enlargement, 1665). Leipzig, New Church (new organ, 1704). —Brandis (near Leipzig; new organ, 1705; partially preserved).

Literature: Schering 1926, 256; Dähnert 1980, 301; Hüttel 1980a, 541; Glöckner 1990, 19–20.

· **Christoph Jr.** (b. December 2, 1659, d. June 15, 1713)

Documented as working with his father on the organ for the New Church in Leipzig (1704) and in Brandis (1705).

Literature: Schering 1926, 256; Dähnert 1980, 301; Glöckner 1990, 19–20; Hüttel 2001.

· **Johann Jacob Jr.** (baptized October 15, 1715, still active in 1767)

Son of Johann Jacob Donati. Organ builder in Zwickau.

Literature: BDOK V, no. B586b.

Dressel (Dreßler), Christoph

(b. ca. 1640, d. August 6, 1686)

Resident of Leipzig from 1679; for a time associated with Christoph Donat.

Organs: Part I. A: Leipzig, St. Thomas's, main organ (repairs, 1681). Leipzig, St. Thomas's, harpsichord (1675). Weißenfels, palace church (new positive, 1682).

Literature: Gerber I, 937; Schering 1926, 256; Hüttel 1980b; Fischer 2001.

Dropa, Mathias

(b. ca. 1656 in Sienbenbürgen, buried September 25, 1732, in Lüneburg)

Journeyman with Arp Schnitger; founded his own workshop in 1692 in Hamburg; moved the workshop to Lüneburg in 1705.

Organs: Part I. A: Lüneburg, St. John's (enlargement, 1715; preserved). Lüneburg, St. Michael's (new organ, 1707).

Literature: Fock 1974, 120–22.

Förner, Christian

(b. ca. 1609 in Wettin [Saale] oder Löbejün, d. ca. 1678)

Taught by his brother-in-law, Johann Wilhelm Stegmann, mayor of Wettin (grandfather of Johann Caspar Trost Jr.). "Royal Organ Builder in Magdeburg" in 1667. Students included Johann Tobias Gottfried Trost, Johann Caspar Trost Jr., and Bernhard Schmidt (later active in England as Bernard Smith). Trained in the sciences, in 1667 Förner invented the wind gauge as a means of precisely measuring wind pressure in organs.

Organs: Part I. A: Weißenfels, palace church (new organ, 1673; case preserved).

Literature: Trost 1677; Dreyhaupt 1755; Adlung 1768; Kümmerle II, 413–14; Serauky 1935, 271 and 273; Friedrich 2001b.

Fritzsche, Gottfried

(b. 1578 in Meißen, d. March 10, 1638, in Ottensen)

Apparently a student of Johann (Hanß) Lange in Kamenz. He was "Electoral Saxon Court Organ Builder." From 1619 to 1627 he was in Wolfenbüttel, then in Hamburg, where he took over contracts of the deceased Hans Scherer II. His son-in-law Friedrich Stellwagen was organ builder in Lübeck.

Organs: Part I. A: Hamburg, St. Catherine's (rebuilds, 1633 and 1636).

Literature: Gurlitt 1913; Gurlitt 1937; Gurlitt 1938, 163; Hackel/Klotz 2002.

Greutzscher (Grützscher, Groitzscher, Gretzscher), Ezechiel

(b. ca. 1575/80, d. after 1625)

Along with his son of the same name, he was organ builder in Erfurt, Stadtilm, and Eisleben.

Organs: Part I. A: Arnstadt, Church of the Barefoot Friars (new organ, 1611). Arnstadt, Our Lady's (new organ, 1624). Sangerhausen, St. Jacobi (new organ, 1603). Gera, Palace Chapel (new organ, 1610).

Sources/Literature: Stadt- und Kreisarchiv Arnstadt, Nr. 394–02–1: *Organist u. Orgelb. Georg Raabe.* —Maul 2006, 197–200.

Hantelmann, Hans

(b. ca. 1655 in Celle, d. April 15, 1733, in Lübeck)

Was working in 1682 with Arp Schnitger; built, among other instruments, the cathedral organ in Lübeck in 1696–99, and became a citizen of Lübeck in 1697. In 1707 he became privileged organ builder to the court of Mecklenburg.

Organs: Part I. A: Lübeck, St. Mary's, "Totentanz" organ (repair, 1701). Part I. B: Lübeck, Cathedral (new organ, 1699; key desk survives).

Literature: Fock 1974, 185–86.

Held, Johann Balthasar

(b. ca. 1640 in Lüneburg, d. 1710 in Stettin)

Apprenticed with Arp Schnitger in 1682–90. According to Buxtehude, in 1685 he repaired and tuned the St. Mary's organ in Lübeck, which was "so very unreliable, out-of-tune and false" (Snyder 2007). He settled in Stettin, where he received a "concession and freedom throughout Swedish Pomerania."

Organs: Part I. A: Lüneburg, St. Michael's, choir organ (new organ, 1701).

Literature: Fock 1974, 186–87; Snyder 2007, 468.

Herbst, Heinrich Gottlieb

(b. May 1, 1689, d. after 1732)

Member of a Magdeburg organ-building family, known because of his work in Lahm/Itzgrund (new organ, 1732; preserved).

Literature: Adlung 1768, 237–39; Gerber II, 639.

Hering, Bartold (Berlt?)

(b. ca. 1480, d. October, 1556)

An organ builder named Berlt Hering was active in Lübeck in ca. 1530 who also was active between 1500 and 1508 in and around Nordhausen as well as in Erfurt. Whether he built the organ in the St. Catherine's Church in Hamburg is unclear.

Organs: Nordhausen, Prediger Church (new organ, ca.1500–1506). Monastery Church Himmelpforten (new organ,1506–1508). Erfurt, Merchants' Church (new organ, 1508–1512).

Literature: Praetorius 1619, 165; Stahl 1931; Ortgies 2004, 70–74; Lobenstein 2003, 216–17.

Herold, Peter

(d. 1700)

Organ builder in Apolda. His only known instrument: Buttstädt, St. Michael's (new organ, 1700; completed by Finke).

Literature: Schmidt-Mannheim 2004, 156.

Hohlbeck (auch Holbeck, Hollbeck), Severin

(b. ca. 1640 in Fredericia, Denmark, d. 1700 in Zella-Mehlis)

Became citizen of Zwickau in 1687; his daughter, Maria Margaretha, married Johann Jacob Donati Sr., who himself became a citizen of Zwickau in 1711.

Organs: Part I. A: Gotha, palace church (new organ, 1692; case preserved).
Literature: Dähnert 1980, 304; Ernst 1983, 13–14.

Hoyer, Dirk

(Sixteenth century, no dates known)

Son-in-law of Jacob Scherer. In 1576, built a Rückpositiv for the St. Jacobi organ in Hamburg, and was the first to put pedal stops in independent towers beside the Rückpositiv (the so-called Hamburg facade). He cannot be documented in Hamburg after 1582.

Organs: Part I. A: Hamburg, St. Jacobi (enlargement, 1570 and 1576; partly preserved). Lüneburg, St. John's (enlargement, 1576; partly preserved). Lüneburg, St. Michael's (repairs, 1580).
Literature: Fock 1939/1997, 17 and 30–33.

Johannsen, Jasper

(d. 1558)

Partner in 1544 with Hendrik Niehoff; together they built the organ in Lüneburg's St. John's Church, which was built in the latest style with a Rückpositiv. (Niehoff/Johannsen stops that survive: Rohrflöte 8', Nasat 3', Gemshorn 2' in Oberwerk; in Rückpositiv, pitches g^1–c^2 of the Principal 8').

Organs: Part I. A: Hamburg, St. Catherine's (enlargement, 1552). Lüneburg, St. John's (new organ, 1553; partly preserved).
Literature: Vente 1958, 64–67; Fock 1967, 14; van Biezen 1995.

Junge, Christoph

(b. ca. 1610 in Schweinitz, d. 1687 in Erfurt)

Organ builder in Weimar. Identified as "organ builder born in Schwei[d]nitz in Silesia" in the 1675 contract for a new organ in Sonderhausen's Trinity Church. From 1674 he was active in Merseburg; in 1683 he settled in Erfurt. He died while building the organs in Erfurt's cathedral and Merchants' Church (the organs were completed, respectively, by David Merker and Johannes Albrecht).

Organs: Part I. A: Arnstadt, Church of the Barefoot Friars (rebuild, 1678). Weimar, City Church of St. Peter and Paul's (new organ, 1685).
Literature: Gerber II, 820; Kümmerle II, 700; Orth 1972, 1697–98; Lobenstein 2003, 220–21; Kirchner 2006, 267–69.

Lange, Johann (Hanß)

(b. 1543 in Wesselburen, d. November 17, 1616, in Kamenz)

Became a citizen of Kamenz (Lausitz) in 1578. Dähnert suggested Jacob Scherer and his son Hans Scherer I as teachers. Lange was Saxony's most important sixteenth-century organ builder.

Organs: Part I. A: Leipzig, St. Nicholas's (new organ, 1598). Leipzig, St. Thomas's, main organ (enlargement, 1599).

Literature: Rubardt/Jentsch 1952, 12–16. Dähnert 1980, 305. Kuhlmann 1981, 197–98.

Lehmann, Blasius

(d. ca. 1543 in Bautzen)

In 1499 he worked with Burckhardt Dinstlinger on the cathedral organ in Bautzen. His workshop was at first in Bautzen, then in Leipzig. Last known work was a new organ in Zwickau in 1542.

Organs: Part I. A: Leipzig, St. Thomas's (new organ, 1511).

Literature: Dähnert 1980, 306.

Lehmann, Kaspar (Caspar)

(d. 1679 in Suhl)

Student of Johann Georg Künzinger, organ builder in Suhl.

Organs: Part I. A: Ohrdruf, St. Michael's (new organ, 1679).

Literature: Fischer/Wohnhaas 1994.

Müller, Johann Heinrich

(ca. 1700, dates unknown)

According to Hartmann, Müller "lived in Köthen at the expense of the prince, proving his skill with, among others, the organs in Kalbe and Könnern."

Organs: Part I. A: Köthen, St. Agnus's (new organ, 1708).

Literature: Hartmann 1799, 19; Rust 1878, vi; Fock 1974, 127; Henkel 1985, 22 (fn. 35).

Niehoff, Hendrik

(b. ca. 1495, d. December 1560)

He was an apprentice with Johann von Koblenz (Jan van Covelen) ca. 1520 in Amsterdam, independent from 1533, and from 1538 in s'Hertogenbosch. His partner after 1544 was Jasper Johannsen; together they built a number of organs in Hamburg and Lüneburg.

Organs: Part I. A: Hamburg, St. Catherine's (enlargement, 1552). Lüneburg, St. John's (new organ, 1553; partly preserved).

Literature: Fock 1939/1997, 10–18; Vente 1958, 63–67 and 76–91; Fock 1967, 14; Peeters 2004, 1079.

Oehme, Georg

(b. ca. 1646, d. October 24, 1708, in Gatzen)

From 1669, school attendant in Gatzen; 1693 also cantor and organ builder.

Organs: Part I. A: Stöntzsch (new positive, 1678).

Literature: Dähnert 1980, 306; BDOK II, commentary to no. 298; Schrammek 1983, 42.

Reichel, Georg

(b. ca. 1628 in Glashütte, d. 1684 Halle [Saale])

Became citizen in Halle (Saale) in 1655 and was given "Privilege of his learned art of organ building for the district of Saal" by Duke August. He was active as organist in Glaucha.

Organs: Part I. A: Halle (Saale), Market Church (enlargement, 1654/55). Halle (Saale), Market Church (new organ, 1664; preserved).

Literature: Serauky 1935, 288–90, 296–97, 382; Stüven 1964, 45–46 and 89.

Röder, Johann Michael

(b. ca. 1670, d. ca. 1750)

From 1713, organ builder in Berlin and Potsdam. In 1688–94 he apprenticed with Arp Schnitger; in 1711 he undertook repair of the Scherer organ in St. Steven's, Tangermünde; according to Vincent Lübeck, he had left the Schnitger workshop "through the back door."

Organs: Part I. B: Potsdam, Garrison Church (new organ, 1713).

Literature: Kümmerle III, 88; BDOK II, 435; Fock 1967, 20; Fock 1974, 211–13.

Rücker, Georg (Johann) Bernhardt

(seventeenth century; no dates known)

Organ builder in Weimar, Jena, and Naumburg. In 1683 built an inferior organ for the City Church of St. Peter and Paul's in Weimar and fled before it was finished. Parts were reused in 1685 by Christoph Junge for the new organ that Johann Gottfried Walther later played.

Literature: Smets 1931, 70.

Scherer, family of organ builders

· Hans I (the Elder) (b. ca. 1525 in Hamburg, d. 161: in Hamburg)

Son and student of Jacob Scherer; active in Hamburg and its environs. The Scherers expanded the manual compass from $F–g^2a^2$ to $C–c^3$, the pedal compass to $CD–d^1$, thereby creating a new standard.

Organs: Part I. A: Hamburg, St. Catherine's (major renovation, 1605–6). Hamburg, St. Jacobi (renovations, 1592 and 1605; pipes preserved). Lüneburg, St. John's (rebuild, 1587; pipes preserved). Lüneburg, St. Michael's (various rebuilds).

Literature: Fock 1939/1997, 35–48; Fock 1963a, 1674–75; Fock 1967, 13; Grapenthin 2007, 174–81.

· Hans II (b. before 1580 in Hamburg, d. 1631 or 1632)

Son of Hans I, first documented working with his father in 1593 on the rebuild of the organ in Bergedorf. Became citizen of Hamburg in 1606 and was working in Kassel between 1607 and 1612 for landgrave Moritz of Hesse. His last documented work was in 1631 in Itzehoe.

Organs: Part I. A: Hamburg, St. Jacobi (rebuild together with his father, 1605). Kassel, St. Martin's (1612).

Literature: Fock 1939/1997, 49–56; Fock 1963a, 1675; Fock 1967, 12–13.

· **Friedrich** (sixteenth to seventeenth centuries; no dates known)

Son of Hans Scherer I; worked together with his brother Hans II between 1603 and 1606 in Kassel.

· **Jacob** (d. 1574 in Hamburg)

Organ builder in Hamburg. Worked with his son and Hans Bockelmann in north Germany. He purchased land in Hamburg in 1543 and a house in 1555. A further house was given as a dowry to his son-in-law Dirk Hoyer, with whom he worked from 1556.

Organs: Part I. A: Hamburg, St. Catherine's (repairs, 1559). Hamburg, St. Jacobi (various repairs). Lüneburg, St. Michael's (various repairs). Lübeck, St. Mary's, main organ (renovation, 1561). Lübeck, St. Mary's, "Totentanz" organ (various repairs).

Literature: Fock 1939/1997, 19–30; Fock 1963a, 1674–75; Fock 1967, 13.

Schnitger, Arp

(Baptized July 9, 1648, in Golzwarden, buried July 28, 1719, in Neuenfelde (Hamburg-Neuenfelde)

Learned joinery with his father; from 1666 he learned organ building with his cousin Berendt Huß in Glückstadt/Holstein. He moved to Hamburg in 1682 in order to build the new organ there for St. Nicholas's and became a citizen. His four sons worked with him. Schnitger built or substantially rebuilt some 170 organs, some of which he delivered as far away as Moscow, England, Spain, and Portugal. Schnitger's pew and coat-of-arms can still be seen behind the altar in the church in Neuenfelde.

Organs: Part I. A: Hamburg, St. Jacobi (new organ using some stops from previous organ, 1693; partly preserved).

Literature: Niedt 1721; Adlung 1768; Rubardt 1928; Fock 1939/1997; Fock 1963b, 1913–17; Pape 1971; Fock 1974; Reinitzer 1995; Edwards 2001; Ortgies 2005; Edskes/Vogel 2009.

Stellwagen, Friedrich

(d. ca. 1660)

Moved with Gottfried Fritzsche ca. 1630 from Halle (Saale) to Hamburg, where he married Fritzsche's daughter. In 1635 he established himself as an independent builder in Lübeck. He carried on the tradition of the Scherers and Fritzsche, adopting new color into the disposition by building, among other stops, the Tierce Zimbel.

Organs: Part I. A: Hamburg, St. Catherine's (rebuild, 1647). Lübeck, St. Mary's, main organ (enlargement, 1641). Lübeck, St. Mary's, "Totentanz" organ (repairs, 1655). Lüneburg, St. John's (enlargement, 1652).

Literature: Fock 1939/1997, 68–71; Klotz 1980c, 115.

Thayßner (Deißner, Tayßner, Teißner), family of organ builders

· **Zacharias** (b. between 1640 and 1655 in Löbejun, d. after 1705)

Son of Hans Thayßner, organ builder in Quedlinburg. In Merseburg from 1695, when he was named "Electoral Saxon Architect and Organ Builder."

Organs: Part I. A: Köthen, St. Jacob's (new organ, 1676). Leipzig, St. Nicholas's (rebuild, 1694). Naumburg, St. Wenceslas's (rebuild, 1705). Part I. B: Merseburg, Cathedral (enlargement, 1705).

Literature: Gerber IV, 330; Engel 1855; Stüven 1964, 89; Fock 1974, 190; Henkel 1985, 8–9.

· **Andreas** (baptized July 28, 1652, in Löbejün, d. 1708 in Halle [Saale])

Son of Hans Thayßner; worked with his brother Zacharias on larger organ projects; in 1684 succeeded Georg Reichel as organ examiner for the city of Halle.

Organs: Part I. A: Köthen, St. Jacob's (new organ together with his brother Zacharias, 1676). Leipzig, St. Nicholas's (rebuild together with his brother Zacharias, 1694). Naumburg, St. Wenceslas's (rebuild together with his brother Zacharias, 1705).

Literature: Gerber IV, 330; Stüven 1964, 89; Henkel 1985, 8.

Weißhaupt, Johann Conrad

(b. 1657, d. 1727 in Seebergen)

Organ builder in Seebergen near Gotha; built organs in the Gotha, Erfurt, and Weimar area.

Zuberbier (Zoberbier), family of organ builders

· **David** (b. before 1700 in Bernburg, d. before 1743)

Became citizen in Bernburg in 1716, and was named "Privileged Organ and Instrument Builder" by the Anhalt court in Köthen. From 1730, active in Köthen, where he took care of the organ in the St. Agnus's Church until 1742.

Organs: Part I. A: Köthen, St. Jacob's (various repairs). Köthen, Palace Church (new organ, 1733).

Literature: Stüven 1964, 57–71; Henkel 1985, 9.

· **Johann Christoph** (b. ca. 1713, d. ca. 1780)

Son of David; from 1745 to 1746 was paid annually for maintaining the organs in Köthen. In 1748 he became citizen of Köthen, and after 1743 he was privileged "Court Instrument and Organ Builder in Köthen." He became responsible for organs in Halle; in 1770, with another commission, he moved his workshop to Neumarkt.

Organs: Part I. A: Köthen, St. Jacob's (rebuild, 1768). Köthen, St. Agnus's (rebuild, 1742). Thurau/Anhalt (new organ 1754; since 1991 in the palace church in Köthen).

Literature: Hartmann 1799, 29; Stüven 1964, 66–71; Henkel 1958, 9 and 26 (fn. 82); Pape 2003, 81–82.

Other Organ Builders and Organ-Building Firms

Ahrend, Jürgen (b. 1930), Leer-Loga. Firm founded 1954 with Gerhard Brunzema; single proprietorship from 1972; in 2005, direction taken over by Hendrik Ahrend.

Beckerath, Hamburg. Founded 1949 by Rudolf von Beckerath (1907–1976).

Besser, Johann Friedrich (ca. 1655–1693), Braunschweig.

Böhm, Gerhard, proprietor of organ-building firm Rudolf Böhm. Founded 1888; in Gotha since 1900.

Brunner, Heinrich, Sandersleben. Second half of seventeenth century.

Damm (Thamm), Frankfurt/Oder. Middle of eighteenth century.

Decker, David, Jr., Görlitz. First half of eighteenth century.

Eule Orgelbau, Bautzen. Founded 1872 by Hermann Eule (1972–1990, VEB Eule-Orgelbau Bautzen).

Flentrop Orgelbouw, Zaandam. Founded 1903. Since 2009, directed by Frits Eishout.

Förster & Nicolaus, Lich (Oberhessen). Founded 1842 by Johann Georg Förster; Karl Nicolaus became partner in 1889.

Führer, Alfred (1905–1974), Wilhelmshaven. Founded 1933, closed 2004.

Furtwängler & Hammer. Founded 1822; in Arnum (Hannover) since 1962.

Gesell, Carl Ludwig, Potsdam. 1847, takeover of organ-building workshop of Gottlieb Heise; taken over by Alexander Schuke in 1894.

Große, Johann Friedrich, Mühlhausen (Thuringia). Mid-nineteenth century. Student of Schulze (Paulinzella).

Haseborg, Martin ter, Uplengen (Ostfriesland). Apparently founded in the 1990s.

Helfenbein, Wiegand, Gotha. In 1919 took over the business of his father-in-law, Alwin Hickmann.

Hoffmann Orgelbau, Ostheim (Rhön). Founded 1848 by Johann Georg Markert.

Holland, Schmiedefeld. Johann Caspar Holland took over the Wagner workshop in 1790; family workshop closed in 1872.

Ibach, Josias (d. 1639), Grimma, Leipzig, and Altenburg.

Iversand, Jacob (d. ca. 1537), Hamburg.

Jacobus, Andreas, Gottsbüren. 1717, official city organ builder; probably an associate of Christoph Heeren.

Jehmlich, Dresden. Founded 1808 by Carl Gottlieb, Friedrich Gotthelf, and Johann Gotthold Jehmlich (1973–1989, VEB Orgelbau Dresden).

Johannsen, Gottschalk, also Borchert (d. 1597 in Lübeck), Husum. According to Praetorius, he was from the Netherlands.

Kaltschmidt, Joachim Christoph (ca. 1717–1806), Wismar.

Kemper, Lübeck. Founded 1868 by Emanuel Philipp Kemper; closed in 1978.

Kern, Alfred (1910–1989), Straßburg. Founded 1953; since 1977 under direction of his son Daniel; in 2003, merger with "Manufacture d'Orgues Alsacienne" (Gaston Kern), Hattmatt (Alsace).

Kretzschmar, Franz Theodor, Hamburg. Student of Gottfried Fritzsche, middle of seventeenth century.

Kröger, Henning, Wismar. Student of Arp Schnitger ca. 1700.

Ladegast, Friedrich (1818–1905), Weißenfels.

Lehnert, Johann Jacob, Hamburg. Middle of eighteenth century.

Mahn, Matthias, Buxtehude. Late sixteenth century.

Marcussen & Son, Aabrenaa, Denmark; founded 1806 by Jürgen Marcussen.

Mare, Marten de (d. 1612), Bremen.

Mathis Orgelbau, Näfels (Switzerland). Founded 1960 by Manfred Mathis, since 1977 a family business.

Mauer, Johann Gottlieb, Leipzig. Son-in-law of Johann Christian Immanuel Schweinefleisch, from 1771 university organ builder in Leipzig.

Mende, Johann Gottlieb (1787–1850), Leipzig.

Mitteldeutscher Orgelbau Voigt, Bad Liebenwerda. Founded 1905 by Arno Voigt (1876–1930).

Müller, Johann Georg, Köthen. First half of eighteenth century.

Offenhauer, Eduard (1825–1904), Delitzsch.

Orgelbau Waltershausen. Founded in 1991 by Bernhard Kutter, Stephan Krause, Joachim Stade, and Dietmar Ullman.

Ott, Paul (1903–1991), Göttingen. Student of Steinmeyer and Carl Giesecke (Göttingen), founded 1930.

Pape, Jost, Göttingen. Second half of sixteenth century.

Petersilie, Otto, Langensalza. Closed ca. 1914/18.

Poppe, Gebr., organ-building family in Stadtroda. Oldest known member of this family is Christian Friedrich Poppe (1751–1812). Made organs until 1897; business closed in 1917.

Ratzmann Gebr., Ohrdruf. Founded by Georg Franz Ratzmann (1771–1846); in 1841 Wilhelm August Ratzmann (1812–1880) established a branch in Gelnhausen. Since 1921, Orgelbau Richard Schmitt (now Andreas Schmidt).

Richborn, Joachim (known to be active 1663–84), Hamburg.

Röver, Ernst (1857–1923), Hausneindorf. Took over the Adolf Reubke workshop in 1884.

Rühlmann, Wilhelm (1842–1922), Zörbig. Took over his father's workshop in 1866, closed sometime after 1945.

Sauer, Wilhelm (1831–1916), Frankfurt/Oder. Founded 1857 by Wilhelm Sauer; taken over in 1916 by Oscar Walcker. Since then it has been known as Wilhelm Sauer (Oscar Walcker, owner); Frankfurter VEB Orgelbau Sauer, 1972–90; Orgelbau Sauer (Werner Walcker-Mayer, owner), 1990–99. Since 1994, located in Müllrose. 2000, founding of W. Sauer Orgelbau Müllrose GmbH.

Schäfer (Schaeffer), Jost Friedrich (b. between 1642 and 1656, d. after 1706), Kirchheiligen/Langensalza.

Schauenberg, Georg. Second half of sixteenth century, between Thuringian Woods and the Harz Mountains.

Scheffler, Christian (b. 1954), Frankfurt/Oder. Certified Restorer (FH); shop founded 1990.

Schlag & Söhne, founded by Christian Gottlieb Schlag (1803–1889). Since 1834 in Schweidnitz; closed in 1923.

Schmieder, Johann Christoph, Möllis. First half of eighteenth century.

Schubert, David (1719–1772), from 1747 apprentice with Gottfried Silbermann.

Schuke Orgelbau, Potsdam. Alexander Schuke (1870–1933) took over the workshop of Carl Ludwig Gesell in 1894. 1972–1990, VEB Potsdamer Schuke-Orgelbau; since 1990, Alexander Schuke Potsdam Orgelbau GmbH; moved to Werder/Havel in 2004.

Schulz, Carl (d. 1870), Crossen/Oder. Apprenticed with Carl Ludwig Gesell of Potsdam in 1848, then became independent.

Schulze, Johann Friedrich (1793–1858). Business founded in 1815; in Paulinzella since 1825; closed in 1880.

Silbermann, Johann George (1698–1749), nephew and apprentice of Gottfried Silbermann.

Steinmeyer Orgelbau, Oettingen. Founded by Georg Friedrich Steinmeyer; taken over by Karl Göckel (b. 1957) in 2003.

Stephani, Johannes, Lübeck. Second half of fifteenth century.

Stephani, Johann Gottlieb Ehregot, Leipzig. University organ builder at the end of the eighteenth century.

Stüven, Harmen, Hamburg. First third of sixteenth century.

Trampeli, Gebr., Adorf. Johann Paul Trampel (1708–1764) took over the workshop of Adam Heinrich Gruber in 1734; his sons Johann Gottlob and Christian Wilhelm continued the business; at death of Johann Gottlob in 1812, business carried on by Friedrich Wilhelm, son of Christian Wilhelm; business closed in 1832.

Treutmann, Christoph (1673/74–1757), Magdeburg. Student of Arp Schnitger; active as organ builder from 1710. Joachim Wagner was one of his students.

Vogel, Gregorius (b. in Brabant, d. 1549 in Hamburg), Magdeburg, Braunschweig, and Hamburg.

Volckland, Franciscus (1696–1779), Erfurt. Student of Johann Georg Schröter.

Wagner Bros. (Johann Michael and Johann Christoph Wagner), Schmiedefeld. Firm taken over in 1790 by J. C. Holland.

Walcker, E.F., & Cie, Ludwigsburg. Founded in 1820 by Eberhard Friedrich Walcker (1794–1872). Bankruptcy in 1999; dissolved in 2004.

Wegscheider, Kristian (b. 1954), Dresden. Certified restorer (FH); shop founded 1989.

Weise, Johann Anton (1672–1750), Arnstadt. Took over the workshop of his father, Johann Moritz Weise.

Werner, Andreas, Wittenberg. Middle of seventeenth century.

Wilhelmi, Johann Christoph, Dörna. Middle of nineteenth century.

Woehl, Gerald (b. 1940), Marburg. Firm founded 1966.

Zippelius, Johann Georg, Halberstadt. First half of eighteenth century.

Zschugk, Joachim (d. after 1632), active in Plauen (Vogtland) from 1600. Student of Johann Lange.

sources and Literature cited

ABBREVIATIONS

BJ   *Bach-Jahrbuch*, ed. Alfred Dürr and Werner Neumann (1953–74); Hans-Joachim Schulze and Christoph Wolff (1975–2004); Peter Wollny (since 2005). Leipzig: Neue Bachgesellschaft.

BDOK   *Bach-Dokumente*. 8 vols. Kassel: Bärenreiter, 1963–2010.

BDOK I   *Schriftstücke von der Hand Johann Sebastian Bachs*, ed. Werner Neumann and Hans-Joachim Schulze. Kassel: Bärenreiter, 1963 and 1982.

BDOK II   *Fremdschriftliche und gedruckte Dokumente zur Lebensgeschichte Johann Sebastian Bachs 1685–1750*, ed. Werner Neumann and Hans-Joachim Schulze. Kassel: Bärenreiter, 1969.

BDOK III   *Dokumente zum Nachwirken Johann Sebastian Bachs 1750–1800*, ed. Hans-Joachim Schulze. Kassel: Bärenreiter, 1984.

BDOK IV   *Bilddokumente zur Lebensgeschichte Johann Sebastian Bachs*, ed. Werner Neumann. Kassel: Bärenreiter, 1979.

BDOK V   *Dokumente zu Leben, Werk, Nachwirken 1685–1800*, ed. Hans-Joachim Schulze and Andreas Glöckner. Kassel: Bärenreiter, 2007.

BWV   *Thematisch-systematisches Verzeichnis der musikalischen Werke von Johann Sebastian Bach* [Bach-Werke-Verzeichnis, BWV], ed. Wolfgang Schmieder. 2nd ed. Wiesbaden: Breitkopf & Härtel, 1990.

Dresden Ms.   *Orgeldispositionen: Eine Handschrift aus dem XVIII. Jahrhundert, im Besitz der Sächsischen Landesbibliothek, Dresden*, ed. Paul Smets. Kassel: Bärenreiter, 1931.

Gerber   Gerber, Ernst Ludwig. *Neues historisch-biographisches Lexikon der Tonkünstler*. 4 vols. Leipzig, 1812–14.

Grove   *The New Grove Dictionary of Music and Musicians*, ed. Stanley Sadie. London: Macmillan, 1980.

Grove²   *The New Grove Dictionary of Music and Musicians*, ed. Stanley Sadie. 2nd ed. London: Macmillan, 2001.

MGG	*Die Musik in Geschichte und Gegenwart: Allgemeine Enzyklopädie der Musik,* ed. Friedrich
	Blume. Kassel: Bärenreiter, 1949–1986.
MGG²	*Die Musik in Geschichte und Gegenwart: Personenteil,* ed. Ludwig Finscher. 2nd rev.
	ed. 17 vols. Kassel: Bärenreiter, 1999–2007.
SeN	*Sammlung einiger Nachrichten von berühmten Orgelwercken in Teutschland mit vieler*
	Mühe aufgesetzt von einem Liebhaber der Musik. Breslau: Carl Gottfried Meyer, 1757.

ARCHIVAL SOURCES

Archiv der Superintendentur Borna, no. 5.722.

Bach-Archiv Leipzig:

    Go. S. 123.

    Rara II, 204.

Stadt- und Kreisarchiv Arnstadt, Bestand Nr. 394-02-1: *Organist u. Orgelb. Georg Raabe.*

Stadtarchiv Langewiesen, Orgel der Marienkirche, Bestand 3478.

Stadtarchiv Mühlhausen: *Chronik. Fragment 1533–1802,* Sign. 61/18.

Thüringisches Hauptstaatsarchiv Rudolstadt:

    Bestand Konsistorium Arnstadt, *Die Orgel in der Oberkirche zu Arnstadt,* 1610–1713.

    Bestand Unterkonsistorium Gehren, Nr.351: *Die Erbauung eines neuen Orgelwerckes in der Kirche*
    zu Langewiesen betr., 1784–1801.

Thüringisches Staatsarchiv Gotha, Gemeinschaftliches Hohenlohisches Archiv.

Thüringisches Staatsarchiv Weimar:

    Bestand B 4342: *Den Bau der Orgel in der Stadtkirche zu Weimar und die deshalb entstandene Irrung*
    zwischen dem Oberconsistorium und dem Stadtrathe betr., 1660.

    Bestand B 4351: *Gutachten Johann Eschleben Organisten zu Erfurt über die Orgeln in der Schloßkirche*
    und in der Stadtkirche, 1678.

    Bestand B 4367a: *1734, 1738 Schloßorgel zu Weimar betr.*

    Bestand Eisenacher Archiv, Konsistorialsachen Nr. 246: *Die nöthige Reparatur und Veränderung*
    der Orgel in der Kirche zu S. Georgen, 1696–1724.

REFERENCE LIST

Adlung, Jacob. 1768. *Musica mechanica organoedi,* ed. posthumously by Johann Lorenz Albrecht with
    contributions by Johann Friedrich Agricola. Berlin: F. W. Birnstiel. Facsimile, with afterword
    by Christhard Mahrenholz. Kassel: Bärenreiter, 1931.

Adolph, Wolfgang, et al. 2002. *Organ: Journal für die Orgel* 5, no. 4 (issue devoted to reconstruction
    of Arp Schnitger's 1699 organ for the cathedral in Lübeck).

Albrecht, Christlieb. 1938. *Bestandsaufnahme von 21 Orgeln in Potsdam und Umgebung.* Babelsberg:
    typescript.

Aumüller, Gerhard, Wolf Hobohm and Dorothea Schröder. 2010. Harmonie des Klanglichen und
    der Erscheinungsform—Die Bedeutung der Orgelbauerfamilien Beck und Compenius für die
    mitteldeutsche Orgelkunst der Ziet vor Heinrich Schütz. *Schütz Jahrbuch* 32:51–105.

Barth, Dietrich. 1974. Das 250-jährige Jubiläum der Orgel in Störmthal. *Musik und Kirche* 44:22.

Belotti, Michael. 1997. *Die freien Orgelwerke Dieterich Buxtehudes: Überlieferungsgeschichtliche und stilkritische Studien.* European University Studies (Musicology) 136. 2nd ed. Frankfurt/Main: Peter Lang.

———. 1999. Registration. In Johann Pachelbel, *Complete Works for Keyboard Instruments,* vol. 1, *Preludes and Toccatas,* ed. Michael Belotti, xix–xxiii. Colfax, N.C.: Wayne Leupold Editions.

Bernsdorff-Engelbrecht, Christiane. 1967. Kasseler Orgelbaugeschichte. *Acta Organologica* 1:113–26.

Biezen, Jan van. 1995. *Het nederlandse Orgel in de Renaissance en de Barock, in het bijzonder de school van Jan van Covelens.* 2 vols. Utrecht: Koninklijke Vereniging voor Nederlandse Musiekgeschiedenis.

Blanchard, Homer D. 1985. *The Bach Organ Book.* Delaware, Ohio: Praestant Press.

Böhme, Ullrich. 2005. Die Bach-Orgel. In *Die Orgeln der Thomaskirche zu Leipzig,* ed. Christian Wolff, 47–87. Leipzig: Evangelische Verlagsanstalt.

Börner, Walter, and Karl H. Schubert. 2005. Zu Johann Sebastian Bachs Aufenthalt in Weißensee (Thüringen). BJ 91:287–90.

Boxberg, Christian Ludwig. 1704. *Ausführliche Beschreibung der großen neuen Orgel in der Kirchen zu St. Petri und Pauli allhie zu Görlitz.* Facsimile in Günter Lade, ed. Die Sonnenorgel der evangelischen Pfarrkirche St. Peter und Paul zu Görlitz: *Festschrift zur Orgelweihe.* Görlitz, 1997. Trans. by Mary Murrell Faulkner as *Christian Ludwig Boxberg's Ausführliche Beschreibung . . . An English Translation with Commentary.* DMA diss., University of Nebraska, 2000.

Brandt, Konrad. 1996. Zur Geschichte der Reichel-Orgel in der Marktkirche. *Händel-Haus Mitteilungen,* no. 2, 14–20.

Braun, Werner. 1999. Ein unbekanntes Orgelbau-Attestat von Johann Sebastian Bach. BJ 85:19–33.

Brinkmann, Ernst. 1950. *Die Musikerfamilie Bach in Mühlhausen.* Mühlhausen: Rat der Stadt Mühlhausen.

Busch, Hermann J. 1993. Die Arp-Schnitger-Orgel der Hauptkirche St. Jacobi zu Hamburg. *Ars Organi* 41:156–61.

Butler, Lynn Edwards. 2004. Johann Christoph Bach's New Organ for Eisenach's Georgenkirche. *Bach: Journal of the Bach Riemenschneider Institute Baldwin Wallace College* 25: 42–60.

———. 2008. Johann Christoph Bach und die von Georg Christoph Stertzing erbaute große Orgel der Georgenkirche in Eisenach. BJ 94:229–69.

———. 2011. Leipzig's Organs in the Time of Bach. *Keyboard Perspectives* 3:87–101.

Butler, Lynn Edwards, and Gregory Butler. 2006. "Rare, Newly Invented Stops": Scheibe's Organ for St. Paul's Church, Leipzig. In *Orphei Organi: Essays in Honor of Harald Vogel,* ed. Cleveland Johnson, 285–306. Orcas, Wash.: Westfield.

Carspecken, Ferdinand. 1968. *Fünfhundert Jahre Kasseler Orgeln: Ein Beitrag zur Kultur- und Kunstgeschichte der Stadt Kassel.* Kassel: Bärenreiter.

Dähnert, Ulrich. 1962. *Der Orgel- und Instrumentenbauer Zacharias Hildebrandt.* Leipzig: Breitkopf & Härtel.

———. 1980. *Historische Orgeln in Sachsen: Ein Orgelinventar.* Frankfurt am Main: Verlag das Musikinstrument.

———. 1983. *Historische Orgeln in Sachsen: Ein Orgelinventar.* Leipzig: VEB Deutscher Verlag für Musik.

———. 1986. Organs Played and Tested by J. S. Bach. In *J. S. Bach as Organist: His Instruments, Music, and Performance Practices,* ed. George Stauffer and Ernest May, 3–24. Bloomington: Indiana University Press.

Dauer, Horst. 1992. Exkurs zur Zuberbier'schen Schloßkapell-Orgel von 1731. *Cöthener Bach-Hefte* 5:26–31.

David, Werner. 1951. *Johann Sebastian Bach's Orgeln*. Berlin: Berliner Musikinstrumenten-Sammlung.

Dehio, Georg. 1994. *Handbuch der Deutschen Kunstdenkmäler: Hamburg; Schleswig-Holstein*, ed. Johannes Habich et al. Munich: Deutscher Kunstverlag.

———. 1996a. *Handbuch der deutschen Kunstdenkmäler: Sachsen I; Regierungsbezirke Dresden*, ed. Barbara Bechter et al. Munich: Deutscher Kunstverlag.

———. 1996b. *Handbuch der deutschen Kunstdenkmäler: Sachsen II; Regierungsbezirke Leipzig und Chemnitz*, ed. Barbara Bechter et al. Munich: Deutscher Kunstverlag.

———. 1998. *Handbuch der deutschen Kunstdenkmäler: Sachsen II; Regierungsbezirke Leipzig und Chemnitz*, ed. Barbara Bechter. 2nd ed. Munich: Deutscher Kunstverlag.

———. 1999a. *Handbuch der deutschen Kunstdenkmäler: Sachsen-Anhalt II; Regierungsbezirk Dessau und Halle*, ed. Ute Bednarz et al. Munich: Deutscher Kunstverlag.

———. 1999b. *Handbuch der deutschen Kunstdenkmäler: Franken; Die Regierungsbezirke Oberfranken, Mittelfranken und Unterfranken*, ed. Tilmann Breuer et al. 2nd ed. Munich: Deutscher Kunstverlag.

———. 2000a. *Handbuch der deutschen Kunstdenkmäler: Berlin*, ed. Sibylle Badstübner-Gröger et al. 2nd ed. Munich: Deutscher Kunstverlag.

———. 2000b. *Handbuch der deutschen Kunstdenkmäler: Brandenburg*, ed. Gerhard Vinken et al. Munich: Deutscher Kunstverlag.

———. 2003. *Handbuch der deutschen Kunstdenkmäler: Thüringen*, ed. Stephanie Eißing et al. 2nd ed. Munich: Deutscher Kunstverlag.

Drechsel, Berit, ed. 2007. *Die Gottfried-Silbermann-Orgel der Petrikirche zu Freiberg: Entstehung, Veränderung, Rekonstruktion*. Dresden: Sandstein Verlag.

Dreyhaupt, Johann Christoph von. 1755/1772. *Pagus Neletici et Nudzici, oder, Ausführliche diplomatisch-historische Beschreibung des zum ehemaligen Primat und Ertz-Stifft, nunmehr aber durch westphälischen Friedensschluß secularisierten Herzogthum Magdeburg gehörigen Saal-Kreyses*. 3 vols. Halle: Verlag des Wäysenhauses.

Edskes, Cornelius H., and Harald Vogel. 2009. *Arp Schnitger und sein Werk*. Bremen: H. M. Hauschild.

Edwards, Lynn. 2001. Schnitger, Arp. *Grove*[2] 22:563–64.

Engel, David Hermann. 1855. *Beitrag zur Geschichte des Orgelbauwesens: Eine Denkschrift zur Einweihung der durch Herrn Friedrich Ladegast erbauten großen Dom-Orgel zu Merseburg*. Erfurt: G. W. Körner.

Ernst, Peter H. 1983. Die Gothaer Hof- und Landorgelmacher des 15.-18. Jahrhunderts. In *Gothaer Museumheft: Beiträge zur Regionalgeschichte*, 11–24.

———. 1987. Joh. Seb. Bachs Wirken am ehemaligen Mühlhäuser Augustinerinnenkloster und das Schicksal seiner Wender-Orgel. *BJ* 73:75–83.

Fischer, Hermann. 1969. Die Beziehungen Mainfrankens zu anderen Orgellandschaften. *Acta organologica* 3:13–68.

———. 2001. Christoph Dressel. In *MGG*[2] 5:1401.

Fischer, Hermann, and Theodor Wohnhaas. 1994. *Lexikon süddeutscher Orgelbauer*. Taschenbücher zur Musikwissenschaft 116. Wilhelmshaven: Florian Noetzel Verlag.

Flade, Ernst. 1926. *Der Orgelbauer Gottfried Silbermann: Ein Beitrag zur Geschichte des deutschen Orgelbaus im Zeitalter Bachs*. Leipzig: Fr. Kistner & C. W. Siegel.

———. 1952. Casparini, Eugenio. MGG²:889–92.

———. 1953. *Gottfried Silbermann: Ein Beitrag zur Geschichte des deutschen Orgel- und Klavierbaus im Zeitalter Bachs*. Leipzig: Breitkopf & Härtel.

Fock, Gustav. 1939/1997. Hamburgs Anteil am Orgelbau im Niederdeutschen Kulturgebiet. *Zeitschrift des Vereins für Hamburgische Geschichte* 38:289–373. Trans. and ed. by Lynn Edwards and Edwards Pepe as *Hamburg's Role in Northern European Organ Building*. Easthampton, Mass.: The Westfield Center.

———. 1950. *Der junge Bach in Lüneburg 1700 bis 1702*. Hamburg: Merseburger.

———. 1963a. Scherer. MGG, 1674–76.

———. 1963b. Schnitger, Arp. MGG, 1913–19.

———. 1967. Der historische Orgelbau im Küstengebiet zwischen Hamburg und Groningen (16.–18. Jahrhundert). *Acta organologica* 1:11–20.

———. 1974. *Arp Schnitger und seine Schule: Ein Beitrag zur Geschichte des Orgelbaues im Nord- und Ostseeküstengebiet*. Kassel: Bärenreiter, 1974.

Friedrich, Felix. 1989. *Der Orgelbauer Heinrich Gottfried Trost: Leben-Werk-Leistung*. Wiesbaden: Breitkopf & Härtel.

———, ed. 1998. *Die Trost-Orgel in der Schloßkirche Altenburg*. 3rd ed. Altenburg: Stadtverwaltung Altenburg, Schloßverwaltung.

———. 2001a. Fincke [Finke, Finck]. Grove² 8:825.

———. 2001b. Förner, Christian. MGG² 6:1477–78.

———. 2001c. Christian Förner und die Orgel der Schloßkirche zu Weißenfels. *Acta organologica* 27:21–35.

———. 2002. Hildebrandt, Zacharias. MGG² 8:1530–31.

———. 2005a. Der Orgelbauer Franciscus Volckland. In *Dulce Melos Organorum: Festschrift Alfred Reichling zum 70. Geburtstag*, ed. Roland Behrens and Christoph Grohmann, 191–216. Mettlach, Germany: Gesellschaft der Orgelfreunde.

———. 2005b. Aufführungspraktische Beobachtungen am Orgelschaffen Johann Peter Kellners im Zusammenhang mit der Orgel von Johann Anton Weise in Gräfenroda. *Ars Organi* 53:214–18.

———. 2009. Der Orgelbauer Tobias Heinrich Gottfried Trost: Zum 250. Todestag 2009. *Ars Organi* 57 (June):102–6.

Gailit, Michael. 2002. Drei Wagner-Orgeln und eine Simplifikation: Zur Berliner Orgelwelt in Mendelssohns Jugendjahren. *Orgel International* 6:140–49.

Glöckner, Andreas. 1990. Die Musikpflege an der Leipziger Neukirche zur Zeit Johann Sebastian Bachs. *Beiträge zur Bach-Forschung* 8:1–170.

Gramlich, Sybille, Andreas Bernhard, Andreas Cante, et al. 2002. *Denkmaltopographie Bundesrepublik Deutschland*. Denkmale in Brandenburg 3. Worms am Rhein: Werner.

Grapenthin, Ulf. 2007. The Catharinen Organ during Scheidemann's Tenure. In Pieter Dirksen, *Heinrich Scheidemann's Keyboard Music: Transmission, Style and Chronology*, 169–98. Burlington, Vt.: Ashgate.

Greß, Frank-Harald. 1989. *Die Klanggestalt der Orgeln Gottfried Silbermanns*. Frankfurt (Main): Breitkopf & Härtel.

———. 1994. *Die Orgeln der Frauenkirche zu Dresden*. Freiberg: Gottfried Silbermann Gesellschaft.

——. 2001. *Die Orgeln Gottfried Silbermanns.* 2nd ed. Dresden: Ostdeutschen Sparkassenstiftung im Freistaat Sachsen.

Grohs, Gernot. 2000. Köthen. In *Das Bach-Lexikon,* ed. Michael Heinemann, 307–9. Laaber: Laaber Verlag.

Grosmane, Elita. 2003. Die Tätigkeit des Orgelbauers Heinrich Andreas Contius in Deutschland und Lettland. In *Studien zur Kunstgeschichte im Baltikum,* ed. Lars Olof Larsson, 43–64. Kiel: Martin Carl Adolf Böckler Stiftung.

Großmann, Dieter. 1968. Wender, Johann Friedrich. MGG 14:463–64.

Gurlitt, Wilibald. 1913. Zwei archivalische Beiträge zur Geschichte des Orgelbaues in Braunschweig aus den Jahren 1626 und 1631. *Braunschweigisches Magazin* 9:80–84, 89–91.

——. 1937. Der Kursächsische Hoforgelmacher Gottfried Fritzsche. In *Festschrift Arnold Schering zum sechzigsten Geburtstag,* ed. Helmut Osthoff, Walter Serauky, and Adam Adrio, 106–24. Berlin: s.n.

——. 1938. Zum Schülerkreis des kursächsischen Hoforgelmachers Gottfried Fritzsche. *Musik und Kirche* 10:158–69.

Hackel, Wolfram, and Hans Klotz. 2002. Fritzsche, Gottfried. MGG² 7:168–69.

Haetge, Ernst, ed. 1931. *Die Stadt Erfurt, Band 2: Allerheiligenkirche, Andreaskirche, Augustinerkirche, Barfüsserkirche.* Burg: August Hopfer Verlag.

——. 1943. *Die Kunstdenkmale der Stadt und des Landes Köthen.* Burg: August Hopfer Verlag.

Häfner, Ludwig. 2006. Neue Erkentnisse zur "Berkaer Bach-Orgel." BJ 92:291–93.

Harder, Peter. 2005. Die Kellner-Weise-Orgel von 1736 in Gräfenroda und der Wandel der Klangvorstellungen. *Ars Organi* 53:154–61.

Hartmann, Christian Friedrich, ed. 1799. *Geschichte der evangelisch lutherischen St. Agnuskirche in Cöthen.* Köthen.

Haupt, Harmut. 1989. *Orgeln im Bezirk Gera. Eine Übersicht über die Orgellandschaft Ostthüringen.* Gera: Rat des Bezirkes Gera.

——. 1998. *Orgeln in Nord- und Westthüringen.* Bad Homburg: Verlag Ausbildung + Wissen.

Heinke, Theophil, ed. 1998. *Die Trost-Orgel und Stadtkirche "Zur Gotteshilfe" Waltershausen. Festschrift zur Orgelweihe und 275-jährigem Jubiläum der Stadtkirche.* Waltershausen: Evang.-Luth. Stadtkirchgemeinde Waltershausen.

Henkel, Hubert. 1985. Die Orgeln der Köthener Kirchen zur Zeit Johann Sebastian Bachs und ihre Geschichte (Teil I). *Cöthener Bach-Hefte* 3:5–28.

——. 1986. Zur Geschichte der Scheibe-Orgel in der Leipziger Johannis-Kirche. *Bach-Studien* 9:44–50.

Hennings, Johann, and Wilhelm Stahl. 1952. *Musikgeschichte Lübecks,* vol. 2, *Geistliche Musik.* Kassel: Bärenreiter.

Hepworth, William. 1905/6. Die Orgel der St. Jacobikirche in Hamburg. *Zeitschrift für Instrumentenbau* 26:258–64.

Hoffman, Horst. 1999. Zwei Bach-Orgeln. *Orgel International* 3:478–83.

Hoppe, Günther. 1992. Die Wiederherstellung der Schloßkapelle Köthen als barocke Emporenkirche (1988–1991). *Cöthener Bach-Hefte* 5:100–127.

Hunstock, Erhard. 1997. *897 Ambraha—1997 Ammern: Festschrift zur 1100 Jahrfeier des Dorfes Ammern.* Ammern: privately printed.

Hüttel, Walter. 1980a. Donat, Christoph. Grove² 5:541.

———. 1980b. Dressel, Christoph. Grove² 5:629.

———. 2001. Donat, Christoph Jr. MGG² 5:1242.

Hütter, Elisabeth, Heinrich Magirius, and Winfried Werner. 1995. Evangelisch-lutherische Universitätskirche St. Pauli, ehem. Augustusplatz. In *Bau- und Kunstdenkmäler von Sachsen: Stadt Leipzig; Die Sakralbauten*, 483–677. Munich: Landesamt für Denkmalpflege Sachsen.

Jauernig, Reinhold. 1950. Johann Sebastian Bach in Weimar: Neue Forschungsergebnisse aus Weimarer Quellen. In *Johann Sebastian Bach in Thüringen: Festgabe zum Gedenkjahr 1950*, ed. Heinrich Besseler and Günter Kraft, 49–107. Weimar: Thüringer Volksverlag.

Kaufmann, Michael Gerhard. 2000. "... alles tüchtig, fleißig und wohl erbauet..." Johann Sebastian Bachs Prüfung der Scheibe-Orgel in Zschortau. *Orgel International* 4:404–9.

Kirchner, Christhard. 2006. Der mitteldeutsche Orgelbauer Christoph Junge. *Acta organologica* 29:267–308.

Kitschke, Andreas. 1993. Die Orgelbauten Joachim Wagners. *Acta organologica* 23:197–240.

———. 2011. Der Lehrmeister von Joachim Wagner. *Ars Organi* 59:200.

Klée Gobert, Renata. 1968a. Hamburg, St. Katharinen. In *Die Bau- und Kunstdenkmale der Freien und Hansestadt Hamburg*, vol. 3, *Innenstadt: Die Hauptkirchen St. Petri, St. Katharinen, St. Jacobi*, ed. Renata Klée-Gobert and Peter Wiek, 101–54. Hamburg: Christian Wagner.

———. 1968b. Hamburg, St. Jacobi. In *Bau- und Kunstdenkmale der Freien und Hansestadt Hamburg*, vol. 3, *Innenstadt: Die Hauptkirchen St. Petri, St. Katharinen, St. Jacobi*, ed. Renata Klée-Gobert and Peter Wiek, 155–234. Hamburg: Christian Wagner.

Klotz, Hans. 1950. Bachs Orgeln und seine Orgelmusik. *Musikforschung* 3:189–201.

———. 1952. Compenius. MGG 2:1591–92.

———. 1980a. Scheibe, Johann. Grove 16:599.

———. 1980b. Schröter, Johann Georg. Grove 16:749.

———. 1980c. Stellwagen, Friedrich. Grove 18:115.

———. 1980d. Trost, Heinrich Gottfried. Grove 19:188.

König, Ernst. 1963/64. Zu J. S. Bachs Wirken in Köthen. BJ 50:53–60.

Koschel, Alexander. 2002. Christian Förner und seine Orgel in der Schloßkirche St. Trinitatis zu Weißenfels. *Ars Organi* 50:9–14.

Kröhner, Christine. 1995. Johann Sebastian Bach und Johann Friedrich Bach als Orgelexaminatoren im Gebiet der freien Reichsstadt Mühlhausen nach 1708. BJ 81:83–91.

Krüger, Franz, and Wilhelm Reinecke. 1906. *Die Kunstdenkmäler der Provinz Hannover: Regierungsbezirk Lüneburg, Stadt Lüneburg*. Hannover: T. Schulz.

Kuhlmann, Erich. 1981. Johann Lange: Ein Orgelbauer aus Dithmarschen. *Nordelbingen: Beiträge zur Kunst- und Kulturgeschichte* 50:197–201.

Kümmerle, Salomon, ed. 1888–1895. *Encyklopädie der evangelischen Kirchenmusik*. 4 vols. Gütersloh: Bertelsmann.

Lade, Günther, ed. 1997. *Die Sonnenorgel der Evang. Pfarrkirche St. Peter und Paul zu Görlitz*. Görlitz: Edition-Lade.

Lehfeldt, Paul, and Georg Voss, eds. 1888–1917. *Die Bau- und Kunst-Denkmäler Thüringens*. 41 vols. Jena: Gustav Fischer.

Ley, Hermann. 1906/7. Die Totentanzorgel in der St. Marienkirche zu Lübeck. *Zeitschrift für Instrumentenbau* 27:280–82.

Linde. *See* van de Linde.

Lobenstein, Albrecht. 2003. Die Orgelbauer Berlt Hering († 1556), Ludwig Compenius († 1671) und Christoph Junge († 1687) in der Erfurter Kaufmannskirche. *Ars Organi* 51:216–23.

Löffler, Hans. 1925. J. S. Bachs Orgelprüfungen. BJ 22:93–100.

——. 1926. Johann Sebastian Bach und der Weimarer Orgelbauer Trebs. BJ 23:156–58.

——. 1928. J. S. Bach und die Orgeln seiner Zeit. In *Bericht über die dritte Tagung für deutsche Orgelkunst in Freiberg/Sachsen vom 2. bis 7. Oktober 1927*, ed. Christhard Mahrenholz, 122–32. Kassel: Bärenreiter.

——. 1931. Ein unbekanntes Thüringer Orgelmanuskript von 1798. *Musik und Kirche* 3:140–43.

Lützkendorf, Thilo. 1991. Orgeln in Halle/Saale. *Ars Organi* 39:166–78.

Lux, Eduard. 1926. Das Orgelwerk in St. Michaelis zu Ohrdruf zur Zeit des Aufenthalts Johann Sebastian Bachs daselbst, 1695–1700. BJ 23:145–55.

Magirius, Heinrich. 1995a. Evangelisch-lutherische Stadtpfarrkirche St. Nicolai, Nikolaikirchhof. In *Die Bau- und Kunstdenkmäler von Sachsen: Stadt Leipzig; Die Sakralbauten*, 337–473. Munich: Landesamt für Denkmalpflege Sachsen.

——. 1995b. Evangelisch-lutherisch Stadtpfarrkirche St. Thomas, Thomaskirchhof. In *Die Bau- und Kunstdenkmäler von Sachsen: Stadt Leipzig; Die Sakralbauten*, 153–335. Munich: Landesamt für Denkmalpflege Sachsen.

Mai, Hartmut. 1995. Johanniskirche. In *Die Bau- und Kunstdenkmäler von Sachsen: Stadt Leipzig; Die Sakralbauten*, 809–69. Munich: Landesamt für Denkmalpflege Sachsen.

Mai, Hartmut, and Herbert Küas. 1995. Evangelisch-lutherische Matthäikirche, ehem. Matthäikirchhof 22/23. In *Die Bau- und Kunstdenkmäler von Sachsen: Stadt Leipzig; Die Sakralbauten*, 679–96. Munich and Berlin: Landesamt für Denkmalpflege Sachsen.

Mattheson, Johann. 1725. Johann Kuhnau to Johann Mattheson, 8 December 1717. In Johann Mattheson, *Critica musica*, 2:229–39. Hamburg: privately printed.

Maul, Michael. 2004a. Johann Sebastian Bachs Besuche in der Residenzstadt Gera. BJ 90:101–19.

——. 2004b. Frühe Urteile über Johann Christoph und Johann Nikolaus Bach, mitgeteilt anläßlich der Besetzung der Organistenstelle an der Jenaer Kollegienkirche (1709). BJ 90:157–68.

——. 2005. "Alles mit Gott und nichts ohn' ihn": Eine neue aufgefundene Aria von Johann Sebastian Bach. BJ 91:7–34.

——. 2006. Scheidt-Dokumente aus der Lutherstadt Eisleben. In *Samuel Scheidt (1587–1654): Werk und Wirkung*. Schriften des Händel-Hauses in Halle 20, ed. Konstanze Musketa and Wolfgang Ruf, 193–213. Halle (Saale): Händel-Haus.

——. 2010. Johann Adolph Scheibes Bach-Kritik: Hintergründe und Schauplätze einer musikalischen Kontroverse. BJ 96:153–98.

Maul, Michael, and Peter Wollny, eds. 2007. Preface. In *Weimarer Orgeltabulatur: Die frühesten Notenhandschriften Johann Sebastian Bachs, sowie Abschriften seines Schülers Johann Martin Schubart, mit Werken von Dietrich Buxtehude, Johann Adam Reinken und Johann Pachelbel*, xxi–xxxv. Kassel: Bärenreiter.

Mehl, Johannes G. 1953. Die Barockorgel in Lahm/Itzgrund, im Zusammenhang des nord- und süddeutschen Orgelbaues ihrer Zeit und die Probleme ihrer Restaurierung. In *Kongreßbericht: Gesellschaft für Musikforschung*, 78–82. Kassel: Bärenreiter.

Müller, Werner. 1982. *Gottfried Silberman: Persönlichkeit und Werk: Eine Dokumentation*. Leipzig: Deutscher Verlag für Musik.

——. 1999. *Gottfried Silbermann 1683–1753: Beiträge zum Leben und Wirken des sächsischen Orgelbauers*. Frauenstein: Gottfried Silbermann Museum.

Mundt, Hermann. 1907/08. Historische Nachrichten über die Kirchenorgeln in Halle a.S. *Zeitschrift für Instrumentenbau* 28:392.

——. 1925/26. Orgel und Glockenspiel der Kgl. Hof- und Garnisonkirche in Potsdam. *Zeitschrift für Instrumentenbau* 46:275–76.

——. 1928. Joachim Wagner, ein Altberliner Orgelbauer. In *Bericht über die dritte Tagung für deutsche Orgelkunst in Freiberg/Sachsen vom 2. bis 7. Oktober 1927*, ed. Christhard Mahrenholz, 139–48. Kassel: Bärenreiter.

Nentwig, Franziska, ed. 2004. *"Ich habe fleißig sein müssen:" Johann Sebastian Bach und seine Kindheit in Eisenach*. Eisenach: Edition Bachhaus.

Niedt, Friedrich Erhardt. 1721. Anhang: Von den Dispositionen etlicher LX (Mehrentheils) Berühmter Orgel-Wercke Itziger Zeit. In *Friedrich Erhardt Niedtens Musikalische Handleitung anderer Theil, von der Variation des General-Basses*, ed. Johann Mattheson, 156–204. Hamburg: Benjamin Schiller's Widow and Johann Christoph Kiszner of Dohm. Trans. by Pamela L. Poulin and Irmgard C. Taylor as "Appendix of More than 60 Organ Specifications." In Friedrich Erhardt Niedt, *The Musical Guide*. Oxford: Clarendon Press, 1989. [All references are to the German edition.]

Oefner, Claus. 1996. *Die Musikerfamilie Bach in Eisenach*. Schriften zur Musikgeschichte Thüringens 1. 2nd ed. Eisenach: Bachhaus Eisenach.

Oertel, Alfred. 1950. Johann Sebastian Bach in Ohrdruf. In *Festschrift zum Bachjahr 1950*, 7–10. Ohrdruf: Bachausschuß der Stadt Ohrdruf.

Ortgies, Ibo. 2004. Bartold Hering: Organist und Orgelbauer in Lübeck? *Ars Organi* 52:70–74.

——. 2004. *Die Praxis der Orgelstimmung in Norddeutschland im 17. und 18. Jahrhundert und ihr Verhältnis zur zeitgenössischen Musikpraxis*. PhD diss., Universität Göteborg.

——. 2005. Schnitger. MGG[2] 14:1529–32.

——. 2006. Über den Umbau der großen Orgel der Marienkirche zu Lübeck durch Friedrich Stellwagen, 1637–41. In *Orphei Organi Antiqui: Essays in Honor of Harald Vogel*, ed. Cleveland Johnson, 313–36. Orcas, Wash.: The Westfield Center.

Orth, Siegfried. 1972. Der Schweidnitzer Orgelbauer Christoph Junge in Erfurt 1684–1687. *Ars Organi* 20:1697–99.

Pape, Uwe. 1971. Arp Schnitger. *ISO-Information* 5 (February):357–76.

——. 2000. Neue Orgel für die St. Marien-Kirche in Berlin. *Ars Organi* 48:175–76.

——. 2002. Zur Rekonstruktion der Mensuren von Joachim Wagner in der neuen Orgel der St. Marien-Kirche in Berlin. *Orgel International* 6:150–59.

——. 2003. Ergänzungen zum Stammbaum der Orgelbauerfamilie Zuberbier. *Ars Organi* 51:81–82.

Peeters, Paul. 2004. Niehoff, Hendrik. MGG[2] 12:1079.

Petzoldt, Martin. 2000. *Bachstätten. Ein Reiseführer zu Johann Sebastian Bach*. Frankfurt am Main: Insel Verlag.

Praetorius, Michael. 1619. *De Organographia*. Vol. 2 of *Syntagma musicum*. Wolfenbüttel. Facsimile, Kassel: Bärenreiter, 1958.

Preller, Gottfried. 2002. Die Orgeln der Johann-Sebastian-Bach-Kirche zu Arnstadt. In *Perspectives on Organ Playing and Musical Interpretation: Pedagogical, Historical, and Instrumental Studies; A Festschrift for Heinrich Fleischer at 90*, ed. Ames Anderson et al., 138–46. New Ulm, Minn.: Graphic Arts, Martin Luther College.

Rathey, Markus. 2001. Die Temperierung der Divi-Blasii-Orgel in Mühlhausen. BJ 87:163–71.

Ratte, Franz-Josef. 2000. Temperatur. In *Das Bach-Lexikon*, ed. Michael Heinemann, 510. Laaber: Laaber Verlag.

Rehm, Gottfried. 2002. *Die Compenius-Orgel zu Kroppenstedt: Geschichte der 1603 bis 1613 von Esaias Compenius d.Ä. erbauten Orgel in der St.-Martini-Kirche zu Kroppenstedt.* Niebüll: Verlag Videel.

Reichling, Alfred. 2000. *Die Hildebrandt-Orgel zu Naumburg, St. Wenzel. Festschrift anläßlich der Wiedereinweihung nach vollendeter Restaurierung am 3. Dezember 2000.* Naumburg: Saaledruck Naumburg.

Reichling, Alfred, and Jan Janka. 2000. Casparini, Eugenio. MGG² 4:371–72.

Reinitzer, Heimo, ed. 1995. *Die Arp Schnitger-Orgel der Hauptkirche St. Jacobi in Hamburg.* Hamburg: Christians Verlag.

Rubardt, Paul. 1928. Arp Schnitger. In *Bericht über die dritte Tagung für deutsche Orgelkunst in Freiberg/Sachsen vom 2. bis 7. Oktober 1927*, ed. Christhard Mahrenholz, 149–75. Kassel: Bärenreiter.

——. 1936/37. Die Bach-Orgel zu Zschortau. *Die Musik* 29:272–74.

——. 1961. Zwei Orgeldispositionen J. S. Bachs. In *Festschrift Heinrich Besseler zum sechzigsten Geburtstag*, ed. Eberhardt Klemm, 495–503. Leipzig: Deutscher Verlag für Musik.

——. 1963. Scheibe, Johann. MGG 11:1616–17.

——. 2005. Scheibe, Johann. MGG² 14:1202.

Rubardt, Paul, and Ernst Jentsch. 1952. *Kamenzer Orgel-Buch.* Kamenz: Oberlausitzer Druckwerkstätten, Werk Kamenz.

Rühle, Wieland. 1992. Über die Restaurierung und teilweise Rekonstruktion der 1754 von Johann Christoph Zuberbier für die Kirche in Thurau/Anhalt gebauten Orgel. *Cöthener Bach-Hefte* 5:5–25.

Rust, Wilhelm. 1878. Vorwort. In *Johann Sebastian Bach's Werke*, vol. 25/2, v–ix, Leipzig: Neue Bach-Gesellschaft.

Schaefer, Marc, ed. 1994. *Das Silbermann-Archiv: Der handschriftliche Nachlaß des Orgelmachers Johann Andreas Silbermann (1712–1783).* Prattica Musicale: Veröffentlichungen der Schola Cantorum Basiliensis 4. Winterthur, Switzerland: Amadeus.

——. 1995. Der handschriftliche Nachlaß des Orgelbauers Johann Andreas Silbermann. In *Die Elsässische Orgelreform: Bericht über das neunte Colloquium der Walcker-Stiftung für orgelwissenschaftliche Forschung*, ed. Hans Heinrich Eggebrecht, 83–94. Kleinbittersdorf: Walcker-Stiftung.

Schaefer, Marc, and Frank-Harald Greß. 2001. Silbermann. In Grove² 23:383–84.

Scherer-Hall, Richard. 1998. Die neue Sonnenorgel zu Görlitz. *Ars Organi* 46:43–48.

Schering, Arnold. 1926. *Musikgeschichte der Stadt Leipzig*, vol. 2, *Von 1650 bis 1723.* Leipzig: F. Kistner & C. F. W. Siegel.

Schindler, Jürgen-Peter. 1985. Die Herbst-Orgel der Schloßkirche zu Lahm. *Ars Organi* 33:112–21.

Schlepphorst, Winfried. 2000. Compenius. MGG² 4:1440–41.

Schmidt, Julius, ed. 1882. *Beschreibende Darstellung der älteren Bau- und Kunstdenkmäler des Kreises Sangerhausen, mit einer Glockenschau von Gustav Sommer* (= Beschreibende Darstellung der älteren Bau- und Kunstdenkmäler der Provinz Sachsen 5). Halle (Saale): Hendel.

Schmidt-Mannheim, Hans. 2004. Die Peter-Heroldt-Orgel in Buttstädt: Auf den Spuren von Johann Tobias und Johann Ludwig Krebs. *Acta organologica* 28:155–88.

Schneider, Thekla. 1937. Die Orgelbauerfamilie Compenius. *Archiv für Musikforschung* 2:8–73.

Schrammek, Winfried. 1983a. *Bach-Orgeln in Thüringen und Sachsen.* Beiträge zur Bach-Pflege der DDR 11. Leipzig: Nationale Forschungs- und Gedenkstätten Johann Sebastian Bach der DDR.

———. 1983b. Zur Geschichte der großen Orgel in der Thomaskirche zu Leipzig von 1601 bis 1885. *Beiträge zur Bach-Forschung* 2:46–55.

———. 1985. Johann Sebastian Bachs Stellung zu Orgelpedalregistern im 32-Fuß-Ton. BJ 71: 147–54.

———. 1988. Orgel, Positiv, Clavicymbel und Glocken der Schloßkirche zu Weimar 1658 bis 1774. In *Bach-Händel-Schütz-Ehrung 1985 der Deutschen Demokratischen Republik. Bericht über die Wissenschaftliche Konferenz zum V. Internationalen Bachfest der Neuen Bachgesellschaft,* ed. Winfried Hoffmann and Armin Schneiderheinze, 99–111. Leipzig: VEB Deutscher Verlag für Musik.

———. 2001. Die durch Hermann Eule Orgelbau Bautzen wiederhergestellte Bach-Orgel von Zacharias Hildebrandt in der Wenzelskirche zu Naumburg. *Ars Organi* 49:27–30.

Schuke Orgelbau (Potsdam). *The Complete Worklist since 1820.* http://www.schuke.com/englisch/index_englisch.html.

Schulze, Claus-Peter. 1968. Wagner, Joachim. MGG 14:77–78.

Schulze, Hans-Joachim. 1981. Über die unvermeidlichen Lücken in Bachs Lebensbeschreibung. In *Bachforschung und Bachinterpretation heute: Wissenschaftler und Praktiker im Dialog: Bericht über das Bachfest-Symposium 1978 der Philipps-Universität Marburg,* ed. Reinhold Brinkmann, 32–42. Kassel: Bärenreiter.

———. 1984. *Studien zur Bach-Überlieferung im 18. Jahrhundert.* Leipzig: Edition Peters.

Seeliger, Reinhard. 1992. Die Sonnenorgel in St. Peter und Paul zu Görlitz an der Neiße. *Ars Organi* 40:16–18.

Seggermann, Günter. 2001. Kleine Orgelgeschichte der Hamburger Hauptkirche St. Katharinen. *Ars Organi* 40:142–50.

Seidel, Johann Julius. 1844. *Die Orgel und ihr Bau: Ein systematisches Handbuch für Cantoren, Organisten, Schullehrer, Musikstudirende etc. so wie für Geistliche, Kirchenvorsteher und alle Freunde der Orgel und des Orgelspiels.* 2nd ed. Breslau: F. E. C. Leuckart. Trans. J. J. Seidel as *The Organ and Its Construction: A Systematic Handbook for Organists, Organ Builders, &c.* London: Ewer, 1855. [References are to the German edition.]

Selle, Liselotte. 1970. Die Orgelbauerfamilie Gloger (1). *Acta organologica* 4:59–116.

Serauky, Walter. 1935. *Musikgeschichte der Stadt Halle 1: Von den Anfängen bis zum Beginn des 17. Jahrhunderts.* Halle/Saale. Repr. Hildesheim: Georg Olms, 1971.

———. 1939. *Musikgeschichte der Stadt Halle 2/1: Von Samuel Scheidt bis in die Zeit Georg Friedrich Händels und Johann Sebastian Bachs.* Halle/Saale. Repr. Hildesheim: Georg Olms, 1971.

Sicul, Christoph Ernst. 1718. *Andere Beylage zu dem Leipziger Jahrbuche, auf Jahr 1718.* Leipzig.

Silbermann: Geschichte und Legende einer Orgelbauerfamilie. 2006. Badisches Landesmuseum Karlsruhe and Franziskanermuseum Villingen-Schwenningen. Published in conjunction with the exhibition "Silbermann: Geschichte und Legende einer Orgelbauerfamilie," shown at the Franziskanermuseum of Villingen-Schwenningen, the Badisches Landesmuseum of Karlsruhe, and the Archives de la Ville et de la Communauté Urbaine of Straßburg.

Smets, Paul, ed. 1931. *Orgeldispositionen: Eine Handschrift aus dem XVIII. Jahrhundert, im Besitz der Sächsischen Landesbibliothek, Dresden* [Dresden Ms.]. Kassel: Bärenreiter.

Snyder, Kerala. 1985. Buxtehude's Organs: Helsingsør, Helsingborg, Lübeck. *Musical Times* 126 (July):427–34.

———. 1986. Bach and Buxtehude at the Large Organ of St. Mary's in Lübeck. In *Charles Brenton Fisk, Organ Builder*, vol. 1, *Essays in His Honor*, ed. Fenner Douglass, Owen Jander, and Barbara Owen, 175–90. Easthampton, Mass.: Westfield Center, 1986.

———. 2002. Ein Lübecker Vier-Personen-Stück: Buxtehude, Schnitger, Hantelmann, Nordtmann und die Lübecker Domorgel. *Orgel: Journal für die Orgel* 5:38–43.

———. 2007. *Dieterich Buxtehude: Organist in Lübeck*. Rev. ed. Rochester, N.Y.: University of Rochester Press.

Sommer, Gustav, ed. 1882. *Beschreibende Darstellung der älteren Bau- und Kunstdenkmäler der Provinz Sachsen*, vol. 1, *Die Kreise Zeitz, Langensalza, Weißenfels, Mühlhausen und Sangerhausen*. Halle/Saale: Hendel.

Sprondel, Friedrich. 2000. Orgelparadies an der Pleiße: Ein Gespräch mit dem Thomasorganisten Ullrich Böhme. *Orgel International* 4:390–93.

Stade, Joachim. 2005. Zur Restaurierung in Gräfenroda. *Ars Organi* 53:161–64.

Stahl, Wilhelm. 1931. *Geschichte der Kirchenmusik in Lübeck bis zum Anfang des 19. Jahrhunderts*. Lübeck: Quizow.

———. 1939. *Lübecks Orgeln*. Lübeck: E. Robert.

Sterzik, Torsten. 1998. Was wäre gewesen, wenn nicht Heinrich Gottfried Trost diese Orgel gebaut hätte? In *Die Trost-Orgel und Stadtkirche "Zur Gotteshilfe" Waltershausen: Festschrift zur Orgelweihe und 275-jährigem Jubiläum der Stadtkirche*, ed. Theophil Heinke, 38–47. Waltershausen: Evang.-Luth. Stadtkirchgemeinde Waltershausen.

Steves, Heinz. 1939. Der Orgelbauer Joachim Wagner. *Archiv für Musikforschung* 4:321–58.

Stüven, Wilfried. 1964. *Orgel und Orgelbauer im Halleschen Land vor 1800*. Wiesbaden: Breitkopf & Härtel.

Tettau, Wilhelm Freiherr von, ed. 1890. *Beschreibende Darstellung der älteren Bau- und Kunstdenkmäler der Stadt Erfurt und des Erfurter Landkreises*. Halle/Saale: Hendel.

Theobald, Hans Wolfgang. 1986. Zur Geschichte der 1746 von Johann Sebastian Bach geprüften Johann-Scheibe-Orgel in Zschortau bei Leipzig. *BJ* 72:81–89.

Thiele, Georg. 1927/28. Die Bachorgel der Divi-Blasii-Kirche in Mühlhausen. *Mühlhäuser Geschichtsblätter: Zeitschrift des Altertumsvereins für Mühlhausen, Thüringen und Umgegend* 28:142–52.

Thom, Eitelfriedrich, ed. 1990. *Der Orgelbauer Joachim Wagner, 1690–1749*. Dokumentationen der Kultur- und Forschungsstätte Michaelstein 24. Michaelstein, Blankenburg: Kultur- und Forschungsstätte Michaelstein.

Trost, Johann Caspar. 1677. *Ausführliche Beschreibung deß Neuen Orgelwercks auf der Augustus-Burg zu Weissenfels, worinnen zugleich enthalten was zu der Orgelmacher Kunst gehöre*. Facsimile in *Acta organologica* 27 (2001):36–108.

van Biezen. *See Biezen*.

van de Linde, Koos. 2002. Organs in Sweelinck's Time. In *Sweelinck Studies: Proceedings of the International Sweelinck Symposium Utrecht 1999*, ed. Pieter Dirksen, 199–218. Utrecht: STIMU, Foundation for Historical Performance Practice.

Vente, Maarten Albert. 1958. *Die Brabanter Orgel: Zur Geschichte der Orgelkunst in Belgien und Holland im Zeitalter der Gotik und der Renaissance*. Amsterdam: Paris.

Vogel, Harald. 1997. A History of the Organs in St. Catharinen, Hamburg, from c. 1520 to 1743. In Gustav Fock, *Hamburg's Role in Northern European Organ Building*, trans. Lynn Edwards and Edward C. Pepe, 95–108. Easthampton, Mass.: Westfield Center.

——. 1999. Waltershausen: Encounter with a Bach Organ. *Newsletter of the Westfield Center* 12/2 (1999):1–3, 6. Also published as "Begegnung mit einer Bach-Orgel," *Orgel International* 6:43.

Vogel, Harald, Günter Lade, and Nicola Borger-Keweloh. 1997. *Orgeln in Niedersachsen*. Bremen: H. M. Hauschild.

Vogel, Johann Jacob. n.d. *Leipzigisches Chronicon, Das ist: Gründ- und Ausführliche Beschreibung der Churfürstl. Sächs. Welt-bekandten Handels-Stadt Leipzig*.

Voigt, Dieter. 2004. Die Voigt-Orgel von 1985 in der Schloßkapelle zu Weißenfels: Ein Beitrag zur Orgelbaugeschichte in der DDR. *Ars Organi* 52:81–87.

Wagener, Heinrich. 1863/64. Die Heiliggeist-Kirche. *Mitteilungen des Vereins für die Geschichte Potsdams* 1 (no. 26):2.

Walther, Johann Gottfried. 1732. *Musicalisches Lexikon*. Facsimile. Kassel: Bärenreiter, 1953.

Wenke, Wolfgang. 1985. Der Spieltisch der Arnstädter Bachorgel: Restaurierung und Rekonstruktion vom Museumsmöbel aus der Zeit um 1864 zum Bestandteil der Wender-Orgel von 1699/1703. In *Bericht über das 5. Symposium zu Fragen des Orgelbaus im 17./18. Jahrhundert*. Beiheft zu den Studien zur Aufführungspraxis und Interpretation der Musik des 18. Jahrhunderts, ed. Eitelfriedrich Thom, 82–85. Blankenburg, Michaelstein: Kultur- und Forschungsstätte Michaelstein.

Wennig, Erich. 1937. *Chronik des musikalischen Lebens der Stadt Jena*, Part 1, *Von den Anfängen bis zum Jahre 1750*. Jena.

Werckmeister, Andreas. 1698/1976. *Werckmeister's Erweiterte und Verbesserte Orgelprobe in English*. Trans. Gerhard Krapf. Raleigh, N.C.: Sunbury Press.

——. 1705. *Organum Gruningense redivivum*. Quedlinburg and Aschersleben: Gottlob Erst Struntz. Repr. ed. Paul Smets, Mainz: Rheingold, 1932.

Werner, Helmut. 2000. Die Königen unter den "Bach-Orgeln": Zur Restaurierung der Hildebrandt-Orgel in der Stadtkirche St. Wenzel zu Naumburg. *Orgel International* 4:396–402.

Wette, Gottfried Albin. 1737. *Historischen Nachrichten von der berühmten Residentz-Stadt Weimar*. Weimar: S. H. Hoffmann.

Williams, Peter. 1982. J. S. Bach: Orgelsachverständiger unter dem Einfluß Andreas Werckmeisters? BJ 68:131–42.

Wit, Paul de. 1898/1899. Bach-Orgel der alten Johanniskirche in Leipzig. *Zeitschrift für Instrumentenbau* 19:801.

——. 1899/1900. Bach-Orgel der alten Johanniskirche in Leipzig [continued]. Leipzig. *Zeitschrift für Instrumentenbau* 20:989.

Wolff, Christian, ed. 2005. *Die Orgeln der Thomaskirche zu Leipzig*. Leipzig: Evangelische Verlagsanstalt.

Wolff, Christoph. 1998. "Eine recht große und recht schöne Orgel": Die neue Bach-Orgel für die Thomaskirche in Leipzig. *Orgel International* 2 (no. 5):20–22.

——. 2000. *Johann Sebastian Bach: The Learned Musician*. New York: Norton.

——. 2005a. *Johann Sebastian Bach*. Rev. ed. Frankfurt am Main: S. Fischer Verlag.

———. 2005b. Die historichen Orgeln der Thomaskirche. In *Die Orgeln der Thomaskirche zu Leipzig*, ed. Christian Wolff, 9–20. Leipzig: Evangelische Verlagsanstalt.

Wolfheim, Werner. 1915. Die ehemalige Orgel. In *Bau- und Kunst-Denkmäler Thüringens 1: Großherzogtum Sachsen-Weimar-Eisenach 3*, vol. 1, *Abtheilung: Verwaltungsbezirk Eisenach 1*, ed. P. Lehfeldt and G. Voss, 230. Jena: Fischer Verlag.

Wollny, Peter. 2005. Über die Hintergründe von Johann Sebastian Bachs Bewerbung in Arnstadt. BJ 91:83–94.

Zietz, Hermann. 1969. *Quellenkritische Untersuchungen an den Bach-Handschriften P 801, P 802 und P 803 as dem "Kreb'schen Nachlaß" unter besonderer Berücksichtigung der Choralbearbeitungen des jungen J. S. Bach*. Hamburger Beiträge zur Musikwissenschaft 1, ed. Georg van Dadelsen. Hamburg: Karl Dieter Wagner.

Ziller, Ernst. 1935. *Der Erfurter Organist Johann Heinrich Buttstädt, 1666–1727*. Repr. Hildesheim: Olms, 1971.

photograph credits

1. Bach-Archiv Leipzig
2. Bach-Archiv Leipzig, ektachrome from Tokyo, Sign. 140
3. Bach-Archiv Leipzig, Sign. A 1039; photograph: Constantin Beyer, Bodelschwinghstr. 63, 99423 Weimar
4. Bach-Archiv Leipzig, Sign. A 1040; photograph by Constantin Beyer, Bodelschwinghstr. 63, 99423 Weimar
5. Bach-Archiv Leipzig
6. Bach-Archiv Leipzig, Sign. DK VIII 18a/7, © Deutsche Fotothek Dresden
7. Staatliche Kunstsammlungen Dresden, Kupferstich-Kabinett, Inventar-Nr. C 4335 in Sax top. I–IV, 28
8. Bach-Archiv Leipzig, Sign. DK VIII 18a/8, © Deutsche Fotothek Dresden
9. Bach-Archiv Leipzig, Sign. DK I
10. Evangelisch-Lutherische Superintendentur und Kirchgemeinde Eisenach
11. SLUB Dresden/Abt. Deutsche Fotothek; photograph: Dankelmann, 1926
12. Bach-Archiv Leipzig, Sign. DK XIII I/8, photograph: Ernst Schäfer, Weimar
13. Martin Doering, Berlin
14. Martin Doering, Berlin
15. Bildarchiv Hamburg
16. Hauptkirche St. Jacobi, Kirchenvorstand
17. Hauptkirche St. Jacobi, Kirchenbüro, © Thomas Helms
18. Bildarchiv Foto Marburg
19. Landesamt für Denkmalpflege und Archäologie Sachsen-Anhalt
20. Bach-Archiv Leipzig, Sign. DK VII 2/7; photograph: Foto-Schmähmann, Köthen/Anhalt
21. Silbermann-Archiv, Vorlage: Prof. Dr. Marc Schaefer, Strasbourg
22. Stadtarchiv Leipzig, Aquarell by Karl Benjamin Schwarz
23. Archiv Ullrich Böhme, Leipzig
24. Hermann Walter, ca. 1880
25. Bach-Museum Leipzig, 2010

26. Bach-Archiv Leipzig, from the Vogler-Chronik (Rara II 227, S. 111), Sign. DK VIII 11/7

27. Postcard, Archiv Markus Zepf

28. Museen für Kunst- und Kulturgeschichte der Hansestadt Lübeck

29. Postcard, Archiv Markus Zepf

30. Museen für Kunst- und Kulturgeschichte der Hansestadt Lübeck

31. St. Johannis Lüneburg

32. Stadtmuseum Lüneburg

33. Courtesy Museum am Lindenbühl, Mühlhausen

34. Sammlung Stadtarchiv Mühlhausen/Th.

35. Stadtarchiv Mühlhausen/Th. 10/X, Nr. 19, fol. 18v–18r (= Notulbuch von 1708–1709)

36. Kristian Wegscheider, Dresden

37. Bach-Archiv Leipzig; photograph: Uwe Wolf

38. Bundesarchiv, Bild 170–139/Max Bauer/CC-BY-SA

39. Werner Tonn, Sangerhausen

40. Bach-Archiv Leipzig, Sign. DK VIII 18c/34; photograph: Ernst Schäfer, Weimar

41. Hermann Eule Orgelbau, Bautzen

42. bpk/Musikabteilung, Staatsbibliothek zu Berlin–Preussischer Kulturbesitz/ Mus. Tb. 64/10 R

43. Klassik Stiftung Weimar

44. Mitteldeutscher Orgelbau Voigt

45. Mitteldeutscher Orgelbau Voigt

46. Gregor Heimrich, Zschortau

47. Uwe Pape, Berlin

48. SLUB Dresden/Deutsche Fotothek/Walther

49. Martin Doering, Berlin

50. Stadt- und Bergbaumuseum Freiberg

51. Otto Schröder, Freiberg

52. Bach-Archiv Leipzig, DK VIII, 18a/13

53. Klaus-Peter Albrecht, Gotha

54. Orgelbaugesellschaft Waltershausen

55. Pfarramt Lahm (Itzgrund)

56. Bach-Archiv Leipzig

57. Bildarchiv Foto Marburg

58. Museum für Kunst- und Kulturgeschichte der Hansestadt Lübeck

59. Freundeskreis Musik und Denkmalpflege in Kirchen des Merseburger Landes e.V.; photograph: Gert Mothes, Leipzig

60. Punctum, photograph: Peter Franke

61. Punctum, photograph: Peter Franke

62. Punctum, photograph: Peter Franke

63. Orgelbaugesellschaft Waltershausen

Translator's Note

An English translation of Christoph Wolff and Markus Zepf's *Die Orgeln J. S. Bachs: Ein Handbuch* (Leipzig, 2006) has allowed for corrections, additions, updates, and revisions to the original text, so that as far as possible this revised edition represents the most recent research in the field. Literature citations have been updated to include sources in English. Thus the reader will find references to entries in *The New Bach Reader* as well as to entries in the *Bach-Dokumente* series; references to Christoph Wolff's biography of Bach are to the English edition (or to supplemental material that appears only in the German edition); and the bibliography includes translations of works such as Werckmeister's *Orgel-Probe* and Gustav Fock's *Hamburgs Anteil am Orgelbau im Niederdeutschen Kulturgebiet*. I have followed the translations that appear in *The New Bach Reader* closely but have also revised these texts in places, especially when organ-building terms or references were unclear.

I am grateful to Martin Pasi, John and Christa Brombaugh, and Edward Pepe for assisting me with a number of thorny translation questions; to Gregory Butler for reading the first and subsequent drafts and offering numerous helpful suggestions; to Christoph Wolff and Markus Zepf for recommending that I undertake this project; and to George Stauffer, the American Bach Society, and University of Illinois Press for their unqualified support.

Lynn Edwards Butler

index

Müller, Johann Georg (first half eighteenth c.), 42, 175

Müller, Johann Heinrich (first half eighteenth c.), 43, 135, 170

Müller, Johann Jacob (first half eighteenth c.), 41

Musikalische Bibliothek (Mizler, 1754), xv

Mylius, Johann Anton (1657–1724), 102

Naumburg, 74–77; City Church of St. Wenceslas, xxv, 75; Hildebrandt organ (1746), xix, xxv, 74, 75–77, 133, 139, 148

Neidhardt, Johann Georg (ca. 1680–1739), 2, 6, 76, 112

Nicolai, David (1702–1764), 26

Niedt, Friedrich Erhard (1674–1708), 56, 60

Niehoff, Hendrik (ca. 1495–1560), 34, 64, 133, 170

Nordtmann, Johann Jacob (d. 1724), 119

obbligato organ, in Leipzig cantatas, xvii, 47

obbligato pedal, xvii

Oehme, Georg (ca. 1646–1708), 86, 87, 170

Offenhauer, Eduard (1825–1904), 98, 175

Ohrdruf, xxi, 78–80

—Castle Chapel, 80

—St. Michael's Church, 78; Lehmann/Brunner organ (1693), 12, 78–79, 135

—Trinity Church, 78, 79; Brunner organ (1679), 79–80, 135

Olearius, Johann Gottfried (1635–1711), 31

organ: construction of, 149–53; design and internal layout of, 105, 140, 143, 146, 149, 150; protection of, 147; tuning of, 34, 52, 58, 62, 75, 142, 144, 146, 152, 168 (*see also* temperament); use as church instrument, xvii, 5, 47, 54, 62

organ continuo or parts, xvii, 47; transposition of, 2, 3; use of Fagotto 16,' 141; use of Stillgedackt or Lieblich Gedackt 8,' xix, 2, 56, 57, 142

organ examinations, xix–xx, 12, 13, 18, 24, 91, 108, 119, 139–48, 164; instructions for, 149–53. *See also* Bach as organ expert and examiner

organists, "Figural" vs. "Choral," xvii, xviii

organ playing: art of, xv, xvi, xvii. *See also* Bach as performer

organ-recital repertoire, xviii, 15

organ-stop descriptions: Chalumeau, 49; Fagotto 16', 24, 141; Fleute Allemande, 49; Flöte douce 4', 24, 163; Gedackt 8', 24; Geigenprincipal 4', 130; Große Hell-Quinten Bass, 50; Hohl Fleute 3', 100; Jubal, 49; Lar[i]go[t], 49; Oboe d'amore 8', 79; Posaune 32', 34, 141; Posaunen Baß 16', 100, 141, 152; Principal 8', 24; Principal 32', 34; Quinta Thön 1', 100; reeds at St. Catherine's, Hamburg, 34, 140; Schweitzer Pfeiffe, 49; Sertin, 49; Sordino 8', 124; Stillgedackt 8', xix, 142; tremulant, 25, 46, 142; Trompetenbass 8', 25; Unda maris 8', 130; Viol di Gamba 8', 100, 141; Violdigambenbaß 16', 24, 152; Vox humana II, 24; Weite Pfeiffe, 49

Orgel oder Instrument Tabulatur (Ammerbach, 1571), xvi

Orgel-Probe, Erweiterte und verbesserte (Werckmeister, 1698), 141

Orgelprobe, oder kurze Beschreibung, wie . . . man die Orgelwerke . . . annehmen, probiren, untersuchen . . . solle (Werckmeister, 1681), 141

Ott, Paul (1903–1991), 116, 175

Pachelbel, Johann (1653–1706), xxi, 22, 78, 105, 113

Pape, Jost (2nd half sixteenth c.), 71, 175

Pestel, Gottfried Ernst (1654–1732), 5, 108, 122

Petersilie, Otto (organ building firm, until 1914/1918), 98, 175

Petzold, Christian (b. 1677), 15

Petzold, Sebald (mentioned 1728/29), 23

pipework: metal alloy of, xix, 142, 144, 152; scaling of, 152; sound of, 144; thickness of, 144; voicing of, xix, xx, 144, 146, 148, 152

Pisendel, Johann Georg (1687–1755), 18

pitch, 1–2; lowering of, 31, 74, 88. *See also* Chorton, Kammerton

Poppe, Gebr. (organ building firm until 1917), 25, 175

Posaune (Groß Posaune, Posaunenbass) 32' (in dispositions), 6, 20, 31, 35, 36, 40, 65, 70, 117, 120, 122, 130

CHRISTOPH WOLFF is Adams University Professor at Harvard University and director of the Bach-Archiv Leipzig.

MARKUS ZEPF, a musicologist and organist, is on the staff of the Germanic National Museum in Nuremberg.

LYNN EDWARDS BUTLER has published numerous articles on the organ and is a practicing organist with special familiarity with restored baroque organs in north and central Germany.

The University of Illinois Press
is a founding member of the
Association of American University Presses.

Designed by Jim Proefrock
Composed in 10/13 Filosophia
at the University of Illinois Press
Manufactured by Bang Printing

University of Illinois Press
1325 South Oak Street
Champaign, IL 61820-6903
www.press.uillinois.edu